Legally Blind Luck

Legally Blind Luck

Braxton Campus Mystery Book 7

James J. Cudney

Acknowledgments

Writing a book is not an achievement an individual person can accomplish on his or her own. There are always people who contribute in a multitude of ways, sometimes unwittingly, throughout the journey from discovering the idea to drafting the last word. *Legally Blind Luck*, the seventh book in my *Braxton Campus Mysteries* series, has had many supporters since its inception in the fall 2020, but before the concept even sparked in my mind, others nurtured my passion for writing.

First thanks go to my parents, Jim and Pat, for always believing in me as a writer and teaching me how to become the person I am today. Their unconditional love and support have been the primary reason I accomplish my goals. Through the guidance of my extended family and friends, who consistently encourage me to pursue my passions, I found the confidence to take chances in life. Thank you to Roda for all the kindness and fun a *big sister* provides. With Winston and

Baxter by my side, I was granted the opportunity to make my dreams of publishing this novel come true. I'm appreciative to them for inspiring me each day to complete this book.

Legally Blind Luck was cultivated through the interaction with and feedback from several talented alpha and beta readers who volunteered to read an early draft of the book. These amazing nine readers and friends found most of my proofreading misses, grammar mistakes, and awkward phrases. I couldn't have completed this wonderful story without Shalini, Lisa, Nina, Didi, Misty, Anne, Laura, Anne, and Valerie. A major thanks to them for encouraging me to be stronger in my word choice and providing several pages of suggestions to convert good language into fantastic language. I'm grateful for their kindness and big-heartedness to play such an integral role in catching the things my eyes and mind completely overlook. They've also supplied insight and perspective during the development of the story, setting, and character arcs. I am indebted to them for countless conversations and multiple readings that have helped me to fine-tune every aspect of this tale. You really learn who you friends are when they offer to do so much to help you.

Thank you to Next Chapter for publishing *Legally Blind Luck* and paving the road for additional books to come. Their support and focus on my novels in the past three-and-a-half years have been a key reason I'm able to keep on writing more. I look forward to our continued partnership.

Overview of the Braxton Campus Mysteries

When I decided to write a cozy mystery series, I adhered to all the main rules (light investigations, minimal violence or foul language, no sexual content, murder happens off-screen, protagonist is an amateur sleuth, and set in a quiet, small town). Some authors push the boundaries with variations, and in the Braxton Campus Mysteries, I followed the same route... just differently. Kellan, my protagonist, is a thirtyish single father, whereas traditionally a woman is the main character. Children aren't often seen in most series, but Kellan's family is important to the story. Kellan is also witty and snarky, but intended in a lovable and charming way, just like his eccentric grandmother, Nana D. Both are friendly, happy, and eager to help others, and they have a sarcastic or sassy way of interacting and building relationships... hopefully adding to the humor and tone of the books. Cozy mysteries are different from hard-boiled investigations, thrillers, and suspense novels; the side stories, surrounding town, and background characters are equally important to building a vibrant world in which readers can escape. I hope you enjoy my alternative take on this classic sub-genre.

Legally Blind Luck: Death via Curse is the 7th book in the series, and the title, as always, is a play on words: Legally Blind and Blind Luck. I trust you'll figure out all the connections within the mystery. This story isn't based on any known curse that I've come across, but I wanted to add a little flavor to the series in this latest book. Queen Tessa and Governor Yeardley are fictional, yet the impacts of apartheid and the history of the South African tribes in the last four centuries are real.

While each book's main mystery is stand-alone, I recommend reading the series in order because of the side stories and character progression. I provide a summary of the key characters at the beginning of each book because there are a lot to remember. To date in the series, we're at 135 characters. In this book, I keep it to under 40, some of whom are minor connections to the past. Don't get overwhelmed! I'm only trying to create a family and setting we fall in love with and want to repeatedly visit. I hope you enjoy this book.

-Jay

Welcome to Braxton, Wharton County
(Map drawn by Timothy J. R. Rains, Cartographer)

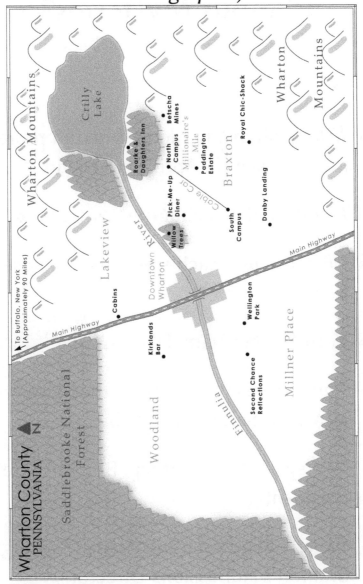

Who's Who in the Braxton Campus Mysteries?

Ayrwick Family

- *Kellan*: Main Character, Braxton professor, amateur sleuth, April's boyfriend

- *Emma*: Kellan's daughter with Francesca

- *Ulan Danby*: Zach's son, being raised by Kellan

- *Zach Danby*: Nana D's son, Ulan's father

- *Nana D*: Kellan's grandmother, also known as Mayor Seraphina Danby

- *Wesley*: Kellan's father, Braxton's retired President

- *Violet*: Kellan's mother, Nana D's daughter, Braxton's Admissions Director

- *Deirdre Danby*: Nana D's daughter, Zach's sister

- *Eleanor*: Kellan's younger sister, owns Pick-Me-Up Diner

- *Hampton*: Kellan's older brother, attorney, Natasha's husband

- *Natasha Reed Ayrwick*: Hampton's wife

Wharton County Administration & Residents

- *April Montague*: Wharton County Sheriff, Kellan's girlfriend, Fox's estranged wife

- *Augie Montague*: April's younger brother

- *Connor Hawkins*: Wharton County Detective, Kellan's best friend, Maggie's boyfriend, Victor's son

- *Maggie Roarke*: Braxton's Head Librarian, Connor's girlfriend

- *Francesca Castigliano*: Kellan's ex-wife, Emma's mother, Cristiano's girlfriend

- *Cristiano Vargas*: Francesca's boyfriend, former mafia head

- *Officer Flatman*: Wharton County Police Officer

- *Ursula Power*: Braxton's President, Myriam's Wife

- *Myriam Castle*: Braxton's Chair of Communications Dept., Kellan's boss, Ursula's wife

- *Fern Terry*: Braxton's Dean of Academics, Jordan's aunt, Ivy's sister

- *Eustacia Paddington*: Head of Paddington family, Nana D's frenemy

- *Fox Terrell*: April's estranged husband, Wharton County Judge

- *Constance Garibaldi*: Psychic medium (Madam Zenya)

The World of South African Art & Mysterious Curses

- *Queen Tessa*: Ancient high priestess (Deceased)

- *Governor Yeardley*: Savage colonial (Deceased)

- *Peter & Gemma Hawkins*: Connor's South African grandparents (Deceased)

- *Victor Hawkins*: Connor's South African father

- *Renee*: Zach's South African girlfriend

- *Lindsey Endicott*: Cain's father, Nana D's ex-boyfriend

- *Kathy Endicott*: Cain's mother, Orlando flight attendant

- *Cain Endicott*: Lindsey & Kathy's son, Chair of Braxton's Art Department

- *Sawyer Jaccard*: Bitsy's husband, art importer/exporter

- *Bitsy Jaccard*: Sawyer's wife, museum curator

- *Rhett Ballantine*: Ivy's ex-husband, Jordan's father

- *Jordan Ballantine*: Rhett & Ivy's son, MBA student

- *Ivy Natcher*: Jordan's mother, Tobias's wife, Fern's sister, Rhett's ex-wife

- *Tobias Natcher*: Ivy's husband, business-man

- *Giovanni*: FBI / ICE agent

Chapter 1

"Are you *certain* she didn't kill him? Let's postpone until next week." I scraped several cinnamon roll crumbs off the coffee table, concerned the feisty secretary would bestow her trademark death look upon me again. Three times in under ten minutes had broken her record.

"Pop a squat and settle that keister, Kellan. Your incessant pacing has inflamed my arthritis. President Power will oust Cain Endicott in a jiffy." Prior to stomping toward the door, Ursula's dictatorial and ornery assistant switched off her Victorian lamp and locked her vintage mirrored desk. "If that rocky discussion shudders your innards," she added, flicking her pearl-adorned neck in the opposite direction, "yesterday's bickering would've ruptured your blood vessels. Professors and students congregated outside the building to identify the source of the ruckus."

I shrugged noncommittally while she hastily escaped Prentiss Hall in her high-performance jogging shoes, charcoal-gray pantsuit, and festive pashmina, precariously dangling four-inch pumps and a bedazzled handbag from her fingertips. A terse mention of her husband purchasing almost-impossible-to-locate theater tickets for that night accompanied her plummy voice. Attending a hot new musical sounded way more appetizing than performing my imminent song and dance routine.

After tossing the dirty napkin into the trash bin, I tiptoed closer to Ursula's door to listen for any death blows signaling the end of their argument. I wasn't normally prone to eavesdropping, but snooping occasionally happened when something important—okay, yes, it was true—I listened to other people's conversations ad nauseam. Nana D suggested I inherited my nosiness from her, but mostly I believed it was my adorable charm and unique dedication to pursuing the truth. An occupational hazard for academic folks with a keen love of mysteries and drama. After fifteen months back home, I fully embraced my innate tendency to solve unusual homicide cases, only because I couldn't retain any self-control for minding my own business.

Behind the wood-paneled interior door, Ursula shouted something about *thousands of dollars over budget* and *lacking the proper authority*, to which Cain retorted, "African art is expensive. Did you honestly think I would be the laughingstock of all the institutions in our immediate academic circle? Come on, President Power, this is unnecessary. Surely you'd agree I am capable of...." His voice dropped too low, so I pressed my five-foot-nine frame against the door to overhear the remaining conversation.

As Ursula responded, the outer door from the main hallway blasted open, and Dean Fern Terry raced inside like a galloping giraffe. A single drop of sweat trailed the center of her creased forehead. We were both scheduled to meet with Braxton's esteemed president, but I wanted to disappear like the rabbit in a cheesy magic trick to avoid whatever hell fury was about to rain down. Especially when Fern trapped her foot under the corner of a leather ottoman, tumbled to the floor, and inadvertently hurled her giant stack of folders in my direction. Ursula and Cain must've heard the commotion, because within the subsequent five seconds I fell backward against the interior office door just as Cain opened it. I landed spread eagle on the carpet, littered with Fern's ridiculous paraphernalia, and cringed as Cain's cup of hot tea puddled on the front of my khakis—in an overly sensitive and embarrassing spot.

"Argh! What the—"

Cain interrupted my soon-to-be blasphemous outburst with his profusive apology, brushing back a rogue chunk of blackish-brown curls from his high and broad forehead. "I'm so sorry. What happened out here? Looks like a tornado swept through the office." Among his classic Roman features—wide-set eyes, a hooked nose, and a powerful jaw—lurked an inquisitive yet angry gaze.

"There can only be one reason you're in the fetal position, Kellan," Ursula chastised in be-tween chuckling and offering me a bunch of wadded up tissues. Her almond-shaped emerald eyes sparkled from the sun piercing through the windowpanes. "You're a magnet for unnatural disasters. I hope you understand if I don't help clean that mess. I'm dealing with enough HR issues these days. Pour some club soda on it before it stains."

Fern organized her papers while I blotted and spritzed water on my pants. Ursula had readily handed over a spray bottle, filled to the brim explicitly for painstakingly misting her exotic plant collection. I sighed before yielding like a trapped critter, then uttered, "No worries. I've got this one all by myself. Maybe we should defer our chat until the inclement weather subsides?"

"Huh? It's sunny and clear out. What are you babbling about?" A moment later, Cain craned his neck and realized I was being facetious. He vigorously shook his head, stretched for his briefcase, and pointed an accusatory finger in Ursula's direction. "Over my dead body will I concede. You know I'm right, President Power. We're shelving it tonight and will address what's best for Braxton on Monday."

While Ursula and Cain exchanged a handful of professional but incisive jibes, Fern and I regained our composures inside the presidential office and scouted for two spots near the bay window. We'd been asked to show up for a six o'clock discussion but had no knowledge of the meeting's purpose. All Ursula's austere secretary had articulated that morning was, "She asks. You appear. Need I explain more?"

I'd reached an unbearable limit of authoritarian women. Our spring graduation had just concluded, and my boss, the doughty and acerbic Dr. Myriam Castle, insisted I cover the next term even though I'd been assured no classes that summer. Braxton would soon convert from a college into a university, and I sat on the committee to facilitate the relaunch. I had non-existent time to teach a six-week compacted lecture in foreign literature and films, but when the irritable despot who also happened to be married to the college president mandated something, the word *no* wasn't an option.

As if Myriam weren't slinging enough abuse, Nana D—my spitfire grandmother, also the mayor of our secluded north-central Pennsylvania county—had stepped up her regular harassment routine and prodded me daily on several *urgent* matters. Ever felt two red-hot pokers jabbing your derriere like twin needles on a sewing machine? Not a pretty sight! Given the recent immense tragedy in my life, I craved essential downtime before my head exploded from stress and sorrow.

While I settled into an uncomfortably petite sofa, Cain stormed out of Ursula's office, and she gracefully ensconced herself behind a white pine desk. "That man has a death wish!" Performing a calming yoga technique, she switched gears and said, "I've always loved this building. So much history! Don't you agree?"

"Over two hundred years old. Must be difficult to concentrate with everything to admire."

Prentiss Hall, an architecturally stunning, four-story Georgian structure overlooking the South Campus cable car system, housed many of Braxton's vital administrative departments. Resplendent with exquisite symmetry, the exterior masonry boasted dozens of pediments, arches, and columns, including an English ivy-covered facade. Ursula's office commandeered the penthouse level, which had been divided into the presidential suite, encompassing a private bathroom and bedroom; an octagonal antechamber, accommodating the secretary's desk and a waiting area for guests; and a large conference room, used for board meetings and other executive-level summits. With a flair for European minimalism, aerodynamic design, and pale, airy, and lustrous decor, she insisted on spending her own money rather than Braxton's. The room's color scheme primarily drew from blue, gray, and beige tones, easily relaxing guests and suggesting a place of harmony. Except, apparently, for that day.

"I agree. It's vastly different from my dreary offices on North Campus." Fern glanced back and forth between Ursula and me, then hiccupped. "Excuse me," she softly added, humbly requesting a pardon for her bluntness, and chugged from her eco-friendly water bottle. "What's on the agenda this Friday evening, President Power?"

"Let's take a minute to center ourselves. I apologize for the tirade you've just witnessed. We are at a crossroads with Braxton's forthcoming exhibition." Ursula explained that Cain Endicott, the chair of the art department, had submitted an unorthodox proposal to her months ago, claiming it would bring a plethora of rich donors to Braxton. His unsubstantiated theory projected that they'd exceed the funds required to complete the fall rebranding as Braxton University.

Fern tugged on her ear, a nervous tick she'd stopped trying to control, and grinned as wide as her quarterback-size shoulders. Her pixie hairdo, pallid complexion, and menacing linebacker body frame kept the student population in control, primarily out of fear and respect. "It's quite thrilling. I've heard so much about next week's opening." When Ursula nodded, Fern mentioned her brother-in-law would speak at a session in the controversial event.

"I forgot about your connection to the panel of revered guests. Maybe he'll contribute something about that infamous African idol." Ursula crossed her long, shapely legs and arched her back. Somewhere in her forties, she was Braxton's youngest president. She'd already piloted the campus for a year, deemed an impressive successor to the former head—my father, Wesley Ayrwick.

Dad had retired in parallel to convincing me to return home and teach at Braxton for a year. I'd recently signed on for another term, something I still aggressively debated in my soul every waking moment. Money versus sanity. Family versus relaxation. Happiness versus potential incarceration because I locked them in an underground storm shelter simply to gain an ounce of privacy and a much-deserved break from their lunacy.

Upon checking my watch and realizing I only had thirty minutes before another pressing engagement, I awkwardly cleared my throat. "Not to be rude, but I have to be somewhere soon. Could we address the reason you asked to meet?"

Although Ursula erred on the down-to-earth and open-minded range of personalities, Braxton's president wielded the upper hand in all conversations. She extended me more leeway than most other professors and administrative staff, and I tried my best not to exploit such charity. "Of course, this shouldn't take too long. It's imperative someone get Cain back in line. His grand plans and lavish spending for the upcoming art exhibition have run amok, and I don't have the time to babysit him." Ursula explained that his ideas had originally impressed her, and she'd granted him a tad too much slack in the previous weeks. Everything needed to align with our meticulously designed marketing program for the university's future.

Fern eagerly agreed to sort through the chaos with Cain, despite her primary role as Dean of Students. Our Dean of Academics had resigned, and the influential and much-coveted position was still unoccupied, so Ursula juggled more than usual. I failed to understand why they'd roped me into the melodrama. "Is there any specific value that I offer here? I'm a professor in the communications department. My specialty is film and series productions. I'm not sure what I have to do with Cain's request for more money."

Fern released a disturbing guffaw. "Well, I suppose one could say you often motivate others to do the right thing. Your natural charm and wit put people at ease. They ardently trust you."

"Quite true. You also pose an intelligent and obvious question, Kellan. I'd planned to tap someone else, but he took an unexpected family leave this summer," countered Ursula, flipping her honey tresses off her shoulders. "Myriam suggested you'd be the perfect replacement candidate. Something about the fortuitous connection between the art exhibition and the impending literature and film seminar you'll teach. I assume that means something to you. I, unfortunately, am not familiar with every course in the curriculum this semester." Ursula dispensed two folders, indicating they contained all the details on the exhibition's budget, schedule, panel of guest speakers, and her specific goals and objectives.

If I weren't so fantastically adept at solving murders, I'd maim and kill my boss. Knowing my luck, I'd resort to helping the sheriff, coincidentally also my girlfriend, arrest and prosecute myself for Myriam's untimely demise. Images of Myriam drowning in a sea of Shakespearean quotes—she expertly inserted one into every conversation—triggered me to stifle a childish giggle. "I will have to thank her for this... generous... vote of confidence. I should buy a nice plant for her office. Is your wife fond of poison ivy or foxglove?"

Ursula released an unexpected snort as I spat out the words through gritted teeth. "Are you two still at each other's throats? I trust you'll continue to improve your relationship to show students the importance of respectfully disagreeing but nevertheless moving the dial forward. Part of me thinks you inspire one another to excel in your respective areas of expertise." As she stood, an unspoken sign implying the meeting's conclusion, Ursula added, "Also, some business school friends have agreed to guide Braxton's interests in next week's exhibition. I'll give them your contact information. Don't be fooled by your initial impressions. This is one situation where it won't benefit you to judge a pair of books by its covers. I'm sure the Jaccards will be in touch after I take them to a new restaurant in Woodland this evening. Have a great weekend."

Fern enthusiastically grabbed my hand and ushered us both out of Ursula's office before I could object, whine, or throw a tantrum. "This will be exciting! My sister taught me oodles about paintings and sculptures. We're having dinner after her flight lands tomorrow. She and her husband are frequent intercontinental travelers. I can hardly keep track of my own life these days, especially with a new grandchild."

"Hmmm… you and I have drastically opposing definitions of exciting," I barked back as we scurried to the parking lot and arranged our meeting for the following day.

"Oh, Kellan, you're entirely too dramatic for a man in his early thirties. How do you put up with yourself?" Fern withdrew a car key from her pant pocket and sneered in jest at me.

"A modern wonder, huh?" With a cheesy grin and two thumbs up, I encouraged a handful of dedicated runners obsessing about their heart rate monitors. They'd just crossed the pedestrian bridge over a man-made pond the science department had dug the previous year. Though deep enough to stock a few species of fish, it wasn't large enough for students to swim in or fraternities and sororities to conduct illegal hazing practices. As Fern shut the car door, I queried, "Any idea what she meant about the Jaccards' appearance? Are we being punked?"

"No clue. Maybe they're one of those mismatch couples... you know... where they are total extreme opposites but click perfectly well together?" While rolling up her window and nearly trapping my fingers, Fern ruefully tossed her hands in the air.

"Hmmm… somehow, I don't think that's what she implied. See ya tomorrow."

I'd luckily scheduled myself off for the entire weekend, mostly so I could plan the summer class Myriam had dropped in my lap. All my free moments belonged to others; none remained at my discretion except spending quality time with loved ones—the only activity keeping me sane since the Orlando airport catastrophe had struck ten weeks earlier. Since then, I'd spent an inordinate amount of time investigating my family's life-changing tragedy. My mind and body were exhausted, but my heart and soul had suffered indelibly upon learning of Uncle Zach's death in a devastating explosion.

Chapter 2

My mother's younger brother, a big-game veterinarian, had lived in South Africa for the previous two years, protecting a rare species of elephants from extinction. After the first year's commitment, Uncle Zach sent his teenager to live with me, citing little time to focus on his son's welfare. Ulan had been in my care for six months when he flew to Disney World with my parents and daughter for Spring Break. Uncle Zach had arranged a surprise appearance at the Orlando airport—where he'd subsequently return with the family to our Pennsylvania hometown—while things would theoretically be under control at the elephant camp. Unfortunately, after Uncle Zach had deplaned and rented a car, an explosion in the short-term parking lot permanently changed those plans.

A lot of rumors had surfaced about Uncle Zach's demise. Truthfully, it wasn't clear to any of us. A taciturn FBI or Immigrations and Customs Enforcement (ICE) agent—we weren't certain at which government institution he worked—had tracked us down at the hospital just as we'd brought in my sister-in-law to recover from a lunatic who'd shoved her off a cliff. As Natasha hovered between life and death, a family friend and psychic, Constance Garibaldi, hysterically darted into the hospital waiting room to inform us that her tragic predictions weren't over and that we still faced impending doom. None of us could've anticipated she'd foreseen Uncle Zach's death.

The government had been following Uncle Zach because they thought he'd stolen a priceless tribal figurine before leaving South Africa. Upon finding no traces of it in the remains of the car or his luggage, they concluded he wasn't guilty and abandoned their investigation. Although we were all grateful Natasha had survived the tumble, and we hoped she would regain the use of her legs, saying a permanent goodbye to Uncle Zach had wrecked us. Nana D holed up in her farmhouse for days, refusing to talk to anyone but me, and even that came in limited quantities. Unfortunately for the authorities, she demanded answers and summoned the big guns to apply pressure. My grandmother wouldn't believe the randomness of his accident, noting Uncle Zach had not been himself in the days preceding his flights to the US. "My son was afraid of someone. This is an unequivocal fact. He all but said the words," Nana D had insisted when she crawled out of her temporary recluse, eyes swollen and hair torn astray.

Was my uncle's death truly the result of a clerical error—that someone had forgotten to repair a leaky fuel line on his rental car? Or had someone else followed him, secretly engineered the explosion, and pilfered the rare African idol? Maybe Nana D had overlooked critical information Uncle Zach revealed on their calls. Poor Ulan had fixated on playing his favorite video game for forty-eight straight hours without any sleep after his father's death. While I frequently soothed my cousin, I also further helicopter-parented my own child who'd been nearby during a second explosion in the parking lot.

While pacing Braxton Elementary's designated pickup area and waiting for Emma to finish an after-school program, I dialed Nana D. We usually chatted a few times each week, but following Uncle Zach's accident, I talked to my grandmother every morning and again around dinnertime. After ten weeks, she'd painstakingly obscured her grief to the exterior world, but I knew instantly how ravaged she was by the tone of her voice. "What's the four-one-one, Nana D? I hope your current agency temp made it through the full week." Since her previous assistant had run off with a foreign husband, she hired and fired the woman's replacement weekly as an outlet for her heartache.

"Canned. She had the nerve to ask if I needed help with the latest updates on my iPhone."

"Isn't that what assistants do?" I rolled my eyes and bent forward to hug Emma as she approached the car.

My daughter assertively shook her head and stepped to the side so I couldn't reach her. With one hand on her hip and the other scolding me in a waving motion, she also gave me the stink eye. *What was her problem?* Luckily, when she tried to escape, I snagged the back of her hoodie and pointed to the door. After I whispered, "Nana D," she relented, and her playful espresso-colored pigtails bounced in unison with her lengthy stride as she climbed into the backseat. If she grew any taller—one of the beneficial traits she'd inherited from her mother, along with flawless olive skin and impeccable bone structure—she'd surpass Nana D's five-foot stature. Emma's dark-brown eyes mushroomed like giant bugs as she formulated a strange half-smile and half-grimace. I'd ask her about the mini tantrum once the call ended with Nana D.

In the background, my grandmother operated a blender on a low enough speed that we could still hear one another. Margarita Fridays with Eustacia Paddington had become a tradition at Danby Landing the previous month—nothing like alcohol and humor as one's emotional therapy. "That paper-pusher rudely hinted I'm too ancient to do it myself. Goodbye. Adios. All feet are insane."

That line perplexed me. "Do you mean *Auf Wiedersehen*? The German words for goodbye?"

"Pish! I know what I said. Her crazy feet can do some walking!" The blender stopped chopping ice long enough for her to invite me over for cocktails and to express her pent-up anguish. "I miss my son, Kellan. Mothers aren't equipped

20

to send their children out of the world. Only to bring them into it. This is unnatural."

When I heard Eustacia consoling her in the background, I gently declined the invitation. "I won't pretend to understand, only support you as best I can. Your great-granddaughter wants to say a brief hello while we drive home. But first, how was your day?" As Emma snapped her seatbelt, I pulled away from the curb.

"I suppose I'm coping," replied Nana D before notifying me that Eustacia had spilled a third drink on her blouse and torn off her bra. "We're making plans to visit South Africa. I want to find out what my son was up to before he got on that plane to Orlando. I need to do something to process my feelings. I've got survivor's guilt." The bleak crack and lilt in her voice were heartbreaking on multiple levels.

Losing one of her kids in the prime of his life, fifty-two, had devastated my grandmother. Parents weren't supposed to outlive their offspring. Besides him and my mother, Nana D had also raised two other children—Deirdre and Campbell—both of whom lived outside Braxton. Aunt Deirdre had gotten married and given birth to her first baby the prior year, and she and her husband continued to reside in England and occasionally travel to the US. She wrote romance novels, and he was the CEO of a major corporation, Paddington Enterprises. Campbell was a more complicated story for a different day.

"One day at a time. Book nothing until we coordinate schedules. I told you I'd take you there when things subside this summer." I convinced Nana D to behave herself and to focus on connecting with the rest of her children.

Between Uncle Zach's shocking death and Natasha's paralysis, my entire family barely held it together. Hampton had managed his wife's company, ReedWell Corporation, since the tragic murders earlier that year. My grouchy older sibling would soon meet a potential buyer, which could generate a positive trajectory for their future. Leading the business, watching over his partially incapacitated wife, and caring for their four young children had undoubtedly taken its toll on him. Even though we rarely got along, I did all I could to comfort him in his misery.

"The facts don't add up at the rental agency. They were too eager to offer a settlement and close the investigation." Nana D hollered something at Eustacia about not plugging in the hair dryer near the sink. "Help! She's gonna burn down my house, Kellan."

"Please do not electrify yourselves. I've had enough issues this year." I agreed that the car company's responses were strangely generous. Even our sheriff had dug into it but failed to elicit anything valuable in her conversations with the local police. When we finished speaking, I handed the phone to my daughter so she could comfort Nana D. "You're in charge, Emma. Make her listen to you."

"Of course, I'm always the boss. My teacher says so!" she stated, snickering in response before addressing her great-grandmother. "You should see Daddy right now. He's a hot mess!"

After Emma hung up with Nana D a few minutes later, I asked why she'd run away outside the school. "Eh, embarrassment, Daddy. You must've had a rough week." During the remainder of our drive home, Emma informed me about her day, culminating with a strange request. "Now it'll cost fifty dollars to join the new club.

Nana D said you better cough up the dough, or she won't bake you any pies."

I parked in the driveway and unloaded our belongings. "That's nice, honey. Don't listen to Nana D anymore. Her brain has extended its hiatus." Obsessed with hazarding guesses over Emma's puzzling comments, I sidestepped her appeal for the funds. I'd recently bought a run-down Victorian, newly renamed Garzenwyck, and renovated both the interior and the exterior. Money was tight. Upon entering the front hall, I swooned at my appalling reflection in a floor-to-ceiling mirror. Despite my classic baby blues, high cheekbones, and radiant dimples, a few disastrous problems refused to be snubbed. Not only were Cain's tea stains showing on my crotch, but I must've dropped catsup from my fries at lunch down the front of my shirt, and my wavy blond hair rivaled a ransacked bird's nest. No wonder my eight-year-old daughter had done a double take and darted away in the parking lot. "Fine, you win. I'll pay for your new club. What was it again?"

"Yippee! Archery. I get to shoot arrows at real targets." Emma immediately dragged Baxter, our black-and-tan shiba inu dog who harbored a tendency to eat socks and randomly growl at the basement and attic doors, outside for playtime before dinner.

"Please don't kill anyone I know. Or me!" I dropped my satchel on the floor and sighed with exasperation. Ulan had already returned home to prepare our meal. Latching on to cooking and baking had temporarily centered his concentration on something other than his father's death. I approached while he obsessively stirred a pot that smelled amazing. "Hey kiddo. What's on tonight's menu?"

After shaving his hair earlier that year to support a friend who'd been diagnosed with cancer, a bunch of brown sprouts clung to Ulan's oval-shaped head. His swimmer's build and chocolate-brown puppy dog eyes often lit a fire in the hearts of all the girls at Braxton High. I'd fended most of them off during his dad's funeral service, at his request, so he could focus on his own emotions. "I didn't hear you come in. Ummm… a variety of seafood dishes. My dad's favorite. I invented a bunch of sauces, and I've got a shrimp boil simmering on the stove and a dozen parmesan-baked clams in the broiler."

Ulan would turn sixteen during the summer, and I knew he missed his father terribly. For every prior birthday, they'd taken an excursion to a remote island to study its wildlife. New Zealand had been on tap for later that year. It would no longer happen.

I wrapped one arm around his shoulder and nudged him closer to my chest. "Your dad would be proud of you. Let's consider a trip to South Africa in August with Nana D. It won't be the same as your past explorations, but it might offer some closure."

He sucked in a whoosh of air while turning off the burner. "It would be really cool to show you where we lived. I could plan a safari too." With his head a little wobbly and his eyes glistening, he swallowed a heavy lump in his throat.

"Only if you're ready. I mean, we have to go at some point, but I've talked to a contact who's checking on your dad's apartment." I'd only been a parent to Emma for eight years—a learning experience every single day, especially since I'd raised my little girl by myself for most of her life. Mentoring a teenage boy on the cusp of becoming a man—indisputably sooner than necessary—was a scarier and more arduous task.

Ulan poured the pot's contents through a colander in the sink, carefully keeping most of the broth for his sauce. Steam enveloped us, mirroring the fuzziness manifesting inside our brains these days. "You've been awesome, Kellan. I don't know how I could've gotten through this without you." He'd regularly assured me that being around family prevented him from crumbling over his father's death, but he rarely expressed the fullness of his devastation. Ulan's mother died in childbirth, and it had been just himself and his dad from that tragedy forward. The woman had been estranged from her family for many years. Ulan and Uncle Zach lived in various cities around the world, which meant he hardly called a single place home. "I'm only supposed to stay here three more months, but are you gonna... I mean, do I have to... leave?"

My heart excruciatingly disintegrated into pieces. I wasn't the most touchy-feely guy, especially being the middle child in the Ayrwick family. I'd mostly felt lost and ignored, so I kept

27

to myself—bookish nerd met prankster met Curious George. I transferred the shrimp pot from Ulan to the counter and pulled him into my arms. Then I hugged him as though I were preventing the force of gravity from stealing my soul. "You don't have to go anywhere. I've seen what happens when a kid's mother passes away, but I can't imagine what it's like to also lose your dad at such an early age. I won't ever replace your parents, but you're welcome to live with me as long as you want."

During the preceding months, I'd gained someone else to mentor—an orphan within a large extended family. Ulan desperately needed an advocate in his corner, someone to steer him on the proper course. Was I really in a position to function as a stable pseudo-dad to him? When Nana D and I had discussed the topic over some freshly baked Snickerdoodle cookies the previous week, she encouraged me to let Ulan decide his fate. "Trial by fire," she'd declared while huffing heaps of cinnamon. "Got three years before he graduates from high school and becomes an adult."

When Ulan pulled away, I shared how much Emma also loved having him around and how Nana D thought we should handle decisions incrementally. "We need you just as much as you need us."

"Meaning, if I'd like to live here sometimes, I can. And if Nana D wants company, I could stay there too?" Ulan wiped his cheek, clarifying he wasn't afraid to weep in front of me. "My dad taught me it's okay to cry, even for a man. I wanna do him proud, Kellan."

"You couldn't disappoint him no matter what, kiddo. You're his greatest achievement."

Uncle Zach and I had briefly chatted a day before he left South Africa. I'd thought the conversation was odd, especially when he asked if I would keep Ulan permanently should anything happen to him. But I was so wrapped up in my own dramas, I hadn't understood any potential veiled messages. I'd thought Uncle Zach was keen to ensure his son had a guardian in case he suffered a freak heart attack or plane accident. Was my uncle worried something awful like murder could fell him? Had I disregarded a significant clue?

Ulan confirmed he was eager to stay with me for the immediate future. "Once we figure out what truly happened to my dad, we can talk about next steps, okay?"

I hesitated before responding, unwilling to let his strange comment linger without an explanation. "What do you mean, *figure out what truly happened*? The Orlando Airport's official statement confirmed your dad's death was related to a fuel line issue with the car. The insurance company has agreed to settle, and you will get a lot of money from them, Ulan."

Emma wandered back inside with Baxter and kneeled on the floor to remove his leash. I smiled at her, uncertain how to react to Ulan's mystifying expression. All I wanted to do was snap my fingers, travel back in time, and reroute Uncle Zach's plane to anywhere else.

"I'd give all the money away if I could uncover the real facts, Kellan. I've been thinking about it a lot today. His girlfriend called during my lunch break. She convinced me to trust my instincts. To seek the truth. I've made a major decision." With his back toward us, Ulan spooned dinner onto our plates.

I wasn't aware Uncle Zach had begun dating a new woman. "I'm unsure I understand what she has to do with your dad's accident or your newfound instincts." In that precise moment, my ringing cell prevented me from further responding to his bold announcement. "Hold that thought for one minute." I picked up the phone and strode in the opposite direction. "Hey, gorgeous. I'm thrilled you're back."

April Montague had just returned home from an out-of-town convention for state law enforcement personnel. "Me too. I can't wait to see you. Give me thirty minutes?"

As the sheriff of Wharton County—a hidden gem located ninety miles south of Buffalo, New York in north-central Pennsylvania—April oversaw the police force for four primary towns. Fully surrounded by the Wharton Mountains and Saddlebrooke National Forest, our welcoming haven boasted a residency of ten thousand citizens. Woodland was the most affluent of all the municipalities, followed by Braxton. Both claimed well-respected colleges and regularly competed against one another. Lakeview and Millner Place had smaller schools and populations but proffered stunning escapes from urban life. Between Crilly Lake and the central downtown shopping district, the entire area represented an oasis of beauty and a balance of all the natural elements.

I slipped into the mudroom, ensuring Ulan couldn't hear me. I quickly told April what he'd revealed less than five minutes ago. "We should hold off on getting together tonight. I need to find the underlying cause of this shocker while he's keen to talk about it."

"Not a problem. I could use the sleep." April graciously offered to swing by first thing in the morning. "You owe me one, babe. I plan to collect on it too. Don't forget… I can be a creative woman."

Once we hung up and my body cooled down, I approached the kitchen and squeezed the back of my cousin's neck. "So, that's a lot to digest. Care to explain what's going on?"

Ulan rotated one-hundred-and-eighty degrees and gawped directly at me with renewed confidence. He spoke in a startling, emphatic voice. "My dad's girlfriend convinced me that he was murdered. Renee claims to have proof, and she's on her way to Braxton to beg you to find his killer. I think we need to seek justice. You'll fix this, right?"

Chapter 3

As much as I'd wanted to make up for lost time with my girlfriend, eliciting what Ulan knew about Renee was the prior night's priority. Although April and Ulan had bonded extraordinarily well, I worried he might not say much in front of her, especially since she'd previously shouted from the rooftops to stop my foolish habit of investigating murders.

April and I were officially dating for six months, and during most of the early courting days, we'd been jointly involved in a bunch of homicide cases. She legally investigated them as the Sheriff of Wharton County while I conveniently poked around and pontificated about the alternative paths she'd missed. Not so much missed as avoided leads she couldn't follow because she lacked the warrant, motive, or justification for interrogating others. I could get away with unofficial inquiries because I'd formerly directed a TV crime show in Los Angeles. I technically still consulted for *Dark Reality*, but a good friend had taken over my responsibilities and run with them. April, on the other hand, rarely valued my input and had all but handcuffed and thrown me in jail when I interjected myself. A healthy American man had a constitutional right to his wicked and wild fantasies. But she made it indisputably clear I wouldn't enjoy the ones she considered as options to keep me in check.

"Good morning, sunshine. That coffee smells heavenly." April let herself in the back door while I scrambled eggs and cheese. "Did you get any sleep? I did, but only after I found an old Matchbox Twenty t-shirt you left behind."

"To drape on your pillow, so you could smell my manly musk?" I growled to make my point.

"No, to wear... like we were spooning, you fool." April reminded me my most recent scent had been her vanilla body crème that I'd slathered on my neck to rid myself of dry skin.

"Don't tempt me from throwing you on the floor right now, woman! Grrr...." I relaxed as she hugged me from behind, turned my body to face hers, and kissed me with such smoldering enthusiasm I weakened at the knees. "I missed you this week. I promise we'll remedy *that* over the week-end."

April's intense lime-green eyes, unarguably one of her best attributes, shimmered like precious gemstones. To the public, she resembled a no-nonsense autocrat who wore minimal makeup and held her own with all the tough guys at the precinct. In private, she embraced a feminine side that needed only a small amount of convincing to spring from hiding. We were both three inches shy of six feet, and a healthy volume of gym time had led to her toned but curvy body. I'd been stunned the first occasion we were intimate, and whenever I saw her in a frumpy blazer, I beamed because I knew the secret beauty that lurked underneath it.

"Good. Tell me again what you learned last night," she directed after pouring coffee and massaging my shoulders. "You're very tense. I think we need some private time before breakfast."

My heart jumped several beats as she slid her hand in between two buttons on my shirt and tickled my bare chest. "Emma is at Francesca's new place in Lakeview. I'll pick her up tomorrow. Ulan is upstairs sleeping, though. Maybe we should be careful?"

"Four wretched days have separated us, and it was no fun being the only female sheriff among a bunch of chauvinistic men. My place, tonight. That's not a suggestion. It's an order." April grunted before removing two plates from the cabinet and setting the table. "Augie and Ulan are hanging out with some kids from the swim team. I checked it out. Parents are clean. The boys will be home by eleven."

I squinted at her with increasing doubt. Augie was the younger brother whom she'd been raising since her abusive, alcoholic father kicked the bucket. Although Augie was a couple of years older than Ulan, they'd hit it off and become fast friends. Ulan would miss Augie when he attended Braxton University as a freshman in the fall. "Ulan's curfew is ten o'clock. You wouldn't be undermining my rules, sheriff, would you?"

April sighed expressively. "We've debated this before. I decide the rules on the weekend. I permit you to *suggest* the rules during the week. We can let them socialize longer tonight. I think it's necessary, don't you? Ulan needs to be around friends." As she inched away and smirked, her hand lingered on my belt and yanked me closer. "Get my drift?"

I nodded and pressed my lips against hers again. Some sort of cherry lip balm teased me in return. "Yep, you are the boss. I'm not opposed to you taking the dominant role in this relationship as long as I get my way sometimes."

"I won't dignify that with a response." She poured us two glasses of juice, then buttered slices of cinnamon-raisin toast. "So, ready to cover Ulan's news?"

"Ugh! I still can't believe this is happening."

"Your poor family. How long were Zach and Renee seeing each other?"

"Nine months. They'd started dating before Uncle Zach sent Ulan to live with me, which was—"

"Last August," she replied, finishing my words—a common routine these days.

I explained the facts and theories I'd learned from my cousin the prior night. Zach and Renee had met when she attended his lecture at a local veterinary school in South Africa. Two weeks later, Ulan left the country. After a couple more dates, Zach introduced Ulan to Renee via a *Zoom* video meet-and-greet. During the call, Renee and Ulan bonded over a mutual love of reggae music, spicy food, and swimming. Although they had just thirty minutes online, he thought she was genuinely nice, extremely pretty, and highly intelligent. Renee had advanced knowledge of modern technology, African culture and history, and various forms of martial arts. Since then, she'd frequently worked or traveled during Ulan's calls, and he only heard from his father twice each month. Then Uncle Zach died, ending their last chance at connecting again.

"Why did she suddenly contact Ulan now?" When April bit into her toast, a trail of butter slid down her chin.

"You're a mess! I never could've imagined this side of you existed. At the precinct, you're a robot… at home, you actually let down your guard and…." Noticing her grimace, I stopped myself from finishing that statement. Before she could swipe her napkin, I reached out my hand and wiped away the drip. "Ulan didn't get all the details. Renee was keen to hang up quickly."

"Well, what exactly did she mean by suggesting Zach was murdered? We all thought that at first too, but the lab results confirmed it was an accident. Is she suggesting that the Orlando police got it wrong? The rental agency is paying the claim, so it's not like they're hiding anything." April unlocked her tablet and pulled up the final report that her Orlando contact had shared the prior month.

After landing at the airport, Uncle Zach had called my mother to indicate he'd rented a car to drive back to Pennsylvania with his son rather than fly home with the rest of the family, to give them some quality time together. He told her that his luggage hadn't yet made it to Baggage Claim, so he would return to his terminal to collect it after locating Ulan. Uncle Zach then parked in the short-term lot and waited for my mother in the Departure's drop-off area just outside her terminal. While Ulan remained inside the airport with my father to check in and print out their tickets, my mother secretly brought his luggage outside. Uncle Zach wanted to store it in the car before he surprised Ulan. As my uncle rolled it through the short-term parking lot, my mother realized she'd left Aunt Deirdre's latest book in Ulan's suitcase. She and Emma chased after Uncle Zach and were twenty feet away when Uncle Zach pressed the remote to unlock his car.

At the same time, despite my objections, my ex-wife had landed in Orlando and tracked them down in the parking lot. Francesca shouted at Emma, who changed directions and sprinted for her mother. Uncle Zach had pressed the automatic engine starter and was opening the trunk to store Ulan's luggage when the car exploded. Francesca dashed toward them, threw Emma to the ground, and jumped on top of her as a second explosion occurred. While my ex-wife dragged Emma to safety, my mother collapsed to the pavement and covered her head. After she barricaded herself behind a concrete divider and regained some of her hearing from the blast, she called 9-1-1. When airport security arrived, they determined Uncle Zach had died instantly. Ulan never got to see his dad.

"It's kind of strange. Renee indicated she's been in hiding for weeks because someone tried to attack her too," I noted.

"Does that mean she finally felt safe enough to fly to the US?"

"I suppose so." When April's inquisitive eyes narrowed in my direction, I added, "I bet I know what you're thinking. And the answer is yes."

"Nice. You captured Renee's incoming number?" April futzed with a mound of eggs on her plate while rereading the report.

"Not exactly. Unknown caller. Wow, we're truly reading one another's minds. Maybe you should offer me a part-time job at—"

"Not on your life. We'd kill one another, babe." She winked at me and traced her foot up my leg to divert my attention. "You said Renee claimed Zach carried a priceless figurine with him, but she couldn't reveal anything about it, in case someone was listening."

I grabbed her toes to stop her from teasing me. "I'm annoyed that this Renee woman would call a fifteen-year-old kid to tell him his father was murdered. She could've talked to me first or at least waited until she got here." I had no clue about the missing artifact, and the pithy FBI agent had refused to share any valuable information. After abruptly terminating the investi-

42

gation, he only cautioned us to be on the lookout for a package from South Africa, lest something odd showed up, whatever that meant. Mostly, he insisted the case was no longer active and instructed us to forget everything we'd learned.

"How's Ulan handling the news?" April slowly blinked, conveying her unwavering support and sympathy for me. Massaging her foot had probably helped too.

I wobbled my head. "He went to bed directly after dinner last night. Ulan is a strong boy, but now he wants to know who killed his father. I'm not even sure Renee is legitimate. What if she's only after Uncle Zach's insurance payout or hunting down the African figurine?"

"Good point. Got a last name to look up?"

"Ulan didn't know it. He'd only met her online on the one occasion and spoken to her on the phone a few times. No emails directly with her. Uncle Zach had no connections on social media with a woman named Renee. Maybe we might find something in his papers in South Africa."

April reminded me we wouldn't have access to them until later in the summer. "Does Ulan know specifically when she'll arrive?"

"Nope, she'll find him when the timing is right. I'm sticking close, purely in case Renee causes trouble." I advised April that Aunt Deirdre and her new husband had visited Uncle Zach in South Africa on their honeymoon the prior summer. "Maybe they might remember something?" I noted that I'd also ask my other family members at Sunday brunch if they'd heard of Renee.

"If there is more to this missing African figurine, then perhaps your aunt overheard Zach talking to someone back then." April inquired about any connections between the missing artifact and the upcoming Braxton art exhibition.

"Not that I'm aware of, but frankly, I haven't read all the materials Ursula gave me yesterday." If my uncle were involved, he would've mentioned a meeting with Braxton's art department or Cain.

April gathered our plates and shuffled toward the sink. Underneath the clatter of the dishes against the ceramic basin, she mumbled something twice.

"Either I'm going deaf or you're purposely speaking like that low-talker from the *Seinfeld* episode we watched last month. Out with it," I in-

44

sisted as Baxter scarfed down a small scrap from the frying pan. Eggs weren't bad for dogs, at least not in moderation.

April spun around and swept her brassy blonde bangs from her forehead. I'd once innocently suggested she grow her hair longer, and after a lengthy argument about femininity and a woman's appearance being solely her prerogative, we'd finally reached a compromise. I'd merely wanted to see what it might look like, and she'd agreed to acquiesce if I committed to growing some facial hair. A month into my new scruffy style, I begged April to let me shave, citing the extreme itchiness and spotty sections on my right cheek. April caved, but she also kept her hair longer the last time she'd gone to the salon. Relationships had their benefits, especially when we respected each other's decisions.

"You're not going to like what I said." April puckered her lips and tapped her fingers on the granite countertop. After intentionally drawing out the silence long enough that Baxter barked just to hear some modicum of noise, she relented. "Do you want me to ask Fox if he knows anything about Zach's girlfriend?"

Yep, she went there. To the dark, dark place where her not-yet-ex-husband tortured me regularly. After a mistake with the divorce decree over a decade ago, April and Fox Terrell remained legally married. She'd refiled against his wishes, and we waited for the paperwork to be completed. Unfortunately, Fox wooed her regularly. He was a former lawyer, security expert, trained investigator, god to all women and hordes of men—including my brother Gabriel, who informed us the previous year that he was gay and suggested Fox was gorgeous man-candy. Sacrilegious traitor!

"Sure. Why don't we meet Fox for a drink and ask him this weekend? Then you don't have to be around him on your own, and I can keep a trace on the dirty rat." I loudly dropped the remaining pans into the dishwasher, scooted Baxter out the mudroom door into the backyard, and reminded April that she'd be late for her meeting if she didn't hurry.

"The divorce will be final by the end of the month. You and I are solid. Besides, I heard a rumor about Fox while I was away." April grabbed her tablet and car keys, then pseudo-tackled me with a Machiavellian grin. "He went on a date earlier this week with someone familiar. One of my patrolmen, Officer Flatman, saw them kissing up a storm at Simply Stoddard. If they wanted no one to discover them, they shouldn't have been so indiscreet."

Simply Stoddard, a high-end dining establishment that had opened the previous year, was April's go-to spot when we needed a night away from all the drama in our lives. Boasting the Finnulia River as its gorgeous backdrop, the restaurant overlooked a lighthouse that Constance Garibaldi, the town seer who had predicted tragedy for my family, inherited from her parents.

"Who was Fox snogging? Don't leave me hanging!" I ran through countless eligible young women in my mind but couldn't pinpoint a confident guess. "Please tell me it's not someone I like or respect. I'd have to kidnap and brainwash her." I repeatedly pressed my fingertips together like a mad scientist conjuring a new mysterious formula destined to change the world.

"Small secrets are good for a couple to intrigue one another. Nothing big, just enough to

ignite the sparks. It's how I keep you in line."
April pecked my cheek, then the super sensitive
spot under my chin, and finally my impatient
lips. "But I'll give you a few hints. She's several
decades older than him, not to mention possibly
unavailable. Also, she's well connected in Wharton County and comes from humble roots." April
traced her fingers down the back of my neck,
generating a wicked cascade of shivers and hot
flashes. "So, I'll text Fox a time and place to meet
us tomorrow. Maybe by then, you'll figure out
the woman's identity. Love ya!"

Before I could balk, April slipped away and
strutted through the back door, unintentionally letting Baxter back inside. He immediately
jumped all over me, nearly knocking me to the
floor. By the time I got away, she was pulling
out of the driveway. "You're in so much trouble,
April! Don't think I won't solve it before we pump
that instigator for details!" I threatened as she in-
souciantly waved her hand through the driver's
window like the Queen of England.

I considered all the women I knew who were
at least in their mid-fifties. Fox was about the
same age as my older brother, Hampton, who

had turned thirty-seven that year. I couldn't figure out the mystery lover's identity until various outlandish thoughts collided in my excessively cramped brain. Either Fox's little mistress was already married, or April hinted that the woman in the parking lot was Nana D. She wouldn't dare!

To squelch the brewing tension, I texted my grandmother, acting like one of Ulan's sassy love interests. Nana D would find my line of questioning comical. Being the mayor was a daunting job most days, and if I could provoke her to chuckle, it was well worth the trouble.

Me: *Forgive me for being blunt and not waiting until Sunday brunch, but were you behaving like a silly little tart at Simply Stoddard?*
Nana D: *Be more specific. What is it you think I've done? It's been a hectic week.*
Me: *You're my grandmother and the mayor. Please don't make me spell it out.*
Nana D: *Then yes, it was me. Who told you?*
Me: *Seriously? I have no words. Wait… I do. You're a horrid old woman who needs therapy.*
Nana D: *Pish! Are we talking apples and oranges, brilliant one? Must I draw pictures again?*

Me: *Excuse me while I vomit uncontrollably.*
Nana D: *You're an immature ninny. I'm on a call with the governor fixing a problem. Go torture your sheriff girlfriend and stay out of my business or I'll slap your bottom silly. Gotta run. Hugs and Kisses.*

That provided as much help as tweezers in a knife fight! Maybe she and I weren't in sync about smooching a repellant jerk in a dimly lit parking lot. Although breakfast was debating whether to propel itself up my esophagus, I couldn't help but crave a slice of coconut cream pie and a chocolate milkshake. Why was I addicted to desserts? Better yet, what was I going to do about Fox if he was sleeping with my grandmother? If they got married, he'd be my step-grandfather. That was the thought that clinched it; breakfast won the battle, and I hustled to the bathroom to offer some contributions to the porcelain throne.

Chapter 4

Once my self-exorcism ridded me of the vulgar imagery, I stormed Diamond Hall to drop off a file with a colleague. As I passed by Cain Endicott's office, several hot-and-heavy moans poured from behind his walls. Our term had ended earlier that month, and summer classes wouldn't begin again for another week. Who was inside with him? I'd heard rumors about his naughty student hookups in the past, but I wanted to believe they were exaggerated. I snatched a sheet of paper from my desk and swiftly shoved a note under his door that read: *Score - six out of ten from the judges. Yep, we all know what you're doing wrong in there!*

I felt awful for causing any embarrassment, but someone had to confront him, albeit in a passive-aggressive manner. My budding angst over Renee's allusion that Uncle Zach was murdered had become too much to process. Every cell in my body compelled me to believe her, but

I needed to talk to someone as equally involved with my uncle at the time of his death.

After sneaking down the steps and unsuccessfully contemplating the options, I met Fern at the Pick-Me-Up Diner. We ordered sandwiches, gossiped over Cain's secret lover, and chatted with my sister Eleanor about her future wedding plans—she was growing frustrated with my mother's insistence on a big wedding. When Fern went to the restroom, my prayers about finding someone who'd been connected with Uncle Zach were unexpectedly answered.

Giovanni, the infamous FBI/ICE agent, bustled across the parking lot with a lanky man sporting a thin mustache and dark suit. As the man slipped into their car, his jacket caught on the seatbelt, revealing a revolver strapped to his side. What was happening in our quiet and peaceful hometown? Their dual presence convinced me I'd stumbled upon a crucial puzzle piece in my uncle's death. Unfortunately, by the time I rushed outside, they'd disappeared. Somehow, I had to corner that agent; he knew something important. As Nana D often said, "My bones are creaking... someone's got a story that needs a peeking."

Fern and I subsequently walked off our meal on the way to Braxton's sprawling North Campus. We'd decided to make use of Memorial Library's lower-level conference rooms to spread out the art exhibition materials rather than risk spilling lunch on them at the diner.

The Paddington family had originally built Memorial Library, but a fire destroyed a substantial portion years ago. After recently amassing enough funds for its rehabilitation, they razed much of the older section. Most of the new wing had been erected that spring, and the construction crew was preparing to work on the interior aspects next. I was curious to see their progress given it would reopen for the fall semester. The head librarian had also offered me a private tour that afternoon.

"So, the entire show lasts one week. The goal is to put Braxton on the map as we join the next tier of university rankings. It's primarily focused on African art's historical influence within our culture." I stared at a photo collection of tribal figurines, antique parchments, and rustic pottery from several centuries ago. "Where did it all come from?"

Fern flipped through the papers. "The art department was lucky to secure several prize pieces that are usually only shown in high-end auctions or galleries. Apparently, Cain formerly worked in a museum and brokered advantageous connections."

Ursula's materials implied that while Cain had obtained sizable donations to offset the cost of securing the expensive collections, he'd fallen short of his initial projections. That's when Ursula had convinced two former business school associates, Sawyer and Bitsy Jaccard, to monitor the college's investment and grandiose plans. Sawyer was an importer/exporter who often expedited the sale and transfer of expensive art and other collectibles between countries. Bitsy had previously been the curator at a historically significant Eastern European museum. Bitsy and Sawyer, who'd been married for over a decade, encouraged Ursula and Cain to implement additional security at Glass Hall, where the art exhibition would be held. Cain initially refused to work with anyone else besides his previous colleagues and contacts, and he fought the idea of security guards monitoring everyone's moves. Eventually, he caved and began listening to the Jaccards' requests and Ursula's direction. Ursula had told him he needed to review everything with Fern and me so that someone else on campus understood the entire event schedule—the inciting factor of the prior day's argument in her office.

I wondered whether Cain had originally listed the mysterious African figurine in the itemized inventory. Several other pieces from that collection filled the sheets, but the famous one that the FBI thought my uncle had stolen wasn't included. Given it was still missing, he'd likely eliminated its presence in the final catalog. From his notes, I understood it had substantial cultural value to the South African people as well as monetary value for collectors and historians. If my uncle had taken the figurine, had he intended to hand-deliver it to Cain but somehow been forced to stash it in one of the airports?

Once Fern and I discussed the remaining background on the upcoming art exhibition, including the bare bones of a supposed curse once placed on the missing object, she said, "Ursula instructed Cain to loop us in before our follow-up meeting on Monday. How's tomorrow at three?"

I checked my calendar and determined I was free. I also saw that April had settled on a time for our tête-à-tête with Fox. Since Emma and Ulan planned to spend the day with others after our regular Sunday family brunch, I could accomplish some work, coordinate next steps with Cain, and have drinks with Fox and April. Foremost, I'd corner and grill Nana D when she was preparing our meal, to find out why she'd betrayed me and become Fox's newest conquest.

While pondering the possibility of those two secretly dating, I deemed it more foolish than sickening. Nana D was seventy-five years old, twice his age. Even though she'd gone on a few dates since my grandpop met his maker a decade earlier, she'd always claimed she was too busy for clandestine trysts. Cain's father and Nana D had been an exclusive item until she dumped Lindsey upon learning about his dual interest in her best friend, Eustacia Paddington. Nana D and Eustacia had deemed themselves frenemies from that point forward; they desperately loved and supported one another as besties, but they also checked their backs for sharp knives whenever the other exited the room. Or poisoned margaritas!

Fern repeated her question. "Earth to Kellan. Does that time work?"

"Sorry, got distracted for a moment. Sure, I'm having drinks with my lothario of an enemy at five o'clock, so it'll be a banner day!"

"Enemy? I presume you mean Fox Terrell," Fern noted as we walked toward Memorial Library's administrative offices.

"Long story. Family drama. The usual." I was preparing to say goodbye when I remembered Fern's sister's flight that afternoon. "Has your family arrived?"

"Yes. I offered to pick them up in Philadelphia, but Ivy's husband hired a car. Tobias is a little snooty, if you ask me." Fern frowned as she scrolled through her mobile phone in search of something.

I'd taught Ivy's son, Jordan Ballantine, my first semester at Braxton. He'd been on the Braxton Bears baseball team and gone off to earn an MBA rather than pursue a career in professional baseball. Last I heard, he was permanently remaining in New Orleans. "I don't think I've met your sister. Tell me about her."

"Ivy is several years younger than me. She and her first husband were high school sweethearts, but Ivy disappeared after graduation and took a gap year. After college, they found their way back to each other and got married," Fern explained as she showed me a photograph of a svelte brunette with demure features and rabbit fur wrapped around her shoulders. "Ivy didn't always look like that. When Jordan's father started traveling more often, my sister suspected he was having an affair and divorced him. Truthfully, he was married to his job for most of their relationship."

"It's good to hear people can fall back in love with one another... even if it ends again." I'd always wondered what had happened between Fern and her husband. They weren't together anymore, but I had no details of their separation, nor did I want to pry.

"I suppose... anyway, Ivy called me one day from the hospital and begged for a ride home." Fern pursed her lips and explained that her sister

58

had undergone several plastic surgeries to alter her appearance, to make her pretty again, in Ivy's words. Ivy had always been the beautiful one, resembling their mother, a former Miss Pennsylvania runner-up in the 1950s. Fern had inherited their father's stockier and more structured appearance. It only further proved that beautiful women had self-esteem issues too.

"She's still gorgeous, even if the surgery is a tinge obvious." I'd considered having a minor procedure when I lived in Los Angeles. My nose had a slight bend from a teenage soccer ball skirmish, but it gave me character, so I left it alone.

"Now she's addicted to it. Tobias, that's Ivy's new husband, encourages the physical alterations too. For Christmas last year, he gifted her a brow lift and a lip augmentation." Fern pulled another photo from her wallet and giggled. "No surgeries at that point."

"Wow! She was perfect back then. Is Tobias a toxic influence?"

Fern shook her head. "No, he seems like a nice guy. They both turn fifty later this year and simply enjoy looking at beauty more than substance.

After the divorce from Jordan's dad, Ivy will do anything to make her marriage work."

Fern confirmed that Tobias Natcher was a self-made millionaire. He'd run several mid-size financial companies in the past, then opened his own investment firm. After expanding internationally, he developed an interest in rare art and the occult. Tobias had agreed to speak at the upcoming exhibition about his experience traveling the world in search of important pieces of historical art, and Ivy was planning to spend quality time with her sister and her son. Since classes had ended, Jordan would fly home for an extended break before commencing his summer internship at a major investment firm. Tobias had secured the opportunity for his stepson earlier that semester.

Fern promised to schedule our discussion with Cain, then left the library in a hurry to babysit her grandson. I entered the administrative offices with a renewed attitude and excitement for our excursion. Maggie's door popped open, and Connor Hawkins, one of April's detectives at the sheriff's office, waved at me. "Hey, bruddah!

Maggie is finishing a call. Then she'll take us on the tour. What's happening?"

We'd grown up together in Braxton and been best friends since pre-school. Both of his parents had emigrated from other countries and originally settled in Anguilla. When he turned two, they left their sun-soaked island filled with ecologically significant coral reefs and an excess of goats. After moving to Braxton and completing the appropriate immigration processes, they'd become American citizens and remained in town for two decades. While I'd moved to Los Angeles after graduation and lost touch with Connor, his parents relocated to the Caribbean for a calmer life. Connor chose to stay in Pennsylvania and focus on his career in security and law enforcement. At just over six foot, he was heavily tanned, chiseled to perfection, and known to flaunt it. Most women considered him their Adonis, and most men knew not to mess with a man built like a brick house.

After our secret fraternity handshake—yes, we once were quite the pair of campus hooligans... okay, I was the troublemaker and he regularly got me out of jams—Connor joined me at a nearby conference table. I scratched at my chin, curious to discover what was going on in his life these days. Given the trauma of my uncle's death and sister-in-law's accident, we'd hardly spent time together at the gym or grabbing a few beers, our cherished three-times-a-week routine.

"Miss ya man. How's your dad doing? Still loving Anguilla?"

Connor smirked. "Yep. Pop and Ma are planning to visit me this summer. They want to see Maggie again." He reminded me they'd met Connor's girlfriend during our college days but hadn't spoken to her in over ten years. "Pop is even thinking about traveling back to South Africa this fall. Ma has never gone there with him, and he's been tracing his roots now that he's retired from his job."

"My dad tried that for a while. Got sidetracked with golf, then tennis, and now volunteer work at the state accreditation facility. Wesley Ayrwick, a man who refuses to sit still!" I loved my father, even though we had a perplexing relationship. He and my older siblings were much closer, like my mother was to my younger siblings. As I mentioned previously, I mostly took after Nana

D. "Speaking of South Africa, are you attending Braxton's art exhibition next week? It's showcasing several artifacts that might honor your family's heritage."

Connor concurred, then examined the calendar on his phone. "Yep, Maggie sold me on it. We're going to the opening on Monday, then again later in the week when they reveal some long-lost pieces from the apartheid period. My family lived through that, from what Pop told me."

I shared with Connor what I'd read in Cain and Ursula's program materials. I'd grown more interested in the exhibition once I learned about the African artifacts included in a special session, and Renee's story had made me curious to dig into potential connections. So far, I hadn't been lucky enough to find anything. I'd suffered through stranger things that year, including secret double identities, killers with an affinity for spray-painted calla lilies, and ancient ghosts living in my house. Was a stolen African figurine with a bizarre curse all that far out of the realm of possibilities?

"Your dad and his parents were all born in South Africa?"

"Yeah. Pop's father died young, and it forced my grandma to raise him on her own. Her name was Gemma Hawkins. She ended up working for a wealthy man who drowned in a boating accident." Connor explained that he'd never met his grandmother because she'd passed away the year he was born. Grandma Gemma had frequently regaled Connor's dad with various anecdotes about the unique African tribes of their region, including one who claimed to be descended from a powerful blind queen or chief priestess. "Her name was Tessa, I believe."

"Are you talking about a woman who put curses on people or like... a strong warrior queen?" I'd read a few details about Queen Tessa in the art exhibition paraphernalia but not enough to know the full story; perhaps it was the same woman Gemma had told Connor's father about.

"I'm not really sure. Two warring factions feuded for decades, maybe centuries. Everyone's fascination quiets down for several years, then pops up again occasionally. Has something to do with revenge, but it might be a bunch of rumors. If it's important, I can ask Pop," he replied.

As Connor agreed to check, Maggie opened the door and invited us both in. Dressed in a pretty, flowery blouse and silk skirt, she looked elegant against the wall of bookshelves behind her. "Thanks for waiting. Wow! Have I got a message for you, Kellan." A wily glint overtook her deep brown saucer eyes. "Your boss didn't seem pleased to hear you were socializing right now."

"This ought to be good." I braced for the impact of a tyrant's fury. "Bring it on. I'm ready."

Chapter 5

"It's been a rough day for me too. I spent most of the morning helping my parents," Maggie replied, complaining about several guests who had checked into their bed-and-breakfast, the Roarke and Daughters Inn. "They're already causing problems. One larger-than-life couple fought like cats and dogs. The other was obnoxious and fussy. Both will speak at the exhibition tomorrow. I might have to skip their talks. Avoid the Jaccards and Natchers if you see them!"

Great! Four of the people I had to converse with as part of my commitment to Ursula and Myriam. The week couldn't get any worse. "So, what did the she-devil want?"

Maggie covered her lips to stop herself from laughing. "First, she confirmed the budget on the new library wing. But then the conversation took a drastically different turn."

"Ah, yes, my wonderful boss strikes again. I met with her yesterday about my forthcoming syllabus, and she conveniently signed me up

66

to help with the art show. Myriam told Ursula that—"

Maggie held her hand up. "Oh, you won't believe this one. Myriam offered very explicit instructions for your weekend plans."

Connor slapped his thigh, sending an echo throughout the wooden rafters of the room's lofty ceiling. "Dragon Lady beckons her minions. Classic!"

I guffawed. "I am not one of her minions. I'm stuck dealing with a barracuda intent on swallowing me whole." After rolling my eyes in hyperbolic circles, I released a burst of warm air and repeatedly flicked my tongue against the roof of my mouth. "Stop teasing me! What did Beelzebub's reincarnation demand this time?"

After shooing us out of the office and pointing toward the distant hallway, Maggie pulled her door shut. "A reminder that Bitsy and Sawyer were not to be ignored. She said, and I quote, 'Inform Professor Ayrwick that he is to take them to lunch or dinner tomorrow. Somewhere chic and impressive. Not any family-owned restaurants or side-of-the-road wiener stands.' Then she hung up to meet with a nurse at Willow Trees."

Willow Trees, an expansive complex offering a collection of elder care services, contained a rehabilitation center, nursing home, and senior citizen residential living quarters. I'd learned recently that Myriam's dad was a patient in the facility. Maybe she was born of humans!

My face flushed bright red. "I don't even eat hot dogs! What is wrong with that woman?"

Connor quipped, "Maybe she's developed a secret crush on you. Little boys and girls often tease each other when they like them."

"Myriam is not a little girl. I think she knew Moses." I embellished the truth; she was somewhere in her mid to late forties.

Maggie smacked a palm to her forehead as we drifted down the hallway to the construction entrance. "Oh, please. She's been married to Ursula for an awfully long time. I highly doubt she's suddenly switched teams or willing to risk her marriage. And really, Kellan would not be her type. That's hilarious but ludicrous, Connor." Her laughter accompanied us through the narrow corridor as if we'd begun traipsing the Yellow Brick Road. If Maggie were Dorothy, and

Connor the Tin Man, did that make me the Cowardly Lion or the Brainless Scarecrow?

Connor roared with a deep belly grumble that rivaled a volcanic explosion. "Totally true."

"Whoa! I wholeheartedly agree that Myriam wouldn't abruptly decide she wants to be with a man instead of a woman; however, and this is an especially important question..." I stated, pausing for dramatic effect. "What is wrong with me that I wouldn't be her type?" Maggie's proclamation offended me, as did Connor's extreme support of said false decree. Not that I'd ever been attracted to my boss, who on most occasions rivaled Cruella de Vil, but I also needed to know why she wouldn't be enthralled by my exhilarating presence. I turned women's heads when I walked down the street, as long as Connor wasn't hovering nearby to soak up all the adoration. Even Maggie's sister had called me a snack once, which wasn't exactly the ideal bandwagon for me to hop on.

"After falling in love with an exotic Scandinavian beauty like Ursula Power, do you imagine Myriam would be convinced to cross to the other side so she could test the waters with a...." Maggie hesitated and, in the silence, looked to Connor with a pleading expression for a suggestion.

"A sensible scoop of vanilla ice cream that one tolerates after consuming a seven-course dinner fit for a goddess?" Connor shrugged indecisively before pushing open the door to the new wing.

I had to agree with him on vanilla; it was not a real flavor or culmination to a magnificent meal, at least not to me. Desserts involved chocolate and lots of it. "Vanilla ice cream goes with a lot of things. Fruit pies. Hot fudge. Apple crisps. Butterscotch brownies. But I am much more than vanilla ice cream. I'm... I'm like... I'm like a Baked Alaska topped with Cherries Jubilee and a ten-layer princess cake covered in scrumptious marzipan." Ugh! Nana D had been way too big of an influence on me as a child. Even I knew I'd just dug my own grave and buried myself under a thousand sheets of embarrassment.

"Need I say more?" Connor shook his head, as he had during most of our youth when I'd developed a case of verbal diarrhea. "You are high maintenance. Myriam has learned exactly how to rile you up. She knows you'll take the Jaccards to a gourmet restaurant, but she jabs you relentlessly to keep you in line. Clearly, the woman is in love with her wife, and you are merely a toy she enjoys winding up to watch it chase its own tail."

"Seriously, who needs best friends like the two of you? When this tour is done, I'm out of here." I followed them through the tight passageway and conjured various retaliatory methods against my boss. While daydreaming about roasting the woman like a marshmallow over an open fire and exploring the astonishing new library wing, my phone buzzed with a message from an unknown number.

Hello, love. Ursie tells me you're a doll and that you're gonna escort little old me around town this week. We're gonna be besties. I can just feel it. Toodles!

Attached to the message was a photo the sender had clearly just snapped on her camera phone, followed by a voice message introducing herself. I couldn't help but recognize how remarkably similar she looked to a cartoon vamp who'd once given me nightmares. Jessica Rabbit had nothing on Bitsy Jaccard, but at the same time the woman's voice also sounded exactly like Betty

Boop. What had Ursula told me not to do... judge a book by its cover? What if the book resembled a caricature of two animated characters I couldn't stand? Oh, it was not gonna end well. Why had Ursula and Myriam involved me in a Draconian nightmare!?!

* * *

After picking up Emma from Francesca's on Sunday morning, we met my parents at church and drove to Danby Landing, Nana D's organic orchard and farm. I'd begun inviting April to my grandmother's weekly tradition the month before, once I'd come clean about our relationship to my family. Mostly, they were happy for me, but a trace of disappointment lined the perimeter of my mother's voice concerning the relationship. We hadn't yet discussed the reason, and I wasn't looking forward to popping that lid off her container of crazy. Nonetheless, April had too much going on at the sheriff's office given her four-day absence, so she skipped brunch that week. We'd more than made up for her time away the prior night, but as a gentleman who was taught not to kiss and tell, my lips were zipper-locked and sealed.

Upon arrival, we recounted heartwarming stories about Uncle Zach, including tons of humorous and touching tales from his childhood when my mother would babysit him, and he'd insist on playing *Hide-and-Seek*. My personal favorite—he'd crawled into the horse barn and fallen asleep in their food buckets. A pregnant mare had even taken a liking to him and kept him safe during the beginning of a snowstorm.

Nana D teared up a few times, then escaped to finish preparations. While my father tutored Ulan for his calculus final exam, my mother assembled a puzzle of African safari animals with Emma. I'd bought one the prior week because I made a point of teaching my daughter about diverse topics, attempting to align her education with my courses at Braxton. I quietly sneaked into the kitchen, even though Nana D insisted on handling all the cooking herself, to learn more about the incident in the Simply Stoddard parking lot with Fox Terrell. Six hours remained before he'd grace April and me with his presence.

Walking into that confounded rigamarole being ill-prepared wasn't an option.

"So, are you gonna explain yourself, or do I have to locate Emma's crayons and let you doodle stick figures acting out your dirty little secret?" I leaned over Nana D's shoulder, an exceptionally effortless task given she barely hit the five-foot mark and, truth be told, shrank each year.

She grabbed the saltshaker and aggressively tossed a ton of grains in my direction. "Oopsie, I didn't see you there, brilliant one. Just making a little wish that I prepare a tasty brunch today."

I swatted most of it off the collar of my royal-blue polo, refusing to let her hijinks fluster me. "Answer my question, you crafty miniature Elf-on-the-Shelf."

"It's inappropriate to refer to your loving, cherished nana or the venerated mayor of our wonderful county like that." Nana D sprinkled salt into the hash browns and commanded me to pour coffee—from the industrial size machine my parents had given her and that she'd hated to no end—into a silver serving pot. "You get more and more like Grandpop every day; God rest his soul. He used to challenge me all the time. Never worked, though. You've got to step up your game, Kellan."

"Uncle Zach was a good man, all because of you and Grandpop. Never forget that you're the backbone of this family. We are here for you, no matter what," I said, kissing her forehead and drying her tears—a rare occurrence from a pillar of strength.

"I know, honey. We gotta find out the truth, okay? I'm not admitting my age... but losing my boy has added a decade when I can barely afford a year. Grandpop doesn't need me up there that badly!" She pointedly stared at me until I told her about Renee and agreed to do everything I could to find Uncle Zach's supposed killer. "Zach must've been keeping her a secret from me. I want to meet this floozy if she dares show her face in town. Anyway, don't get me started again... you had something to ask, if I remember correctly, brilliant one."

While my heartache brewed over her words, I filled the coffee pot and gently placed it on the serving tray, clasped my hands together, and sat on the banquette in the adjacent corner. "Yes, please help me understand why you'd make out with a ridiculous interloper who intentionally aggravates me. Fox is worse than that recurring boil on your bum you complained about last year, but you still had to go canoodling there. Why?"

"Canoodling? Stop appropriating words that belong to my generation. And while we're focused on curbing your bad behaviors, you're beginning to annoy me by always bringing up Fox! Grow up. Grow smarter. Grow a pair." Nana D accidentally dropped the giant metal spoon she'd just taken out of the drawer and shouted a word she'd taught me never to say as a child. "Sorry, not sorry. Anyway, have you lost your mind? What on earth are you blathering about?"

"You confessed in the text message yesterday."

"I did not." Her upper lip curled in such a way I thought she had morphed into Morticia's mother from *The Addams Family*. "You're a few pennies short of a dollar. Sipping at the sherry a little too early, Boozy?"

I ignored her insults and expressively read aloud our chain of text messages, hoping Nana D hadn't developed a case of Alzheimer's or multiple personalities. "Does any of this ring a bell?

Am I talking to myself, or have the cylinders begun spinning properly again?" I stood, tapped two fingers gently on her noggin, and closed my eyes, patiently waiting for a response.

After whacking my rear end with the slotted spoon, which would leave a giant red welt I'd have to explain to April that evening, Nana D solved the riddle. "You and I obviously had a misunderstanding. Yes, I visited Simply Stoddard's parking lot this week, but not for the reason you've implied." Nana D indicated that she'd been present the night of Fox's infamous smooch, and she'd already told April about it.

"Wait a minute! You told my girlfriend that her husband was kissing some other woman, but you failed to tell me? That's messed up, even for you!" I rubbed the spot where she'd spanked me just as Emma walked into the kitchen.

"Can I have a glass of…" Emma began, changing her train of thought when she caught me peeling back my jeans to check if my bum had already bruised. "Did you just make an air biscuit, Daddy?"

My eyes bulged so far out of their sockets they'd never pop back in. Before I could respond,

Nana D chortled like a cackling fool and my mother dashed into the kitchen. Nana D pulled Emma closer to her waist and nodded feverishly. "He sure did. Big stinky one too. They heard and smelled it over in Woodland. Thought the fertilizer factory imploded. He's got no class, that father of yours!"

Emma pinched her nose and buried her face in Nana D's immaculate apron. "Ewww… rude."

"Honey, where did you learn that expression?" cautiously asked my mother, who must've caught the tail end of the conversation as she waltzed into the room.

"Ulan said Augie lets them loose all the time," Emma stated, still holding her nose. "And sometimes he makes his farts sound like a horn playing Jingle Bells."

"That does it! I'm never coming to brunch again." My mother snatched a real biscuit from the counter, clutched Emma's hand, and dragged her back to the living room. "Little girl, you need to stop repeating everything those two hooligans say and do. They are not the role models a little princess should emulate."

Grateful for the moment of levity and distraction, I sighed heavily, accepting the role of 'punchline in her jokes' as an avenue to help Nana D address her grief. Predictably, Nana D never admitted who she'd seen Fox kissing or what she'd thought she was confessing to in the first place. "Okay, now that we're more absurd than a *National Lampoon's* farce, care to explain yourself?"

Nana D put the finishing touches on our extravagant brunch and rattled off all the details. She'd gone to the restaurant on a rainy evening to pick up a to-go plate for dinner. When she stepped out of the car, she accidentally dropped her umbrella in a giant puddle. An attractive, middle-aged gentleman kindly stopped to help, and when he handed her the umbrella, she planted a kiss on his cheek as a thank you. After he slipped away, she rushed inside to collect her chicken Milanese. On the way back out, Nana D caught Fox in an intimate embrace with Kathy Endicott, Cain's mother.

"You've got to be kidding me! Lindsey Endicott's ex-wife? Your former boyfriend, Lindsey? But Kathy is old enough to be Fox's mother. Fox and Cain are about the same age. Heck, those two kinda look like one another too." As the words dribbled from my mouth, I squirmed with nausea.

"Ewww," replied Nana D as she shook violently and made the most unattractive face I'd ever seen. "Yeah, Cain and Fox are both dark-haired, tall, and in exquisite shape, if you like that sort of thing. And I do... they sure razz my berries!" For a scary moment, Nana D glazed over as she entertained some sort of daydream and uttered unspeakable noises.

"I get it. Everyone I know is hot. Can we stick to the pertinent facts? Did he see you watching them kiss?" It really didn't bother me that the women in my life constantly remarked about all the gorgeous men in our town. Okay, it tangentially bugged me a bit. I was tired of always being cast as the cute, fun, and friendly boy next door; never the stud who revved a woman's engines until she overheated and stripped naked in the town fountain. Not that I knew anyone who'd achieved that feat. Nevertheless, my point was valid. Maybe I needed some therapy too.

"You seem a little jealous. Didn't your parents compliment you enough when you were a child? Green isn't an attractive color on you, brilliant one." Nana D poked her head into the living room and ordered the troops to congregate at the dining room table.

I pulled her aside before we consumed brunch. "Listen up, old woman... I love you more than I should... did Fox or did Fox *not* see you?"

"Yep, and he smiled real big when he pulled away from Kathy and watched me standing there, shocked as a precious little lamb encountering a hangry bear." Nana D informed me that Fox had waved to her, escorted Kathy to her car, and tore off on his motorcycle.

"Maybe he'll leave April alone now. Thanks for the info. It might come in handy later." I hadn't realized Kathy Endicott was in town. While Lindsey had married several additional women and fathered more children after their divorce, Kathy had become a flight attendant and worked Orlando's international routes. She'd have some insight into what everyone was saying about the explosion that had killed my uncle.

Since weekends were my sister's busiest days at the Pick-Me-Up Diner, Eleanor wouldn't arrive until the end of our meal. She'd also agreed to bring Ulan back to her eatery that afternoon for his new part-time job as a busboy. It would hardly distract his mind from his dad's death, but a couple of hours a week were bound to encourage some positive impact. Whenever they left, Eleanor and Ulan would also drop off some of Nana D's home-cooking at the Royal Chic-Shack, the affectionate name for our parents' remodeled log cabin. Hampton and his family had been living there with my parents for a few months, so someone could help Natasha throughout the day. Although he had hired a physical therapist and a part-time nurse to focus on Natasha's recovery, my sister-in-law wasn't ready to appear in public. She also preferred to enjoy quiet time alone with her immediate family whenever my parents disappeared for several hours. After brunch, my mother and father were planning to attend a concert in Philadelphia for the evening.

The rest of the afternoon went as well as expected, given my brother Gabriel had skipped that weekend to be with Sam in Dallas. He'd typically received the brunt of my parents' criticisms, which meant I incurred their wrath in his absence. Emma and Ulan hung out with Eleanor once she showed up. My sister seemed to avoid all the adults for some reason. My mother asked lots of questions about the upcoming art exhibition. And Nana D only spilled two drinks on Dad's lap. Usually, she *accidentally* tripped over an invisible object and sent a sharp knife soaring into his lap. On that day, he survived with no wounds, headaches, or verbal lashings. She must've been slipping in her old age.

While I packed Emma's puzzle and prepared to leave, Fern rang my phone. "Cain delayed our meeting. Claimed something important got in the way. When I reminded him about Ursula's frustrations, he just laughed."

"Are you serious? He's becoming a problem," I noted, thinking back to the noises I'd heard in his office. "Someone better put that impervious man out of his misery."

"And get this... in the background, a woman told him to take off his pants before she stripped 'em like a pole dancer!" Fern awkwardly revealed that she'd turned six different shades of red and silently disconnected their call rather than over-hear anything too salacious.

"We'll do the work ourselves. Like normal!"

"Listen, I found something in Cain's papers that we missed yesterday. Just to give you some advanced warning," Fern said, a tinge of worry in her voice. "A sticky note in his handwriting that mentions your uncle's name, a car rental, and a strange code or number."

"What? I'll be there pronto." I grabbed a pint of rum from Nana D's liquor cabinet on the way out of Danby Landing. While I wouldn't drink any until I safely arrived at my destination, liquid courage offered the only way to endure the bal-ance of the day. Had Fern connected Cain with Uncle Zach's death?

Chapter 6

After dropping Emma off at gymnastics practice with a friend from school, I met Fern on campus. She'd arrived first and prepared all the remaining accounts, expenses, and proposals for our discussion with Cain. We convened in the art department's conference room, despite his unprofessional delay. "Let me see the sticky note."

Fern slid a document across the table. "It was attached to this short bio on a seventeenth century governor named Yeardley. Be right back."

I read both while Fern ambled to the kitchen and retrieved two bottles of water. The sticky note said: *FL1162. Possible car rental. Send photo of article to Zach.* The bio contained only a few sentences and appeared to be a photocopy of something from an encyclopedia or library book. All I'd learned of value was that Governor Yeardley had overseen several colonies in southern Africa and was held in high regard by his people. He'd died during his forty-ninth year from a venomous snake bite and left behind several daughters who vied for control of his empire. I typed the code into my phone's browser and determined it was a flight number for a plane traveling from Orlando to Philadelphia.

"Does it mean anything to you?" Fern handed me one of the bottles and pulled her chair closer.

I shared my discovery, keen to further research Governor Yeardley on the Internet. Was the missing African figure connected to him? "Cain has a lot of explaining to do. This is the same number of my uncle's original flight out of Orlando. Before he canceled it and rented a car instead. I don't get it."

Fern suggested that Cain might've been working with my uncle on the art exhibition and coordinated the car rental for him. "Were they friends?"

"Not that I know of. Cain didn't come to Uncle Zach's funeral service or burial ceremony." I decided to look more closely at all of Cain's papers in case anything else popped up. If not, I would update April afterward and spend time investigating the Yeardley notation that evening. "Thanks for finding the sticky note. It might be a perfect lead. Let's get through the exhibition planning. That okay?"

"Sure, no worries. I'm anxious to spend more time with my sister."

"Ah... how are things with Ivy and Tobias? Any new plastic surgery surprises?" I continued smirking in Fern's direction even though she scowled at me.

"No. In fact, she looked more relaxed than last time. We only met for drinks. Tobias had an unexpected business meeting. Ivy was eager to return to the inn to see how it went."

"I'm sure Ivy is excited to see her son. Will Jordan stay with them at the Roarke and Daughters Inn?" I remembered that Ivy had sold their family home when Jordan left Wharton County to begin his MBA program. She and Tobias had purchased a permanent residence in London and rented in the US when they stayed for extended trips.

"Since my son moved out when he got married last year, I have the extra space. We turned Arthur's room into a guest area. Jordan crashes there when he visits." Fern reminded me that Jordan's father, Rhett Ballantine, traveled internationally on a regular basis and hardly saw his son much.

"I always liked Jordan, even if he was slightly cocky. I assumed the behavior resulted from his parents' divorce. Teenagers struggle to accept things like that until later in life." I flipped through Cain's detailed expense register, and from what I could tell, he was fifty-thousand dollars over budget given the amount he owed to museums and private collectors. "Do you have the tour schedule?"

"Yes, one sec." Fern handed it to me and fiddled with her phone.

Most of the next day's opening festivities included introductions and a couple of lectures from visiting professors. We wanted a walkthrough of Glass Hall to verify the facility was ready, but Cain had told us the cleaning crew would perform a last sweep that afternoon. We intended to head there for a brief tour once the meeting with him concluded. While I perused the tour schedule, Fern noted that Cain was an hour late. "Should we call?"

"Sure, go ahead. I hardly know him. We've exchanged pleasantries at faculty or administrative meetings, and we briefly chatted at his father's holiday event last year, but I don't have his number."

While Fern tried to reach Cain, I leafed through the remaining timetable. The Jaccards appeared on the schedule for the following morning as well as Tobias in the afternoon. Bitsy and I had exchanged a series of text messages during the prior twenty-four hours. Given her preparation for the art show, she couldn't arrange a lunch or dinner as Myriam had demanded, but we planned to meet for coffee before the exhibition opened. Several conference calls would sidetrack Sawyer, and she thought it would be beneficial for us to meet alone. I had no clue why, but until meeting her in person I reserved judgment, just as Ursula had recommended.

When I glanced up, Fern was coddling someone on her phone. She must've gotten hold of Cain to determine when he'd grace us with his presence. A minute later, she disconnected and cocked her head sideways. "That was Cain's mother, Kathy. He left his cell at home today. She's staying with him while visiting from Orlando. He never showed for their lunch date, and when she returned home and found his phone, panic set in. Kathy picked up, hoping it was her son, but he's vanished."

"Ursula definitely has a valid reason to worry. Hopefully, he's securing more funds to remedy his fifty-thousand-dollar shortfall. Unless the Jaccards fixed that already. Shall we wait for Cain to reach out to us?" I asked Fern for Kathy's phone number so I could determine whether she had any information about my uncle's car explosion.

Luckily, Fern had saved the woman's contact details from a prior book club. "No. Want to walk over to Glass Hall? I don't have my keys with me, but if Cain or BCS are on site, they could let us in."

Braxton Campus Security (BCS) patrolled the campus regularly and monitored the safety of students and staff. Most academic halls were closed on Sundays, and Braxton hadn't switched the structure to an automated access control system. The facilities department would open and shut down all the buildings each morning and night. Although they worked twenty-four-seven,

BCS rarely posted security guards at individual buildings. They'd only hired extra temporarily for the exhibition.

When we reached Glass Hall across the courtyard, we found the side entrances locked. A security guard at the front door indicated no one was inside the building. Given neither of us knew exactly how the exhibits should be set up, we agreed to sync up later that night after Fern got hold of Cain. She would be dining with Ivy and her husband and needed to change into more formal attire. Tobias had insisted on a Michelin-star restaurant located somewhere between Braxton and Philadelphia, about an hour's drive.

Once she exited, I checked on Ulan's first day of work. He enjoyed bussing tables and still hadn't heard a peep from Renee, his father's mysterious girlfriend. He planned to finish some schoolwork in my sister's tiny office at the back of the diner. Augie would swing by to pick him up after collecting Emma from gymnastics practice. April confirmed she'd meet me at a nearby Irish pub to talk to Fox; she'd been detained with a couple of reports that had to be filed by the following morning.

I headed to Kirklands and prepared myself for all its debauchery. Over the years, the famed Irish tavern had transitioned into a trashy twenty-and-thirty-something singles hangout. During Happy Hours, patrons could order two-dollar beers and five-dollar cocktails while listening to a wide range of loud, diverse music. It was the type of place you could temporarily hide from your boyfriend or girlfriend until they showed up ready for a brawl with your name first on their list. Sticky tabletops. Peanut shells on the floors. Couples making out in the corner. I avoided the place myself, but if I ever needed to meet someone on the down low, it was the perfect ramshackle dive.

When I arrived, Fox was deeply engrossed in a conversation with the FBI/ICE agent I'd met a couple of months earlier and seen at the Pick-Me-Up Diner. A mere few inches shorter than me, the enigmatic Giovanni had medium-brown skin, a noticeable scar on his neck, and went by only his given name, a la Madonna, Cher, and Sting.

In our last conversation at the hospital on the day of Natasha's accident, I'd learned that he partnered with Fox to conduct several discrete traces on my family. He'd also dug into my uncle's background to confirm whether he concealed information on an African figurine. As a government agent, Giovanni had been assigned to the case when unknown sources verified that the missing object would secretly be sold to a US citizen. Given the strain placed on America's relationship with South Africa because of the figurine's loss, it was his job to find and return it before tensions escalated. At least that was what he'd claimed. I continued to worry his explanation was an erroneous fabrication.

Eager to ask about his investigation into Uncle Zach's supposed larceny, I stomped my way through a boisterous crowd toward their table. Before I descended upon them, Giovanni noticed me and immediately picked up his phone. He hung up quickly and muttered something to Fox, who winked at me in his usual intolerable manner. As I attempted to convince a pair of twenty-something baseball enthusiasts arguing over an umpire's calls to step aside, my phone buzzed. I quickly retrieved it from my pocket and slipped by the Phillies fans to blast whoever had interrupted my stroke of luck.

Bitsy Jaccard. Per Myriam's instructions, ignoring the woman equaled death by awful class assignments. She'd explicitly directed me to watch out for Bitsy while she was in town, noting the woman habitually landed herself in hot water. After I kindly answered Bitsy's repetitive questions about how to find Glass Hall—we'd also discussed it twice already the night before—she ordered me to hold on while she located a piece of paper. In the background, she argued with her husband. I knew because she hollered his name twice in a loud whisper, then complained when he asked her to fix him a Martini. She capped and shook a cocktail shaker while Sawyer refused to answer her questions.

Finally, Bitsy returned to the call and apologized for the interruption. As I clarified our location for the following morning, she declared she had to meet Ursula and Myriam for dinner. "Toodles, my hunky-dunky little friend!"

The capricious woman skidded close to aggravating my last nerve. How would I survive an entire week with her? After shoving thoughts of her high-pitched voice and wacky speech pattern out of my head, I continued striding toward Fox and Giovanni. In the five minutes I'd gotten distracted by Bitsy, Giovanni had disappeared, and April was approaching Fox from the opposite side of the room. Somehow, I'd missed her entry into Kirklands and lost my opportunity to corner the agent.

"Where did he go?" I blasted Fox, practically crowding his face when I reached the booth.

With a single hand against my chest, he pushed me away. "You don't want to start something here, do you?"

April snapped her fingers like a machine gun, then pointed to the seat beside her. "Enough. We're not doing this again. Sit down, Kellan. Who are you looking for?"

"Giovanni was here moments ago. He might know more about my uncle's death and this missing African figurine. I want to understand what it looks like."

April glared at Fox. "I assume you're intimately acquainted with this priceless artifact?"

"Maybe. But it'll cost you," he jested, affectionately resting his hand against her forearm as I slid into the booth opposite him. "I'm sure we can work out a deal to exchange information. We were always good with sharing… right, doll?"

A fury built up inside me, but I knew tempering it would net the best outcome, especially if April and I planned to walk away with critical information. "Look, something funny is going on with this whole situation. I want to believe you're an honest guy, Fox. Really… this rivalry between us is useless and maddening. April has informed you she loves me. Nana D told us about your dalliance with Kathy Endicott. If you agree to stop, I'll stop too."

Fox flexed his pecs and shrewdly beamed, refusing to acknowledge anything I'd mentioned. He shifted positions against the padded cushion when April ripped her arm away from him, then motioned to the waitress who passed by with a carefully balanced drink order. "Three local brews this time. My friends are planning to take advantage of my good nature this evening. Thanks, honey."

April waited for the scantily clad woman to disperse before adding more color to the conversation. "Fox is generally a good guy, even though he likes to instigate trouble. As two intelligent and mature individuals, I'm confident you can play nicely together in this sandbox." Using her admirable negotiation skills, somehow, she persuaded him to tell us everything he knew. Or at least more than we'd learned to date. He was the kind of guy who'd conveniently leave out a few facts to ensure we'd have to visit him another time.

"Trust me. I don't know Giovanni well. Quid pro quo when I need some help. The figurine he's looking for is from three or four centuries ago, and no, I never saw a picture. You should know it's called a talisman, and this particular spiritual object has wreaked havoc on many people to date."

April cocked her head in his direction and clomped on his foot. "Quit mansplaining. Just tell us the entire story, Fudnucker." Oh, she'd used his real first name, at least before he'd legally changed his embarrassing moniker.

"Okay, okay… relax. Giovanni didn't want to release all the details, only a brief description so I could keep my gorgeous peepers out for it. He indicated it would be obvious if I ever came across the monstrosity." Fox then shed some remaining light on the elusive agent's curious tale, including a potent connection with the famous Governor Yeardley. His story enthralled and terrified me at all once.

Chapter 7

In the mid-1600s, a beloved queen named Tessa ruled one of the chief tribes in the South African sub-continent. She was born blind but had become a skilled negotiator and facilitator who united several divisive clans during her early rule. While European settlers attempted to conquer the area, she led her tribe to victory for many years. Queen Tessa had a talisman she claimed the gods had bequeathed to her when she'd gone on a spiritual walk through the coastal mountains. She fastidiously wore the twelve-inch figurine around her neck, and according to legend, a golden nectar inside a hidden chamber protected them from the ruthless invaders. One day, Queen Tessa left on a mystical journey to ask the gods for assistance to defend her people from the new weapons being used to hunt them. During the walk, she was kidnapped by a group of mercenaries who'd banded together to conquer her tribe. They savagely beat and burned her body. Before killing the treasured queen, the vandals drained her blood and re-placed the nectar in her talisman with some of it. Governor Yeardley, the leader of the largest colony masterminding the plot, sent the talis-man back to Queen Tessa's tribe with a message that they had lost the war and it was time to surrender.

Fox's eyes ignited like firecrackers when he regaled us with the story, as if he believed in its magical history like children did Santa Claus and the Easter Bunny. "Queen Tessa had told her daughters that this would happen one day. She could often predict the future, a gift the gods had bestowed upon her with the original talisman. Knowing minimal opportunity persisted to pro-tect her people, Queen Tessa placed a dark curse on the figurine before Governor Yeardley massa-cred her."

April kept silent as Fox reveled in all his glory. I shimmied closer to her on the bench, not so much to remind him she and I were dating but because Fox's news had unsettled me. "I read a bit about this curse. Queen Tessa vowed that one day her family would return to power and expel the invaders, so she instructed her children to pass the talisman to the eldest daughter in each new generation, right?"

Fox nodded. "She supposedly placed two specific curses on the object. Giovanni heard an equivalent story from multiple museum curators, as well as a mysterious contact who had connections with many high-ranking US officials and someone in the South African embassy. Unfortunately, he wouldn't tell me the name of his primary contact, nor did he know the exact details of each curse. The family buried the particulars over the years. And not everyone believes in such foolish things."

April interjected, keen to limit our time with her soon-to-be ex-husband. "What happened to the talisman between the time Queen Tessa gave it to her eldest daughter and it possibly ending up in Zach Danby's hands?"

"Patience, darling," Fox scolded with a fleeting, displeased scowl. He gently clocked her chin in jest. To April's credit, she didn't flinch. Instead, she lifted her jacket panel to remind him of *Old Betsy*, the gun strapped to her waist. Fox licked his lips and blew her a kiss. "All Giovanni conveyed was that the tribe maintained

their land for two centuries, but eventually negotiations disintegrated. Although each daughter
passed the talisman to her eldest daughter, the
facts of the curse became blurrier and the family
took many risks to remain in hiding. It's become
a bit of an old wives' tale now."

While Fox clarified his opinions, I wondered
how much he had embellished. Every few generations, one of the eldest daughters had been born
blind, like her powerful ancestor, Queen Tessa.
The new baby was also named Tessa in honor
of the late queen who'd led the tribe to victory
on so many occasions. As each generation unfolded, they married into different races and eth-
nicities across the continent and from the European colonies. Once more Caucasians settled in
their enclave and dangerous civil wars broke out
across the region, the tribe shrank until merely
one line existed.

The last surviving Tessa had only given birth
to a son, whom she named Ludovicus after his father, a German who hailed from Bavaria. Ludovicus looked nothing at all like his maternal ancestor, Queen Tessa; in fact, he'd appeared a hundred percent Caucasian despite having a quarter

of his DNA originating from African roots. He'd married a young woman whom his mother had insisted would provide him a daughter to carry on the family tradition and inherit the cursed talisman. But sadly, rebels had stolen the figurine from Tessa, Ludovicus, and his wife during the crux of apartheid. "Rumor is that the rebels were descendants of Governor Yeardley too."

"If I'm not mistaken, isn't there some truth to the curse?" I wasn't sure exactly why they thought Uncle Zach had gotten a hold of the talisman, but hopefully Cain, Fox, or Giovanni could supply that information. If not, Renee would know more, assuming the mysterious woman ever showed face. I grew more certain my uncle had been murdered, that the car explosion wasn't an accident.

"Yes. Giovanni's research verified that ever since the sixties, when the talisman was taken from Queen Tessa's heirs, it brought disaster to anyone who came in contact with it. Many of these people died strange deaths throughout the last fifty years. Horrific and unusual final moments like falling off buildings, drowning in low tide, dying in unprovoked safari attacks, and being struck by lightning. A few of the victims could trace their lineage back to Governor Yeardley, but not all of them. Yeardley only had female children. His family had daughtered out, making his ancestry a bit murky. After each victim died, the talisman disappeared for a few years until someone new claimed to discover it, and the cycle began again. I'm more inclined to believe the deaths were coincidental if I'm being honest." Fox eventually confirmed that the talisman showed up in a bidding war earlier that year, but the person who bought it never received the object from the seller. Giovanni had been assigned to recover the stolen figurine, and during that investigation, he had become acquainted with Uncle Zach in South Africa a few days before he left the country.

"And you think Kellan's uncle arranged to steal it from the seller. Or was he the seller? For what purpose?" April sat back, puzzled at all the latest information, and sipped from her beer.

"That's the peculiar part," Fox cautiously replied, scratching his head and shifting his gaze. "Giovanni never told me why. Just that he was certain Zach had possessed the talisman. Perhaps he was a fence or the middleman to transfer it to someone else. When they couldn't find the object in Zach's luggage at the airport, and no traces of it appeared in the ruins of the car explosion, Giovanni explored other avenues. He hasn't offered any additional details since then."

When Fox indicated he had no other information, April subsequently grilled him about the divorce and his foolish behavior with Kathy Endicott. Fox confessed he was merely keeping himself entertained until April changed her mind about their marriage. She told him to vamoose before she arrested him for some trumped-up charge, and for some reason, Fox listened to her and swaggered out of the bar. Then the waitress dropped off his check, which I had to pay. That man was an abomination! But he had provided some intriguing leads to follow up on.

"Something doesn't seem right here, does it?" April rubbed both her temples and sighed from the confusion.

"It doesn't. Either my uncle was involved in the theft of Queen Tessa's talisman, or someone set him up so he or she could make off with it before the explosion. Clearly, his death wasn't an accident. It's critical to uncover the identity of the mysterious seller who never surrendered the talisman. I bet that's who killed Uncle Zach to keep him from talking."

April tentatively nodded. "I'm also wondering what connection this might have to the upcoming art exhibition at Braxton. From what I gather, a bunch of artsy folks are gonna be here soon. Possibly someone's trying to resell it this week. We need to learn more about the extent of this curse."

I relayed the news about Cain's sticky note to April. "Not to mention Giovanni's deception, Cain failing to show up for our meeting earlier, and his mother's job at the Orlando airport where Uncle Zach's car blew up. Too many coincidences. Kathy might know something important."

Was April going to support me on the investigation or insist I back down? Although we'd found a middle ground to deal with it in the past, she wasn't responsible for investigating Uncle Zach's death. It had happened outside of her territory, yet she was equally suspicious of facts that weren't adding up.

April's words pulled me from deep thought. "You know what I'm thinking, Kellan?"

"That we have just enough time at home before the kids return?" I waggled my eyebrows and traced my foot along her calf. "Maybe I could take you there to—"

"Yeah, that's definitely gonna happen. But first, we should recognize this as a sign to do a little sleuthing together." April swigged the remnants of her beer, latched on to both my hands, and eagerly led me away from the booth. As we crossed through the rowdy baseball fans, she stopped to check the score. "Home team's ahead. Nice!"

Despite having a keen interest in baseball, all I could think about was the fun that would ensue when we got to my place. Then it hit me. "Wait, are you actually telling me to pursue a homicide case? Who are you and what have you done with my girlfriend?"

April was about to respond when my cell buzzed again. She stopped short and folded her arms against her chest. Her eyes glowered like laser beams intent on burning a hole through my skin. "Wanna get that interruption? Make it brief... you're gonna be tied up for a while."

Her prurient expression immediately convinced me to accept the call and make plans to hang up as quickly as possible. I recognized the number but couldn't remember why it seemed familiar. "Hello. Who's this? Can't really talk right now."

"Hi... are you Kellan Ayrwick?" inquired a soft-spoken but sophisticated voice.

"Yes, and you are?" I wondered if Renee, who had offered to contact me soon, obtained my number from Ulan.

"It's Kathy Endicott. We met when you were a young boy at the Endicott family summer barbecues. I used to be married to—"

"Lindsey Endicott. You're Cain's mother. He and I work together. My friend Fern called earlier to track your son down. Have you located him yet?" I covered the speaker and conveyed to April the name of the person who'd interrupted our impending private time.

"No, Cain hasn't contacted me. I'm sure he'll be home soon; we're supposed to cook dinner together this evening. But I was..." she expressed hesitantly before briefly considering her thoughts. A touch of nervous tension filled the silence. "I called to tell you that something arrived here. It belongs to someone you know."

I had no idea what she was talking about, nor did I care at that moment. Pictures of April in next to nothing, like the new red negligee she'd teased me about, kept popping up inside my head. "Oh, well, as I said... I'm busy right now, but we could meet for coffee tomorrow. I have some questions about the Orlando airport incident and my uncle's death. I heard you were around that day. Thought you might clarify a few fuzzy points."

"Yes, that's why I'm calling. I'm not sure if you knew, but I was the flight attendant on Zach's plane from Amsterdam. He'd traveled from South Africa to the Netherlands, then he boarded the second leg destined for Orlando."

I updated April, who persuaded me to remain on the call. "Really? I wasn't aware. How's tomorrow morning around eight thirty?" I wasn't meeting Bitsy until nine o'clock, which meant I'd have thirty minutes to talk with each of them before locating Fern at the art exhibition. "We could connect at The Big Beanery."

"That sounds good. Should I bring it with me?"

"Bring what?" I played dumb, hoping she might present a clue. A nagging suspicion convinced me she had the African figurine in her possession. Were she and Cain involved in something together?

"It's your uncle's suitcase. It looks just like mine. They got mixed up. I guess I'll see you tomorrow." Kathy promised to clarify everything when we met the following day.

After agreeing to call her if Cain showed up, I pivoted to April. "Do you think she stole Queen Tessa's talisman and is planning to return his luggage without it?"

"Only one way to find out. Looks like tomorrow's gonna be a big day for you. But not as big as tonight. March your lucky self home, boyfriend. We're gonna carve out a few minutes to ourselves before the kids get back and we dig into Cain's sticky note and Governor Yeardley's history."

Unfortunately, April and I ended up with zero alone time when we arrived home. All three of the kids were starving, and Ulan tested another recipe, which flopped worse than *The Exorcist* sequel. As hard as we tried to swallow the overcooked yet somehow still raw-in-some-spots-we-hoped-it-was-beef dish, Augie caved and ordered a couple of pizzas. Emma, Augie, and Ulan opted for the healthier route with peppers and spinach. April and I snagged a pepperoni and sausage special, then added a layer of ham. We'd work it off in the future. Instead, we focused on enjoying time together as family, a strange and twisted one where siblings raised younger brothers and cousins considered adopting their cousins.

After Augie departed to *chill with some friends*, Ulan volunteered to help Emma with her homework. April and I scoured the Internet for details about Governor Yeardley and Queen Tessa. Little information was available, and most of what we stumbled upon, we'd already known. Apparently, the history between the two had only been generically documented given there were several tribes and colonies throughout Africa that had battled for control over the centuries. The only unique element between the two was the cursed figurine. Any secrets about their descendants and the curse were probably kept close to the vest by their families and those who'd been brought into the fold.

April offered to assign her crew to keep a lookout for Cain that night. We agreed to sync up the following morning after the exhibition kicked off. "When I get to Glass Hall, we'll talk to Cain together to find out what his sticky note about Zach meant. If he's involved, we'll nail him to the wall. I promise."

Once April left, I finalized the forthcoming lectures that Myriam had requested to approve in advance. Before falling asleep, I focused on my unyielding desire to hunt down all the mysterious people who were avoiding me at all costs. Why did I fear that the only way to solve my uncle's murder would be to corner and force Giovanni, Renee, and Cain in a room together to confess the truth?

* * *

Monday morning descended upon me like a plague of tornadoes. I'd barely slept during the night. Dreams of African tribal dances, mysterious death curses, and evil lifelike dolls with Queen Tessa's blood boiling inside them kept jolting me upright in a sweaty frenzy. Every time a tree branch scratched the roof, or an owl hooted, I thought someone was breaking into the house. When the sun finally blasted through the curtains, I propelled myself out of bed and organized my day as though my life depended on it.

At breakfast, Ulan reminded me he would be on campus that day. His art class was previewing a handful of exhibits and having lunch with Braxton's admissions staff as part of an early college credit program. Ulan swore to text me when he was around so I could pop over and say hello. Once the kids were delivered safely to school, and Ulan received a direct warning not to engage with Renee if she tried to contact him, I took off for work.

Kathy and I were meeting at The Big Beanery, Braxton's popular coffee shop on South Campus, not too far from Diamond Hall. With thirty minutes to spare before my eight thirty appointment, I decided to drop off my briefcase and a bunch of reference books in my office before heading over.

Diamond Hall, a historic colonial-style mansion built in the 1870s, had been transformed into classrooms and offices for the communications, arts, media, and English departments. Limestone excavated from the nearby Betscha quarries encompassed all three stories of the remarkable facade. The front entrance, flanked by gorgeous arched windows and framed with ornate burgundy shutters, was accessible via a meandering stone trail that boasted several giant rhododendron bushes and cast-iron benches. The pathway rambled all around the courtyard and its primary buildings, including Prentiss Hall, the executive administration tower housing Ursula's office; Paddington's Play House, the campus theater; Stanton Concert Hall, the musical performance center; and Glass Hall, a large convention venue where Braxton held exhibitions, conferences, and important campus events.

As I entered the foyer and climbed the curved marble staircase, footsteps approached me. When the person turned the corner, I recognized him. Finally, fate had done me a solid and offset the calamity at Kirklands. A Zen calm descended, and I prepared to discover the truth.

"Giovanni, what a surprise! I've been hoping to talk to you. You and I are gonna solve a co-nundrum that's pestered me for ten weeks!" I would undoubtedly find out who the agent was and why he continued to stalk my family. My grandmother and Ulan demanded justice for Uncle Zach's death, and disappointing them was not an option.

Chapter 8

Besides his irritated expression, Giovanni carried a leather satchel in one hand and his phone in the other. "Kellan, I'm in a rush. We'll chat another time."

Although the man attempted to scurry past me, I held onto his arm. "Just a couple of minutes. We're talking about my uncle *now*."

Giovanni grunted. "Look, can we meet later? I'm searching for Dr. Endicott, but he wasn't in his office. A rude woman quoted Shakespeare and told me to check Glass Hall. Are you meeting him too?"

"If Cain isn't in his office, then he's most likely at Glass Hall. The exhibition opens today, and he's in charge of it." I was worried that Fern still hadn't located Cain, and Kathy had never updated me if her son returned home the previous night. Hopefully, she'd have news when I met her at The Big Beanery in twenty-five minutes. I would not tell Giovanni that, though. "Fine, we can meet later, but answer one question for me?"

Giovanni huffed loudly and yanked his arm away. "Okay, just one. If I don't find Dr. Endicott this morning, we're going to have a tremendous problem."

"Why did you think Zach Danby stole the African figurine? I can't figure out what my uncle has to do with this theft, but I'm worried it's connected to the car explosion that killed him." I didn't exactly trust Giovanni, especially with that scar and his cloak-and-dagger activities. He'd once mentioned his wound had resulted from a knife fight while he was in pursuit of an illegal immigrant who had tried to escape. I suspected it was a bald-faced lie.

"Listen, it's a much longer story, and you don't have the proper clearance for me to share any of the details. I can only tell you that your uncle hosted a dinner party at his apartment in South Africa. About ten of us attended it, and during the evening he presented the missing talisman." Giovanni explained that Uncle Zach had offered everyone an opportunity to bid on the object. At the end of the dinner, he announced someone had won the auction, but he wouldn't reveal the purchaser's identity. "The next day, Zach Danby fled the country, and I learned the figurine went missing during the night. I suspected Zach was playing games, trying to steal it or double-cross the bid winner. I followed him to Amsterdam and monitored his movements. He never answered the door to his hotel room, and I didn't have a warrant to break inside. I lost track of him for fifteen minutes when a cleaning person attempted to enter my room. But shortly afterward, I received word that Zach had purchased flight tickets and was heading to the US." Giovanni indicated that was when he'd flown to Braxton and coordinated with Fox to keep tabs on my family, not realizing Uncle Zach had altered his destination at the last minute. Giovanni had already landed in Braxton by then and couldn't get to Orlando in time for Uncle Zach's arrival. During the interim days between their trips, he'd helped Fox with the ReedWell financial investigation, met with a colleague about the fraudulent sale of the talisman, and tracked Uncle Zach's flight to Orlando.

"Tell me again why you stopped pursuing him."

"A colleague searched his luggage when it arrived in Orlando. He had one checked bag and one carry-on item. The figurine wasn't in the suitcase he'd checked, and we found no traces of it in the car explosion. There's a chance he transferred it to someone else in Amsterdam, or he truly had nothing to do with the theft. Either way, other leads came up, and we've been focused on those. Just drop it, okay? Your uncle's death was an accident. The car rental agency confirmed it was their fault." The aloof government agent muttered a hurried goodbye and sprinted down the steps.

I barely had a chance to yell in his direction, "He might've had a third piece of luggage." It was useless; he'd already raced through the courtyard and approached the entrance to Glass Hall. Giovanni was super intent on locating Cain Endicott. As were we all these days.

How well did Cain and Uncle Zach know one another? Had Cain bought Queen Tessa's talisman in the blind auction, then killed my uncle for some reason? If Kathy were on the same flight as Uncle Zach, he might've transferred the talisman to her and been killed by someone else.

I'd get more insight in a few minutes, but first I needed to pop by my office and address some administrative responsibilities.

When I reached the second floor, I bumped into only one other person who'd be on site that early when no terms were in session—my steadfast boss, Dr. Myriam Castle. She'd obviously been the rude person quoting Shakespeare to Giovanni. As I passed her office, she craned her neck in my direction. "Hello, Professor Ayrwick. I trust you're taking diligent care of Sawyer and Bitsy Jaccard. Be sure to keep them both happy and out of trouble! I also sincerely hope you've fixed the issues with Cain Endicott's financial mishap."

Myriam could best be described as a harsh-looking woman with short, spiky salt-and-pepper hair that most people mistook for a wig. She wore tortoise-shell glasses and designer suits, had a petite frame yet was obscenely strong, and flaunted excessive knowledge of everything under the sun. I knew little about her other than that she came from money, was married to and dearly loved Ursula, and had been raised solely by her father. She never explained all the details, and I never felt the urge to ask. But she once mentioned that he'd suffered a massive coronary embolism on her thirtieth birthday when she'd told him she was marrying Ursula. While doctors assured her that he was in extremely poor health and it had nothing to do with her news, the event had forever changed her. He had been confined to a nursing home for over a decade, and she visited him every Saturday morning.

"Yes, you have nothing to worry about. I'm meeting Cain in the next hour. Bitsy and I are having coffee in about thirty minutes," I confidently stated, handing her print-outs of half my lesson plans for the upcoming summer course. "And this should keep you busy reading for a few days. Consider it a collection of stories and customs of African life that aligns the goals of our art exhibition with my upcoming lectures."

"*Life … is a tale told by an idiot, full of sound and fury, signifying nothing.*" Myriam indicated I should place the folder in the inbox tray on her desk's corner. She rarely accepted things directly from others, claiming people shouldn't spend prolonged time touching one another because germs could be dangerous. "Please tell me you know that tragedy."

"*Macbeth*?" My overly critical boss loved her Shakespeare quotes more than life, as far as I suspected. I'd learned to ignore the aggravating lessons most days.

"Correct. I'll provide corrections to you by midweek. That's all. I'm quite busy this morning. Keep yourself in line, Kellan. I'm paying close attention to your teaching methods this year. I only extended your contract because Ursula convinced me you deserve our gratitude for helping her out of that minor spot last year."

I simply smiled and walked three doors down to my office. Dr. Myriam Castle delivered a uniquely special brand of cantankerous poppycock that was best left ignored if you valued your sanity. I unloaded the books and my briefcase, grabbed a spiral notebook from the desk drawer, and took off for The Big Beanery. It was time to extract the truth from Kathy, Bitsy, and Cain.

When I arrived, Kathy waved in my direction from a high-top table near the counter containing various creamers and sugars. "You look just like Seraphina, Kellan. How is Nana D?" Kathy shakily stood from her seat and hugged me for way too long. She smelled like cinnamon and vodka. That's when I noticed the coffee cake and Bloody Mary on the table. The Big Beanery didn't serve alcohol. I assumed she'd brought her own flask or ten of those adorable airplane bottles.

My grandmother's official name was Seraphina Gretchen Betscha Danby, but most people called her Nana D or Madam Mayor. Betscha being her maiden name and Danby her married one. Rarely did parents name their children Seraphina or Gretchen these days. I wasn't sure whether looking like my grandmother was a compliment or a detriment, but debating it seemed counterproductive to our more important topics for discussion. "She's wonderful. Back on speaking terms with Lindsey. Have you seen him since you returned?"

"My ex-husband and I are having a family dinner with Cain tonight. That is, if my son ever shows up." Although Kathy was in her mid-fifties, as far as I understood, she had aged well. Vodka that early agreed with the woman. Barely noticeable fine lines around the corners of her eyes and plump lips existed, but her hair was still a vibrant mahogany brown that she'd kept long and layered. All the walking up and down the airplane aisle ensured she maintained dynamite legs. Given her knee-length skirt and short-sleeve silk blouse, the remarkable definition in her bronzed arms and calves stood out.

"Does that mean he never returned home yesterday evening?" I began to worry about her son. He was avoiding several people based on what Giovanni and Fern had mentioned.

Kathy winced a skosh. "No, I'm fairly sure he did. I received his text about working late on the exhibition. I met a friend instead for dinner last night. When I got home, I crashed. Heard some noise in the middle of the night in Cain's bedroom, so he must've returned home." She indicated he'd departed earlier that morning and left another message that he'd meet his parents for dinner after the show.

I assumed by *friend*, Kathy meant Fox. I wasn't sure how to ask without being impolite, but again, my rival's taste in women wasn't the primary reason for our discourse. "So, you mentioned something about Uncle Zach's suitcase.

By the way, did Cain and my uncle know one another?"

"I don't believe they did." Kathy located another tiny bottle of vodka from her pocket and poured its entire contents into her glass. "Do you want to order anything before I tell you about the suitcase? It's such a crazy story."

I nodded and turned toward the main register area. When the barista looked over at me, I ordered my usual dark-roast coffee and the special pastry of the day. I'd pick up a slice of pie or a batch of cookies to bring back to Glass Hall as sustenance before my next meeting with Bitsy Jaccard, assuming she even ate desserts. "I'm curious how you came into possession of Uncle Zach's luggage." I also desperately wanted to know whether it contained the missing African talisman or if she'd rifled through the contents and was responsible for the theft.

"I'm not a hundred percent certain. I'll tell you what I think happened, though." Kathy scooped some of her hair between her hands and twisted it on top of her head with a scrunchie. "I was working his flight from Amsterdam to Orlando. While he was being a chatty Cathy with my colleague at the gate, I arrived and stored my rollaboard suitcase and carry-on tote near the entry door to the bridge."

Kathy explained that she'd recognized Uncle Zach. Although she was a couple of years older than him, they'd attended high school together when she was a senior and he was a freshman. After graduation, she'd married Lindsey on her eighteenth birthday and soon gave birth to Cain. They'd lost touch when he moved around the world and she'd become a flight attendant. The two old friends caught up for a few minutes, then she noticed that Zach's suitcase was too big to fit inside the cabin's overhead compartments. Kathy informed Uncle Zach that he'd have to check it. My uncle didn't want to, but Kathy convinced him to buy a new one at a store in the terminal since he'd mentioned having items that he needed access to during the flight.

"So, you're saying he bought the same specific one as you?" It seemed possible. We could download Uncle Zach's credit card statement, assuming he hadn't paid cash.

"Exactly, but not everything would fit inside it. While I checked the passenger lists, Zach transferred some things he needed on the plane to the new suitcase and left a bunch in the old one. I was showing him how I took advantage of all the different pockets and cubbies in my suitcase when my colleague called me over to verify something." Kathy indicated she'd only kept a few worn uniforms and non-essentials in her rollaboard that day; all her identification, important items, and toiletries were stored in her carry-on tote. She'd temporarily abandoned her rollaboard, chatted with her colleague, and then returned to Uncle Zach.

"Did he tell you what was so essential to keep with him on the plane?" I thanked the barista for dropping off my coffee and swallowed a large gulp.

Kathy shook her head. "No. We were so busy catching up, I didn't think to ask. Anyway, I fetched my suitcase, opened the bridge door… after following all our normal safety procedures, of course… and boarded passengers on the plane." She confirmed that when she checked Zach onto the aircraft, she tagged his old luggage and told him to leave it at the end of the jet bridge.

"For the crew to store below?" When Kathy nodded, I understood why Giovanni had said he'd confirmed there was no trace of the talisman in the luggage that had never been picked up at Baggage Claim. "Okay, so Uncle Zach got on the plane with his new rollaboard. Then what happened?"

"Transferring the items into his new suitcase had prevented Zach from boarding in his group. Since he was the last person to walk on the plane, the overhead storage bins were already filled. I had to hold it upfront in my area." Kathy explained that normally she wouldn't have, but knowing my uncle made it less risky. She promised that she'd help him retrieve anything from it during the flight, but he never requested her assistance.

"Did he ever go near his luggage?" I was convinced Uncle Zach had the talisman at that point. It made no sense for him to worry about his luggage unless he'd hidden something valuable inside it. Could he have sold the figurine to someone at the dinner, taken the buyer's money to cover his personal debts, and disappeared without giving it to them? How had he come across it in the first place?

"I don't believe so. I asked if he needed anything, but he declined and kept a close watch on it. He inquired if he could exit the plane first. Now that I think about it, he was behaving a little funny on the flight. Kept looking behind him at a couple of people." Kathy tore off and nibbled on a piece of my Baklava, indiscreetly moaning with pleasure. "Divine! These are almost as good as the ones in Greece!"

I smiled, reluctant to appear unfriendly. "Definitely. Did he point anyone out specifically?"

"No, I got the feeling he recognized someone but was concerned about being late for meeting his son," noted Kathy before taking a deep breath. "Oh, that poor boy. Zach and I talked about how much he loved Ulan and couldn't wait to surprise him in Orlando."

I didn't want to press Kathy too obviously, but she was close to telling me exactly how she'd ended up with Uncle Zach's luggage. I could feel it against my leg under the table and frantically wanted to rip it open. Truthfully, as much as I believed Kathy's version of the story, a small part of me wondered whether she was an incredibly talented actress attempting to throw me off the scent.

"Ulan is devastated. I'm glad you ended up with something of his dad's. You haven't said yet how it happened. Can we focus on that part?" Smooth, Kellan; the woman must have thought I was being insensitive about my uncle's death.

"Oh, right. Here's what I assume occurred. In my haste to off-board him first, I grabbed the wrong suitcase from the closet. Zach was in such a hurry, he sped down the bridge." Kathy indicated that my uncle had asked her twice if she retrieved the right one, and she confirmed that she did, but later she realized another attendant had previously removed both pieces to access someone else's bag. "I guess she put them back in the opposite spots, and so I gave Zach mine, and I ended up with his."

Her explanation sounded logical, and I couldn't imagine she'd generated a crazy lie on her own. Nor would she return the luggage if she'd been the one to steal it. "Okay, so I get how Uncle Zach took the wrong one, but didn't you realize sooner that you had his luggage? It's been over two months."

"You'd think so. After I finished my shift at the Orlando gate, the airport went into lockdown when everyone heard about the car explosion." Kathy confirmed she'd brought her rollaboard to an office area where her airline let them rest in between flights. She stored it in an employee locker, keeping only her carry-on tote with her, while she waited for news. "Once they declared the airport safe, my supervisor asked me to work several shifts for someone who'd gotten ill."

"Did you know it was Uncle Zach who'd been in the explosion?"

Kathy verified she didn't know who'd been injured or killed. She also clarified that she was asked to travel to a different climate and for a much longer period. She accepted the new assignment and rushed home to pack, realizing she had no time to collect the rollaboard she'd stored in the locker or to wash her worn uniforms. Instead, she gathered new ones from her bedroom closet. Kathy later returned to the airport to board the evening flight. "Since I needed to switch to a bigger suitcase, I never retrieved my rollaboard from the storage locker. Luckily, I had all my essentials in the carry-on tote I'd originally kept with me. I figured someone could send the rollaboard once I finished covering for my colleague."

"That was still the day of Uncle Zach's accident, right?" I was missing a critical piece of information.

"True. Since they wanted me to spend several weeks running flights from Eastern Europe to London, I decided to use some of my leave time. Cain was busy preparing for the art exhibition. I'm single these days. So, I booked a few extra weeks at various hostels and toured the Balkans." Kathy had arrived in Pennsylvania a week earlier and remembered her rollaboard in Orlando. She'd asked them to send it to Braxton, and when the baggage arrived, Kathy realized her mistake.

Now I fully understood. "Did you go through my uncle's suitcase?"

"Briefly. As soon as I opened it, I recognized a sweatshirt I'd seen Zach repacking in the Amsterdam airport. I talked to Lindsey, and he mentioned you were looking after Ulan, so that's why

I called you first." Kathy bent downward and tapped Zach's suitcase, noting she hadn't lost much in the car explosion, given Zach had taken her suitcase at the time. "All yours! I hope it will give Ulan some comfort to have his dad's things."

Kathy and I spoke until just before nine o'clock when I noticed Jessica Rabbit's twin AKA Bitsy Jaccard slink into The Big Beanery. She and I were supposed to meet at Glass Hall. What had changed our plans? And how did a woman who couldn't get directions straight find me? I hesitantly waved at Bitsy, then informed Kathy that I had to end our conversation. Bitsy pointed at the restroom and dashed across the café. Her heels clacked on the tile floor as she darted around the order line and pushed her way past a group of cranky patrons.

I switched my focus back to Kathy. "Are you meeting Cain now?"

"In a few minutes. I'm catching up with a new guy I met the other day. Phew, don't tell anyone, Kellan, but he's the same age as my son. I guess they'd call me a cougar, huh?" She innocently giggled as she collected her pocketbook and Bloody Mary glass. "Then I'll head over to Glass Hall for the exhibition. Cain told me they're only letting in Braxton staff or guest speakers before ten o'clock, the official opening time. Even hired additional security to check everyone at the entrance. Some of the art is really expensive and rare, apparently."

I knew she was meeting Fox. "Anything serious? I'm sure things will work out as they should."

Kathy's smile stretched ear to ear. "Oh, whatever happens is fine. We're just getting to know one another. Cain wouldn't embrace a new stepfather at his age. I'm too young not to have fun, and I'm a touch too old to consider marriage again. Wouldn't you agree?"

I declined to answer that question. Once she left, I bent under the table to unzip the rollaboard. Unfortunately, it wouldn't easily open without its contents falling out the side. I was about to change its position when someone tapped me on the back. "Yoo-hoo! Plant some sugar on me, you gorgeous man!" announced the irritating voice of a Betty Boop soundalike.

The day couldn't get any worse, could it? I'd been saying that all too often lately. Check, please!

Chapter 9

I zipped up the suitcase, frustrated that I'd have to wait another thirty minutes before searching for the African talisman. "Hello Mrs. Jaccard. How lovely to meet you in person," I replied, rising and bracing for impact. She practically toppled me over with her greeting ritual. I backed into the high-top to support myself and suddenly felt her super moist lips practically vacuuming mine off my face. When she stepped away, I removed my glasses and cleaned the fog settling on the lenses.

Bitsy's massive cascade of tight bottle-blonde curls sent the room spinning endlessly. "Oh, we are just gonna have an amazing week together. Tell me all about yourself. Ursie raves about you all the time. MirMir, not so often. I get the feeling she doesn't like you very much." She grabbed my rear end as I stabilized myself and stepped away from the table. Wow! She was strong for a petite thing. "Now, don't run too far, sugar cakes. Call me Bitsy. None of that formal stuff for two people who are gonna be so intimate this week, everyone will think we're married!"

Did she call Myriam *MirMir* to her face? I couldn't believe my boss allowed herself to be around Bitsy for a hot second. Then again, I was instructed not to judge the woman on first impressions. Where was April when I needed her? She'd keep Bitsy Jaccard under control by using a taser to simmer the boil.

"I'll escort you to Glass Hall for the art exhibit, but I have classes to prepare for this week. We won't be able to spend too much time together, unfortunately. I'm sure Ursie and MirMir would be terribly upset with me if I ditched my job." Oh, lord, I'd already adopted Bitsy's pet nicknames. What had I done wrong to deserve this?

"I'll talk to them. Bitsy always gets what Bitsy wants, darling," she teased, gently tapping her ring-clad index finger hand on my nose three times. "Ursie and I go way back. Did she tell you I saved her from choking on a grape in business school? Ever since then, she's been my best bosom buddy in the whole wide world. Owes me her life. Can't ever say no to me! Especially with all the cash I throw at Braxton." Her throaty, seductive chortle caused several heads to snap in our direction.

The lifesaving story explained the nature of their relationship. Assuming Bitsy donated a lot of money to the college, Ursula wouldn't dare dismiss their friendship. I chose a different tactic next as I meandered to the other side of the table to allocate sufficient space between us. "Plus, I have a young daughter and… a teenage son… to look after this week too." Ulan technically wasn't my son, but I really didn't want to explain all the details of my family life to the exuberant woman.

Bitsy leaned forward and cupped both my cheeks with her hands. She had the softest skin I'd ever felt in my life. A heavenly perfume scent of jasmine and vanilla wafted around us, almost mesmerizing me into silent obedience. "Oh, Kellan. Children adore me. I can't wait to meet them. Sawyer and I couldn't have babies after a nasty medical issue when I was younger. We tried for a few years, but it seems my ovaries are all too happy playing hard to get with his little swimmers."

TMI. Quick, how else could I get out of the debacle? Just as I'd thought of another excuse,

I noticed a two-inch smudge of red on her white leather purse and a scratch on her right hand's index finger. At first, I thought she'd cut herself or injured me when she hugged me so tightly. Then I noticed that she'd fastened a Band-Aid to her finger. Part of the injury was still exposed and must've bled on her purse. It seemed like a lot of blood for a small wound. I casually reached for her wrist and asked her to hold still. "You have something on—"

"Oh, look at that. We've barely met and the boy's already getting as fresh as a jailbird just sprung from prison. You must know Bitsy likes it when a handsome devil gets physical with her." She pulled her shawl over the full length of her arm. "Don't worry about it! I bumped into something… a strawberry or cherry pie over yonder… on the way to the restroom."

"Are you sure?" It didn't look like any sort of jelly or filling from a dessert, and I was well versed in my desserts. I edged closer to check it out, but she yanked her hand away.

"Why don't we sit, cutie patootie? I want to shoot the breeze about this exhibition before you and I inspect it ourselves."

As we sat at the same high-top I'd shared with Kathy, Bitsy hung the strap of her purse on the chair and dragged herself within inches of me. My insides considered charging her rent. In the process, I noticed she'd already secured her ID badge for entry into Glass Hall. We hadn't mailed them out in advance, which meant she must've already gone inside the building. "I thought we were meeting near the Glass Hall lobby this morning. Did you already go there before stopping at The Big Beanery?"

Bitsy blushed and glanced to the front door, then back at me. "Oh no, honeykins. I haven't been there yet. I was dreadfully in need of caffeine, so I came here first to buy a hot tea. I'm desperate to quell this scratchy throat from the stifling air on my flight."

"But you have an ID badge already. And you've ordered nothing to drink."

"Oh, silly me," she explained, reaching for the plastic ID attached to her purse. "Sawyer picked them up earlier and gave me mine when I arrived. I've got a little teensy-weensy headache now, so I think I'll skip the caffeine. They'll have some at the exhibition, I'm sure."

I acknowledged her dubious reasoning and offered to escort her to the campus store to buy an aspirin, but she declined. Instead, she jumped right into the details of the conference. As soon as she started asking questions, it became obvious what Ursula and Myriam had meant by not judging the woman on initial impressions.

Bitsy Jaccard was eloquent, intelligent, cultured, and extremely professional. An entirely different person burst forth when we focused on the art world. So much so, she'd quoted a dozen examples from the itemized list of artifacts, including the prices and pedigrees leading to their authentication. Within ten minutes, she'd rearranged the order of most speakers on the panel, postponed revealing two artifacts from the inventory until the last day, where she suggested we hold them for a final surprise appearance, and rattled off the name of four major players who'd committed to providing generous donations.

"You're quite an impressive woman, Bitsy," I noted, despite the potential risk of delivering a compliment. "And you used to be a curator in Greece, right?"

"A few years ago. Sawyer spends so much time traveling, we decided it would be better if I accompanied him on all his trips rather than stay home." Bitsy clarified that she'd hand-selected her replacement and focused her energy on searching for rare African pieces to add to their collection. "I'm hopeful to find out what happened to Queen Tessa's missing talisman. I met your late uncle when he showed it at a dinner party months ago. Are you familiar with it?"

My leg developed a painful cramp when she mentioned the very object that could be hiding in the suitcase below our table. Was she the buyer who had been angry when Uncle Zach disappeared with it? Or was she involved in its theft with my uncle? "Wait! You knew Uncle Zach?"

"Just from the fab dinner party. That's all. Barely had a moment to talk with him."

I would ask detailed questions about the dinner party when we didn't need to open the art exhibition. "Yes, I've heard a few stories about the figurine. Do you think it's here in Braxton?"

Bitsy shook her head. "I'm not entirely sure, but I plan to conduct my own search this week, snookums. Oh, dear me… I suppose I should level with you."

I couldn't imagine what she was about to unleash next. "Of course, that would be helpful. I admit… I'm definitely out of my element in the art world."

Bitsy enlightened me that she'd never been taken seriously when she was younger because of her appearance and indelicate upbringing. Her father had been a film director and her mother a famous actress. Both had died in their late forties from a horrific car accident when Bitsy was only seventeen years old. "You probably wouldn't know much about them. You seem like an innocent, vanilla guy."

Not again! Ugh, she'd totally thrown me for a loop. I worked in Hollywood and had a firm knowledge of the industry. "I have my moments. I was wilder in my twenties."

"Kellan, I'm only telling you this because Ursula promised I could trust you." She explained that her father directed pornographic film shoots and her mother was the top paid performer in the sixties and seventies. "She had the biggest chest and smallest waist that Hollywood had ever seen. My parents became quite wealthy, and then I came along unexpectedly." Bitsy had a tough childhood being passed around from friend to friend while her parents made movie after movie and ignored her. When they died, she'd come into a lot of money.

"I'm so sorry. That must've been rough." I felt dreadful for laughing at her the prior weekend, even surprised that she was in her late forties. Bitsy looked amazing.

"As you can see, I inherited my mother's body. I also inherited my father's talents. Instead of working in the film industry, I threw myself into the art world. I worked my way up the museum circuit until finally, everyone took me seriously." Her distinctive edge was the bubbly personality she outwardly depicted to garner attention, but once she got to know someone, she tossed away all the garish makeup, silly voices, and expressions. "I can't do much about this hourglass, yet I have to admit, it has come in handy a few times."

I wasn't exactly sure how to respond. "Well, you're clearly gorgeous, and I'm sure people judge you harshly based on your appearance. Women should be proud of their looks and figures, even if they might border on the…." I stopped, hesitant to offend her.

"Likes of Jessica Rabbit? That's the most prevalent insult. Or I sound like Betty Boop. You can't imagine the names people fabricate," she added, anguish and disappointment cresting in her voice.

I slapped my forehead for imagining the same awful things when I'd seen her picture and heard her voice message. "Oh, you're clearly smart enough to ignore those idiots." Hopefully, I hadn't turned bright red. "Men can be jerks. Even the good ones, sometimes."

"Precisely. And that's what helped me become the secret weapon I am today. Most people ignore me. Think I'll add two plus two and come up with the letter D." She laughed demurely and relaxed into her chair, showing her true nature, one that I considerably admired.

Before we could finish the conversation, Fern approached us. "There you are, Kellan. We need to get hold of Cain before he kicks off the show. It's nine thirty now. You haven't been to Glass Hall to see him yet, have you?"

I indicated I had not. At Cain's name, Bitsy's voice grew energetic. "He seems like one of the good guys, not those types of men we just spoke about, Kellan. Oh, silly me... I better fix my makeup before my Sawyer sees me looking a frightful mess. See you over there, stud muffin."

Bitsy gathered her purse, adjusted her shawl, and swiftly departed The Big Beanery before I could introduce Fern. She'd also reverted to her vivacious personality given a stranger approached.

"Stud muffin? Does April know you've found yourself a coquettish admirer?"

"No. You're barking up the wrong tree, Fern... just like Bitsy Jaccard!"

I begged her to grant me a minute to check the luggage. I didn't articulate its potential contents, only because I needed to know the truth and to find out what my uncle had been up to. I couldn't risk him acquiring a terrible reputation without a way to defend himself.

"We have no time, Kellan. Cain's opening remarks are in thirty minutes, and if we don't tell him what to change, Ursula will kick us to the curb."

"Not to mention Bitsy. She suggested a bunch of ways to fix this exhibition. Come on, I'll share a few on the way over." I hopped off the stool and collected the rollaboard, confident I could shake Fern loose once we entered Glass Hall. I would return to my office with the suitcase, check its contents, and decide how to proceed.

"Bitsy seemed rude, if I do say so myself. I know Ursula told us not to judge her, but women like that should cover themselves up as much as possible. I know she can't help what God gave her, but really, that's a lot to handle all at once. Is it me, or did she sound exactly like that cartoon character from the thirties… what's her name—"

"Oh, Fern… I expected better of you. Women bashing women? Seriously, the poor lady must get so much flack, you really ought to be nicer… like I've been. What about the #MeToo movement and Women's Liberation? You're setting your gender back by decades!" I shook my head with extreme exaggeration, flouting my guilt for developing the same impressions about Bitsy and for not telling Fern I'd acted similarly judgmental. "And I think you mean Betty Boop."

Now that I'd met Bitsy, I wondered what could be in store when I stumbled upon Sawyer. Which famous cartoon character would he resemble? Bugs Bunny? Elmer Fudd? Wile E. Coyote?

Fern dipped her head in shame. "I know, I'm dreadful. I guess we all need a wake-up call sometimes."

While we wandered to Glass Hall, I updated Fern on Bitsy's true temperament and confessed to making the same gaffe. Fern promised to get even with me, but she also agreed not to reveal Bitsy's secret.

Glass Hall resided on the westernmost section of South Campus, behind Paddington's Play House and Diamond Hall. A large institutional-looking structure, its red-brick exterior was emblazoned with four giant columns and steep entry steps into a grand foyer. Inside the building were three floors and a basement level lacking any external access points. The main lobby boasted gorgeous casement and transom windows in the entryway, and at both ends of the building were marble staircases that led to the basement or the higher levels. The interior décor reminded me of a 1950s elementary school's cement hallways and a time when students rushed under their desks to practice safety from nuclear attacks.

By the time we showed our IDs and entered the building, we were back on track to kick off the exhibition. As we navigated the basement hallways in search of the classroom where Cain had temporarily set up shop, excitement peaked for the impending demonstration. I implored myself to separate from Fern as soon as we found Cain, so I could open Uncle Zach's luggage. If she started providing instructions to Cain, I could excuse myself to use the restroom and search for the talisman. A little panic consumed me, contemplating whether I should even touch the object if it brought danger to non-members of Queen Tessa's bloodline.

We reached the end of the main hallway, both uncertain whether the security guard had told us to go left or right. Fern chose right. I went left. We agreed to check for Cain in the rooms on either side, then regroup.

After shuffling through the eastern hallway, idle tension materialized inside my body. Lights flickered above me, and I swore I heard footsteps in one of the nearby rooms. Uncle Zach's suitcase had a squeaky wheel, which added to the anxiety building up around me. "Cain, is that you?" I called out in a slightly high-pitched voice. No one answered, but the lightbulb above me cast strange shadows before blinking erratically and going dark.

I flinched yet held in the scream I really wanted to let loose. I reached the first room and knocked on the closed door. No one answered, of course. What was I thinking? I rolled the suitcase to the concrete wall and pushed open the heavy metal door. I'd poke my head in only to confirm whether Cain was working farther inside and had turned off the overhead lighting.

When I entered the chilled room, several ancient statues and clay pottery were piled together on a table. A couple of paintings were laid out on cloth. I flipped on the front section of the ceiling's lights and scanned the rear area of the room. It contained several leftover artifacts that weren't being displayed that day. I noticed some paperwork strewn across the student desks, and when I picked up one document, I learned that the items originated from the South African collection and had at one point belonged to Queen Tessa's tribe. The museum where Bitsy previously worked had donated the antiquities. One paper was streaked with a red stain on its corner. It reminded me of the blemish I'd seen on Bitsy's purse. Had she been in the room when cutting herself?

I walked a few more feet, noticing a faint glow in the closet about fifteen yards away. When I stepped closer, I could see through a narrow crack between the door and its frame that the enclosed space contained several tribal weapons. Long pieces of cylindrical wood shafts with metal arrows tied tightly to one end hung from a hook on a higher shelf. From what I'd read about its value, the stuff should've been locked in the closet.

All the entries to the building were sealed shut and had security personnel standing guard. Guests were only allowed access through the main part of the building, where Fern and I had entered. No one could get in or out without going through those doorways, and none of the artwork or historical pieces were permitted to leave the building. It required the signature of Cain

Endicott, the chief security guard, and someone from Ursula's direct staff.

Something gnawed at my composure, raising all the little hairs on my arms. It appeared like Cain had gone down there to collect a piece and forgotten to lock everything back up. I decided to transfer a few items into the closet and shut the door, just to be safe. Cain would be in a lot of trouble when I finally tracked him down. As I approached the dimly lit storage area, something blocked the door from being pushed inward. A sudden sense of doom enveloped me as my stomach plummeted and my eyes glanced to the floor.

I saw the shoes poking out near the doorjamb first. It couldn't be another one! I convinced myself to inspect the other side of the door, stirring nothing in the process. Could the feet be part of the exhibit, attached to a fake body that demonstrated replicas of various tribe members? Then I realized African tribesmen from the 1600s didn't own fancy dress shoes with laces and metal clasps.

I stifled a scream and called out to Fern. "Get in here quickly. Don't touch anything, though. I just need you to verify what I'm seeing!"

I leaned forward and stuck my head through the gap between the open door and its frame. With a bit of luck, someone wouldn't be standing there about to chop it off. I had a suspicious feeling Cain lay supine on the floor. When I finally pushed through far enough, I studied the victim's entire body, keenly aware of the spear thrust into his abdomen. Was this where the blotch of blood on Bitsy's purse and the drops on the documents had come from? While scanning from the guy's gaping wound up to his face, I shrieked and stumbled backward. "This can't be happening!"

The body didn't belong to Cain. Sprawled on the cold linoleum tile behind the closet door was Giovanni, the no-last-name government agent with the nasty scar who'd been hunting down Uncle Zach and the missing talisman. Based on the amount of blood pooling around his waist, Death had unquestionably claimed another soul on my watch. Maybe even the only chance to discover who had killed my uncle too!

Chapter 10

My head grappled with a caustic mix of anger, sadness, and disbelief. First, I needed to confirm whether Giovanni was still alive. Although sensitive not to contaminate any evidence, I squeezed through the small gap where the door was slightly ajar and entered the walk-in closet. My body naturally tensed up, almost stopping me from breathing as I knelt between a standing shelf unit and Giovanni. No matter how many times I'd encountered a dead body, the raw pain at knowing someone's life had been terminated in a vulgar and horrific manner prompted the desire to retch. I held it back and focused on my immediate priority.

As I carefully leaned my head closer to confirm Giovanni wasn't breathing, the warmth of his body was still evident. No pulse. No rising in his chest. And cold, lifeless pupils. I closed my eyes and silently prayed for him, for his family, whoever they might be. Then I curled my fists even tighter, furious that the one person who could share the truth about Uncle Zach's death was gone. Renee had promised to visit, and Cain was still missing, but I worried either had something to do with one or both deaths. It was time to notify April of the dire and distressing event I'd found myself embroiled in once again.

Knowing April wouldn't let me back inside once the police arrived, I quickly scouted for any obvious clues or mysterious messages. I saw no other signs of a struggle. Giovanni's attacker must've caught him inside the walk-in closet and thrust the spear into his stomach. Giovanni's left hand grasped a section of the spear and his other arm was bent at an odd angle behind his head. The fist on his right hand was scrunched together as if he held something in its grip. Wouldn't he have attempted to stop his attacker from plunging the spear into his abdomen? If he had, his efforts had clearly failed. Perhaps he'd been hit by surprise. The poor man didn't deserve this type of horrid, painful ending, even if he had kept something important about my uncle's murder from me, or worse yet, lied to me and intentionally caused his death. I retreated into the main room, avoiding the pool of blood and a strange piece of jewelry tucked under his left knee.

April answered on the first ring, but I could barely get any words out when Fern raced to the room. She stopped short at the door upon seeing my confused and harried panic. I held up a hand to her, then informed my girlfriend of what I'd discovered. "I... I called you first... what do you want me to do?"

April relayed a few comforting words and promised to rush over instantly. "Sit tight. You've been through this before. Don't let anyone in the room, okay?"

"Yes, get here quickly, please." As soon as we hung up, I loudly instructed Fern, "Don't come any closer." Frustration burgeoned over recognizing that I'd already disturbed evidence when I picked up the documents and nudged the walk-in closet door.

Heavy footsteps echoed in the hallway behind Fern as she cautiously stepped into the room. "What happened? I found Cain. He was strolling down the main hallway when I heard you screaming."

"Someone's had an accident. It's a terrible sight." I was glad Cain had reappeared.

Fern yelped and held up her arm to stop him from running past her into the room. Cain yelled, "Who's inside? No one is supposed to be down here. This is my prep area, and it's off-limits."

I joined them in the middle of the room, watching Cain scan the desks and all the scattered paperwork. "A man's been injured by one of the artifacts. I've met him before, but I don't know if you two would recognize him." I explained the little I knew about Giovanni, unclear why or how he'd gotten into Glass Hall before the exhibition opened.

Fern, who'd turned a dull shade of green, shook her head. "That's the guy you mentioned was at the hospital when the news alert popped on about the Orlando explosion."

As I nodded, the color drained from Cain's cheeks. He bit his bottom lip and sloped to the side so we couldn't see his face. "No, I don't think I've met him before."

Cain was lying. The hesitancy and distant gaze before he'd turned had easily given him away. "Somehow Giovanni broke in here. I don't

157

know if he was trying to snatch or prevent some-one else from stealing the art. We should wait outside for the police—"

Before I finished speaking, Connor zipped into the room with Officer Flatman and directed us to leave. "We'll catch up in a few minutes, but we need to see the body and secure the premises."

As Cain and Fern discussed the art exhibition, he noted, "I'm supposed to make my opening re-marks right now. I should go upstairs and pre-pare."

Fern looked to me for assistance. "Perhaps we should postpone. Wouldn't you agree, Kellan?"

Cain's lack of empathy for someone's death astounded me. Clearly, we couldn't pretend a dead body wasn't hiding in the basement while we bragged about the wonderful artifacts on the campus that week. Based on what I'd observed in the closet, Giovanni must've been stabbed very recently. I'd seen him in Diamond Hall two hours earlier, so his killer was potentially still inside Glass Hall.

"Cain, I agree with Fern. The police won't let more people into the building. It'll be sealed off, at least for today, so they can investigate what happened." I paused, curious where Cain had been disappearing to. "Maybe you could answer another question for me?"

As he rotated toward us, Cain adjusted the sleeve on his coat. When he pulled his dress shirt down to cover his wrist, a cufflink sparkled from the overhead light. It looked identical to the piece of jewelry I'd seen near Giovanni's body. Had Cain been the one to thrust the spear into the agent?

"What's that? I'm really not up for talking right now, Kellan. I'm in shock."

"I found a note in your exhibition paperwork. It referenced my uncle's flight and car rental. Can you explain what that's all about?" I studied his face for any odd reactions.

"Huh? What does he have to do with this mess?" Cain clenched his jaw.

"I'm not sure. You tell me."

Cain shrugged. "Zach and I talked about some of the African art in the exhibit. He mentioned his flight to Philadelphia airport. I considered meeting him there, but then he changed his plans." His responses were too weak and hiding the whole story.

Fern glanced at us, somehow picking up the thoughts circulating inside my head. "I know this is a horrible thing to say, but the police will want to know where everyone was this morning. We've been trying to reach you for most of the last day, Cain."

Cain's jaw dropped lower. "Are you implying I had something to do with the man's accident? I don't even know the guy who's bleeding all over the floor, probably ruining some of the art we were lucky enough to secure."

I slanted my eyes at Uncle Zach's suitcase just outside the room. I couldn't risk the police thinking it was evidence, so I walked over and placed my palm on the handle. Then I raised the bar and rolled it closer toward us. "Of course, that's a huge issue too, but the priority is going to be figuring out what happened to the dead man. And I still have questions about your sticky note. Why would you care about his car rental?"

"I don't know anything about these deaths," Cain repeated, insistent that he was as stunned as us. A strange flash in his eyes told me otherwise. He was undeniably lying. Whether it was knowing Giovanni's identity, the reason for my uncle's car explosion, or being involved in either death, I couldn't say for sure.

"Tell us where you've been disappearing to. You never showed up to our meeting yesterday afternoon." I also reminded him that his mother told us she couldn't get hold of him the previous night.

"You talked to her? What does she have to do with this situation?" Cain leaned against the tiled wall and slowly shrank to the floor until he sat with his knees pulled up to his chest and his arms blanketed across them. When he stretched his upper body, I noticed the other sleeve on his bright white dress shirt was conspicuously missing a cufflink.

"Kathy picked up your phone when Fern contacted you yesterday afternoon, and then she followed up with a call to me on a different topic last night. We just met this morning for breakfast. She's worried about you." I soon heard April's voice calling Connor's name outside in the hallway.

Before Cain could respond, April and a pair of EMTs rushed down the corridor. "Kellan," April hollered when she saw us at the opposite end. "Has Connor arrived?"

"Yes, he's inside with Flatman. We're too late. Giovanni is dead. It's terrible in there." I wanted to pull my girlfriend in for a hug but knew better. When she was on official business, we played it safe, especially in a public setting.

The EMTs hustled into the room and greeted Connor. Flatman updated his boss on what he'd already discovered, then instructed the security guard not to let anyone in or out without his authorization. April studied the interaction between Fern and Cain, then said, "Dean Terry, we need to lock down all entrances and exits to this building. Coordinate with Officer Flatman and the other police officers upstairs to put a plan in place. Now, please."

Fern nodded and exited with Flatman. Cain awkwardly stood and addressed April. "Sheriff, I should update the other panel members. And my boss. President Power is going to be livid."

April indicated she would let him make a few calls shortly. "Let's find a place for my team to set up shop. Is there a classroom we can temporarily use as a base?"

"Yes, I have a makeshift office in the other hallway. I've been using it to catalog the incoming art. Just like in this room," Cain explained.

While Cain and April worked out the details, Connor strolled toward me. "We'll document your official statement later, but what have you already picked up?"

I filled in Connor on how I'd stumbled upon Giovanni, that he'd been looking for Cain in Diamond Hall earlier, and about the sticky note. "You also need to check Cain's shirtsleeves. He's missing a cufflink, and I'm certain that's the piece of jewelry near the victim's body. He's somehow involved in this mess. Does it seem like he's stalling?"

"You're suggesting Cain killed both men? Did they all know one another?" Connor scratched at his chin. He'd agreed to grow out his facial hair the previous month in a show of solidarity with me. But where I'd given up and shaved, he said Maggie preferred the scruffy look and that it was staying put.

"I'm not really sure. Cain said he didn't, but Giovanni led me to believe earlier that they did. I think this has to do with a missing African talis-

man. The one you told me about the other day."
I wanted to update him that it might be inside
Uncle Zach's luggage, but I needed to check for
myself first.

"I emailed my dad to ask a few questions
last night. I'll let you know what I find out." He
directed a police photographer to begin working inside the room. "Touch nothing!" When he
looked back at me, he said, "Anything else you
can add in the meantime?"

"No. Should I help Fern get things under control?" When Connor agreed that my proposal
was acceptable, I grasped the suitcase's handle-
bar and rolled it down the hallway.

"That's not evidence, I assume?" Connor
didn't look at me when he asked the question.

Without turning around, I confidently replied,
"I brought it with me. Wasn't in the room, that's
for sure."

"Okay. Don't leave Glass Hall until we catch
up. I need to have my team search this entire
building and gather folks in the same room so
we can address everyone." Connor informed me
he'd be ready in thirty minutes and asked me to
find a place for him to speak.

"Will do." I rounded the corner and passed another police officer while trudging up the stairs. Once I was safely alone in a vestibule on the second floor, I slipped into an empty office and hurriedly unzipped the suitcase. I needed the first look at anything to help identify my uncle's killer.

Several pairs of pants, a few button-down shirts, and other items of clothing were folded and stacked at the top. Beneath them I found a foot-long velvet satchel secured with a leather string. Before I untied the knot, I felt the object contained inside the cloth. My heart plunged into my stomach and set off an alarm bell. I knew what I was about to find, and it frightened me to no end. As I pulled the mysterious object out of the bag, I saw for the first time what I believed was Queen Tessa's cursed talisman. I refused to touch the figurine; even holding onto the velvet bag gave me the willies, but I needed to be certain. I held the bottom of the strange deity, using the velvet bag as a protective glove, and studied the no-longer-lost African treasure.

Constructed from cloth, wood, and various jewels, its exaggerated features were astronomically scary. I suspected the talisman's eyes were made from diamonds as they glistened and sparkled brilliantly. But the black stitches above gave it a menacing appearance. The wooden elements, representing the doll's neck and four limbs, were interspersed with a creamy white coating at each joint. In the center where the stomach should have been, underneath a few layers of fabric that I delicately lifted, was another diamond-like tube filled with brownish flakes. Queen Tessa's blood? Over the years, the natural reddish color would've turned a different shade and eventually dried out, then broken down into mere particles like the ones in the tube. The object everyone had been searching for was strangely in my possession. Had I unintentionally become its new keeper?

If Kathy hadn't taken the talisman from the luggage, then she probably wasn't involved in its theft nor working with Cain in the background. What was so special about this thing? How valuable was it? Before I could slip it back into the velvet satchel, the door squeaked open. I looked up with shaky confidence. Myriam and Ursula stared back at me, offering startled expressions.

I forced myself to respond as if everything was perfectly normal. "Hi. I was just on my way to the lobby to find you both. I assume you've heard the awful news?"

When Myriam focused on the talisman, she immediately cocked her head and said, "Are you playing with dolls in a room all by yourself, Professor Ayrwick?"

"Not exactly," I replied, summoning the most appropriate explanation that wouldn't generate a far worse dilemma. "Just something I brought to work today."

"*To thine own self be true. And it must follow, as the night the day, thou canst not then be false to any man.*" Myriam narrowed her judgmental gaze in my direction and sighed. "I should've expected you'd have a strange hobby."

"Polonius. I remember that one from *Hamlet*." Ursula covered her mouth and whispered, "Wait! Is that one of the pieces we're displaying in the exhibition? I'm intrigued by ancient cultural traditions, but that thing is frightening beyond any expectations. It looks angry and vengeful."

I delicately pulled the velvet sack around the talisman and gently set it back in the luggage.

"It is ugly, I agree. Ummm…" I hesitated, feeling uncertain how many lies I could continue to tell. "No, this isn't in the show. Someone else gave it to me… thought I'd present it to Cain today for comparative purposes." I zipped up Uncle Zach's luggage and stood it firmly on the ground.

A bewildered pout occupied Myriam's face. "That doll reminds me of something I've seen before… I… can't place it, though. Maybe it'll come back to me later."

It was the first time I'd ever seen that expression on my boss. "Anyway, Detective Hawkins wants to speak in about fifteen minutes. They're locking down the entire building. I was just coming by to tell you we need to gather everyone together."

Ursula indignantly shook her head. "This is not what we needed today. Do you have any idea who was killed downstairs? All the police would tell me is that a man died sometime this morning."

"I don't know his last name, but he was upstairs in Diamond Hall with Myriam earlier." I described Giovanni's appearance, focusing on his scar and facial features, then mentioned he had been searching for Cain.

"Yes, that man was knocking on Dr. Endicott's door about two hours ago. I asked him to stop disturbing the entire building. He was very rude, I might add." Myriam smoothed a wrinkle on her steel-gray pencil skirt and uttered a *tsk tsk* sound. "He implied it was urgent, but given he didn't belong on campus, I directed him to leave before I called security."

"I ran into him too. I've seen him around town a few times. He's an ICE agent who's been working with the FBI on a couple of cases. He had concerns about the art exhibition." I tugged the suitcase a little closer to my body. Lying wasn't the right path, but until I could find out what the heck was going on, I needed to keep any news of the talisman hidden.

"Just what we need. I knew Cain would cause a problem. Haven't you coerced him back in line, Kellan? Bitsy thought you were wonderful, by the way." Ursula composed an email on her phone when she finished speaking.

I noted Cain had avoided me the previous days. "He's rather elusive. Finally saw him today."

"Come along, Ursula. You need to notify Public Relations about this incident while I find Dean Terry and send out a campus-wide alert that the exhibition is temporarily closed." Myriam slipped her glasses down the bridge of her nose before addressing me. "And you, Professor Ayrwick, better get this situation under control. You're in charge of finding a place for the police to address us."

In no mood to extend the conversation, I kept silent as they descended the nearby stairs to the basement level. I went in search of April, who'd come up the other stairwell and walked through the main lobby. She could only offer me a sixty-second news briefing, citing she'd already been in touch with the FBI and ICE about the agent's death and that the pressure to keep things contained was intensifying. About thirty people remained in the building, and she had sealed off all the entrances and exits.

"It's a disaster. Some cartoonish woman and her husband are having an enormous fit about being forced to stay inside. Threatened to contact the governor if I kept them any longer." April hated when people threw their wealth and connections in her face, but she was vigilant about observing all rules and guidelines.

I took the opportunity to tell her the truth about Cain's responses and Queen Tessa's talisman. I couldn't lie anymore. "Sorry, I should've waited for you to grill Cain. I'm also certain this is the figurine everyone's been looking for, but it wasn't here when Giovanni was killed. What should we do with it?"

"Damn it! I know you don't intend to make my life more difficult, but seriously, you are *The Unlikely Death Locator*, Kellan." April highlighted the demeaning nickname someone had coined in the past when we'd merely been dancing around our attraction to one another. But I took no offense to it anymore. Even I thought I was cursed like the talisman.

"I can't change the facts. This proves my uncle was somehow involved in the figurine's theft." I explained everything Kathy had shared with me earlier that morning. "Now we've discovered that the dead guy in the basement is the agent who was searching for Uncle Zach and the figurine. Again, what do you want me to do with it?"

"Why don't you shove it where..." April began, hesitating before responding further.

"Oh, that's not very ladylike. You're approaching the danger zone now!"

Chapter 11

Once April deigned to speak to me again, her advice was highly unforeseen. "Take it to your office. Do you still have that locked compartment in the bottom of your desk?" When I nodded, she continued to provide instructions. "Let me finish here in a couple of hours, then we can assemble a plan of attack."

I was glad we were on the same side. "Can you share anything else about his death?"

"Not much." Based on her initial conversation with the EMTs—who were typically reliable about guessing the time of death, even though they should've waited for the coroner—Giovanni had been killed less than two hours earlier. "The body is still warm, so it's very recent."

I mentally tabulated the math. "So, between eight thirty and nine thirty?"

"Probably." April reconfirmed that Uncle Zach's luggage was in my possession when Giovanni had been murdered, then scribbled something on a piece of paper and handed it to me. "Give this to the officer at the front entrance. He'll let you leave with the suitcase."

After taking the note, I updated her about the red splotch on Bitsy's purse, including how a paper cut wouldn't generate that large amount of blood. "Cain's cufflink was next to Giovanni's body too. Could they be involved in it together?"

"I really don't know at this juncture. My priority is to ensure this crime scene is as clean as possible. Once Connor addresses everyone, head back to your office. We can regroup later, and Kellan, be sure not to—"

"Say anything to anyone at any point today. I know… you've taught me well." I verified no one was nearby and leaned in to kiss her. "I love you. See you soon." She held my hand for an extra ten seconds, as if to convey her understanding of my regret and concerns about what this all meant.

Once April dashed away, I entered the main lobby with the rollaboard and instructed everyone to gather. With that, I turned toward the crowd and anticipated the disaster that awaited me. Hopefully, the worst of the day was already behind me. Too bad the déjà vu feeling settling in my bones told me otherwise. Seeing everyone flocking together reminded me of the times I'd found bodies in Memorial Library and Paddington's Play House. Large masses had watched as I explained who died, practically in my arms or mere feet from where I stood, in those instances. It never got easier.

Tiny droplets of sweat formed at my temples. My eyes glazed over, but I persisted. "If everyone could remain here in the lobby, we'll notify you what's happened. I'm just waiting for Detective Hawkins. Should be five minutes and we'll explain why the police are on site."

Everyone nodded or shared some malleable sense of acknowledgement. Across from me, Fern chatted with her sister and brother-in-law. In person, Ivy was even more beautiful than the picture Fern had shown me the previous day. Tobias, who stood just under six foot tall, had dark hair, brutally angular features, and a suntanned complexion.

On the opposite side of the group, Bitsy chatted with a man in a dark suit who boasted an old-fashioned mustache. He reminded me of Clark Gable from *Gone with the Wind*, one of my all-time favorite films. He might've been the same guy Giovanni had spoken with at the Pick-Me-Up Diner. Was that Bitsy's husband? Or was he a panel speaker I hadn't yet met? Bitsy waved at me, then scrunched her face to imply I shouldn't interrupt.

Strangely, Kathy Endicott lingered near one of the far tables with her ex-husband, Lindsey. I hadn't expected to see Cain's father there with everyone else, but he'd generously donated to the college in the past and was potentially a special guest. I walked toward the hallway restroom to splash water on my face, eager to cease carting around the ticking time bomb hiding in Uncle Zach's rollaboard, but stopped when someone called my name. I glanced to the side only to find Nana D and my mother deep in conversation and shaking two fingers in my direction.

Nana D had dressed in her dark-green linen suit, a perfect combination to offset her henna-rinsed hair, which was tightly woven together in a braid that measured over three feet long. Mom wore a striking black pantsuit. Both had no inkling of what I'd discovered or that I would soon drop a bombshell that our prospective lead for learning more about Uncle Zach's death had gone up in smoke.

"What are you two doing here?" Neither had told me she'd be attending the opening of the art exhibition. My mother oversaw student admissions for Braxton, so she could easily get into Glass Hall with no one making a big deal. Of course, Nana D was the mayor and retained unlimited access, but why hadn't they mentioned it at brunch the prior day.

"I texted you forty-five minutes ago, brilliant one. You never returned my messages. What a shame! I could've fallen and hurt myself. Some help you are!" Nana D tapped her foot repeatedly, and when that didn't capture my attention, she whacked me with her Costco-size pocketbook. "You're my least favorite grandchild. And I've got, what, fifteen now? Who knows how many kids Campbell has these days!"

"Oh, Mother! No one believes you when you say things like that. Really, let's not exaggerate." Violet, my own mother, had said that line; she tried her best to keep quiet when Nana D embellished things, but rarely could. "I invited your nana to come with me, Kellan. She wanted to explore some collections but had no other time this week."

Nana D rolled her eyes at her daughter. She and my mother couldn't have been more different from one another. "Sure, sure. Kellan knows what I mean. He expects me to answer the phone immediately but struggles to do the same in return. Pish! What twaddle!"

"Nana D, that's simply not true. The last two times I didn't pick up were because I was teaching. And we'd spoken thirty minutes prior to that... when I distinctly told you I was going to class and not to disturb me." Not only did I need to deal with another murder, but a maniacal grandmother who loved to torture me.

"And the time before that? You were probably distracted by some hanky-panky activities with the sheriff." Nana D stomped her foot while waiting for me to respond, which I refused to do, especially in front of my mother and because I couldn't stop images of the bloody spear from manifesting inside my head. My interfering granny was only trying to get a rise out of me because it tickled her pink. "Cat got your tongue? Anyway, what kind of trouble did you cause now?"

Before I could respond to her litany of questions, my mother interrupted. "Why can't we leave the room, honey?"

I painstakingly shared as much as I could about Giovanni's death, without providing any gory details of what I'd seen. I noted that Kathy had just given me Uncle Zach's luggage but didn't explain what I'd found in it. Nana D picked up on my clues when I nonchalantly mentioned getting an African doll for Emma's next birthday. A hint of underlying anger and frustration in her words revealed her genuine distress. Any death these days would immediately bring up thoughts of Uncle Zach.

After we comforted one another over the loss, Nana D elbowed me in the ribs, her way of confirming she'd understood my hints. We had a secret code the rest of the family rarely understood "Speaking of Africa, I got hold of Deirdre last night. She and her husband visited Zach in South Africa while they were on their honeymoon."

My mother pulled a compact mirror from her purse and tried to fix her makeup. A few of the tears she'd shed had left a trail of mascara. She could be a bit vain, which I fully admitted was one of the limited traits I had inherited from her. "Oh, yes. She loved that trip. Spent an entire day with our brother before dashing off on a safari. I just can't believe Zach's gone. And now this!"

Nana D cast an empathetic look at my mother. "I was going to tell you, Kellan. Deirdre talked to Zach a lot in the months before he was killed. She was about to share something important with me about Renee, but then the new baby got fussy and she hung up. I think you should call her to find out what they discussed."

My nana was distraught over Uncle Zach's death and wanted answers—she wouldn't accept that it had just been a random car explosion. I would be careful with any future details I revealed so as not to raise her hopes until I had solid evidence. At the same time, Nana D could often elicit information from others that I wouldn't be privy to, so we worked together to solve cases in the past. With the death hitting so close to home, things were different.

"I'll call Aunt Deirdre this evening. Thanks for the tip." I was about to rest my hand on Nana

D's shoulder when she produced her phone and pressed a bunch of buttons.

A second later, she yelled, "Deirdre, that you? You sound like you're whispering in a tunnel. Speak up, for heaven's sake. I'm almost seventy-six years old and standing in a crowded room full of blowhard academics." She then turned to us and said, "No offense, dearies."

My mother and I exchanged harried and out-raged looks. Nana D never admitted any medical issues, and the voices around us were barely murmurs.

"That's better. Tell that sweet baby to stop waking you up at night. Really, daughter of mine, I raised four children to adulthood. You're old enough to be this kid's grandmother. I know what I'm talking about. Give the little devil some bourbon before his nap. Worked on Kellan all the time. Noisiest crybaby I ever heard," Nana D shouted into her device again after putting it on speakerphone. "Still is sometimes. Whines until he gets his way. Not sure where he got that from. Maybe his father."

When I grimaced and opened my mouth to object, my mother tut-tutted. "It's true. You were a handful. Your father even asked if they'd switched babies at the hospital. Your older siblings never cried as infants. Must've come from Wesley's side of the family. Not mine!"

"Pish! No, Deirdre, I'm not telling you what to do. I'm speaking the truth. It's up to you if you choose to do the right thing or screw it up." Nana D palmed her forehead before staring at me. "First-time mothers never listen." She returned to the call with my aunt. "Kellan is coming by at five o'clock. Tell him what you and Zach talked about. Everything. Gotta go. The sheriff's about to speak to me. I'm the most important person in this building, you know."

Nana D disconnected and pointed to the corner of the room. Connor and April had stepped inside and were waving everyone closer together. I couldn't believe my grandmother had scheduled me to meet with Aunt Deirdre and never asked if I was available. "I told you I'd call her later. What's eating you today?"

"Put your underwear on too tight again? Must cut off the circulation to your brain. Answer my question, please. Are you free to meet her, or is this just useless obstinance, brilliant one?" she inquired with a soured expression.

I glanced at my calendar and verified I didn't have to pick up Emma until six o'clock. "Well, yes, but that's not the point. I told you I'd call—"

"I expect more from you each time you find yourself embroiled in another scandalous murder. This is your true calling. Consider this an order from the mayor." Nana D held up one hand and pretended to close her lips with a zipper using the other. I let it go since she was still grieving my uncle's death. And our attention was diverted elsewhere.

April instructed everyone to listen to Detective Hawkins. Once Connor advised everyone of what had happened and organized the group so he and another officer could interview them, April signaled it was time for me to leave. As I marched toward the front doors with the rollaboard, Connor was questioning a disgruntled Tobias Natcher. Ivy, Fern's sister, had just initiated a conversation with the strange man boasting the Clark Gable mustache. It seemed everyone in the art world knew one another.

I muttered a hasty goodbye to Nana D and my mother, who volunteered to take Emma to the mall later in the week. Having a family who stepped in to care for my daughter was something I tried not to take for granted too often. For the first six years of Emma's life, I'd been a single parent in Los Angeles and had very few trusted friends who could babysit when I was busy with work. Ever since my dead wife had risen from the ashes, I'd been forced to allow Francesca two days a week with our little girl.

While striding through the courtyard toward Diamond Hall, my phone buzzed with a message from Ulan asking me to contact him as soon as possible. He was supposed to notify me when he was on campus so I could meet with his teacher. Was he ready?

I called him. "Hey, kiddo. I'm just heading back to my office. Where are you?"

Ulan replied in a nervous tone, "Ummm… I'm sorry, I know you told me not to talk to her, but she just showed up."

"Who? What are you talking about?"

"Renee, Dad's girlfriend. My friends and I were huddled together on the terrace outside the student union building. She was sitting at a table and some guy called out my name." Ulan explained that he'd turned around and remembered her because of the dark glasses she'd worn both times.

"Dark glasses? But it's overcast and foggy today. Please tell me you instructed her to leave you alone and contact me instead." The woman really irritated me, but if she were on campus earlier, she could've been involved in Giovanni's death. She had been the one to mention the African figurine, and that was quickly proving to be the reason my uncle had been killed.

"I'm sorry. We did talk for a bit. I learned something about her that I didn't realize last time." Ulan paused, his silence adding an unnecessarily dramatic effect to the conversation. I was confident I knew from where he'd picked up that attribute. Nana D was the queen of sensational performances. Thankfully, it hadn't impacted me!

"Stay there. I'm coming over as soon as I lock something up in my office. What did you realize?"

"Renee is blind. That's why she wears those glasses."

In a matter of seconds, every alarm inside my head blasted uncontrollably. Queen Tessa had been blind, as were many of her descendants. The latest generation of daughters had gone missing and supposedly died in the 1960s. Renee was hunting down the talisman and had somehow involved Uncle Zach. Was she related to Queen Tessa and searching for her family's heirloom?

Chapter 12

After locking the cursed talisman and the suitcase in my desk, I located Ulan in the student union building and briefly excused him for a family emergency. Knowing he'd recently lost his father, his teacher allowed us the time while his classmates toured the school's bookstore.

"Are you angry that I spoke with her?" inquired Ulan as we wandered across the quad. Since the summer session was significantly less crowded, none of the sports teams or large classes occupied the space. Lush green grass, colorful flower gardens, and a bevy of benches and ornate tables filled the field. On our foggy day, I sorely missed the pristine view of the Wharton Mountains and Crilly Lake.

"No way! She tracked you down. But please tell me everything she said. I'm not sure we can trust her yet, and no matter what, it's my job to look out for you." I affectionately slapped his back and gripped his shoulder. "I promise to keep an open mind and determine whether someone intentionally harmed your dad."

"Thanks, Kellan. I think she's legit. Really." Ulan conveyed what had occurred in their five minutes together.

Renee was sitting on the veranda overlooking the quad across from a tall, muscular man when Ulan and his friends strolled by them. He'd briefly noticed her because she wore a short skirt, and her silky legs caught his teenage attention. When Ulan almost walked into another student, his friends elbowed and teased him that the hot lady was watching him like a hawk. Then the man called out his name. None of his friends had used his name, and Ulan wasn't a common American moniker. He assumed she was someone he knew, so he moved closer to her. That's when he recognized Renee, even though he'd only seen her once on a past video chat.

Renee expressed heartbreak over Uncle Zach's death, indicating she'd been detained before coming to the US. They'd been scheduled to fly together to Orlando to meet Ulan, but at the last minute, plans had changed, and Renee was stuck in Amsterdam. She'd attempted to reach

Uncle Zach many times, but he never answered his phone. A few days later, she learned about the explosion at the airport and knew it had been engineered by the same person who had tried to kill her. Renee had more information but insisted it was safer if she spoke with me about it. Ulan begged her to share everything she knew about his father's accident, but Renee only hugged him tightly and apologized profusely for dragging Uncle Zach into the fiasco.

"And that's when my teacher saw me talking to someone she didn't recognize and insisted I join the group. As we shuffled away, Renee told me she was in a lot of danger and wouldn't risk contacting me again." Ulan stopped pacing and turned to me. "But she asked me for your phone number. I gave it to her. Did I do the right thing?"

"Of course, definitely." Part of me was grateful that Renee had only informed Ulan of some details. Despite his maturity for his age, she had no right to tell a teenager why a horrible criminal had blown his father to smithereens. I led us back on the path toward the student union building. "Did she say who was after her?"

"No. I asked, but that's when she told me to get you involved."

"Okay, describe her. Maybe I've seen her around town this week." Though a long shot, it was important to extract everything from Ulan's fresh mind.

"I'll do you one better, Kellan. A buddy snapped a photo while we were chatting. Renee's bodyguard never saw him do it." Ulan explained that his friend had air dropped the file to his phone, then showed me Renee's photo.

Although dark glasses covered her eyes, a portion of Renee's face remained visible. Flowing, jet-black hair had been pulled back and tied with a bow. Of mixed race, her skin appeared neither dark nor light, but the photo was slightly pixelated. Renee wore a trim slate-gray suit and large choker that covered most of her neck. Her features seemed awfully familiar, and even though I couldn't exactly place them, she reminded me of someone. "Thanks. Can you send that to me?" When he agreed, I followed it up with a question about whether she'd always been blind.

"Nah, we never got to talk about that. I remember my dad saying she was special, that she had a tough life and accomplished way more than most people despite everything working against her." Ulan hadn't realized what his father meant at the time, but he must've hinted that she was successful at overcoming her disability.

It was imperative I shared the news with April and Connor. With no way of tracking down Renee, I'd have to wait for her to contact me. But the sheriff's office could be on the lookout or ask if anyone had seen her in Glass Hall that morning.

"We'll figure it out. Let me do some digging, and I'll get back to you." I summarized what had transpired that morning, mostly so Ulan understood our potential imminent danger. "Please be careful. I don't know whom to trust. I understand you believe Renee is an ally, that she loved your dad, but people can hide secrets from us until it's too late."

After I escorted Ulan back to his classmates, his teacher agreed not to let him out of sight for the rest of the afternoon. I also forwarded Renee's photo to April. I would explain the background to her when she stopped by my office.

Throughout the next hour, I stared at Uncle Zach's suitcase and wondered whether Queen Tessa's talisman would enact its curse on me. I had no idea exactly how the magic worked, or even if the whole shebang was a bunch of crazy, unsubstantiated theories. All the historical deaths could've been exaggerated or unrelated. Nonetheless, my superstitious nature insisted I solicit input from Constance Garibaldi. Although she was a psychic, which vastly differed from a cursed figurine bestowed by the gods to an African queen, she might convey something of value.

Constance answered on the first ring. "I knew you'd be calling. My gift is rarely wrong, Kellan."

"Yes, you've mentioned that a few times," I replied, eager to talk to the woman yet also careful how long our conversation lasted. In the past, she'd had a habit of popping up too often. I respected and admired the woman, but I much preferred to leave the future in the future. I did not like the anticipation of something bad happening. And for some reason, Constance never brought me positive news. "How are you feeling?

You were convinced you only had weeks to live the last time we spoke."

Nearly eighty years old, Constance had endured several years in an institution when she was younger. Although she'd escaped and transformed into a famous psychic named Madame Zenya, her health continued to languish. As much as the woman could frustrate me, she'd been a comfort on many occasions, and I knew better than anyone how many tragedies she'd suffered through in the past. I needed to make a better effort to check on her in the coming days and weeks; the thought of her not being around added another layer of misery and consternation to my life. Too many good people had died around me this year, and it left me hollowed like a piece of Swiss cheese.

"It is true. I'm not well… but I've lived a generous life. And the answer to your question is no, the curse will not harm you."

Get out! She'd proven her authenticity to me on a handful of occasions, but it was becoming too uncanny. "Seriously, how do you know what I'm about to ask?"

"That doll... a tribal relic... I'm sensing diamonds and elephants, no... that makes little sense. Wait, it's coming to me. Ivory! Diamonds and ivory. It's an evil little idol!" Constance excessively coughed into the phone and asked her partner, Bartleby, the former mayor prior to Nana D's term, to prepare her a cup of peppermint tea.

That clarified the white coating on Queen Tessa's talisman. Ivory from an elephant's tusk. How intriguing that Zach was protecting elephants when the object found its way to him. "You're a hundred percent right! But why do you believe the sacred jinx won't impact me?"

"I'm unsure, just a vibration I'm receiving. An ancient curse was placed on that doll by a powerful woman. Two curses, to be clear. She incorporated some of her hair or clothes inside it... I can't decide which, but part of her physical being is trapped together with that figurine."

I confirmed for Constance everything I knew about the talisman. She'd never heard of Queen Tessa, but she felt vindicated when I explained the chief priestess's blood hidden inside one tube. We determined that elephants were special to Queen Tessa, and because Uncle Zach had been protecting them, her curse wouldn't impact him or anyone he loved. "So, you think it's kosher that I have it right now. I won't die a strange death like all the others?"

"Yes, you will be fine… this time. Zach was murdered, but not because of Queen Tessa's vengeance on those who attacked her tribe." Constance's voice wavered as she finished speaking. "But remember, this curse has been living and breathing for almost four hundred years. I'm feeling the presence of the man who killed her. Queen Tessa did something terrible to him in the past. He wants to end their war."

While I understood what she said, I didn't agree fully. "I don't believe a curse can kill someone. People kill someone. They have ulterior motives like love, revenge, betrayal, money, and jealousy."

"Or fear, Kellan. Don't underestimate the human mind. People believe all sorts of obscure and crazy things when they have darkness in their hearts. Your killer is afraid of this curse. I'm not sure why, but he or she is murdering to protect themselves from something. That's what you must figure out." Constance informed me she was growing tired and needed to rest. "I will always remember how generous you've been to me, Kellan. Never panic... you will have a guardian angel looking after you when I leave this earthly plane."

I thanked Constance for providing me with a different viewpoint and begged her to focus on her health. She made me promise to visit her sometime soon before it was too late. I wondered whether she truly foresaw her own death and hid the exact details from everyone. I'd learned enough from Nana D to read between the lines for similar situations. Some people, like Constance and my grandmother, had the strength to face their fears head on. I admired them greatly and hoped to emulate such hardiness and potency myself in my final years.

While waiting for April, I considered Constance's suggestion that the person who killed Uncle Zach and Giovanni had something important to hide or fear. What could it be? While focusing on it, I devoured a turkey sandwich I'd brought from home and forgotten to eat the prior Friday. Then I removed the suitcase from the desk, so it was ready for April when she arrived. Theorizing potential motives for murder and preparing for next week's impending lectures continued to distract me for a couple of hours. I also entered random searches for Giovanni, the FBI, and ICE into my laptop, hoping to uncover his last name or additional connections. Nothing valuable turned up.

Around midafternoon, Myriam moseyed into my office without knocking and dropped my lesson plans on the desk. "Not bad. Only two mistakes, three missed opportunities, and one suggestion to toughen up the students' exam. If I didn't know better, I'd say you were capable of learning new things."

"You've been such an amazing mentor, Dr. Castle. I'm honored to be in your presence." I did my best not to sound sarcastic, but from her scowl I hadn't succeeded.

"Don't patronize me! I'm not complimenting you as much as I am recognizing you're almost meeting my expectations for the first time since your father forced us to hire you." Myriam sat in the chair across from my desk and waited for me to resume our verbal sparring.

"I'm hoping one day you might accept my presence and be less combative." I flipped through the lesson plans and sorted them into two piles: approved and requiring changes.

"Relax, Professor Ayrwick. I'm softening toward you, but it doesn't mean I can't keep you on your toes." She paused, catching sight of the luggage I'd been carrying earlier in Glass Hall.

"Remind me. Where did that bizarre doll come from?" She leaned forward and yanked the rollaboard toward her.

"It was my uncle's." While considering her motives, I realized I still hadn't met Sawyer Jaccard. I assumed he'd been with Bitsy in Glass Hall's lobby, but I'd never actually seen him. Between him, Tobias Natcher, and the other man with the Clark Gable mustache, I could've confused everyone's identities.

When I asked Myriam if she had a photo of Sawyer, she laughed. "The man is camera shy, but you'll know him when you meet him. How did you come across your uncle's doll again?"

"Someone delivered it to me. Why are you so interested?" I worried she'd developed an inkling about its connection to Giovanni's death and the

success of Braxton's art exhibition. She and Ursula skated on the perimeter of the art world, especially given their close friendship with Sawyer
and Bitsy.

"It looks remarkably familiar. I've been wrack-
ing my brain all morning, but nothing wants to
come out of hiding. Rare... I almost never lose
objects or memories." Myriam certainly wasn't
old enough to claim forgetfulness. Why was she
overly obsessing about it?

"Did you want to see it again?"

"No, that's fine. I'm confident I'll land the
plane soon enough. And you say it came from
Africa?" Myriam glanced at her watch as though
she had somewhere else more important to be.

"Correct. Maybe Bitsy and Sawyer showed
you pictures of the talisman?"

"Perhaps. It's quite a unique piece. Anyway, I
should get home. I've had a boondoggle of a day,
and now that we've officially delayed the exhibition's opening until Wednesday, we must deal
with a bunch of rescheduling." Myriam advised
that I should check in with Fern, who was reor-
ganizing all the events with Cain. The building

would be closed for forty-eight hours while the police conducted a thorough search.

As Myriam sauntered away, April strolled through the hallway. They exchanged a laconic greeting, then April entered my office and closed my door. We spent a few moments kissing and catching up before I explained the picture of Renee and pointed to the rollaboard. "You need to confiscate that talisman from my office ASAP. Check it for prints or unfulfilled death threats."

April snorted while opening the suitcase and gingerly removing the velvet bag. "I'm only planning to check into its rightful owner. As of now, I don't have that answer, nor am I certain it's been stolen. Renee's presence is suspicious, but it's not confirmation. I'll ask Connor if anyone mentioned seeing a blind woman in Glass Hall. That said, I have important news about Cain Endicott."

"Be careful. Remember the curse," I reminded her, recalling Constance's advice.

April promised not to touch the idol. "It's a frightening doll. Between the impeccable stitching and the variety of materials used for all the features, it feels like it's staring back at me, mocking me. I'm impressed something almost four hundred years old has survived this long. I can't imagine anyone wanting to come in contact with it." April vowed to ask Cain more about it once she read everyone's formal interviews and understood what the collective group had to say. "Regarding Cain, he claims to have lost his cufflink in the closet while selecting the final items for today's opening exhibit. He made a last-minute change early this morning and wanted to swap one of the spears for a collection of pottery that showcased a better story."

"So, he admits to being down there. Just not when Giovanni was around?"

April nodded. "Cain showed up at six o'clock and rearranged the exhibits based on input from his colleagues. He temporarily kept the door open while he meandered back and forth between the classroom with the items not on display and the office he was using as a prep area. Given no one else would arrive until eight, he hadn't worried about a thief or killer breaking in."

"Okay, thanks. Whoever did this had to be strong… to puncture Giovanni's abdominal muscles and draw so much blood, right?"

"Definitely. The coroner's report will confirm the extent of the damage. We'll know how much force was necessary." April explained that it would take at least twenty-four hours to find out, which was helpful given the head honchos at the FBI and ICE were already smothering her with inquiries.

April also confirmed Connor had collected the sign-in sheet from the front security guard. They'd scrub it later in the day. The security guard hadn't kept a specific record of what time someone showed up, but he noted who'd come by that morning to collect their ID badges and subsequently entered the building. Shortly after eight, Cain had exited the basement classroom and was finalizing his introductory remarks in the makeshift office in the other hallway. Around eight forty-five, his father came downstairs to find him. Lindsey and Cain spoke for a few minutes, then joined everyone else on the main floor to prepare for the opening. Several guests had seen Cain arrive shortly before nine, and he hadn't exited the lobby until nine forty-five when he remembered he'd left the basement rooms wide open. He returned downstairs to lock both and the walk-in closet. That's when Fern found him loitering in the hallway, and I discovered Giovanni's body.

"Did he ever connect with Giovanni?" I'd sent the man to the building around eight o'clock, which would've been enough time for them to chat, assuming Cain wasn't only in the other hallway.

"No. Cain claims he saw no one else all morning. He'd only included Giovanni on the access list because he'd previously spoken with him on the phone about the theft of Queen Tessa's talisman. Cain agreed to let him attend the pre-exhibition activities as a favor, so Giovanni could ask questions of all the panel members." April carefully set the figurine on a pile of Uncle Zach's clothes. "Cain also confirmed he'd been working late the prior day to set up the exhibits, and that's why he'd missed the meeting with you and Fern. He returned home last night around midnight, which corroborates his mother's statement that someone had come in while she slept off a few glasses of wine."

"Fern and I tried to access the building. The security guard said no one was inside. Maybe Cain paid him to look the other way?"

April agreed to investigate. "This company is usually reliable. That said, I have a lot to focus on this week. At best, the government will allow me seventy-two hours to sort it out on my own."

"I can't imagine what it's like to deal with the FBI. I'll do whatever I can to help without getting in the way. Were you able to ascertain Cain's connection to my uncle?"

"A bit," April noted, shaking her head back and forth. "Cain is being somewhat vague. Claims that Zach reached out to him shortly before his South African dinner party with some art history questions. He wanted Cain's advice after remembering that Kathy had once told him about Cain's job at Braxton."

"So, my uncle initiated the contact. This looks bad for him. Stealing art that belonged in South Africa." I groaned in frustration.

"Maybe not. Cain thinks Zach only asked questions to understand his options while preparing for the benefit and auction." April smiled and encouraged me to toss out any ideas brewing in my mind.

"Did Queen Tessa's figurine come up in their conversation?"

"Yes, but Cain informed Zach that it had been missing for years. Zach never revealed that he had the object. He did, however, ask Cain to send him info about Governor Yeardley."

I absentmindedly tapped the desk. "What about scribbling the other words on the sticky note?"

"Cain wrote down Zach's flight number so he could meet him when it landed. Zach potentially had some less precious art to offer for Braxton's exhibit, but he ended up shipping it ahead of schedule. Zach had also mentioned changing his flight to rent a car in Orlando and inquired if Cain had any recommendations. He recalled that Cain often visited his mother in Orlando." April explained that Cain had completely forgotten about the sticky note once he emailed the Yeardley information and Uncle Zach mailed the less valuable art.

"So, Cain might have nothing to do with the car explosion?" I barely knew him, and he came from a good family. I struggled to believe he could be so vicious and lie to my face about murder.

"I'll keep investigating this angle. But the sticky note seems harmless as of now." April tousled my hair and kissed my forehead. "Let's talk about my next steps. I plan to cross-reference everyone who entered the building with potential disappearances from the main floor."

"Then you'll understand who had access to the basement classroom and walk-in closet." I worked out the timing based on what I'd learned. "If Giovanni left me and signed in at Glass Hall around eight fifteen, and I discovered him at nine forty-five, and he'd been dead at least thirty minutes—"

"Bravo! You're paying attention." Before finishing my thoughts, April congratulated me for remembering all the normal paths she'd previously followed once stumbling upon a dead body. "We'll need to check for anyone who showed up before nine o'clock and disappeared from the main floor for over ten minutes. That would give him or her enough time to sneak down to the basement level, kill Giovanni, and get as far away from the closet as possible. Both Cain and the security guard insist the place was empty on final walkthroughs last night, just before midnight."

"Unless someone hid in a closet or broke in when the guard wasn't looking, you have a full list of everyone with access." The lead meant we could narrow down the potential list of murderers to manageable expectations, even if the motive still weren't clear.

As April studied the doll from afar, she consented. "Connor should have the complete list of visitors and their supposed alibis tomorrow."

"Speaking of lists, can you obtain the passenger list for my uncle's Orlando flight? Kathy said Uncle Zach suspected he'd been followed." I would also check whether Kathy had access to flight manifests as soon as I could.

"Sure, great idea. In the meantime, I want to give some thought to what we're gonna do with this nasty creature. Keep it here until tomorrow. Technically, it's not evidence yet. I've got to update my new best friend at the FBI. They're not gonna patiently wait on the sidelines for me to solve this one."

"True. We need someone trustworthy to examine the figurine. What about Bitsy? Could she explain where it's been or how it came into Uncle Zach's possession?" I encouraged April to drop it in the velvet satchel and return it to the desk until we decided on our next steps.

"I'll talk to Ursula tomorrow. I trust her more than anyone else on site this morning," she noted while snapping a photo and putting the figurine in the rollaboard. "Originally, I was comfortable with you co-investigating your uncle's death because I wasn't responsible for the case."

I saw the *but* coming before she released it. Instead, I jumped in. "But now that a second murder has occurred, this time within your jurisdiction, I need to stay out of it?"

"Well, I might be kept out of it too, babe. The deceased is an ICE agent with former ties to the FBI. This will become a federal case by the end of the week." April confirmed she hadn't yet talked to Connor or scanned the access list to verify Giovanni's surname. They planned to meet in the morning to compare notes. Connor had the lead, and she would handle communications with the college.

Once April exited Diamond Hall, declining to take custody of Queen Tessa's talisman until she talked to Ursula, it was time to visit Aunt Deirdre. I confirmed Emma had been picked up by her friend's mother and would arrive home by six. I'd be back by then, and we could all cook dinner together. I locked the suitcase in the desk cabinet, grateful for our separation until the next day.

Before I left, I turned to the desk in a moment of levity. "Be kind! Don't even think about using that curse against me, Queen Tessa. I'm trying to find your rightful owner."

As I shut the door, I could've sworn several tribal drums began thumping. Was that her way of promising to behave for the evening? Or had she motivated the killer to strike again?

Chapter 13

When I reached Aunt Deirdre's, her husband had just taken the baby for a stroll around their property. They were living at the Paddington estate, one of the grand homes on Millionaire's Mile, a store-lined street connecting North and South campuses via Braxton's cable car system. Though they mostly resided in England, Timothy still ran the family company and had to spend a week each month in Wharton County to strategize with his executive leadership team and key business contacts.

Aunt Deidre had bright blue eyes, was two inches shorter than me, and typically had a trim figure. Having a child late in life had made it difficult for her to return to her pre-baby weight, but she was determined to get there soon. We talked about her new baby, whom she'd named Michael after Grandpop. Aunt Deirdre excitedly relayed the details of her next novel due out that fall. We vented about Nana D's intrusions in our lives, both agreeing she was meddlesome but also our favorite person in the entire world.

My aunt was the first to bring up her brother. "Zach and I are... were... very close. Just like your mother and Campbell used to be. Zach and I chatted every week. When Timothy gave me full control of our honeymoon destination, I scheduled a stopover in South Africa to visit Zach before we went on a week-long safari farther north of him."

"How did he seem while you were there?" I told her what Uncle Zach had said about looking out for Ulan should anything strange happen.

"You know, at the time, I didn't realize it, but something was going on a month before Ulan came to live with you." Aunt Deidre shared a conversation she'd had with her brother during that period.

Uncle Zach had been thinking about staying for a second term to work on his elephant program. He was worried how Ulan would react to another year in South Africa. They were supposed to come back to Braxton so Ulan could attend high school and be around family. Uncle Zach had told Aunt Deirdre about a new girlfriend he'd met, but he never said her name or that she was blind. He also mentioned that he'd run out of savings and couldn't afford to keep spending all his money on the elephant rescue program. Aunt Deirdre had offered to ask her husband, who controlled a successful international company, but Zach refused to accept a handout. He preferred viable donors who held an interest in the preservation of African elephants, culture, and history.

"I suggested he organize a benefit gala or dinner. Something that would attract more financing from rich benefactors. He agreed to let me fund that piece, and simultaneously, we proposed the idea of an auction. I introduced him to some influential people in the art world. Bitsy and Sawyer Jaccard."

Aunt Deirdre knew the Jaccards? "I just met Bitsy this morning. She's… quite a lot to take in the beginning."

My aunt chortled loudly, noting that she'd met the couple on a castle tour during an extended weekend in the Cotswolds. "Oh, you don't know the half of it. We're not particularly chummy, but she's a smart woman who puts on a lively show. Anyway, here's what I remember...."

Aunt Deirdre had connected Uncle Zach with Bitsy and Sawyer before departing on her honeymoon. The Jaccards were excited about the opportunity to work with elephants and introduce various artists to take photos, create custom experiences, et al. Six months later, Uncle Zach had amassed a bunch of donations, and to thank everyone, he'd arranged an elegant dinner party and silent auction with several of the key contributors last spring. Aunt Deirdre's tale was lining up with Giovanni's story, but it didn't explain how Uncle Zach had stumbled upon Queen Tessa's talisman.

"So, basically, you're saying Uncle Zach was short on cash and you connected him with bigwigs in the art world?"

My aunt nodded, adding that he'd eventually told her his financial issues weren't fully resolved, but he was optimistic things would pan out after the benefit dinner. "He never brought it up again, and since we'd originally fought about me giving him money, I decided not to pursue it anymore. I assumed he'd talk to me if he found himself out of options." Aunt Deirdre indicated that she'd only spoken with him once after the dinner party, when he mentioned flying to Amsterdam. Afterward, he sent her a text that he'd be off the grid for a couple of days, working on a few projects and visiting Ulan in Braxton. "I booked a trip to be here the same week so I could see him again, but then... he had the accident in Orlando."

"Do you think it was an accident? Or do you believe something else is going on?" I wasn't sure how much my grandmother had shared with her other children. Nana D tended to keep things to herself, or only tell me, when she was uncertain of the outcome.

"There are lots of unanswered questions, but the Orlando police found nothing suspicious, so I had to side with them. Nana D will come around, I'm sure of it."

Aunt Deirdre reminded me that Francesca had been the only one to see someone with a cigarette skulking a dozen yards from my uncle's car in the parking lot. No one else had mentioned it, and the Orlando cops failed to find any suspects. My aunt confirmed she would meet Bitsy and Sawyer midweek for drinks—only because Timothy had committed them without her input—and then fly back to London for an international conference. I promised to swing by again before she left.

On the way home, I processed everything I'd learned so far. If my uncle was experiencing money problems, was Renee the cause of them? If she were related to Queen Tessa, had she used him to steal the artifact from someone in the art world, then killed him? That made little sense because she would've retrieved the talisman before arranging his car accident. Maybe they were working together to fund his elephant rescue programs and steal the talisman for personal gain. I still wasn't sure how my uncle had come across it, who had won the auction bid, and which attendee was involved in underhanded trading schemes.

Patience was not my strong point, yet I'd have to wait for Renee to contact me. I couldn't fly to South Africa to search through Uncle Zach's belongings and unearth some important clue. My best chance was to learn from April and Connor how Giovanni fit into the puzzle and wait for the coroner's report. Between Cain's cufflink and the possible blood on Bitsy's purse, I had two solid suspects to pursue.

In need of a temporary break, I devoted part of the evening to relaxing with Emma and Ulan. We cooked Frikkadel, a traditional South African dish of baked meatballs prepared with onion, bread, eggs, vinegar and flavorful spices, and mashed potatoes with a sheba tomato sauce, in honor of Ulan's father. While the kids watched a television show, I relived many of my childhood memories of Uncle Zach. He'd been there for me whenever my father scolded me or compared me to Hampton. I would deeply miss the man more than I'd realized.

Once the kids went to sleep, I updated Nana D with everything I'd learned. I'd originally wanted to spare her from suffering through all the details until I had answers, but she could provide some of the missing pieces. "So, now that you know everything… what do you think?"

"Pish! You're in a quandary. Let me ponder this overnight. The FBI reached out to me and asked to chat tomorrow. To ensure I instruct Sheriff Montague to cooperate."

"What did you tell them?" I knew my grandmother wasn't April's biggest fan, and she would do anything to find out the truth about Uncle Zach's death.

"I told them that Wharton Country's three best detectives were on the case, and they needed to trust my talented trifecta!" Nana D also noted that she'd pull in some strings to keep the FBI from taking over the case until the end of the week. "The trifecta will get people to talk more than the FBI will."

I was glad Nana D had stood up for April. "Connor and April are two amazing detectives, but who's the third?"

"Oh, you are definitely not the brilliant one tonight. Go look in the mirror and you'll have your answer." Nana D disconnected, promising to update me after her meeting with the FBI.

As I settled into bed, I realized how lucky I was to have someone like her in my corner. Nana D believed in me, and she was confident I could sort out this mess. Along with Connor and April, we would cover all the angles and capture the mysterious killer. I called April to chat about the evening's activities, but extreme fatigue and a tension headache ensured we had minimal energy to process anything more than the basic facts.

"Did you ask Fox if he knew Giovanni's last name? Surely, he wouldn't associate with someone he couldn't investigate himself?" I knew Fox might have the information, but whether he'd share it was another story entirely. I couldn't force him to, but as the sheriff, April had a solid chance.

"They never exchanged full names. It was why he'd been so successful at his job in the past." April agreed he was just stonewalling, but without a warrant it would be impossible to force Fox's hand. He was the primary judge in Wharton County and had the unyielding support of our governor.

I told April what I'd elicited from my aunt. "Is that enough to check my uncle's banking records?"

April commended me for unearthing more options, but she indicated nothing could reopen Uncle Zach's case with the Orlando police unless we connected his demise to Giovanni's. Until we learned more about Giovanni's identity and how Uncle Zach had gotten possession of Queen Tessa's talisman, we were at a standstill. "Let's meet tomorrow to talk through the list of people who had access to Glass Hall. I should have it on my desk first thing. Minor delays with handling all the evidence prevented me from assembling the names tonight. Connor is accompanying Giovanni's body to the morgue and will check for identification and let me know what he discovers."

When we hung up, I texted Connor to suggest we meet at the gym at seven thirty the following morning. No reason to wait for April when I could insert myself into the situation. I would drop the kids off at school early and head over to campus. We usually worked out together at the Grey Sports Complex a couple of mornings a week, so it wasn't an unusual proposal. He confirmed our plans as my eyes fluttered closed.

Hopefully, I'll be done early enough that I get some sleep. Been a long day. About to sort through Giovanni's clothes now. See ya tomorrow.

* * *

After a ten-minute warm-up the next morning, I set the weight level on the bench press at an amount that would push me but not kill me. Connor handled twice the load, so we'd have to alternate machines to avoid constantly resetting them between sets. Wondering what had detained him, I struggled to get through the routine. Finally, I noticed him practically crawling toward me from across the room.

"Dude, I almost didn't make it. Got home at four o'clock in the morning. I nearly called you too." Connor had dark bags under his eyes—not an attractive look on him. Score one for Team Kellan!

"Sorry. We could've canceled or rescheduled for lunchtime. I can usually get out midday now that the spring term has ended." I wouldn't have been happy about it, but my buddy needed his sleep.

"I couldn't cancel, at least not when I have a name to share. Off the record, of course." Connor added another ten pounds to the machine and reprimanded me for practicing improper form.

"Yeah, I know. I'm a little tired myself today. What did you find out?"

As I pushed the bar upward, Connor spotted me in case it was too much weight. He waited until I finished my first set, then said, "You sure you're ready?"

"Hit me with it." How bad could it be? It's not like I knew the guy from Adam. I began pumping out another set.

"Giovanni's last name is Vargas. As in the Vargas crime family."

My arms immediately turned to jelly. I dropped the weight bar so quickly, it almost landed on my neck. Luckily, Connor had laser-fast reactions and caught it.

"He's related to Francesca's boyfriend... as in my ex-wife's new lover? You can't be serious!"

"Trust me, man... this is not a helpful discovery. I hope it doesn't mean a mob hit or something far worse killed your uncle."

This couldn't be happening all over again. I almost died because of Francesca's rivalry with the Vargas family. What was going on? Once Connor racked the weight bar properly, I thrust myself off the bench and swigged a mouthful of water from a nearby fountain. A spiderweb of various, murky connections percolated inside my head.

Francesca and Cristiano had claimed they flew to Orlando, against my request, to spend time with Emma. But could it have been a cover?

"Connor, what if Cristiano blew up my uncle's rental car while Francesca intentionally hovered nearby to ensure Emma stayed far enough away?" Even I knew my theory was flimsy, especially since I didn't have proof Giovanni was from the same Vargas family.

Connor pulled me to the side and explained that they'd already informed ICE and the FBI to investigate these additional angles. "Listen, I only know what appeared on his identification badge and the sign-in sheet. We don't have any details beyond that. We're also checking records based on his driver's license address."

"What happens next? Someone claims his body, right? You can search his house for clues or evidence." I asked Connor where Giovanni lived, but he only admitted it wasn't in Wharton County.

"Relax. I know this appears suspicious, but if Giovanni were involved in the Vargas crime family, he could be a double agent. Someone else might've killed him for revenge. Totally unrelated to this African talisman, the art exhibition, and Zach's accident." Connor tried to calm me down with other theories, but it wasn't working.

"Were you able to obtain more news from your dad about the curse and the idol's history?" I needed to find out who had killed my uncle and whether Francesca and Cristiano had placed my daughter in danger a second time. It was hitting way too close to home again.

"My dad and I moved our video call to six o'clock. I'll share anything he tells me. Promise." Connor convinced me to focus on our exercise routine, which we did before hitting the showers and beginning our workdays.

After leaving Grey Sports Complex, he bolted to the sheriff's office to examine new test results. I psyched myself up for an art exhibition update with Cain, Fern, and Ursula. She'd postponed our discussion, given the murder at Glass Hall, as we needed to sort through all the financial aspects and the rescheduled opening that week. While riding the cable car from North to South Campus, I called and pressured Francesca for the truth. She swore to me she had nothing to do with Uncle Zach's accident.

"But what about Giovanni Vargas? Is he related to your boyfriend? Is he part of the mob? You promised to keep Emma away from anything dangerous. I'll revisit our custody arrangement if you're lying to me, Francesca." I kept my tone civil, but my ex-wife knew the extent of my wrath.

"Cristiano has a cousin named Giovanni. I've only met him once, and I admit, he had a scar on his neck. It sounds like the same guy, but I don't know for sure." Francesca agreed to talk to Cristiano as soon as he returned from a business meeting. "I'll get back to you tonight."

"I guess I have to be patient." Not my favorite thing in the world!

"Listen, Kellan... I know you're going through a lot right now. Everyone grieves differently. Don't underestimate the impact of something this tragic. It silently gnaws at you, even when you don't recognize it." Francesca attempted to soothe my nervous and frustrated emotions—a kind gesture given our chilly relationship these days. "Trust me for once, okay?"

"I appreciate your help. Thanks, Francesca. I'll do my best." As we hung up, I knew she was right. I had to take care of myself too, and that meant letting others step up. Tonight, I'd summarize everything I'd learned to date. It was time to start poking holes at alibis, search for new clues, and discover all the missing links. Then I would take advantage of the connections in my network who could help solve the murders.

Chapter 14

I disembarked the cable car and sprinted to Diamond Hall. Police tape still wound across the nearby front entrance to Glass Hall, and a burly guard ensured no one accessed the inside. Only a few lectures took place in the building during regular semesters, and since the exhibition was being held there, no one except the art department needed entry that week.

When I reached my office, I checked in with Fern, who was preparing for a separate meeting with Ursula and instructed me to head over to the president's office in thirty minutes. Grateful for the brief reprieve, I greeted my colleague, checked the desk compartment, and verified Queen Tessa's talisman was safely stored inside the suitcase. I was unwilling to continually lug it around or bring it home where it could cast its voodoo curse on me or my family. For now, keeping it in my office seemed ideal. Only April and Nana D knew it was in my possession, so I felt secure enough leaving it there until we had a decision on how to proceed.

Myriam might've connected it with the missing talisman, but she wouldn't think it important enough to tell anyone. Using all of Myriam's input, I executed the last changes to my lesson plans and dropped them off in her office. Unusually, she wasn't on site that morning. Most days, she arrived at sunrise and departed at sunset. The woman was a workaholic, just like her wife. Other than her catatonic father who was sequestered in a nursing home, Myriam had no other relatives in the area. Ursula's one living relation, a nephew named Cheney whose mother owned Simply Stoddard with her husband, hadn't found the time to get to know his aunt. Myriam and Ursula had only each other as family, and a few close friends like the Jaccards made up for their missing relatives. Maybe she'd chosen to spend a plethora of her time with them while they were in town.

Upon scanning my calendar, I remembered my forgotten promise to my brother that I'd swing by for an early lunch with him and Natasha. Hampton confirmed it was still a light day, so I ambled toward Prentiss Hall to get through my discussion with Ursula and Fern. It wasn't too far away from the cable car station, but I'd at least achieve my total step goal early that day. Afterward, I'd hop in my SUV and head to the Royal Chic-Shack to see my brother, his wife, and the kids.

Ursula's door was open, and her obstinate secretary escorted me inside. "Excuse me, President Power," the bitter woman said as she turned to leave. "Cain isn't answering his phone. I'm not sure why he isn't here for the meeting. He agreed to the new time when I rearranged your calendar."

"That's fine. You can close the door, but if he shows up, please send him in." Ursula joined Fern by the picturesque bay windows and sat in a tall wing chair, catty-corner to the fireplace.

Fern patted the sofa, so I sat next to her. "Can't imagine where Cain has disappeared to."

Ursula noted, "He's being interviewed by Sheriff Montague again. Apparently, he might have been the last person to see Giovanni alive yesterday."

Fern repeatedly shook her head. "Awful business. I don't understand what's happened in the last year, but ever since Kellan returned, we've experienced a series of unfortunate incidents."

I wasn't sure how to respond to my *supposed* pal carelessly tossing me to the wolves. "It's definitely not because of me. You're not insinuating I had anything to do with all—"

Fern apologized. "No, I'm simply referring to the peculiar timing. You have a cloud of darkness hanging above you, my friend."

Ursula interjected. "Truthfully, one of those past murder investigations involved my brother. I accept partial guilt too. Coincidence is a powerful motivational tool."

After discussing the history of Braxton's series of murders and thefts, Ursula casually mentioned Sheriff Montague had offered surprising news that morning. Since the homicide happened on campus, she had to report more details to the Board of Trustees. I convinced her to share the information with me. "I'll keep it to myself. Maybe it'll help me protect the college from any wrongdoing."

"Cain originally told us he'd never interacted with Giovanni yesterday morning, but he confessed to Sheriff Montague that he had briefly chatted with the man." Ursula clarified that one of the security guards had overheard the two men in the basement minutes after Giovanni descended upon Glass Hall. "Cain warned Giovanni to stop pestering him about the curse of Queen Tessa's talisman. Giovanni insisted it was super important for him to comprehend the figurine's history." This had happened around eight thirty, which lined up with me sending Giovanni to Glass Hall shortly beforehand.

I felt as if I were missing essential information. "Why did Cain lie?"

Fern's eyes went wide. "We're not sure. Cain swears he left the man in the classroom to look at the remaining African artifacts while he returned to his office in the other hallway."

"At least now we know Giovanni was stabbed with the African spear between eight thirty and nine. You discovered him just before ten o'clock, so minimal people had access," added Ursula.

I promised to extract anything else that might be valuable from April. We promptly focused on rearranging the schedule for the exhibit. The sheriff's office had swept Glass Hall clean that morning and would turn it over to Braxton by dinnertime. Fern and Cain would coordinate with the facilities staff to prepare the building and reopen the following day.

"What else do you need from me?" I inquired, hoping they'd completed most of the tasks. I wasn't avoiding more responsibility, but my personal priority was to find my uncle's killer. I had little doubt that the entire series of events weren't mysteriously connected.

"If you can track down Cain, that would help. Otherwise, we've got the art exhibition under control for now; however," Ursula said, pausing to carefully articulate the next set of instructions, "I also need you to employ your special detective skills to uncover whatever Bitsy is hiding from me."

"But she's *your* good friend. Why would she keep a secret?" I didn't like the direction of our conversation.

"Bitsy hasn't been herself since she arrived. She and Sawyer are fighting constantly, which rarely happens. At dinner yesterday, she clomped out and told him it was the last time she'd believe him." Ursula couldn't convince either of them to talk, but she assured me that her friend had taken a strong liking to me. "Please find some time to poke around and ask a lot of questions about what she's up to."

At the end of our discussion, we'd assembled a solid strategy, including a method to butter up Bitsy for information. "Fern, do Ivy and Tobias know much about Queen Tessa's talisman, or were they friendly with Giovanni or Cain? I'd like to understand how they became involved in the art exhibition."

Fern indicated she wasn't aware of any prior relationships between them and Giovanni. Ivy had revealed that she and Tobias met Cain at a previous art conference, but she wasn't sure of the timing. "Both gave their statements yesterday to Detective Hawkins. Afterward, Tobias attended several business meetings and Ivy met Jordan for dinner. It's the first time she's seen her son in two months. I didn't want to intrude."

"Okay. I need to visit my brother. If you learn anything from them, let me know. Give my regards to Jordan too. Tell him his favorite professor wishes him well in graduate school." I suggested we head out to address each of our priorities.

Fern's office was on North Campus, as was my SUV, which I needed to visit my brother at my parents' house several miles away. While waiting for the cable car's arrival, we relaxed near the running path on the edge of the campus. It traversed the perimeter of a wooded area, where a half-dozen of the benches lined either side of the platform used to board the cable car. In between them, large terracotta urns bursting with flowers, grasses, and trailing leaves offered vibrant colors and pleasant scents.

Our highly reliable cable car system collected and deposited students on each campus twice every hour. During the ride, Fern and I chatted about the plans for the fall university conversion. Sure enough, the cable car brought us back on time, just as we finished addressing a handful of critical issues with the launch. While she ambled to her office, I drove to the Royal Chic-Shack. My dad had taken my mom to lunch in Lakeview, and the babysitter had brought all the kids to the park for the afternoon. It would only be Hampton, Natasha, and me. Hampton had arranged a break in his schedule at ReedWell, so he stayed home to prepare for his meeting with the potential buyers the next afternoon.

When my parents had bought the house, it was an authentic log cabin on twenty acres of untouched land. Over the years, they remodeled and tacked on two additions with vaulted ceilings and endless cedar planks. All the bedrooms except for one were on the second floor, and a deep hunter-green that reminded me of an avocado, a favorite snack of mine, coated the walls. The enormous flagstone fireplace and handcrafted antique furniture offset all the modern conveniences, allowing for compromise between my parents' distinctive design aesthetics.

Upon arrival, I knocked on the front door. Natasha immediately rolled to the foyer in her wheelchair and ushered me inside. She'd recently lost a dozen pounds despite her already petite waist, and her face had unfortunately taken most of the heat. Amplified by icy blue eyes and hollowed cheeks, she appeared gaunt and exhausted. "It's good to see you, Kellan. I'm glad for the company today."

"Too much with the kids and my brother, eh?" I bent down to kiss my sister-in-law's forehead. In the past, she'd been frigid and terse with me. Natasha had come from a pretentious and wealthy family, but after her paralysis, she'd reformed.

"Exactly. I have a newfound respect for you these days. I used to think you exaggerated all those stories about your brother's obnoxious personality. Now that I'm around him twenty-four-seven, it's enlightening." Natasha explained how she loved him to pieces, but among his patronizing attitude, disinterest in listening to what she wanted to accomplish with her therapy, and his controlling methods for finding potential buyers, she wanted to strangle him before noon most days.

"Surely, he isn't that bad? I know how demeaning he sometimes sounds, but he's a good guy deep down when it comes—"

Hampton strolled into the living room, interrupting my carefully balanced words, and shouted a confrontational greeting in my direction. "Good to see you, brother. I presume you're encouraging my wife's objections these days. I'm merely looking out for her best interests. Never one to support me, are you?" In the preceding months, a widow's peak and profound frown lines had formed on his diamond-shaped face.

"No comment." Hampton and I tepidly shook hands; he wasn't the hugging type. The three of us shared a brief conversation in which they each offered their perspectives and validated that they were mostly teasing one another. Natasha knew she needed to sell ReedWell, and she trusted Hampton to make the right decision. She wanted to meet the recommended set of buyers before her husband drafted the paper-work—he was an attorney by trade—and bro-kered an official agreement. In terms of recov-ery, they did their best to negotiate a truce, but whereas Hampton wanted Natasha to take her time, she was adamant about controversial ther-apies and a risky surgery to regain the use of her legs.

"Anytime the doctors go near your spine, there is a tremendous risk, Natasha. I almost lost you once. We can't mess around with unproven no-tions." Hampton steered his wife's chair into the dining room and announced that he'd brought lunch home from a nearby delicatessen. "Waldorf salad, a bread and cheese platter, and fruit cocktail. All approved by your doctor, darling."

Natasha winked at me and smiled at her husband when he complained about napkins missing from the paper bag. "Of course, I understand. We'll figure it out on Friday when we meet with the surgeon. I'm hardly ready to do much. It's only been ten weeks, and I'm not strong enough to undergo anything radical until the six-month mark. We have time to decide on the best approach."

While nibbling on our meal, I casually mentioned the incident at the art exhibition. "You went to high school with Cain, if I remember correctly, Hampton."

Hampton verified they had graduated the same year. "Poor guy. You just missed him."

Natasha reached for the bottle of water but struggled to stretch her fingers far enough across the table. When Hampton rose from his chair to assist, she cautioned him. "I can do it. If I need help, I'll ask." She pushed herself three more inches and finally looped her hand around the neck of the bottle. "See what I can accomplish when you trust me to know my limits?"

I couldn't imagine what they were going through. For years, Natasha had worked at her family's company, leading major divisions and securing lucrative contracts. During the same period, she'd given birth to four children, volunteered in multiple charity organizations, and run several miles each day. Natasha Reed Ayrwick was a persistent enough woman to push through her injuries and achieve a miracle. Her toughest challenge these days involved overcoming the mental obstacles associated with the new physical restrictions of her body.

When enough time had passed, I further inquired about Cain's visit. "He was scheduled to meet with President Power an hour ago, but he never showed up. Did he leave here on time?"

Hampton held the salad bowl while I scooped another spoonful of colorful fruits. "He needed some advice, and I admit, I kept him here a few minutes late." My brother explained that while he wasn't a criminal lawyer by schooling, he knew enough to provide guidance to Cain. "Unfortunately, he's technically hired me to represent him, so I cannot break client-attorney privileges. Your girlfriend and best friend have placed a tremendous amount of pressure on Cain."

I understood that Hampton couldn't say anymore, but if Cain was nervous enough to ask for legal help, there must have been more to the story about why he'd lied. He'd kept something crucial from me when I asked where he'd gone missing to in the previous days, and he'd spoken to Giovanni in Glass Hall less than an hour before the man's death.

"April and Connor are only doing their jobs." I decided not to push my brother for answers, but I noted the potential connection to our uncle's death. "I'm not saying I believe Cain is guilty, but he knows something more than he's saying. He also seems to be avoiding me."

"You should be used to that by now. We all need a break sometimes." After smugly grinning, Hampton promised he was only providing legal advice until something more serious happened. "If they arrest Cain, or he's responsible for hurting Uncle Zach, I'll back off."

"Glad to see you've got an open mind."

As I cleared the table, Hampton followed me into the kitchen and apologized. "Look, I'm just stressed. I know we haven't always been close, but you saved my wife from being murdered. Between that and Uncle Zach's death, I've gotten the wake-up call. I'll try to be nicer. Okay?"

Though tempted to hug him, I let it go. His apology, his terms. "That's all I can ask, Hampster. Thank you. And you're welcome." Using his dreaded childhood nickname was a fair way to balance our complicated relationship. It would be all about marginal gains with my brother—incremental improvements to our relationship. It also was how I'd successfully solve my uncle's murder.

When Hampton stepped away to check the office, I escorted Natasha back to their temporary bedroom so she could rest before the kids returned from the park. After I helped her into bed, she praised me for supporting her during lunch. "I know he means well, but your brother can't do it all. Between leading the company, coordinating my doctor's appointments, and spending free time with the kids, he's running himself ragged."

"Well, it looks like tomorrow might initiate the sale of ReedWell. That'll eliminate one major responsibility." I layered the blanket over Natasha and offered her the television remote.

"Yes. It makes things a lot easier since I know the preferred buyer. Tobias Natcher and my father belonged to the same men's club and used to do business together in the past." Natasha settled into a comfortable position and thanked me for my generosity.

Interesting. That explained why the Natchers were really in town. "How well do you know Tobias? Have you met his wife, Ivy?"

Natasha confirmed she'd attended their wedding several years ago, as Tobias had known her father for years. "Have you met them, Kellan?"

Wow! It was a small world. I hadn't encountered them, but he and Ivy had multiple connections in town. "No. I've heard Tobias is a big arts enthusiast. Just didn't realize he was interested in buying up petroleum businesses." ReedWell was a natural gas and oil company with its primary offices in the south. Natasha's father had opened another office in Pennsylvania the prior year so he could stick closer to his daughter when she returned to Braxton with Hampton.

"Oil and natural gas aren't the only areas piquing his interest. Tobias is quite entrepreneurial and invests in all the major industries." She explained that the man hardly ever slept, had been on a quest for decades to amass a substantial fortune, and often took calculated risks in life.

I peppered my sister-in-law with a few pertinent questions, but she knew nothing of Queen Tessa's talisman or the other man I'd seen at Glass Hall with the Clark Gable mustache. I'd have to review the security list with April, if she agreed to share it. It felt like she'd talked to everyone but me. Then again, she was solving a murder, and her job came first at a time like this. Especially with the bigwigs at the FBI and ICE breathing down her neck.

I left my parents' house feeling puzzled about the numerous connections between all the people involved in the art exhibition and my family. During part of my contemplation on Braxton's South Campus, I lingered at the top of the arched wooden bridge that crossed the new man-made pond, admiring the incredible design that the college had poured into its architecture. When I heard Braxton's clock tower chiming, I knew it was two o'clock. April had planned to swing by after meeting with her team. It was time to return to my office to wait for her and to accomplish additional preparation for the start of next week's classes. I also needed to fulfill my promise to Ursula to determine what Bitsy was hiding. I maintained hope it had nothing to do with Giovanni's death. While the red liquid on her purse might've come from something other than Giovanni's blood, her reaction to my pointing out the splotch had not been convincing.

As I crossed the bridge a final time, my shoe slipped on a wet spot. In the stumble, I accidentally knocked my glasses off my nose. By the time I bent down to pick them up, the lenses were spotted with water droplets. I had no tissues or loose clothing to wipe them dry and would need to walk back to Diamond Hall in a blur. I stepped back onto the main pathway, distracted by a couple of voices giggling near the rear entrance to Paddington's Play House. Through the smudges on my glasses, I saw a woman and a man playfully pushing and pulling each other back and forth. Romance blossomed on campus all the time between students, but even through my hazy vision I could tell the pair was older.

When they separated, I received quite a shock. Not only had I stumbled upon Cain, but I wouldn't have to travel extremely far to locate Bitsy. Recalling all the pressure Ursula and Myriam had placed on me earlier in the week, I made a split-second decision to ramble in their general direction. Had I witnessed a friendly banter between two acquaintances or a woman cheating on her husband? Was she who'd been in Cain's office the prior weekend? Bitsy was the first to notice me. She blushed and stepped away from Cain. He whispered something upon seeing me, but I wasn't close enough to hear the words.

"Cain, I'm glad I found you. Ursula and Fern were disappointed you skipped our morning meeting." I led with a direct statement, hoping to underscore my frustration with the man who'd avoided us way too often lately. I then said to Bitsy, "I need to catch up with you too, Mrs. Jaccard. Might you have a moment?"

Cain swallowed heavily before profusely apologizing to me. "Truly sorry. I completely lost track of time at your brother's place. Sheriff Montague had more questions. Then I realized I left my briefcase at home this morning. If you'll excuse me, I need to call President Power and beg for forgiveness." He turned to Bitsy. "Nice meeting you again. Have a wonderful afternoon, and I look forward to our tour of the exhibition tomorrow."

As he left, Bitsy grabbed a hold of my arm. "Oh, Kellan. It isn't what it looks like. But don't worry, everything will be okay."

I hadn't expected those words from the woman. Keenly aware that Myriam and Ursula had cautioned me to keep the Jaccards out of trouble and to ensure they were looked after properly, I dug a little deeper. "It appeared like you two were quite intimate. Last time I checked, you were married, and he was under suspicion of murder. Is there anything you'd like to discuss, Bitsy?"

"Perhaps I should explain more," she agreed, looping her arm with mine and suggesting we should take a short stroll. "It seems worse, but really, Cain and I have been talking for weeks about the exhibition. Today, we met for the first time, and it was all very innocent. I simply made a mistake letting him kiss me in a weak moment."

"Well, I understand what you're saying. It feels good to flirt with someone occasionally, but it leaves me unsettled." If I had any chance of convincing her to talk, I had to appear as if I were on her side. "I'm still concerned that Cain has been lying to me about a few things. I wouldn't want him to put you in any danger. Maybe you could help me understand what's going on there?"

Bitsy sighed, halting our casual saunter through the courtyard near the beautiful azalea bushes blooming in front of Stanton Concert Hall. "It's like this, Kellan. Every year, I feel a bit older. As much as I understand that's life, I'm not willing to cast away my youth so quickly. Cain and I have been talking for the last three weeks about the art exhibition, and he's quite an attractive man, albeit a few years younger than me. We have a lot in common when it comes to personal interests. Things with Sawyer can get difficult. I'm tired of his underhanded methods and shadiness." Bitsy indicated that she'd only be visiting Braxton for four days, and it was rare to come across a man like Cain, so she permitted herself some harmless fun.

"But you made a big deal of saying you were gonna spend all your time with me. And you still haven't acknowledged that Cain might be responsible for killing a man in the basement of Glass Hall." I was secretly glad she'd switched her attention to another man, and part of her routine might have included testing me, but it was still confusing to comprehend the true story. She could've chosen not to say anything, but Bitsy almost wanted to confess her secrets to someone. Was she feeling guilty for something?

"I have no idea what happened to Giovanni Vargas. I was just as shocked to find out about the murder as everyone else."

Interesting. The police hadn't released the victim's name, and anyone who might've known his first name would have no idea his last name was Vargas, unless he or she knew Giovanni previously. "What about fawning all over me? Wouldn't that bother your husband too?"

"Oh, well… that was just for show. I told you that, Kellan. Remember, everyone thinks I'm this flighty airhead. If Sawyer believes I'm socializing with you, he'll never suspect I sneaked around with Cain today." Bitsy squeezed my hand and rested her head against my shoulder. "Myriam and Ursula have assured Sawyer you wouldn't dare take advantage of me. He's a pussycat, deep down. You won't say anything, darling, will you?" She led me back to the main path again.

"Since I really don't want to get involved in your marriage, I'll keep quiet about what I just saw. But it would be helpful if you could answer a few questions." When she agreed, I explained both the items troubling me recently. "One, exactly what was that red stain on your purse yesterday? Two, do you have any insight into my uncle's death?"

Bitsy stopped so abruptly, I had to catch myself from falling forward. As she turned toward me, the veins in her neck bulged and hands balled into fists. "You don't want me on your bad side, Kellan. I know many people who could cause problems for you. I've told you before… I'm not a silly little tart who can't take care of herself."

I'd apparently hit a major nerve. What was Bitsy hiding from me?

Chapter 15

I trusted my instincts, which had been wrong once or twice in the past. "Really, this isn't my nonchalant method to accuse you of murder. But look at it from my perspective. Everyone's searching for this African talisman, and…." I shared everything I'd learned to date with Bitsy, except I neglected to tell her the figurine had been buried in the suitcase Cain's mother gave me.

"I'm truly sorry your uncle died in that freak accident. I'll tell you the truth, but only because I have nothing to do with the murders, and I can see how much you're hurting, Kellan," said Bitsy.

When Ursula had insisted Cain talk with the Jaccards to secure more donors, Bitsy intended to support the art exhibition because she valued their friendship and had a passion for African culture. She'd been helping her husband search for rare pieces for many years, and the infamous tribal queen's story had enthralled him. She'd wanted to get her paws on Queen Tessa's talisman, but it had been gone from society for such a long time. No one ever expected to find it again. When she'd seen it at Uncle Zach's dinner party, she made an offer to purchase it as a gift for her husband, but she'd lost out to a different bidder. She'd given up on her marriage once Sawyer professed his disappointment in her lack of connections and innovative skills to secure him a piece he'd wanted to own for years. Once Bitsy and Cain ran into one another the previous Friday, a spark ignited. And even though it was risky, she desired as much time with him as possible.

"You deserve the truth. That's why Cain has been late to so many meetings since last weekend. We've been slipping away to enjoy some private moments together. That's all, Kellan. It's also why I didn't tell you the entire truth at the café yesterday morning. Before I arrived at The Big Beanery, Sawyer and I went to Glass Hall to retrieve our identification badges and ask whether Queen Tessa's talisman had shown up. As soon as we got inside, he took off to scour the exhibits. I met Cain in the basement."

"So, you're telling me you two shared some alone time while your husband was in the same building. A little dangerous, don't you think?" I couldn't believe she would act so foolishly.

"That's what heightened the thrill for me. We also discussed some changes Cain should make in the show, and he agreed to them. That's how I cut my finger and the blood got on my purse. We were rushing through all the paperwork to finalize the updates." She insisted it wasn't Giovanni's blood—even when I suggested there was too much on the purse to come from a small papercut—and she'd only hidden it from me because she didn't want me to know she'd been alone with Cain.

"Okay. Let's say this is all true. What times did you enter and exit the basement?" If Cain had brought Giovanni into the classroom at about eight thirty, wouldn't Bitsy have seen him too? I needed to understand the order of the events and what Bitsy's husband was doing while she flirted with Cain.

"Sawyer and I arrived at eight o'clock. I went downstairs immediately and found Cain in the classroom. We were in there for five to ten minutes. When I sliced my finger, Cain took me to his office in the other hallway to get a bandage."

Bitsy showed me the cut on her finger, which still looked red and raw, as proof of her story.

"You know they can test the blood on those papers they took into evidence, and—"

"It will be mine, I swear," she promised, growing irritated with me. "I like you a lot, Kellan, but you've got the wrong idea. Cain and I were in his office together when he realized he left the other classroom door open, so he went back to shut it. While he was gone, Sawyer called to tell me he hadn't come across the talisman. Cain must've met Giovanni while I was on the phone and let him in the classroom." At that point, Bitsy had hung up and met Cain in the hallway just after eight thirty. She told him she had to find Sawyer in the lobby and then meet me at The Big Beanery. Cain said he'd be upstairs in a minute, and he showed up soon after with his father. "That's when I left to locate you. I never saw Cain again until a couple of hours later when everyone gathered in the lobby for the police inquiries."

Everything she'd said could easily be verified, including whether it was her or Giovanni's blood, the call from Bitsy to Cain, and the next one from Sawyer to Bitsy. Could Sawyer have sneaked into the basement and stabbed Giovanni while his wife was on her way to meet me? Had Cain killed Giovanni before his father arrived in the basement? Were Bitsy and Cain covering for one another? Too many unknowns, including why so many people would fight for control of this cursed talisman.

"Well, I'm forced to tell the sheriff what you've just told me. I can probably skip the conversation about your extra-marital rendezvous, but not about being down there," I noted, even though I'd definitely tell April the entire story. She'd find the whole situation amusing.

"Go ahead. I just don't want Sawyer to know about Cain. I'm seeing him again tonight, and nothing's gonna stop me from enjoying this trip before we have to go back to Greece for another series of arguments." Bitsy indicated she wanted to locate her husband and inform him first that she'd been in the basement talking to Cain about the schedule, per Ursula's instructions. "You'll keep my secret from Sawyer, okay? Until I decide if I'm gonna ask for a divorce, please."

I nodded and offered a sympathetic tone. "For now. But please don't lie to me again, Bitsy. Ursula and Myriam have placed immense pressure on me to watch out for you this week. I also need to find out what happened to my uncle. It's important to my family that we get some closure."

Before leaving, Bitsy agreed to be more forthcoming, then mentioned she'd just been to see Myriam and would return later to drop off a donation check. Once Bitsy left, I texted April to confirm her location and arrival estimate. We'd gone back and forth multiple times about whether I'd bring Queen Tessa's talisman to her, or she'd collect it from me, to minimize any risk, but the day had gotten too busy to properly synchronize.

April: *I was on my way, but we just got an alert. There's been an accident at Cain's house.*
Me: *What happened?*
April: *Cain called it in five minutes ago. He returned home. Place broken into. His mother was unconscious.*
Me: *That's horrible. Poor Kathy! Where exactly does he live?*

April: *Two-minute walk from South Campus. On the road that leads to the back steps of the cable car entrance. Near the running path and pond.*

April promised to update me after she arrived at Cain's place. I checked my watch and confirmed that Bitsy and I had been talking in the courtyard for fifteen minutes. He'd been at my brother's until I arrived at eleven thirty. How long were Bitsy and Cain together before I'd found them? If Cain had gone directly home, he had enough time to fake a break-in and distract his mother from seeing him inside her room. Or could he have gone home after visiting Hampton and staged the scene before he met up with Bitsy? I refused to believe he'd do such a preposterous thing as attack his mother, but the crazy art exhibition and his recent behavior were astronomically fishy.

Despite the likelihood he had nothing to do with Giovanni's and my uncle's deaths, my gut instinct insisted he knew more than he'd confessed. How could I force the truth out of him? Showing up at Cain's place wouldn't look good

256

for April or for me. If Kathy had really been attacked, I'd only make the situation worse.

Instead, I popped into The Big Beanery to pick
up my lunch for the following day. My schedule would be super busy, and it'd be easier to
buy and store something in the department's refrigerator. After paying and leaving a tip for the
cashier, I noticed the same guy with the Clark
Gable mustache I'd seen at Glass Hall the previous morning. Was that Sawyer? Like last time, he
wore a dark suit and shiny black tie, but that day
he offered a bright smile and appeared to be enjoying his conversation with Braxton's president.
Before I could catch up to him and Ursula, they
turned the corner and headed into Prentiss Hall.
I'd have to ask her later to verify his identity. If
he wasn't Sawyer, he must've been connected to
the art exhibition, and therefore Cain, somehow.

On the way back to Diamond Hall, Francesca
returned my call and confirmed Emma's schedule for the week. "Cristiano and I chatted between meetings. I know more about his cousin,
Giovanni. Is this an appropriate time?"

"Sure. I appreciate you getting back to me
quickly. What's the deal?" I'd prepared myself to

learn Giovanni had been straddling both sides of the law, that he'd tried to buy the talisman at Uncle Zach's dinner party but failed. What she revealed came totally out of left field!

"Cristiano's uncle and aunt adopted Giovanni a few days after he was born. He's not a member of the Vargas family by blood." Francesca explained that Cristiano's aunt, who'd been married to his father's brother, couldn't have any children. They'd been on a waiting list for a baby for many years when Giovanni's mother gave him up for adoption. He was born in Europe in the late 1980s to a single mother who was young and unable to care for a child.

"Interesting. I'm sorry for Cristiano's loss. It's awful to grieve for a member of your family." I hadn't known Francesca's boyfriend that well, other than the two weeks where he'd stalked me previously, but he'd lost his sister then and his cousin recently. "Was Giovanni's death mob-related?"

"Not everything is connected to the mafia, Kellan. I know you don't want to believe me, but after last year's fiasco, Cristiano and I have done our best to get away from all that drama."

Francesca had always been a little high-strung, but her displeasure had skyrocketed.

"Understand where I'm coming from. Our daughter was almost killed twice. Now my uncle is dead and there's a weird connection to the Vargas family." I asked a bunch more questions that led to a flurry of not-so-pleasant words, and eventually we agreed to cease arguing about it. Both families had suffered tremendously.

"Giovanni joined the FBI because he vehemently opposed the Vargas family business. At some point, he switched over to ICE, but he always remained an honest and dedicated agent."

"I imagine Cristiano is hunting down his cousin's killer?" I sat on the building's steps at the far end of the entranceway so no one would interrupt us.

"Yes, but he's already grilled all his contacts. This wasn't a mob hit or retaliation against the Vargas family. It's probably not even connected to Giovanni's current or past ICE cases." Francesca's generosity offered hope that we'd eventually ease past our issues.

"Was this personal? I'm not sure what you're saying."

"Giovanni was searching for his biological parents. He'd been digging into the adoption records and conducting various DNA tests to locate a match." Francesca confirmed Giovanni had told Cristiano recently that he'd stumbled upon something at an Eastern European nunnery that might identify one of his birth parents. He'd been aggressively pursuing the lead before he was killed.

I was glad he'd made progress, but I worried it had also led to his murder. "Does this have anything to do with that African figurine everyone's fawning over?"

Francesca indicated she wasn't sure about that angle. "The Vargas family knows nothing about it. Their businesses run through the Americas and occasionally Asia. They're not involved in African trades or other projects in that region."

Once my ex-wife's mother called, she had to disconnect. I thanked her for being liberal with her time and information. Mostly, I believed she'd told me the truth. But it still made the situation much more complicated than I'd initially understood. If Giovanni's murder were related to his biological parents, it could have nothing to do with Uncle Zach. Then again, Giovanni was adamant about locating Queen Tessa's talisman and had believed my uncle stole it, which meant there must be a connection between the two deaths, especially given my uncle had hidden it in his luggage.

When I walked through the central hallway of Diamond Hall's second floor, Myriam beckoned me to come by. I poked my head in her office. "Hello. What can I do for you?"

"*Time shall unfold what plighted cunning hides... who cover faults, at last shame them derides.*" She waved a gold pen in her hands and twisted the cap off. "Please tell me you remember that from the King Lear play we worked on together last year."

"I see we're back to riddles. Not sure I understand how this one pertains to me." I plastered a friendly grin across my face as I wasn't in the mood for a battle with my beleaguering boss.

"Never mind. That doll you had the other day. When did you come into possession of it?" Myriam opened her desk drawer and shared a photograph with me. It looked remarkably similar to the one in Uncle Zach's suitcase, at least in terms of coloring and materials. Queen Tessa's talisman was much bigger, and the new idol didn't have the diamond and blood chamber in the center.

"My uncle somehow came across the figurine and flew to Orlando with it. I'm not sure of the previous history, but it was given to me on Monday morning by an airline representative. I was planning to ask Bitsy, but there's a chance it has something to do with my uncle's death, and now possibly Giovanni's murder." I needed to confirm who had bought Queen Tessa's talisman, as people would soon discover it was in my possession. Would the same person come after me to retrieve it? "Where is that picture from?"

"Just something I stumbled upon recently. Nothing for you to worry about. We should chat with Bitsy together about the doll. She's acutely familiar with African art and might explain it all." Myriam returned the photo to her desk drawer and remarked that the remainder of my lesson plans were approved. "I'll coordinate a meeting with Bitsy. You can leave now."

Once Myriam dismissed someone, it was important to walk away with your head held high.

Often, escaping alive and without permanent injuries meant victory—never any goodbyes, and given her perplexing mood and our bizarre conversation, I scampered back to my office. After sitting at the desk, I contacted April. "Any news? I want this crazy cursed figurine out of my hands!"

"They took Kathy Endicott to the hospital. She should be fine; it's just for observation." April indicated that Kathy had been in the shower when she heard the front door alarm. She left the bathroom on the second floor, called out to her son, and began descending the stairs. About a third of the way down, something clunked her on the back of the head. Kathy stumbled down the rest of the staircase but hadn't hurt herself badly.

"Did she ever see her attacker?" I'd always feared someone breaking into my house while I was defenselessly showering. Too many horror movies, which I loved, had also messed with my brain.

"No, unfortunately. She probably has a concussion." April confirmed that as soon as Kathy recovered from landing at the bottom of the stairs, she witnessed a tall figure in a baseball cap rounding the corner of Cain's property.

"Did she call the police or her son first?"

April grunted. "Kathy was dialing 9-1-1 when Cain walked through the back door. She passed out but remembered him looking flushed. He claims he'd jogged back from campus because he'd forgotten a file he needed for the rescheduled opening of tomorrow's art exhibition."

"That sounds too coincidental." I was increasingly distrustful of Cain.

"Exactly. He didn't have on a hat, but Kathy also thought the assailant wasn't as tall as her son." April noted that Kathy was slightly dizzy afterward and wore glasses for distance. "She might not be a reliable witness."

"Not to mention the assailant could've tossed the baseball cap somewhere in the immediate vicinity. You should assign Flatman to methodically check all the garbage cans." I held back a snicker, but it seemed like a logical plan.

"Thanks for telling me how to do my job. Between you and the government bullies, it's been a marvelous day." April's sassy tone marginally conveyed she was only joking.

"Sorry, babe. We'll solve this before they do anything worse. Was anything stolen?"

"No. Only a few drawers in Cain's home office were ransacked. Kathy's pocketbook with her wallet and phone sat untouched on a table in the front hallway." April put me on hold to provide direction to her team.

"So, it wasn't a robbery?" I asked upon her return.

"No, doesn't appear to be. I'm bringing Cain to the precinct. I shouldn't tell you this, but I trust you'll keep it to yourself. His fingerprints were the only ones found on the spear that killed Giovanni Vargas." April verified she'd been able to match them because Cain had served in the military after high school and before enrolling in college. The police wouldn't normally have access to those records, but April had contacts in high places.

I let April know what I'd learned about Giovanni's adoption and seen happening between Bitsy and Cain near the campus pond. She promised to follow up on Bitsy's detailed account of what transpired between her and Cain in the basement the prior morning. "Are you arresting him?"

"It all depends on how Cain answers my questions and the results of the coroner's report. It's due on my desk in thirty minutes. I'll call you when I learn more. We can discuss the report and the list of people who were in the building on the morning of Giovanni's murder." April apologized for the delay in sharing the names and hung up.

I needed to know exactly how long Cain and Bitsy had been together before I'd seen them in an intimate embrace. Obtaining that answer would incur a painful but necessary follow-up conversation with the Dragon Lady. Hopefully, it didn't lead to my premature death!

Chapter 16

I grabbed the schedule for the exhibition's opening and returned to Myriam's office. After standing outside so my boss couldn't see me while she spoke to someone, I heard the distinct click of a receiver slamming its phone base.

Before I could step into her doorway, Myriam announced, "Hasn't President Power warned you about eavesdropping? Really, you've got abominable manners, Kellan."

I peered my head around the corner, momentarily paranoid she might throw an electric pencil sharpener or an extra pointy letter opener in my direction. Truly, the woman wanted me dead; the venomous vibes poured out of her skin regularly. I slunk into her office and pointed at the agenda.

"I was curious... ummm... Bitsy is supposed to speak before the lunch break tomorrow, but when I saw her earlier, she seemed too relaxed, quiet. I wonder whether we should rearrange the sessions and have her introduce the events directly after lunch? Maybe a healthy meal will increase her energy levels and help her inspire the attendees." I knew better than to come right out and ask about Bitsy's whereabouts earlier. She'd claimed to be with Myriam before meeting Cain near Paddington's Play House. But I wanted undeniable proof.

"We will not reprint schedules again. Bitsy is a professional. She was perfectly fine before we ate our meal together today. She even agreed to make another donation to the college." Myriam pinched the bridge of her nose and sighed relentlessly. "What time did you see her?"

"Oh, about one o'clock, I suppose. I assumed she hadn't eaten yet, based on her energy levels." I prayed that my plan to incite Myriam to overcommunicate was working.

"Bitsy and I left campus at eleven twenty-seven and went to a French restaurant near Woodland College. It took us precisely thirteen minutes to arrive. She ordered grilled salmon, asparagus, and brown rice. Drank two glasses of water. Enjoyed a bowl of strawberries with cream afterward. Finished the meal with a cup of lemon tea. I'd say she consumed a sufficient amount of food. She was as lively as she always is. We returned to the office promptly. Why are you wasting my time?"

That was too healthy of a meal for me, but I respected the woman's willpower. "Oh, I'm just thinking too much about it. I'm hoping to ensure this exhibition is productive and lucrative. Ursula trusts me. Perhaps Bitsy was a little tired." I paused, uncertain how to extract the specific time she'd returned to campus. Then a clever idea struck. "The walk back must've exhausted her. It's about two miles from here, isn't it?"

Myriam slammed her fists on the desk. "We did not walk two miles. Bitsy drove to and from the restaurant. I had to return for a one o'clock conference call. She was completely normal and energetic when I deposited her in the very same hallway in which you're standing and antagonizing me." With a creased forehead and painfully soured expression, she gathered a stack of folders and declared that she needed to meet with a colleague. I followed her down the back set of stairs leading to Paddington's Play House, which seemed to further irritate her. "You really ought to control these incessant inquiries into other people's lives. I'm not entirely sure whether you are bored, suffering from a head injury, or lacking the proper emotional intelligence to understand when someone is done speaking with you. Either way, please remedy it post haste!" At the bottom of the steps, she turned back to me with a sneer. "*The miserable have no other medicine, but only hope.*"

When we reached the exit door, I thanked Myriam for her considerate advice and apropos line from *Measure for Measure.* Clearly, she'd been talking about herself. If the woman only knew I'd been analyzing whether her wife's friend was a murderer, she might be grateful. Rather than reveal what idled in my mind, I watched her plod across the courtyard and pondered what I'd learned.

Bitsy played strumpet with Cain around one fifteen, which meant she couldn't have been at his house during the break-in. She might've had time to sprint there and return to campus, assuming she ran as quickly as the last winner of the New York City marathon. That, I highly doubted—she'd worn high heels and looked flawless in the campus courtyard. It would've been impossible for Bitsy to rifle through all the drawers in Kathy's bedroom, prevent Kathy from discovering her identity by clubbing her on the head, and make out with Cain near the pond.

Bitsy and Cain could've colluded on the entire affair. I suspected he realized his mother had Queen Tessa's talisman in her luggage but hadn't known she'd inadvertently transferred it to me. He couldn't search her room or belongings until she went out for the morning, but if she'd been in the shower, he might've had time. Or had he come rushing back after faking the break-in for some other unknown reason, then been celebrating with Bitsy when I found them? I was missing important clues and would need to talk to Kathy myself, depending on what she remembered post-accident.

When I returned to the second floor, a strange man walked out of Myriam's office and hovered near mine. From behind, his thick mane of wild red hair and shiny, leather cowboy boots seemed out of place. I quietly sneaked up behind him, intending to block him from trying to escape. Although it was a risky move, and I had no idea who was loitering in the hallway, I had determination on my side. Knowing the talisman was in my office and two people had been murdered, I wasn't letting a potential suspect get away.

My footsteps must've alerted him to my arrival. Before I could announce myself, the man turned around and aggressively pinned me against the wall so I couldn't see his face. "What the hell do you think you're doing? I've got a good mind to teach you a lesson, boy!"

"You're the one breaking into my office. I think you should explain what it is you're doing!" I mumbled the words as my lips squished against the peeling, rose-colored wallpaper.

As he released my arms, the assailant apologized. "I know how to protect myself and don't appreciate strangers creeping up behind me. I was looking for a friend."

While turning around and shaking loose the adrenaline, I studied his navy-blue suit, goldenrod dress shirt, and thin bolo tie. When I noticed his face, I bit my lip to restrain myself from guffawing. In a strange way, his long and bushy mustache reminded me of Yosemite Sam. I suspected he was Bitsy's husband. No wonder Ursula had cautioned me not to judge her friends during an initial introduction. Both resembled cartoon characters who'd magically sprung to life. If Bitsy were faking her personality, would Sawyer too?

"In my office? I saw you leave someone else's and step into mine." I loosened my shirt collar.

"Dagnammit! I guess I missed the ol' battle-ax," he gruffly hollered, raising his bright, wild crimson eyebrows two inches to meet his hairline. "You seen her, boy?" he then inquired, pointing a grubby finger in my direction.

Anyone who referred to my boss as a battle-ax deserved a second chance. "If you're referring to Myriam Castle, she skedaddled across campus for a meeting a few minutes ago. You must be Sawyer Jaccard." I extended my hand in his direction, cursing myself for using a word like *skedaddled* around him. "I'm Kellan Ayrwick. I met your wife yesterday."

He grabbed mine with gusto, shook it frenetically, and aggressively slapped my shoulder with his other one. "You the varmint she's been spending all her time with, ain't ya?" Sawyer stepped close enough that his breath stung my cheeks. His pasty skin and thick mustache smelled like a combination of beer and cigars. Given his larger-than-life greeting, it appeared like he would again grasp my throat and shove me against the wall to issue a warning about his wife. "I'm just kiddin' ya, Kellan. Bitsy has said many good things about you! You've got my gratitude for keeping the little lady busy while I'm attending the exhibition. Sorry about our little skirmish there."

My stomach settled into a semi-normal position, allowing me the courage to slowly slip between him and the wall and to reclaim my personal space. What was it with men who used their stocky bodies and domineering personalities to control a situation or conversation? While he'd theoretically meant little harm, I couldn't help but assume his abundance of confidence compensated for something else. Guilt? Lack of intelligence? Then again, he was a successful importer and exporter, even if his ethics weren't completely legitimate according to his wife. What had she meant by *underhanded*?

"Welcome to Braxton. Bitsy has been a genuine pleasure to get to know the last two days." The lie spilled from my tongue quickly. I angled toward my door and waved him inside. "She had lunch with Myriam earlier. You just missed her heading off campus to write a donation check."

"That woman likes to spend too much money. I guess she's got plenty of it. And this institution is a fine cause." Sawyer paced the room, ultimately settling his intimidating body against the edge of my desk. Though he wasn't a large man, his bone structure was solid and heavy enough to cause the frame to buckle. Hopefully, if he broke the piece of furniture, all the clothes and the suitcase's rigid plastic exterior would protect Queen Tessa's talisman. He fiddled with something in his pocket, then withdrew a pack of cigarettes and a lighter. "Want one, boy?"

"No, and to be honest, I don't think you're allowed to—"

"Ain't gonna stop me. But I respect a man who knows these things will kill him one day." Sawyer flipped open the silver-plated lid, lit a cigarette, and inhaled a long puff. The smoke trailed the curves of his hollowed and yellowed cheeks, dissipating as they reached his slightly receding, coppery hair. "The Good Lord's coming for me soon. I got no business interfering in his plans."

Changing his mind wasn't an option. Instead, I cracked open the window and activated the air purifier my sister had given me for Christmas. Thankfully, Eleanor had looked out for my holistic wellbeing the prior year. "You look healthy enough to me, Mr. Jaccard. Is there something I can help you with this afternoon?"

"Fifty. I'm turning fifty in a couple of months. Don't come from a healthy family. The ticker's got a bum valve, but two fingers of whiskey kick-starts the ol' engine, as it should. Real men take dangerous risks and demand action." Sawyer mumbled more comments about his doctor's warning to limit his alcohol intake, consume less red meat, and eat more fruits and vegetables. "What will be, will be."

At the risk of repeating myself, I inquired again why he'd visited me. "My boss has a staff meeting in thirty minutes, and I should finalize this report. Happy to help if you need anything, though." Oops, another lie. I would definitely have more than three *Hail Mary prayers* to offer in church that week.

"Bitsy told me she'd be here all afternoon. That woman never could keep her time straight.

Been out gallivanting while I'm working lately. She said you'd be having dinner tonight. That a fact?" Sawyer scanned the room in search of an ashtray which he wouldn't find but seemed not to accept. Finally, after failing, he unlatched the screen, tossed his half-smoked butt out the window, and coughed violently. Had he not scowled and snickered, I would've assumed the smoke caused his excessive choking. Something unexpected had clearly caught his attention on the pathway in the courtyard. "Why don't you and I get us some refreshments? How's this Kirklands pub I've heard all about?"

Either he'd ignored my comment regarding Myriam's meeting, or someone or something outside had infinitely distracted him. Bitsy and I also weren't having dinner. She had plans with Cain. Ugh! Why had she used me as an excuse again? I considered how to best bring up Giovanni, knowing Sawyer had been in Glass Hall at the time of the man's murder. "Perhaps I could take you there soon? It's a shame what happened at yesterday's exhibition opening. Did you know the victim well?"

As Sawyer narrowed his sinister gaze, his lips curled upward. "Met that yahoo a few times. Asked lots of unimportant things. I'm not fond of answering questions. Know what I mean, boy?"

This was going to be harder than I'd anticipated. "I agree. Giovanni was aloof. Did you run into him during the opening yesterday?"

"Nah! Too busy checking out the exhibits. Hoping to find some things to add to my collection, boy. We done with this line of questions?" He absentmindedly struck his lighter a half-dozen times.

"I guess we are. Maybe I should call Myriam for you, see if she's on her way back."

Sawyer brushed some dust off his boots with a handkerchief he'd pulled from inside his jacket. "You're all right for a Yankee. Seem normal. A little on that metrosexual side of the spectrum for me, but some ladies appreciate softness in a man." He fetched another cigarette from his pocket and flicked his lighter on the side of his leg. "One for the road. Before I go, you should know something regarding Bitsy and me. 'Bout our marriage," he added after extinguishing the flame.

Yep, I knew his wife had cheated on him and wanted a divorce. It was not a conversation I needed to pursue. It'd be risky, but I had to ask one more time. "Bitsy seems like a wonderful wife. She told me you two stopped by Glass Hall incredibly early yesterday. Is it possible you saw Giovanni talking to someone who might've followed him to the basement? The sheriff's inclined to catch the murderer as quickly as possible." Optimistically, my questions wouldn't irritate him any further if he knew I thought he was innocent.

Sawyer took another drag as he approached me with a strange confidence and a dangerous change in his countenance. "Saw nothing. Heard nothing. Did nothing. Don't ask me again! Now, about you and my wife, boy...."

I stepped back and threw my hands up in defeat. "Listen, I'm not interested in causing any problems. She's a fine lady, but not my type of—"

He leaned forward, wrinkling his nose and sniffling intensely. "Something wrong with Bitsy? You too good for a woman who knows what she wants and goes after it?"

What was going on? The man threatened me for talking to her, then inquired why I didn't find her attractive? "Hang on! You've got the wrong impression, Mr. Jaccard. I'm simply spending time with her because Ursula and Myriam asked me—"

Sawyer burst out laughing such that his entire girth shook uncontrollably. "Oh, had ya going there now, didn't I, Kellan? As lily white as a ghost who's seen the devil and near pissed himself!"

I half-winced and smiled. "Sure, you're a regular riot. But I'm confused. What do you mean?"

As he strode into the hallway, he slapped his thigh and roared emphatically again. First, he disappeared into Myriam's office and collected his over-the-shoulder bag. Then he stomped back to my door and got in my face. "Bitsy is free to do what she wants. She and I have an arrangement. A few rules, but as long as her fun doesn't embarrass me and she doesn't cozy up to the same fella twice, it's good."

"You approve of this?" Bitsy hadn't exactly told me that part.

"We ain't children. I married that filly because we make each other happy. But we also have our own separate lives. Wild oats need to be sown, boy. You'd best keep that in mind. Don't get trapped into anything too serious." Sawyer stuffed his glowing cigarette between my lips and confidently strutted down the hallway. "Besides... I hired a private dick to watch her. She was none too pleased about that. Cursed me up a storm yesterday. Anyway, thanks a mil, pal. You take care now. I'll be reaching out to grab those drinks, ya hear?" As he descended the steps, the spurs on his boots jangled.

Myriam and Ursula had warned me about the Jaccards. I couldn't help but laugh at their wacky reality. I also failed to understand why they'd ever gotten married, but perhaps when I saw them together, it might become clearer. In the meantime, Bitsy could have her fun as long as she kept me out of it. Let the private investigator report his or her findings to Sawyer. Her dalliances with Cain had broken the rules, if what her husband told me was true. She'd spent more than one day with the sly chairman of Braxton's art department, and I suspected Sawyer wasn't the kind of man who'd let that fact go unnoticed without proper retaliation or revenge.

When my blood pressure dropped within normal range, I put out the cigarette, shut the window, and collapsed into my chair. For May, a surprising chill lingered in the air. At least the man's smoke had evaporated, and I could return to my regular rollercoaster day. I wished I'd learned something valuable about the Jaccards' relationship with Giovanni, but I could always follow up again when Sawyer and I had drinks. If he didn't shoot me in the pub. That future adventure sounded as appealing as voluntary hernia surgery with no anesthesia.

It was time to take the cursed idol to the sheriff's office. When I retrieved the key from my briefcase and opened the desk's outer panel, I received a horrific shock. Not only was the inner door not locked, but it was also ajar. Luckily, the suitcase was still tucked inside the side compartment. I tore it from the cabinet and rifled through its contents. My entire body tensed like a cornered badger who'd been declawed and brought to a fight with a cougar. Someone had stolen Queen Tessa's talisman!

Chapter 17

As soon as I determined the talisman had gone missing in the previous nine hours, I notified April and formally reported the theft. She dispersed a few members of her team to check for fingerprints and file an official report, promising to return my call soon. Clouds of dust and misshapen footprints littered the floor of my office. My desk resembled the bathroom sink after Ulan had shaved all his hair and tossed Talcum powder on his neck to cool off his skin.

Most everyone had already left Diamond Hall for the night. Our department administrator confirmed that Myriam wouldn't be returning to the building, but she was concerned that someone had broken into my office and insisted I notify BCS. Once I coordinated a discussion between them and the sheriff's office, I packed up my briefcase and headed to the parking lot. Ulan was at home with Emma, and he had already arranged with Connor to order Chinese takeout for dinner. Connor wanted to talk about the video call with his dad. I wouldn't be home for dinner for at least another ninety minutes, though. I had one eventual stop before I could call it a night.

April rang me back as soon as she finished her meeting with the town councilmen who were interested in changing zoning restrictions downtown. With several big summer events planned, and the college expansion happening in four months, they wanted to address our important deadlines.

I knew April would ask all the same questions as her team had earlier. But rehashing it one more time might stir up something I'd missed. "The last time I saw it was about nine thirty."

"You're absolutely positive it was in your desk?" inquired April. Her demanding yet curious tone was clearly due to stress at the office and not from me losing potentially vital evidence.

"Yes, shortly after I got back from the gym. I looked at that ugly doll to beg it for a sign identifying Giovanni's killer."

April had earlier agreed I should drop off Queen Tessa's talisman after work that evening so that her team could inspect the luggage and verify Kathy's airport story. But given Kathy had gotten hit on the head later that day, followed by Cain's extended interrogation at the sheriff's office, April wanted to hold off on the exchange until she could personally be at the sheriff's office.

"This is getting ridiculous," commented April. We considered everyone who had access to my office, at least that I'd seen at some point nearby earlier. Anybody could've broken in when I went off site or to a meeting.

"Sawyer was hovering outside my office when I returned from stalking Myriam down the back set of stairs. He had a large enough messenger bag, which coincidentally did not seem like the type of briefcase a man like him would carry, to hide the figurine."

April acknowledged me through several throaty giggles. "My team observed no signs of forced entry. Think carefully. Did Sawyer glance at the desk at all? Make any comments about African art? Anything that hinted he knew you kept it in your office?"

I ran through our conversation in my head, assuming he somehow learned in advance where I'd hidden it. "Not really. I was barely gone for six or seven minutes. He would've had to wait on the front steps while I followed Myriam, pry open the door with a special tool, unzip the luggage, steal Queen Tessa's talisman, and conceal it in his bag. All before I returned."

"Where was he going after your office?"

"To find his wife, I think."

If Sawyer was the thief and potential killer, he was quite crafty. He might've intentionally placed his over-the-shoulder bag in Myriam's office to substantiate his claim that he'd stopped by to visit her. Then, when I'd caught him, he introduced himself to me as an excuse to easily escape with Queen Tessa's talisman. Initially, I was confident he hadn't said or done anything obvious. That's when I suddenly remembered he'd behaved strangely when he looked out the window. I relayed that part of our encounter to April. "What if he was searching for a partner, or he saw someone who would've stopped him from making a quick getaway?"

April assigned Officer Flatman to follow up with Sawyer. "We can ask him whether he witnessed anyone near the building when he exited, so he doesn't think we suspect him. If he's not guilty, perhaps he'll have information to share with us."

"Careful. He doesn't appreciate questions. I almost got my head ripped off."

"That's because you treat everyone like it's the Spanish Inquisition," she countered, noting her team would be much more careful.

"You're hilarious! If it wasn't Sawyer, that means the talisman was stolen earlier in the day while I was visiting my brother or summoned to Ursula's office." I recounted for April my entire schedule, confirming when I was in Diamond Hall and when I'd been away. There had been two or three obvious opportunities for someone to break in, and hopefully we could talk to everyone who'd been in the building and in a position to notice. Bitsy and Cain had accessed my floor, and in between the burglary at his house and their courtyard rendezvous, one or both could've sneaked into my office and stolen the much sought-after object. "How's Kathy Endicott?"

"Still at the hospital. Dr. Betscha will release her this evening or tomorrow. She called her ex-husband to bring her home." April clammed up when I asked about the incident in Cain's house and why Lindsey was helping her. Although they seemed on friendlier terms, Kathy had stayed with her son that week.

"Why isn't Cain bringing Kathy home?" Once I arrived and parked at North Campus, I headed toward Fern's office.

"He's being interrogated. I told you that his fingerprints are the only ones on the spear. Cain lied about Giovanni and had ten minutes alone with him before leaving Bitsy and meeting his father." April shared a few more details, including that she'd formally requested the manifest from Uncle Zach's flight. It could take a few days for necessary approvals and subsequent release. She also indicated that Connor had worked seven days straight and needed an evening off. Since April had been away for the conference, she was making up for lost time and staying late.

"Okay, Connor is coming over for dinner around eight. Maybe we can all catch up about the murder and theft when you're done." Once someone entered April's office with the coroner's final report, I couldn't ask further questions.

Before we disconnected, she promised to call that evening and let me know what it revealed. As soon as I passed the student union building and caught sight of the setting sun, the area suddenly got a little brighter. When the nighttime security lights flickered on, I remembered that we'd installed new cameras on the top of the lampposts all around South Campus. If Sawyer had met someone else in the courtyard, any video recordings we'd captured could provide the person's identity. It could also confirm what he might've seen outside the window. Too bad we had installed none inside Diamond Hall.

As I rounded the corner and approached Fern's office, Ivy Natcher's voice echoed in the hallway. When they saw me idling at the doorway, Fern waved me inside.

"Much appreciated. Ivy, it's a pleasure to meet you. Fern has told me so much about you the last few days." I pulled up another chair from the corner of the room and joined them.

Ivy pressed a hand to her heart and dipped her head toward the floor, calling attention to her slight melancholy and cat-like eyes. "Oh, Kellan. I'm sincerely sorry about your uncle. Zach was a truly kind and generous man, and I will miss him terribly."

"Thank you. I appreciate hearing so many positive accolades from his friends. Were you and my uncle particularly close?" I knew Ivy and her husband had attended my uncle's dinner party, but I wasn't certain whether they'd been friendly outside of that individual event.

Ivy's cheeks reddened. "Yes... Yes, Zach and I used to... oh, I just assumed he'd told you. We were... good friends... back in high school. But then I left town for a while." She explained how they'd reconnected after their separate college graduations and even went on a few dates before she eventually married Jordan's father.

It was news to me. Although my uncle and I had been close, their relationship would've happened around the time I was a toddler. I remembered Fern telling me that her sister had gone away for a year to find herself between high school and college.

"I understand you visited Uncle Zach in South Africa a few months ago. Had you kept in touch the whole time, or was that a more recent connection?" I had no reason to believe Ivy had anything to do with my uncle's death. However, if she had been present at that dinner, there was a strong likelihood she had access to information about Renee or the Jaccards, who'd also been in attendance.

Ivy shook her head. "It's a rather complicated story. Zach and I were close as teenagers. A bunch of us were part of a large group back then. My ex-husband, Rhett Ballantine, and Zach were best friends too." Ivy explained that she and Rhett had been dating for a year and a half, but they had a colossal fight over another girl who had a crush on him. They'd broken up for a few weeks, and during that time, she and Zach had considered becoming more than friends. "But it got very heated, and after a huge blow-up, I ended it with both Zach and Rhett."

"That's when you left for Europe, wasn't it? You refused to talk to any of us that year." Fern rested a hand on Ivy's shoulder, displaying the closeness of their sisterly bond.

"Yes. I needed some time to figure out what I wanted out of life," she said with a hesitant and withdrawn tone. "Rhett and Zach hardly spoke to each other again after that. I always felt awful that I'd come between two good friends." Ivy clarified that Rhett had been the captain of the football team, president of their class, and the most popular boy in school. Uncle Zach was part of their crowd, but he'd also been the type of kid to befriend everyone. "He loved animals even back then. Started a rescue program in Braxton and volunteered at the shelter on weekends too."

I hardly knew much about Rhett Ballantine, Jordan's father and Ivy's ex-husband. It suddenly occurred to me he could've been the man with the Clark Gable mustache whom I'd seen the morning of the art exhibition opening, when Giovanni was killed with the African spear. How ironic that he resembled his own namesake, Rhett Butler from *Gone with the Wind*!

"It's wonderful to hear such caring memories about my uncle. You never said how you got back in touch after returning from Europe. Was that before you and Rhett got married?"

Ivy replied, "Rhett and Zach avoided each other after high school. They blamed one other for my disappearance. Eventually, we all caught up once we came home for college breaks... Braxton is a small town, you know. But then

Rhett and I settled our differences at a home-coming game one autumn. By the following year, we'd fallen back in love, gotten married, and had Jordan." She confirmed that Uncle Zach had traveled around the globe by then, following his love for animals and nature. "When Zach's wife passed away, I reached out to him on *Facebook*. It really upset Rhett that I was being supportive to a former friend, but it felt like the right thing to do."

Fern joked about the benefits and detriments of social media. "Students still haven't learned how to control themselves on all these apps. I've told you to be careful on there too, sis."

Ivy's shoulders slumped lower. "I know. I hardly go on anymore, but back then, it was new and exciting. Zach made me long for the days when we were all friends and less stressed out." She indicated that they'd renewed their friend-ship virtually, but it eventually annoyed Rhett to where he began traveling much more often. When Jordan graduated from high school, his parents divorced. Ivy stayed connected with Un-cle Zach, but once she met Tobias, they'd mostly gone their separate ways.

"Did Rhett and my uncle ever repair their friendship?" While I hardly knew much about the man, he'd been present the morning Giovanni died, wielded a grudge against my uncle, and traveled internationally. It was a weak connection to our mystery, but one I should explore.

Ivy winced. "Definitely not. They had a falling out many years ago and constantly complained about each other. Whenever I was around Zach, he'd make awful jokes about Rhett's super-secret work activities, and Rhett threatened to throw your uncle in prison a few times."

That threw me for a loop. "Is he a cop or a private investigator?" Maybe Sawyer had hired Rhett to follow Bitsy. He had concealed the gun at the Pick-Me-Up Diner on the weekend.

Fern interjected, "No! Never let him hear you say that. He'd be offended... takes his job very seriously. Rhett is an FBI agent based out of Orlando. He's mostly responsible for global operations and tracking issues or crimes related to American citizens who are overseas."

Wow! That changed my theory on Rhett being a feeble suspect in my uncle's and Giovanni's murders. I'd supposed he was an agent when I first saw him but never connected him as Jordan's dad. "Was he working on anything in particular? Connected with Braxton's art exhibition and the murder that happened yesterday?"

A noise near the door prevented her response. "Ah, you must be Professor Ayrwick. My stepson told me all about how you helped him out last year with that grading fiasco." Tobias Natcher leaned against the doorframe, eager to introduce himself with a handshake and a wide smile.

immediately rose and walked toward the man who was dressed as impeccably as a Wall Street stockbroker. A dark pinstripe suit offset his ebony hair, and a gold tie and black loafers with a shiny buckle brought the entire ensemble together. He was the man who'd made the bid to buy ReedWell Corporation from Natasha and Hampton.

"Mr. Natcher, I'd hoped to run into you. You're meeting with my brother Hampton tomorrow?" I shook his hand and waited while he kissed his wife's cheek and nodded a hello to his sister-in-law, Fern.

"That is correct. It appears we know a lot of the same people. I'm deeply sorry about Zach

Danby's death. Your uncle, from what I under-stand?" Tobias reclined on the sofa near the win-dow, crossing one leg on his knee. He waited for me to acknowledge his question, then said, "As far as my wife's ex-husband, Rhett is always mixed up in dangerous situations. I wouldn't doubt it if he'd inadvertently gotten himself in-volved in Giovanni Vargas's death."

Another person who knew Giovanni's last name. "Thank you. It was a significant loss. You were at a dinner party he threw several months ago. How well did you know one another?"

Ivy attempted to respond, but Tobias leaned forward and dismissed her with a flick of his hand. "Zach and I met through a mutual ac-quaintance back in South Africa. I was sell-ing some land that a wildlife rescue foundation bought, and he'd hoped to annex part of it for his elephant camp program. We met casually a few times, and eventually he invited me to par-ticipate as a donor for his research. Then I found out he and my wife knew one another already."

"Are you a big supporter of protecting the ele-phants he was trying to save?" I appreciated To-bias's candor and succinct responses, but the glance at Ivy when she tried to respond was troubling.

"Not any more than the average man. I, of course, wouldn't want to cause a species to go extinct, and I have enough money to do something about it. But ultimately, I was interested in the art Zach Danby had come into contact with earlier this year." Tobias sprawled into the cushions and turned to Fern, his wide-set eyes scanning her and the picture on the nearest wall. "Are you joining us for dinner this evening? I'm in the mood for authentic Greek. Any recommendations?"

Fern replied, "Yes, but I need to meet with Kellan on an important summer program. I could meet you both somewhere." She suggested a popular restaurant in Woodland that had rave reviews in the regional papers.

"Jordan will be with us tonight. He's excited to talk about the internship Tobias arranged for him. You should join us, Kellan," Ivy said, indicating her son had hoped to run into me on his trip.

"Of course, the more, the merrier." Tobias grabbed his wife's jewelry-adorned wrist and stepped away from the sofa. "Come along, Ivy.

I have news to share. After finalizing the plan to purchase ReedWell and my panel discussion in tomorrow's art exhibition, we must fly to South Africa. A deal has fallen through, and I need to fix those negotiations. I'm rescheduling our flights to Thursday."

Fern whimpered. "Oh, no, I was hoping to spend more time with Ivy this week. We had plans on Saturday to go hiking and kayaking with Jordan. Plus, your birthday is this weekend, Tobias."

Ivy gripped her husband's arm a little tighter as they reached the door. "Do I have to go back too? Maybe I could stay through the weekend and meet you there?"

Tobias calmly replied, "It's possible. I might need your charm to help seal the deal, but we can work something out. I know how much you two miss one another." He pulled out a business card from his inner coat pocket and handed it to me. "If you ever need help negotiating or have an interest in making large investments, please call me, Kellan. I'm always happy to help a friend of the family."

While Tobias's facial expressions seemed in-different, he delivered the message with an en-couraging tone. Fern might tell me more about him. "Before you leave, I had a question about Uncle Zach's dinner party. Would you mind?"

Somehow the flash of panic on his face told me he did.

Chapter 18

"Of course not. It was several months ago. Not sure if I'll remember all the specifics." When the pulsing of the blood vessels near his temples subsided, Tobias lovingly stroked his wife's glossy cheek. "Ivy has a terrific memory, though. She might be of help."

I shared with Tobias and Ivy my concern about Uncle Zach's death being connected to Giovanni's murder, noting that both men had died under unusual circumstances. "A priceless figurine went missing. No one's been able to find it, and the FBI once thought my uncle stole it. Would you know anything else?"

Ivy's mouth formed a small circle as she gripped her husband's hand tighter. "Yes, Zach presented Queen Tessa's talisman that night. He was keen to sell it to the highest bidder in the anonymous auction. Tobias and I were hoping to buy it, but we never heard from your uncle about our very generous offer."

Tobias said, "Given Ivy's friendship with Zach, I expected he'd agree to a fair price. I understood he was having some financial difficulties, and I wanted to be of help. Unfortunately, he decided not to accept my bid."

"What was so special about it to you, Tobias?" inquired Fern.

Tobias tossed his head from shoulder to shoulder. "I have several artifacts from all the ancient African tribes across many historical periods. This was one that would make a perfect addition to the collection. Ivy and I even cleared a place in our parlor for it. Such an intriguing past, I wanted to be part of the figurine's remarkable story. I don't believe in all that phooey curse stuff either."

"Did Uncle Zach divulge whom he sold the figurine to?"

"Unfortunately, no. I suspected, at first, he'd given it to that blind woman who was at the dinner. I never understood their connection." Tobias gently ushered his wife through the doorway.

"Zach and Renee had started dating recently, Tobias. I think because she was blind and Queen Tessa was blind, he felt it would be best in her hands." Ivy promptly confirmed the attendees besides her and her husband: Sawyer and Bitsy Jaccard, Rhett Ballantine, Giovanni Vargas, Uncle Zach, Renee, two Australian collectors who'd supplied a large donation and left early, and a few museum curators.

"Were any of the curators or the Australians interested in buying Queen Tessa's talisman?"

"No, they only wanted to see the object, to claim they came close to it once. They all made modest donations and enjoyed socializing with prominent artsy types." Ivy waved to her sister and confirmed she'd received the text with the restaurant's address. "We should head out now. See you later."

Tobias turned to me before approaching the stairs. "Be careful around Renee. She's not who she appears to be, and while I don't know her all that well, I do not trust the woman. She probably manipulated Zach into giving it to her, and when he tried to leave the country, she had him killed."

"Do you think she's hiding Queen Tessa's talisman for a specific reason? What about the curse?"

"Of course. She's playing games. Stole it from your uncle and intends to resell it to the highest bidder. You should use extreme caution if you run into Renee. I suspect she's faking her blindness too." Tobias had little other to share about the curse, citing most of the associated deaths had been found to be total accidents. "People like to believe in the macabre. They live boring lives, and it makes them feel special. Don't be fooled by it. This killer was motivated by the profits of selling Queen Tessa's talisman."

As Tobias and Ivy descended the stairs, I processed their news. I'd ask Connor to check into the unfamiliar people who'd attended the dinner party. Clearly, Tobias disliked Renee, and he was marginally controlling of his wife. Tobias and Ivy also weren't sharing everything they knew. Since Fern didn't know her brother-in-law all that well, we changed topics and focused on the art exhibition's opening the next morning. Within the hour, we sorted out how to handle it ourselves, assuming April might detain Cain for a good part of the day.

On the drive home, I picked up our Chinese takeout. Connor was already at my house playing a video game with Ulan and Emma. My daughter raced into my arms and revealed that she'd beaten Uncle Connor at a virtual reality restaurant war. "He has no idea how to build a burger. He dropped the cheese twice!"

I glanced at Connor, who fidgeted with the controller before tossing it on the couch. "Win some, lose some. The point is... we all had fun, right Emma?" When he took a seat and opened all the containers, she climbed on his lap and kissed his cheek. "Yep. You just need more practice. Are you gonna tell your friends that an eight-year-old beat you really bad?"

Ulan chimed in but quickly looked embarrassed at his own words. "Don't forget to tell them you lost to a girl."

Emma squinted at her cousin, then shouted, "What's wrong with that?" All throughout dinner, she lectured Ulan about not being a jerk and assuming boys were better than girls at video games. Although she won the argument hands down, they quickly forgot his faux pas and took Baxter for his evening walk. It gave Connor and me a chance to catch up about Giovanni's death and the missing talisman.

"I've interviewed everyone who was at Glass Hall yesterday morning. By the time we ruled out any maintenance workers or student assistants with rock solid alibis, we're down to sixteen known persons with access. These are people who couldn't produce a thorough alibi between eight thirty and nine forty-five."

"Because that's the window of opportunity for Giovanni's death. And you're presuming it would take at least fifteen minutes for someone to sneak downstairs to commit the murder and then return to the lobby?" I understood and agreed with his logic. Anyone who couldn't prove they hadn't left the lobby during that time was a potential suspect.

"Yes. Of course, someone might've slipped in overnight and escaped without being noticed. Doubtful, though. The cameras in the courtyard didn't capture anyone other than those people inside the building." Connor pulled out his notepad to rattle off the names, then stuffed it back in his bag when I waved it away.

"Let me guess. Cain and his parents, Lindsey and Kathy Endicott. Ivy and Tobias Natcher. Bitsy and Sawyer Jaccard. Ursula and Myriam.

Fern, but she'd been with me beforehand. Who am I missing?" I tallied them on my fingers and produced only ten.

"You. Your grandmother and mother were both there, although they never left each other's side, so I guess—"

"Do you seriously think someone in my family killed Giovanni Vargas?"

Connor tossed one hand in his pocket and scratched at his chin with the other. "If Giovanni murdered Zach, revenge is a powerful motive... but no, I don't actually count them."

"Oh, Rhett Ballantine. I didn't meet him until yesterday, but I saw him on site in the lobby. And Jordan, his son, was talking to his mother. I neglected him."

Connor nodded. "Yes, he's the fifteenth. Don't forget the blind woman. Both Tobias and Jordan mentioned seeing her at one point. Renee signed in with the security guard, but I couldn't read her last name. I've got a lead I'm pursuing there."

"How could she get around on her own if she were blind? Did her bodyguard escort her?" I wanted to believe Ulan's previous interaction with the woman, but something wasn't adding up. If she'd been familiar with the building, she could've navigated the place on her own. But from what I understood, Renee was completely new to Braxton.

"Jordan claims he ran into her outside Glass Hall near one of the benches in the courtyard. She requested his help, and he escorted her to the front of the building. When he saw his father, Jordan asked if Renee would be okay on her own." Renee had indicated that she was waiting for someone and would be fine in the lobby. The guard had focused on checking identification at the door, so he never paid attention to her comings and goings once inside the building. He'd assumed she was Jordan's guest.

"So, you believe it's possible she's faking her disability?"

Connor waffled his head. "Or she and Giovanni knew one another, and he accompanied her downstairs to look for the talisman. She could've tricked the man, then killed him."

"I'd only buy that scenario if she were faking her blindness. There's no way she could murder a man with an African spear, then maneuver around the building on her own without being seen or getting lost in a giant maze. You said she was gone before we discovered the body, right?" Myriam and Ursula had caught me hiding in a room to open Uncle Zach's suitcase. Someone else would've noticed Renee sneaking around. Then again, Tobias had told me that Renee was unpredictable.

"All I'm saying is that she was inside the building and could've been the person to kill Giovanni. She exited Glass Hall without being seen, except by two people. It looks like she met a man in the courtyard, and they departed together."

"Where did Tobias see her?" If he noticed her downstairs, that meant he'd been in the basement too.

"At the entrance when he was submitting his identification to the guard. But he had to wait for Ivy to find her driver's license. By the time they drifted into the lobby, Renee had disappeared, and he never saw her again." Connor carried the leftover food containers into the kitchen. "No one else knew her last name either. I'm working with several outside sources to track her down. But hold that thought. I have something else that might rock your world. It did mine when I heard about it."

"Okay, well… before we go there, let's eliminate a few people from the list of potential killers. We can agree Fern, Ursula, Myriam, my grandmother, and my mother are innocent. And me. Yes?"

"I suppose. You were the one to find Giovanni's body. If you thought he killed your uncle, perhaps that mad brain of yours exploded." Connor snorted before finishing his words. He also failed to appreciate the inappropriate gesture I made with my fingers.

"That's ten suspects. Cain is being held at the sheriff's office. No one saw Renee except for the five to ten minutes later that morning when she cornered Ulan at the student union building." I wondered why her bodyguard had been present with her then but missing beforehand. Unless he was the guy she'd met in the courtyard according to the camera. "The other eight are—"

"Kathy. Lindsey. Sawyer. Bitsy. Tobias. Ivy. Rhett. Jordan." Connor grabbed two beers from the refrigerator as the kids returned to the house. He waited for them to head up to their bedrooms before asking his next question. "We're bringing them back for another round of inquiries; however, are you ready to hear what I learned from my dad about Queen Tessa's talisman?"

"If that's the reason my uncle and Giovanni were murdered, then something in your father's story will provide us a clue to the killer's identity." I leaned against the counter and swigged from my bottle. One would not cut it that evening. "Hit me with it."

"My grandmother shared this story with my dad days before she died from ovarian cancer. He never lent it much credence in the past, nor had he believed this latest part because he thought his mother was experiencing a touch of dementia. I have to admit, given what I just learned from him a couple of hours ago, April might ask me to recuse myself from the case."

"Huh? How are you connected to everything?" I couldn't wait to hear the explanation.

Connor swallowed the vestiges of his beer, grabbed another, and clinked it on the neck of mine. "Let me tell you about Pop's family first."

Connor's paternal grandparents, Peter and Gemma Hawkins, had fallen in love during the apartheid era, when South Africa made significant efforts to segregate diverse racial groups, specifically the white and black populations. When other nations were looking to end racism in the 1950s, South African policies continued to treat them differently and attempted to reinforce inhumane practices. Laws forbidding the marriage between two different races were enacted, and anyone who violated them lived in constant danger. Peter, a Caucasian white man, was killed during an attack on their remote village, leaving Gemma, an African black woman, to raise their son, Victor, alone. With little income or opportunities, Gemma was forced to accept a job as a maid for a wealthy woman named Tessa Casseldricken.

Tessa, the last known descendant of the famous South African queen who'd owned the talisman and been murdered by Governor Yeardley in the 1600s, was born blind like her namesake. Though she'd come from mixed races, she appeared white to most others. Cherishing her roots and believing in equality, she and her husband sought to provide protections for all the people in their village. Ludovicus, their only child, was an avid sailor and explorer. He eventually married, but his wife failed to provide him with an heir. Tessa believed her son was going to be the last blood member of their family. She feared the ancient curse her namesake had placed on Governor Yeardley's family would finally dissipate because she had no daughters to continue summoning its powers. Since Ludovicus never cared to learn about his many-times-great-grandmother's efforts to protect her tribe, Tessa shared key details about the curse with Gemma Hawkins, the family maid, in her last days.

Connor said, "When Tessa died in the 1960s, Grandma Gemma continued working for the Casseldrickens as a nurse. Ludovicus's wife suffered from a rare blood disorder. At the same time, massive wars erupted in South Africa over apartheid practices. To protect her only child, Gemma insisted that Victor join the navy and leave South Africa when he turned eighteen."

I remembered Connor's parents telling me how they'd met. "Your dad was subsequently dispatched to the Caribbean, where his ship docked at a port in Anguilla. He met and fell in love with your mother. Right?" He nodded and continued telling me the full story.

Back in South Africa, Ludovicus and Gemma had an affair once his wife slipped further into the dark abyss of impending death. When the attacks on their village hit too close to home, Ludovicus decided to escape. Gemma refused to leave her beloved home, and with his own wife near death, Ludovicus gathered all his family's belongings and amassed wealth and set sail off the southern coast of South Africa. He left behind Queen Tessa's talisman with Gemma, instructing her that he would include the location of his destination in a secret internal compartment. Ludovicus left strict instructions for Gemma to give it to his dying wife should she recover and escape the country. And if not, he begged Gemma to change her mind and join him. Unfortunately, the powerful curse Queen Tessa had placed on the talisman took effect the moment it left her family.

Queen Tessa had issued two specific tenets to the curse. Both were passed down to her daughters and to their children, and Ludovicus's mother shared them with Gemma, who relayed most of the details to her son, Victor. One, all the descendants of Governor Yeardley, the man who'd killed Queen Tessa, would experience horrific and painful deaths. Two, only if one of his heirs killed Queen Tessa's last descendant and destroyed the talisman would it break the curse. The night Ludovicus departed on his ship without the talisman, a terrible storm descended upon South Africa and caused his boat to capsize. Several of his family's jewels and relics from Queen Tessa's tribe surfaced on a nearby island, but they never found Ludovicus. Gemma held onto the talisman for seven nights, hoping he would somehow come back to her, but he never did. Days later, she discovered she was pregnant with his child.

Connor paused in his story to confirm I understood the implications. Even though I did, he made sure we were thinking the same thing. "Grandma Gemma gave birth to Ludovicus's child in 1969, but she never told Pop he had a sibling until much later."

I covered my lips. "So, you're saying that—"

"Renee might be my dad's half-sister."

Chapter 19

"That's incredible." I understood now why Connor would have to step away from the investigation. "Did you know you had an aunt you'd never met? Or did you find out today?"

"Just today. Pop had always thought his mother was losing her mind in the end. Grandma Gemma only revealed her secret as a deathbed confession. She'd been too embarrassed and thought he'd be angry on behalf of his late father, who'd died to protect her from apartheid." Connor noted that his father had returned to South Africa only once to visit his mother, and he remembered a young girl whom she'd babysat. Gemma had claimed the child belonged to a neighbor, and Victor believed his mother. "When my grandmother contacted my dad to tell him she was dying in 1986, I'd just been born. Pop couldn't get away to visit her, but she confessed that he had a half-sister who'd left South Africa in search of her father's family. Grandma

Gemma never lived long enough to tell him her name."

"Why is he so certain that Renee is his half-sister?"

"Pop recently remembered that the little girl he'd met on his trip was named Renee, and he believes she was blind. He'd only briefly seen her playing in the field, and someone was leading her around most of the time. It can't be a co-incidence." Connor was certain that his grand-mother had given birth to a blind daughter resulting from her affair with Ludovicus Cas-seldricken and named her Renee. He'd checked with some contacts to find out if the woman who was dating my uncle—and who'd been in Glass Hall when Giovanni was murdered—could be Re-nee Casseldricken or Renee Hawkins, depending on which name she'd taken.

"I think you might be onto something." I rum-maged for the picture Ulan had sent me, but it was too blurry to know with any positivity. "Re-nee could be your missing half-aunt. And there's a possibility she killed two people and stole the talisman from my office this morning."

Connor deposited his beer bottle in the sink and grunted. "This is a giant mess, and I can't figure out what's going on. Do you think Giovanni is secretly descended from Governor Yeardley? That Renee murdered him so he wouldn't kill her and end the curse? People are genuinely jumpy about the validity of this thing. I'm not sure I buy it."

"It seems completely feasible to me. If my uncle had come across the figurine and tried to sell it, Renee must've used him to find Giovanni. Then, she killed my uncle before he could reveal the truth." I just wasn't sure why she'd told Ulan to give me the message at the student union building after she'd already killed Giovanni. "We're missing something critical. Probably about Giovanni's true birth parents. I can't help but wonder why this talisman was so important to everyone else at the dinner party."

"Perhaps it's just the mystery of the curse. Some people revel in those things." Connor and I tossed around a few additional theories, but we were both too exhausted to agree on the most plausible explanation. Neither of us sincerely believed in the curse, but the various strange deaths and unexpected connections had presented enough evidence that we couldn't ignore the possibility. Too many related parties were adamant about finding Queen Tessa's talisman for there not to be some legitimacy to its haunted history. Over the years, Governor Yeardley's family had daughtered out, making it increasingly difficult to keep track of his heirs. That was an area where I could do a bit of research, including determine if there were other motives within these relationships.

Connor promised to discuss everything with April so they could decide whether he needed to turn the investigation over to another detective. "I'm also going to put out an APB on Renee. If she's still in Braxton, we'll find her."

After he exited, I amused and tortured Ulan—video game wars and trivia contests—for an hour. Emma had already gone to bed much earlier. When Ulan shut his door, I phoned April to let her know Connor had updated me about the list of people who'd been inside Glass Hall when Giovanni was murdered. It was well after midnight and she still hadn't left the sheriff's office. April confirmed the flight manifest request had been denied due to the lack of evidence or connection between Uncle Zach's and Giovanni's deaths. "It's circumstantial, but I'm working on the rental car agency angle. They might offer something helpful."

"That's crazy. I'm certain the two murders are related. I guess we'll keep trying to find a stronger link. What did you learn from the coroner's report?"

"Nothing new, honestly. The blade on the spear punctured a vital organ. He died within minutes. No other fingerprints, and no drugs in his system." April noted the non-existence of objects in Giovanni's hand or signs of additional injury to his body. She also clarified that the assailant could be a man or a woman, as long as the individual had enough strength and power to drive the object into Giovanni's abdomen, potentially twisting until it connected with his organs below his ribs and above his pelvic area.

"Okay, thanks for the visceral details. Next time, perhaps just the highlights?" I also mentioned that Connor had something important to talk to her about too. "Give him time as soon as possible."

"I'm not sure I like the tension in your voice. Is this more evidence to implicate Cain Endicott?" April asked, noting she would connect with Connor first thing in the morning.

"Not exactly." As much as I wanted to see April, we were both drained. "I love you very much. Dinner soon, just the two of us?"

"Absolutely. You gonna cook something special for me? I've been super charitable lately, letting you in on confidential information." April paused for me to consider her humorous suggestion. "Don't make *Old Betsy* teach you a valuable lesson! She's got a penchant for hitting her intended targets."

"Of course. Gotta hold up my end of the bargain too." I had every intention of making breakfast for dinner, simply because it was her favorite meal. "Pancakes. Bacon. Sausage. Anything else?"

"Put yourself on that platter for dessert too, babe. All this hard work has made me hungry."

"Consider me a willing servant for the night. Maybe *Old Betsy's* cousins, *Lord and Lady Shackles*, could come out to play again!" Thinking about April's suggestive comments and her infamous pair of handcuffs prompted a ton of intriguing fantasies!

* * *

On Wednesday morning, I dropped the kids off at school. Ulan was nervous about his calculus exam, but Emma reminded him he'd passed the practice tests, so *he'd totally score again* that day. She announced a separate agenda, which included convincing her teacher that she could bring Baxter to class the following week for show and tell. It was not happening, but I lacked the courage to break Emma's little heart. Even if the teacher permitted it, I couldn't. Baxter would destroy the classroom in under ten minutes, and I'd be forced to slink away in humiliation.

On my way to campus, I noticed a black sedan trailing close behind. I thought I'd lost it when I pulled into the parking lot, but while I sprinted to Glass Hall, the driver stepped out of his car and pretended to look at a map. I wasn't in the mood for a confrontation, so I discreetly snapped a photo of the license plate and temporarily let it go.

Given April had kept Cain overnight and was planning to hold him for another twenty-four hours, Fern and I were tasked with kicking off the newly rescheduled art exhibition. That day's agenda comprised opening remarks from our president, Ursula Power, followed by a discussion panel that included the Australian art collectors and two of the professors who'd worked under Cain in the art department. They would provide a historical overview of the different periods in Africa's history, then take groups on a one-hour tour of the collection. After lunch, Tobias Natcher would share a brief talk about his experience traveling the globe in search of rare objects. Then Sawyer and Bitsy Jaccard would discuss the role of museums and international organizations in arranging and promoting a diverse culture.

While the first group was led on a tour, Fern chatted with her sister and Tobias about their looming early departure. Tobias agreed that Ivy could stay through the weekend, but he'd arranged to leave on Friday, so he'd be back in time for a meeting. Given it would take over a day for him to return, he couldn't stay much longer. I wanted to ask Tobias about his sighting of Renee in the lobby, but getting a word in edgewise was impossible. Rather than make a big deal of it, I assumed I could check with him after his speaking engagement. Tasked with introducing him to the audience, I'd easily broker an opportunity to bring up Renee's presence. When I left the chat, they were discussing dinner plans for that evening.

I casually scanned the three tables assembled in a u-shape in the main foyer where a dozen artifacts were locked under glass and a newly installed camera observed the room. Each object came with a story about the people it belonged to, including an arrowhead and crude painting from the same tribe and era as Queen Tessa's talisman. Other than a photograph of the figurine, they would show nothing else in the exhibits. Cain had hoped to display it, had he gotten his hands on the prized possession, but the inventory of included items in the final schedule didn't include the idol. Whoever had stolen it from my office certainly wouldn't offer it up for the viewing at Glass Hall that week.

I looked up to find Rhett Ballantine approaching the table. Impeccably groomed with brightly whitened teeth, he presented the aura of a true gentleman. Rhett carried a booming voice when introducing himself to me. "It's good to meet you, Kellan. My son, Jordan, tells me you were instrumental in helping him pass his film classes last year. I'm grateful for your guidance and support, especially given everything going on with the baseball team back then."

"Indeed. It was a challenging time, but Jordan is a smart kid. How's he doing in New Orleans?" I asked basic questions before diving into the more complicated topics.

We chatted briefly about Jordan's first year, including how he wasn't confident he'd chosen the proper career path. When Tobias had secured the internship for him, he decided to give it a chance that summer. "If he's unhappy at the end of the program, he might consider following me and joining the FBI. I'm trying not to be the assertive father who decides for him."

"Jordan is headstrong, and he goes after what he wants, from what I remember. I hope to run into him soon." I stepped away from the tables to allow other guests to view the art.

Rhett walked to the nearby corner with me. "He'll be on site later. He had a meeting this morning with someone in town. Won't tell me what it's about, but he's a young man in his prime. I'm sure it's connected with a woman."

The last one he'd dated, a member of the ruthless Grey family, had done a number on him before he graduated from Braxton and left town. "It always is. So, what brings you to the exhibition today?" Rather than jump right into my uncle's death or Rhett's presence the morning Giovanni had been killed, I began with an open-ended inquiry. April had always preferred vague questions when grilling a suspect, to allow them to slip up by babbling too much.

"Many reasons, to be honest. The African culture has always fascinated me. I had an art minor in college, but law enforcement and foreign counterintelligence are my passions." Rhett clarified that in addition to visiting his son, he'd come to town to check out a lead with an ongoing case.

"Does the case have anything to do with the death of Giovanni Vargas? I was the one who found his body two days ago. Not sure if you knew that," I noted, hoping it'd encourage him to open up about his specific interests and recent whereabouts.

"I did. Sheriff Montague mentioned it. There is a connection, but unfortunately, I can't comment on active cases."

I brought up Nana D's meeting with the FBI. "What's the current prognosis?"

"Even though your grandmother is applying tons of pressure to grant Wharton County a chance to solve the murder first, I've only permitted forty-eight hours before we take over on Friday morning. Giovanni was a colleague I'd spent a good amount of time with over the years. Deeply sorry to hear what happened to him." A touch of sadness accompanied Rhett's voice as we stood in silence for a few moments. "You've had a loss recently too. Please accept my condolences for your uncle's death."

I thanked him for his sympathy. "Your ex-wife mentioned you and Uncle Zach were buddies years ago, but there had been a falling out." As he sighed, I noticed Tobias, Ivy, and Fern heading down the far staircase to the basement.

"Old business, honestly. He and I made our peace. I'd rather not dredge up history. It's always difficult when former classmates die. An unexpected death reminds us of our own mortality, especially when it's someone close to your age." Rhett checked his watch and appeared shocked at the time it showed. "I won't turn the big five-oh until later this year. Zach was a couple of years ahead of Ivy and me in school. Nonetheless, I'm on the next tour, and I need to attend to some business this afternoon. Please take care of yourself, Kellan. Good meeting you."

I asked him to hold up momentarily. "I'd love to grab lunch this week. Talk about my uncle and the art world. I'm a novice, and your expertise might help me learn a thing or two. Jordan could join us if you'd like?"

"Truthfully, I'm here for another day and then I head to Eastern Europe for an investigation. Another time," he said curtly, making a big show of being late for the beginning of the next tour.

He seemed too casual for an FBI agent. Was he another ticking time bomb? Without a straightforward way to insert myself into his business, I couldn't prevent him from walking away. I'd bring it up to Connor and April later, to find out whether they knew more about his recent whereabouts.

While walking through the lobby, an Australian accent caught my interest. I introduced myself, hoping she was one half of the pair who'd been at my uncle's dinner party. Luck was on my side at first, as she was the Australian art collector; however, she had nothing of value to add about the missing talisman. "My colleague and I were present to fund the elephant rescue program, to be honest. We donated and embarked on our next destination. Sorry, I can't help you, mate." She also had paid little attention to the conversations at the dinner party. Sometimes leads went nowhere.

With only an hour to grab lunch before it was time to introduce Tobias, I returned to my office to eat the food I'd purchased the day before and organized my thoughts. Myriam had closed the office and lent our department administrator to Fern to assist with any coordination for the art exhibition. She and Ursula would attend to ensure the Glass Hall event kicked off with no issues. I let myself onto our floor and flipped on the lights in the hallway where most of the offices resided. As I approached mine, I noticed my door was slightly ajar.

Had the thief returned with the cursed figurine? I debated whether to call BCS, but the cleaning staff could've left it open. No other lights were on. What could someone be doing in the dark? I quietly approached my office, tightly hugging the hallway walls. When I reached my door, I flung it open and shouted, "I've got the police on speed dial! Who are you?"

"No one you need to be afraid of," responded a vibrant feminine voice. "Didn't Ulan inform you I'd contact you this week?"

I stepped into the doorway and glimpsed a woman sitting in my chair. A narrow ray of light peeked through the window shade and settled on Renee's face. A pair of dark glasses covered her eyes, and she wielded a folded walking stick in her hands, which rested on the top of the desk. Finally, we could tackle the important stuff in our mystery.

"How did you know where to find my office?" I flipped on the light switch to better see Renee.

"My bodyguard escorts me around, as needed. He's also my driver these days. You probably didn't notice him, but he's been watching you all morning. It's imperative we speak." Renee indicated that the man had overheard me mention I'd be going to my office shortly, so he collected Renee—who'd been hiding in a black car with tinted windows—and led her to my office. "He's good at picking locks and helping me get situated somewhere unfamiliar."

Her bodyguard must've been the man hovering in the parking lot earlier. While the main entrance to Diamond Hall was open, as it always was during the day, they'd been forced to break into my office. Had they accomplished the same with my desk to steal Queen Tessa's talisman the previous morning?

"I must admit, you've been reckless to involve my fifteen-year-old cousin in this entire debacle. My uncle has already been killed. Are you after his son now too?" I widened my door, so I could easily escape. I wasn't worried that she'd physically attack me, but if she pulled out a gun, I needed an unblocked getaway. If she truly was blind, her other senses were heightened. I suspected Renee's hearing could pinpoint my exact location.

"As I told Ulan, you have nothing to fear from me. I loved Zach very much, and I'm incredibly distraught he's been murdered." After standing, Renee removed her glasses, unfastened a clip on the top of her head, and shook out her long, dark tresses. "Go ahead, get a good look at me. I know you're curious to learn more."

I studied the woman as she appeared before me, inviting an opportunity for intense scrutinization. Only five foot six, she displayed a petite frame and beautiful tawny skin, and she dressed immaculately. Her aqua-colored silk blouse emphasized the intense blue of her eyes, and her reassuring smile was contagious. Delicate facial features suggested innocence, yet her silvery voice was heavily modulated. Uncle Zach had a terrific taste in women, but could I really trust Renee?

"Please, sit. I appreciate the opportunity to momentarily gaze, but I don't want to put you at an unfair advantage." I lolled in my guest chair once she took her seat and restored her glasses.

"Because I'm blind and can't see you?"

"Yes," I cautiously said, not intending to offend her.

"Lean forward, please." Renee did the same as she instructed.

As I did, she placed her strong hands on my face and gently pressed in different spots. First, she confiscated my glasses, then she ran her hands through my hair. When she pressed a finger on my lips, she paused and grinned more widely. "Plump, but not too exaggerated. Soft skin. You normally don't wear cologne, but I can smell the cracked pepper body wash you've chosen." After she finished, she handed me my glasses and leaned back in her seat. "You have your uncle's nose, button-shaped. That tells me you're threatened by people... women... with a powerful will. But you're generous and trusting with the right one. Unlike Zach, you have a semi-structured jawline and full head of thick, wavy hair. Given its texture, I suspect you're a dark-blond or light-brunette."

I swallowed the lump in my throat and a small percentage of my wavering concerns. "You're perceptive. Uncle Zach was fond of the bald look!"

"He was a gorgeous man to me, in every way. I will never get over his death." Renee reached into her pocket and produced a tissue that she used to dry the corner of her eyes. "You must have many questions for me. I can only stay for a few minutes. Someone is intent on killing me, and I cannot risk being unprotected for too long."

I relaxed enough to entertain Renee's way of managing the predicament. She had no reason to harm me, and I had nothing of value to offer her. But she had the answers I sought. "Are you really the daughter of a man named Ludovicus who died in a shipwreck off the coast of South Africa? And do you prefer Casseldricken or Hawkins?"

"Yes, I believe I am. I never knew my father, and my mother only told me the crucial details in the days before she succumbed to ovarian cancer. Because the woman believed in a family curse, she didn't want anyone to know my father's identity. I go by Renee Hawkins, even though that was my mother's married name." Renee moved the walking stick to the side of the desk and clasped her hands together. "But I'm not convinced my father actually perished in the shipwreck."

Chapter 20

My heart raced like an overworked thorough-bred. Connor hadn't told me the part about Ludovicus surviving the shipwreck. "Is he still alive today?"

"To be truthful, I don't think so. My father would be eighty, and no one has heard from him since he disappeared in 1968. Once my mother confessed the truth, I fruitlessly explored the African subcontinent. I've only connected with him and his ancestors through some relics I've come across."

Renee advised that she'd left for the US after finishing high school in South Africa and learned about the dangers of the world. "My mother was very old-fashioned. She believed young girls needed to stay home and care for their husbands. I had grander dreams and disappeared as soon as I could. Hid out in America and Europe." She'd admitted to being a little wild in her youth, but when her mother called to say she was dying, Renee flew home.

"Are you aware your mother had another family before you were born?" I assumed if Gemma had confessed to her son that he had a younger half-sister, she would've also told Renee about her older half-brother.

"Yes, I know his name is Victor, and he moved to Anguilla. But he knows nothing about my father. I suppose one day, I should meet the man, but my prime focus has always been to track down an object that belonged to one of my ancestors. I assume you've heard of Queen Tessa's talisman."

At least I had confirmation she was searching for the figurine. "Yes, it's been quite the popular item around here lately." I didn't want her to know I'd temporarily had custody of it. "What can you tell me about it?"

Renee shared a similar story about its history, confirming many of the facts that Giovanni, Fox, and Connor had revealed. But she had bonus information none of them had been privy to.

"The curse, which I know in full certainty, is quite legitimate. But more elements exist than those you've probably been told about." Renee verified that everyone assumed Ludovicus Casseldricken was the last remaining member of Queen Tessa's family, given none knew about her existence. She also acknowledged that many of the descendants of Governor Yeardley, Queen Tessa's killer, had died very suspicious deaths. "The curse will be broken only when all of Queen Tessa's descendants have been eliminated and someone in Governor Yeardley's family tree destroys the talisman... this is true, but there was a very specific tenet to the second."

I let out a small gulp, pulling together the bigger picture. Renee wanted to find the talisman so she could ensure no one else destroyed it. Once someone exterminated her and the missing object, the curse would be broken. "What's the other tenet?"

"Every descendant of Governor Yeardley always dies before his or her fiftieth birthday. The person who is trying to obtain Queen Tessa's talisman and who wants me dead is approaching that age, and now that he or she has stolen it from Zach, I'm likely next on their list."

My mind raced furiously. "How do I know you're not really one of Yeardley's descendants who's trying to track down the cursed figurine?"

I knew the answer but needed to hear it for my-self.

"I can show you pictures of my father that my mother kept. You'll see the resemblance. I'm blind, just like Queen Tessa. My mother refused to give me Tessa's name to protect my identity and paternal connections." She paused to collect her next set of words. "I loved your uncle more than life. I would never have murdered him. He tried to help me, Kellan."

Renee shared everything about her relation-ship with Uncle Zach. She'd been searching all over South Africa for the stolen talisman in the last two decades, hoping to find the object so that Governor Yeardley's descendants could never obliterate it. She worried it was already destroyed, but the fact that she was still alive meant few knew she existed, or they would've killed her in the past. She'd met my uncle while visiting the elephant camp one afternoon, as she'd heard rumors that the people who'd stolen it from Gemma Hawkins in 1968 had once lived on the property. Over time, she and Zach grew fond of one another. Uncle Zach had gone into debt to protect his elephant rescue programs, and he'd borrowed money from someone who demanded it back unexpectedly. Renee had convinced him to send Ulan to the US the previous summer so he wouldn't be caught in the crossfire.

Earlier that year, Uncle Zach arranged to sell some art he'd come across, including items that Renee had found in her quest to locate Queen Tessa's talisman. She'd never told him about the talisman, though, as she wanted her family secret to remain hidden until she ensured the cursed idol was found. Uncle Zach had been excavating on his property in preparation to build another facility when he discovered Queen Tessa's talisman buried in a treasure chest. He decided to auction it at the dinner party where a dozen investors and art enthusiasts had been invited to anonymously bid. Renee attended the event at the last minute, as she was originally supposed to be away on a work trip.

Uncle Zach enthusiastically presented the idol at the dinner party. By the manner he'd described it and the reactions around the room, Renee realized it was her family heirloom. At the end of the evening, she confessed the truth about it belonging to her family. Uncle Zach wasn't sure who'd won the final bid, as everything had been handled anonymously. Uncle Zach only knew he was supposed to provide bank account information the following week, and when everything was transferred, the winner would collect Queen Tessa's talisman. Instead, once my uncle learned Renee wanted the figurine, he attempted to cancel the transaction. He then received a threatening note that he'd be killed if he didn't acquiesce and deliver the object to the winner.

"Unfortunately, someone else at his event recognized it too," Renee noted while texting her bodyguard-slash-driver that she was ready to leave. "Zach and I decided to escape to the US. We were going to determine what to do with the figurine when we arrived, but that's when trouble unfolded."

"Uncle Zach never told me about his financial problems or the threats." I only knew he'd been worried in those last few days, briefly mentioning something about taking care of his son.

"I know. He was being extra careful. We agreed to fly separately so nothing looked suspicious.

As far as anyone knew at the dinner party, I was merely Zach's disinterested girlfriend. He planned to introduce me to his family when we got to Orlando, and I was going to drive with him and Ulan back here." Renee finished sharing her incredible story just as her bodyguard showed up.

Zach had taken a flight to Amsterdam while Renee arranged for security protection once they both landed in the US. Once arriving, he confirmed everything was on schedule before he boarded the plane to Orlando. Renee left later that day, but local authorities detained her in Amsterdam when her passport went missing. Airport security refused to let her leave the country until they sorted it out. During the time she was stuck, Uncle Zach left a cryptic voicemail that he'd been followed on the Orlando plane, and that was the last communication she'd received from him.

"I tried to reach your uncle, but he never picked up. Finally, someone at the airport found my passport and turned it into security the next morning. Someone obviously stole my passport and intentionally prevented me from getting on that next flight to Orlando. When I learned what happened to Zach on the news, I left the Amsterdam airport and slipped into hiding." Renee verified that she'd been keeping a low profile for the previous two months, hoping to find Queen Tessa's talisman and search for Uncle Zach's killer. She was positive someone had intentionally murdered him and, somehow, arranged for it to look like an accident. She'd checked into the car rental agency's records, and something seemed suspect. The killer had deliberately arranged for my uncle to be loaned a car that was improperly scheduled for repairs, hence why it looked like the explosion was truly an unfortunate mishap.

I considered my options. If I didn't make the offer, Renee might creep away for good. "I'm close friends with Sheriff Montague. I promise she'll listen to your story and protect you. She's keen to talk to you about your presence at Glass Hall the other morning. When Giovanni Vargas was murdered."

Renee declined my offer, but she confirmed Jordan's story about helping her enter the lobby. Her bodyguard was parking the car, and she only attended to find out whether Queen Tessa's talisman was listed on the inventory or mentioned by other guests. Once she corroborated it wasn't, she rushed off with her bodyguard and went back into hiding. "I can't take the risk of this psychopath finding and killing me. You have to trust that I will be in touch again soon."

"Please, won't you give me a chance? For Uncle Zach's sake? I wouldn't do anything to hurt you." I wanted to honor my uncle's memory, and if he loved the woman, she was strangely part of our family. Although unconvinced she'd told the entire truth, I had no choice but to confess what'd happened with the talisman. When I explained the mix-up with Kathy's suitcase and how I'd temporarily been in possession of the idol before it disappeared, Renee grasped my hands tightly.

"Do you know what this means? If the killer has Queen Tessa's talisman, then all they have to do is find me. I must go back into hiding immediately, Kellan." Renee released me, promising to be in touch soon. "I didn't kill Giovanni. He was also at that dinner party. I remember hearing his name, but I didn't get to speak with him.

I stayed in the background and listened to everyone's conversations once I realized Zach had found the talisman."

"Wait! Maybe you heard something important?"

"I've given you a lot to process. I'll be in contact again soon, and we can talk about how to proceed from here. I hope you trust me now. I'm not just worried about myself being killed anymore. I'm concerned that... well... never mind. Another time." Renee skulked into the hallway, cradling her bodyguard's arm as he guided her to the steps. She promised to send me a list of people who'd been present at the dinner party, in case what I'd learned to date was wrong. "If I think of anything, I'll let you know."

As they reached the first-floor landing, Myriam Castle stomped around the corner. She briefly interrogated them, then let them pass once learning they were there to see me about the summer course schedule. Myriam haughtily shook her head in my direction and noted she had no time to gab. As her office door slammed shut, I returned through mine to consider the newly gained information.

Several of the people I'd spoken with had talked about turning fifty years old soon. Ivy and Jordan had mentioned Tobias's upcoming birthday. Rhett was afraid of turning a half century too. Sawyer and Bitsy were somewhere in the late forties, like Myriam. I immediately updated April, who told me to exercise caution around Renee, in case she was lying. She also would turn fifty this year.

"I've discovered something funny about Zach's accident. The car rental agency's final report denoted that he was supposed to receive a smaller model, but he'd been upgraded at the last minute when the car he was originally scheduled to receive hadn't been returned by the previous renter. Someone you've recently met."

"Who? This could be our best lead, April."

"Sawyer Jaccard. After the dinner party in South Africa, he flew to Greece for forty-eight hours, then Orlando, where he rented a car that he'd originally intended to return the day before Zach's flight," replied April.

"But he kept it?"

"For an extra week, then Sawyer flew back to Greece. I'm going to talk to the Orlando police tomorrow to find out how they want to handle this information." Extending a car rental longer than planned was occasionally part of regular business operations. Given what happened in Braxton, exploring all possibilities became necessary. "I'm so sorry it's taken this long to find out the truth."

"It's okay. I appreciate all you're doing to help me. At least this lines up with Renee's theory that someone was trying to kill Uncle Zach. They'd planned to blow up his car and needed it to look like a clerical mistake, not an intentional explosion." I knew something had been strange with how quickly the car agency wanted to settle the claim. Whoever had arranged for the car to explode and kill Uncle Zach must've been involved with the immediate payout. Was Sawyer behind it all?

"I'm pulling some strings to get answers. We might find a link between the list of people at the dinner party, those who were present at the art exhibition's original opening, and the car rental agency. I'm not sure if Sawyer blew up the car himself or hired someone else, but that's my focus tomorrow." Before April hung up to finish her research, she confirmed Cain would be released overnight. She hadn't been able to convince a judge to keep him detained longer than forty-eight hours and was receiving immense pressure from the governor, a close friend of Lindsey Endicott's.

As I left the building, I dialed Nana D for one of our daily check-ins. She'd been in contact with her government cohorts to learn more about Giovanni Vargas and the FBI and ICE's interests in Queen Tessa's talisman. "Please tell me you've uncovered a solid lead?"

"That depends, brilliant one… that depends." Nana D chuckled as she confessed to suckering several connections into revealing some classified information. "Neither agency was hot on finding the talisman. Sure, they wanted to eliminate any growing tensions between South Africa and the US regarding an object that belonged in their country, but Giovanni's quest for the figurine seems to have been more personal."

"Meaning he wasn't authorized to track it down?" I scratched at the back of my head, befuddled over the new scoop.

"Exactly. Giovanni's supervisor instructed him to drop his pursuit, clarifying that he had other priorities and shouldn't use government sources for personal gains." Nana D pitched a momentary fit at the constant bureaucracy she faced in the same vein. "Looks like he was just as much a victim as Zach. You've got to find their killer, brilliant one."

Chapter 21

When I returned to Glass Hall, the building was hopping with art students and staff interested in attending a free campus event. I ran into Ursula and inquired about her conversation with Rhett Ballantine the other day. She noted that he had questions about the fall MBA program, citing potential interest in teaching a course. "Sorry, nothing about the art exhibition came up. By the way, have you seen Myriam today?"

"She locked herself in her office earlier. Not sure what that was about. She seemed out of sorts again. It wasn't the first time this week."

"You know how orderly she can be. As much as she won't admit it to me, Bitsy and Sawyer aren't her favorite people. She's only tolerated them throughout the years because they're my longtime friends." Ursula ran her fingers through her hair and sighed heavily. "The things we do for our loved ones, Kellan... I've put my wife through a lot over the years. Between that business with my brother trying to kill me and now this... I truly feel awful."

"If it's any consolation, I think you two have a beautiful, solid partnership. Everything you do to support one another is obvious. I might believe her personality is on par with Nurse Ratched and Lizzie Borden, but I don't doubt her love for you." I pulled my bottom lip into my mouth and braced for Ursula to dress me down because of my comparisons to her wife.

Ursula covered her mouth, but the hidden laugh was evident. "Oh, I appreciate your candor. You're one of the few who will heroically stand up to her. Myriam would kill me if she knew I told you this, but she very much respects you. At first, she assumed your father's nepotism was the only reason you'd gotten this job. But you've proven yourself a worthy addition to the Braxton campus."

"Does that mean I should press my luck and try harder with our modern-day Lady Macbeth? I try to observe a fair boundary with her being my boss and all...." And I truly did. I only allowed myself to fight back every third time, assuming it'd eventually whittle away her iron exterior.

Before I could respond, Ursula picked up her phone. "Speak of your devil, it's Myriam. Excuse me one moment."

While Ursula spoke with her wife, I stepped to the side to block Tobias Natcher's path. "Pardon, might I bother you for a second?"

"Yes, but aren't you supposed to introduce me in several minutes?" he asked, examining his watch. "I'm just making a quick stop in the restroom."

I looked at the clock above the giant windows in the front of the building, noticing I needed to be at the lectern shortly. "Yes, I'll be brief. I was curious if you've been in Orlando recently. My uncle had been meeting someone there, but I don't know his or her identity." I thought if I could systematically cross names off the list, I'd pinpoint who might've been following Uncle Zach. Tobias seemed like an unlikely candidate, but I had to rule him out.

"Not this year," he replied, both eyebrows knitting together in confusion. "Is that all you wanted to ask?" He released a small laugh, then told me it was an unusual question.

I could check with Ivy later to be sure too. "Sorry... no, one more thing. You mentioned seeing Renee Hawkins at the original opening on Monday. Can you share anymore about that?"

Tobias smiled wide enough for all his teeth to appear. "Ah, is that her last name? I assume you've decided to agree with me that the woman is hiding something."

"I am a little wary. I met her briefly, and well... something isn't exactly clear. She claims she doesn't have the talisman."

"Really? She's shown up again... interesting. I would've thought she hightailed it out of here with the cursed figurine." Tobias cleared his throat. "Don't believe the woman. Watch yourself. At your uncle's dinner, she kept disappearing from the room throughout the night. She had all the access needed to slip away with the golden nugget."

"I'll keep that in mind. Do you remember anything else from Monday morning? Did you ever see her go downstairs?" I was hoping Tobias had forgotten something he'd seen until recently.

He shook his head. "Honestly, no, I wasn't paying much attention. When I saw her and later heard about a man's death, I just assumed she was involved." He excused himself and jokingly instructed me to give him a grand introduction worthy of Queen Tessa.

When we finished talking, Ursula tapped me on the shoulder. "That was very odd. Myriam isn't feeling very well. She just went home to lie down for a while."

"Oh, I'm sorry to hear that. Did she say what's wrong?"

Ursula indicated she hadn't. "Myriam never gets sick. In fact, I can't remember a time she's ever mentioned a headache, stomach issue, or pain in the past."

"Do you think it's serious?" I certainly wouldn't wish anything bad on the woman, despite the many times I considered strangling or poisoning her myself.

"No, I think she's lying to me." Ursula wrinkled her nose and expelled a long, noisy breath. "Anyway, she doesn't intend to return to the exhibition. She'll meet me at the funeral home later, assuming she's feeling better."

"Oh, for Giovanni Vargas's funeral?" I'd forgotten that it was scheduled for this evening.

Cristiano had arranged for a vigil for anyone in the area who'd known his cousin. Then he'd fly the body back to Los Angeles, where the Vargas family lived.

"Yes. Since he died on campus, Myriam and I feel compelled to extend our condolences. I better run, Kellan. Will I see you there?"

"You will. I'll be partnering with Fern here all afternoon. We'll keep the art crowd in check, don't worry. I assume these folks are pretty calm."

Ursula frowned. "Have you forgotten someone was murdered here two days ago? And a priceless figurine was stolen from your office yesterday?"

I acknowledged her irrefutable facts. "Shouldn't that mean nothing else bad will happen?"

"We can only wish. Terrible things happen in triplicate, my friend."

"Ah, true. Quick question?" I didn't want to offend her but had to ask. "Do the Jaccards have any business dealings in Orlando?"

Ursula considered her response. "Not that I'm aware of, but we all vacationed there years ago.

Bitsy enjoys the weather. She goes to a spa near the beach at every change of season."

"Okay, thanks. I should let you go." I needed more information before I accused her friends of arranging my uncle's death. I worried that Bitsy and Sawyer were the ones behind everything. She had access to kill Giovanni, and that smoker might've blown up my uncle.

Ursula exited the foyer, and I navigated to the other room to introduce Tobias to everyone.

As he spoke, Ivy and Fern hovered near the front of the crowd, providing him with the comfort of familiar support. I listened to his opening remarks but became distracted when a noise near the back of the room erupted. While it wasn't intrusive enough to stop Tobias from speaking, I wanted to contain it. I traversed through the throng of guests and approached the doorway. Standing just outside, Lindsey and Kathy Endicott were having a minor spat. She'd been massaging her own neck, just below the bandages that were covering the back of her head.

"You shouldn't have done that, Lindsey. It's the exact reason I couldn't stand being around you anymore." Kathy raised her voice enough that people at the back of the crowd turned around to listen.

"I've been the one protecting our son all his life. You don't understand what it takes to be a good parent sometimes." Lindsey grabbed his ex-wife's hand and squeezed it tightly. Both his bushy caterpillar eyebrows waggled as he spoke. "If I didn't take care of it, we'd all be in a lot more trouble."

"Protecting? You mean covering up his messes, Lindsey." Kathy threw her free hand to her forehead and rubbed her left temple, tugging slightly at the side of the bandage.

I stepped through the arch and pulled the door closed behind me. "Excuse me, please take your discussion down a notch. There's a conference going on in there."

Lindsey released Kathy and waved at me. His paunchy belly failed to be contained by the plaid sports coat he attempted to button. "Kellan, it's always good to see you. I'm so sorry. Kathy was just released from the hospital this morning and she insisted on coming by."

"To see what's happening with the exhibit. Cain is still stuck at the sheriff's office, and I want to let him know later how the event went." Kathy walked closer and gently touched my forearm. "Did you give Zach's luggage to Ulan?"

Lindsey rubbed a palm across his swollen belly. "Sorry for the interruption. Won't happen again. Maybe you can help us out."

I focused on Kathy first. "No, I couldn't give it to Ulan. Turned out the suitcase contained something that might help us understand more about Uncle Zach's death. I had to turn it over to the police. But thank you for providing a potential lead." When she gasped, I switched positions and glanced at Lindsey. "Do you need directions to something inside the exhibition? Or how can I assist?"

"No, no... nothing like that. I thought you might do some of your famous snooping, regarding this shameful murder. Seraphina raves about how you always find the criminals and culprits in this town." Lindsey popped a pill from his pocket and tossed it in his mouth. "Stress prevention. All the women in my life are trying to kill me. So, will you do it?"

"I hardly think I'm in a position to help Cain. My uncle is one of the victims. I'm focused on finding his killer, not proving that your son isn't involved." Although, it could help me uncover more information.

"But Zach died in an accidental car explosion," said Kathy, leaning on Lindsey when the news became too much to handle.

After we escorted her to a private reception area on the far side of the lobby, Lindsey spoke. "Cain has nothing to do with either death. I don't exactly know what you're talking about regarding Zach Danby's connection, but if Seraphina thinks my family tried to hurt hers, she's got another thing coming. I'll march right into her office and—"

"No! That's not what I'm saying." I had little patience left to deal with them that afternoon. "Look, Nana D and I haven't discussed this. I've only just learned that Uncle Zach's death might be connected to Giovanni Vargas's murder. I need to update Sheriff Montague, and then she'll decide if that has any bearing on the case against Cain."

"But you've found a link that could convince her to let my son go?" inquired Kathy.

"I really don't have much to divulge. I'm focused on finding out what happened to my uncle. If there's an opportunity to help Cain along the path, I'll do my best." I asked Kathy what she'd remembered about the break-in.

"I slept in late. Still haven't adjusted to the time changes from all my traveling. Around eleven, I grazed on some oatmeal and noticed he'd left his briefcase at home. I texted my son to see if he wanted me to bring it to campus. He said he'd stop home around lunchtime." Kathy confirmed that she'd taken a shower and was dressing in the bathroom when the house alarm chirped. Assuming Cain was on his way in, she left the bathroom on the second floor and walked toward the stairwell. "I was going to ask if he needed me to shut off the alarm."

Lindsey chimed in. "Foolish woman. What have I always told you to do when you hear a stranger in the house?"

"Get my gun."

"Exactly. And did you get your gun?" Lindsey banged his fist on his knee.

"No, I told you that I—"

Despite Kathy's obvious intent to respond, Lindsey interjected with progressively wilder gesticulations. "No exceptions! Get the gun, be prepared, and call the cops. Honestly, woman."

"You can't talk to me that way anymore. We're not married, and I am sick and tired of it!" She stood and shoved his shoulder several inches.

Lindsey rose to match her stance. "Ain't the point!"

Kathy attempted to slap him but missed when he leaned away. She had a great deal of strength behind her swing. "I left my gun in Orlando. I can't carry it across state lines right now, you moron!"

"Okay!" I shouted, increasingly fatigued by playing arbiter in everyone else's disagreements. "Can we finish the original discussion? What happened when you started descending the steps?"

Kathy emphatically sneered at Lindsey. "I called out to Cain, but when I got down a few, I could see the door was wide open. Cain would never have left it like that, so I paused to think."

She turned to Lindsey. "That's when I remembered my gun!"

"And then what happened?" I didn't wait for Lindsey to respond, only held up my hand in his direction.

"Someone threw a blanket over my head. I started to fall, but luckily, I caught the banister. As I did, the burglar walloped me on the head." Kathy had struggled to pull the blanket off and fell down the steps when the assailant rushed by her. Once she reached the bottom of the steps and stood near the front door, she looked through its glass pane. While only saw a brief glimpse, Kathy was certain the guy she'd noticed near the corner of the property had a baseball cap and wasn't as tall as her son.

"So, you definitely don't think it was Cain."

"No, it couldn't be. A few seconds later, Cain strolled into the living room and saw me collapsed on the floor. I'd gotten woozy from the head injury and practically passed out. There wasn't enough time for Cain to do it. And why would he?"

Kathy had a good point. Cain wouldn't have set the alarm off in his own house. If he were truly scavenging her room to find the talisman, he would've been quiet while she took a shower. The only reason I could rationalize was if he wanted to cast suspicion on someone else, to make it look like he'd been a victim of a crime too. Then the police would think whoever killed Giovanni had also broken into Cain's house to find the talisman.

"I tend to agree with you. Are you sure you don't remember any strange smells? Something identifiable?" I hoped it would trigger a memory.

"Did the assailant have gloves?" added Lindsey.

"I never saw his hands. No cologne or anything, at least not to my memory." Kathy noted that the police had taken fingerprints, but given it was Cain's home, many existed on the banister, doorknobs, and dresser handles. "It'll take them weeks to sort through it all."

I inquired how much either of them knew about Queen Tessa's talisman and the curse she'd imbued on it. Neither knew much other than the bits and pieces Cain had shared while preparing for the art exhibition.

"Honestly, Kellan, I'm flabbergasted. Cain has been teaching in the art world for years. He doesn't collect it. He appreciates it from afar. Sometimes he creates and sells his own pieces. He's made a solid living over the years." Kathy asked Lindsey if he'd take her home, as she wasn't feeling too well.

"My son has never asked for money. He knows he has a hefty inheritance arriving in the future. Cain is a good boy. This is all just a bunch of nonsense. And you better tell your girlfriend to get off his back, you hear?" Lindsey wagged a finger in my direction.

"I'll do what I can. April wouldn't keep him if she didn't have a solid reason. Perhaps she's waiting for him to share additional information, or she's trying to protect him in case someone comes after him next time." I knew it wasn't the latter, but it might get them to back down.

Kathy smiled. "Oh, that's a good point. You're a smart guy. Let us know if you hear anything."

"Will do. Hey... quick question for you about travel," I added, remembering that she'd mentioned visiting the Balkans for a few weeks. Giovanni had been born in a nunnery in Eastern Europe. Could that be the connection I was trying to recall recently? "Have you spent much time in Eastern Europe?"

Kathy's face scrunched together. "It's gorgeous. I've been going since my mid-twenties. After Lindsey and I separated, that was my home away from home. Why do you ask?"

If Kathy had been eighteen when she gave birth to Cain in 1981, that meant she would've been in her mid-twenties when Giovanni was born six years later. Could she be his birth mother? How could I ask such an indelicate question?

Lindsey frowned. "I'd rather not bring those times up, Kathy."

"Fine! I'm heading to Cain's place. A friend will check on me," she replied in a blase tone.

Lindsey scowled at his ex-wife. "Someone I've met before?"

"No." She walked to the front doors without him.

"Then who?" He looked askance at me, shaking his fist. "What did I say earlier about women?"

I tossed my hands in the air, averse to getting further involved. I assumed she meant Fox, but I would not say his name aloud. "Understood, Mr. Endicott. I'll let you know if I hear anything. Oh, neither of you would have ancestors in South Africa, would you?"

Lindsey's eyes bugged out. "What is this, world geography on *Jeopardy*? My family's been in Wharton Country for centuries. Kathy's parents were born in Ireland, and she traced her roots to the last king of Ireland before the English took over. She's had quite the good fortune this year."

"And does Kathy have any other children?" I pushed my luck with the inquiry.

"Not any of mine. She'd have asked for child support if that were the case!"

"I meant, had she met someone after you," I cautiously added.

"Doubtful. She never looked pregnant to me, and I saw her frequently. You know, you're as strange as your grandmother, Kellan. Too nosy for your own good." Lindsey raced after his ex-wife.

After they left, I sat in the corner by myself, puzzled at all the muddled clues I'd stumbled across in the previous few days. I was grasping at straws with guessing Giovanni's biological parents, even if I felt that would offer the best clue to his killer's identity. Normally, it'd be much easier to determine where to start, but it continued to stump me. Between the stolen talisman, Queen Tessa's curse, a common group of people on the perimeter of the case, and my uncle's money problems, there had to be a missing link. Something obvious but hidden well enough to keep me from figuring it out easily.

I'd become obsessed with analyzing all the clues and hardly felt someone jostling my shoulder. "Kellan? You asleep? Yoo-hoo?"

Chapter 22

I jerked myself from the distraction. "Oh, hey… sorry. Was processing some news. How's it going?"

Fern and her sister, Ivy, sat across from me. Ivy squeezed my knee. "Tobias just finished speaking to the crowd. He's talking with two other guests, but he should be done shortly. He has to meet with Hampton and Natasha about the sale of ReedWell. Maybe you need a break?"

"Probably. But there's just too much going on to stop right now. I have a funeral to attend tonight too." I would've loved to stay home with the kids and April, but it wasn't an option. My parents had invited Ulan and Emma to dinner so I could go directly to Whispering Pines for Giovanni's service that evening. I'd collect them on the way home.

Fern said, "Ivy is going to come with me too. She hardly knew Giovanni, only met him briefly at Zach's dinner party."

"We're gonna stop by to pay our respects, then find a lovely restaurant and drink a bottle or two of wine. If Tobias is finished negotiating with your brother early enough, he'll join us too." Ivy searched her pocketbook for her keys.

I remembered that I wanted to verify Tobias's response about Orlando. "Have you and Tobias been to Orlando this year? Simply curious… asking everyone these days. My daughter loved it. Trying to decide if there's enough for adults too."

Ivy clutched a pillow from the couch. "No, we went to New Orleans to see Jordan in March. Come to think of it, right before Zach's accident. I haven't been to Florida in decades."

"I guess Tobias wouldn't have been either, huh?"

"I don't think Orlando is his idea of a vacation. He doesn't have any children for the same reason. Prefers international travel, to be free to come and go as he pleases. Matter of fact, after New Orleans, he headed to London for a last-minute business meeting with Paddington Enterprises." Ivy noted that she'd flown separately to Los Angeles to work with the interior designer on their renovations.

"Thank you. I'll keep checking. I'll see you at the funeral parlor soon. I might go take a quick catnap in my office." I looked around the lobby and saw several people leaving the building. The exhibition would conclude soon, which meant the cleaning crew could come through to prepare for the next morning's activities.

Fern said, "You've got dark circles under your eyes, my friend. I think a nap is a promising idea." She turned to her sister. "You used to get tired like this in the middle of the afternoon when you were pregnant with Jordan. Practically fell asleep talking to me sometimes."

Ivy giggled. "Tell me about it. Thank God I only had to go through that twice." She reached for her sister's hand and stood. "Let's get moving, sis. I could use a cup of tea and a healthy snack."

Fern squinted at her sister, jerking her head sideways before summoning her response. "Ummm... yeah, sure. We can stop at The Big Beanery prior to getting the car."

"See you later, Kellan," replied Ivy as they stepped through the doors and onto the front terrace.

As they left, I noticed them huddled closely together, whispering like two sisters squabbling about a secret they were trying to keep.

I considered what had just transpired and everything else I'd learned to date. Ivy had mentioned two pregnancies, but as far as I knew she only had one child, Jordan. She also frequently changed the topic when I brought up Giovanni Vargas's murder. Giovanni had been searching for his birth parents, and the Vargas family had adopted him in 1987 when he was born. Since Ivy was a couple of years younger than my uncle, she would've been about eighteen the year Giovanni was born, probably graduating from high school. She'd also taken a gap year after high school, and no one had seen her for over nine months. More than enough time to secretly have a baby and give him up for adoption. Had Ivy Natcher just accidentally revealed a hidden connection to the victim? Then again, if she were his mother, she'd never kill her own son. It was a laughable suggestion, unless she didn't know he was her son or didn't want anyone else to know he was her son. That's when the more obvious question made itself known.

Who was Giovanni's birth father? Prior to her gap year, Ivy had been involved with both Uncle Zach and Rhett Ballantine. Which one was Giovanni's biological dad?

Despite being on the verge of a breakthrough, I couldn't get hold of Connor or April to discuss my theory of Ivy being Giovanni's birth mother. Perhaps Fern would know, or at least clarify her sister's remark about two pregnancies. I sent April a text that we needed to chat urgently. I also messaged Connor, but he replied that he was on the phone with his father, who'd remembered something else his mother had once told him. Connor promised to connect with me at Giovanni's funeral service that evening.

I returned to my office and called Aunt Deirdre, who verified that while she had flown to Pennsylvania the week Uncle Zach died, she believed her husband had taken a meeting with Tobias the next day. "Tobias invests in Paddington Enterprises. They're always doing business together."

With that confirmation and two names off my list, I decided to indulge in that nap before heading to the funeral parlor!

* * *

Whispering Pines was one of two funeral homes in Wharton County. The Nutberry family had owned it for many generations, and in the prior year they'd spruced up the place. Gone were their flowery wallpapers and dainty furniture, replaced by more modern, natural colors and textures that brought class and comfort to mourners. Although I'd arrived fifteen minutes early, the funeral parlor would be open, and I needed to talk to Francesca about Emma's schedule while she'd be on a summer holiday the next month. When I found her, she was conversing with her boyfriend, Cristiano, a Latinx man with piercing golden eyes and a cultured, hypnotic accent. It soothed you into believing he wasn't once a major player in the mafia.

Francesca smiled and waved me over. Dark roots had crept into her short, platinum-blonde bob since our last encounter. "Hi, Kellan. It's good of you to stop by tonight. Thank you."

I offered my condolences to Cristiano on the death of his cousin. "It's been a horrible year for you. With a bit of luck, things will get better soon."

"*Muchas gracias*, Kellan. It has been quite *ridículo*, but it's also had some positive moments." He pulled Francesca closer to him and kissed her forehead. "I met this beautiful woman. And you've been flexible about Emma's custody arrangements." His tall, well-built frame towered over mine, and layers of his dark, wavy hair fell across my ex-wife's highly rouged cheek.

I had little choice. Even though it could have disastrous consequences for my daughter, keeping her mother from her would only alienate us in the future. Emma needed to make her own decisions about her mother's choices. Francesca had missed out on several important years of Emma's childhood, and extraordinarily little would make up for it in the year since she'd returned. Hopefully, Francesca and Cristiano stayed on the straight and narrow. I also trusted my daughter's clever observation skills.

"If we all keep up our end of the deal, it should work out." I proposed a schedule, which disappointed them at first, but Cristiano reminded my ex-wife that she was looking to return to work again soon. She'd been a nurse years ago and missed saving people's lives.

"I know you're right, but two days a week is hard. I miss her so much," she said, clutching his hand and biting her lip. "We'll make it work."

Francesca had a point. I needed to be more sensitive to her needs too, even if a constant fear lingered about her underlying intentions. I promised to be more flexible as time progressed. Once we came to an agreement, I inquired whether Cristiano had learned anything new about his cousin's murder. "I really don't think Cain Endicott is guilty. Do you?"

Cristiano mumbled a few Spanish phrases that I barely understood. I knew enough to know they weren't kind ones. "Not unless he's working for someone else. A bunch of connections are looking at the usual players. Francesca is too, and we're hoping—"

Noticing my contrary expression forming, Francesca interrupted. "Relax, Kellan. It's legal stuff. Neither of us is doing anything dangerous or against the law."

"Okay, thanks. Sorry, go ahead, Cristiano." I felt much better after they'd seen the light during the previous months.

"We're hoping to hear tomorrow about Giovanni's adoption paperwork. Technically, it was sealed at the time he'd been given to my aunt and uncle, but now that he's been murdered, the courts are considering the option of lifting the original order." Cristiano invited me to approach the casket.

Although I wasn't interested in viewing the man's dead body, his face might help me confirm a resemblance to Ivy, Rhett, or Uncle Zach. Could I trust Cristiano enough to tell him my theory about Ivy being Giovanni's birth mother? I'd ruled out the possibility of Kathy Endicott, but part of me wondered whether Cain had killed Giovanni upon finding out they were half-brothers. It made little sense, and I had no proof. When we reached the front of the room, he kneeled with Francesca and said a brief prayer.

After he finished, I did the same. I peeked inside the casket and snapped a mental picture of Giovanni's facial features. Nothing clicked right away. I then stood and stepped back.

Francesca squeezed Cristiano's hand. "He looks great. The mortician covered Giovanni's scar enough that you almost don't even see it."

I considered her statement. In the dull light, it was almost gone. "How did he get that scar? I heard it came from chasing a criminal, but I'm not sure if that's the truth."

Cristiano laughed as we shifted toward the side of the room near the flower arrangements. "Giovanni told that lie so often, even he believed it."

"Oh, did it happen another way?" I was curious to hear the explanation.

"Yes. That's actually part of the reason Giovanni went into the FBI and later switched to Immigrations and Customs Enforcement." Cristiano explained the story.

When he and Giovanni were young teenagers, a rival family other than the Castiglianos had kidnapped them and put out a hit on various members of the Vargas mafia. During the ordeal, Cristiano knew to be quiet, as his father had taught him to protect himself in such a situation. Giovanni, whose adoptive parents weren't as involved in the family business, failed to teach their son to remain quiet. Giovanni tried to convince the kidnappers to let them go, which inflamed the situation even further.

Giovanni used to have a birthmark on his neck in the shape of a four-leaf clover. He'd been proud of it, as no one else in the family had such a unique symbol. For years, he'd been referred to as the Lucky Boy. Only when he'd been kidnapped, he wasn't so lucky anymore. The man guarding the two boys became so agitated with Giovanni for his constant disruptions that he shut him up by holding a knife to his throat. "Giovanni struggled to get free. I couldn't do anything. Another man held me down. By the time they were done fighting, the kidnapper had sliced the birthmark off Giovanni's neck and left him with that scar."

"That's horrible. I can understand why he wouldn't want to tell anyone. Easier to say it happened in the line of duty, huh?"

Cristiano agreed. "Exactly. He refused to have plastic surgery to get it fixed. Instead, the scar served as his motivation to join law enforcement. It caused a lot of problems in *la familia*."

Francesca added, "But he promised to stay away from Vargas business. That's why he switched from working in the FBI to ICE. He wouldn't have to worry about arresting one of his relatives."

I hadn't realized how close Francesca had become with Cristiano. If she knew that much about his family, she must really love him. "I'm deeply sorry for your loss. I hardly knew Giovanni, and my encounters weren't always positive, but still... he sounds like a respectable man."

"Thank you, Kellan. If you'll excuse us," Cristiano said, pointing to a couple who had walked into the funeral parlor. "I see some friends of *la familia*."

As he and Francesca navigated across the room, I approached the main hallway to pour a cup of tea. Connor entered through the building's back door. "Glad I ran into you before anyone else. I have news to share from my dad."

"What's that?" I had my own to tell him about my suspicions that Ivy was Giovanni's mother.

"Pop remembered something potentially vital to our investigation of Queen Tessa's curse."

Connor briefly joked that he still struggled to believe in the entire concept, but he accepted it was a central theme and believed in his ancestor's history. "I'm not related to Queen Tessa, but if Renee is my aunt and is truly descended from her tribe, I have to lend it some credibility."

"I know exactly how you feel. Regardless of the validity of the curse, someone murdered my uncle and Giovanni to get a hold of the figurine and break the curse. To rationalize their fear of dying by fifty, I suppose." We needed to determine the person's identity.

"Apparently, the curse Queen Tessa placed on all Governor Yeardley's descendants came with another unique element. Not only would they die before turning fifty, but she wanted to brandish them as villains." Connor pulled me to the side and advised me to keep the information to myself. "If the reason for these murders is truly about finding the talisman to stop his or her own potential death, then this could be the break we need."

"What do you mean by brandishing?" I had a funny inclination about his upcoming revelation.

"Queen Tessa's curse includes a birthmark in the shape of a four-leaf clover on all the descendants. Then her descendants would always know whom to be wary of."

Processing Connor's bizarre news about the four-leaf clover birthmark knocked me for a loop. "Are you serious? It must've been the chief priestess's ironic way of tricking each heir into believing he or she would be lucky enough to escape the curse. In reality, they'd die horrific deaths before turning fifty."

"That's what my dad said. Pop remembered his mother talking about it on her deathbed." Connor confirmed what Gemma Hawkins had seen when the group of vandals attacked her home. A man with a four-leaf clover on his right cheek had stolen the talisman from her days after Ludovicus died in the shipwreck.

Connor's news began to gel. Anyone who stole the figurine from Queen Tessa's family was brutally murdered, at least as far as any documented evidence had implied. The only way to break the curse was to gain possession of the talisman and kill her last descendant. Anyone who'd gotten a hold of the talisman would've died horrible deaths as long as Renee was still alive. The man with the four-leaf clover birthmark who'd stolen the talisman from Gemma Hawkins must've died shortly afterward. And his descendants somehow kept the idol and continued to find ways to break the curse. At some point, the figurine had been lost until Uncle Zach found it in his elephant camp. Even if the curse was only imaginary, and everyone's tragic deaths in the past were coincidental, someone believed it was real and had gone to great lengths to find the figurine and kill Queen Tessa's last descendants.

"Giovanni had a birthmark on his neck underneath the scar. Cristiano just told me about his clover. I don't understand why he was killed then. If he was a descendant of Governor Yeardley, then the only person who would've killed him is Renee." But I mostly believed she was innocent.

Connor shook his head wildly. "We don't have the complete story, Kellan. You'll need to reconsider all the facts and determine who's working for whom here."

"Me?"

"I'm expecting April to formally pull me from the case tomorrow morning. She's processing everything overnight." Connor promised to update me when he had more information to share.

When we walked into the main viewing room, I pointed at Rhett Ballantine. "Should we start with him? He worked with Giovanni, so he must know something about the man's personal life."

"Let's get him to talk about his relationship with Ivy. Maybe we'll figure out whether he's aware of Ivy having a child after they graduated high school." Connor elbowed my side and instructed me to follow his lead.

By the time we reached the far side of the room, Rhett realized we were approaching him. "Good evening, gentlemen. I didn't expect to encounter the two of you at this service."

"Surely an FBI agent operates like a police detective in these circumstances. The killer often attends his or her victim's funeral. They can't help but want to hear what everyone's saying about them." Connor wisely pointed out something obvious to anyone in a similar field.

Rhett guffawed. "We're in no way identical. Cops ultimately want to be members of the FBI,

but most couldn't hack the agency's require-
ments." His sarcasm and arrogance would only
further irritate Connor, who'd no doubt try to
keep his cool.

When Connor breathed in deeply, his chest
puffed out. "Of course, you'd say that because
you're in the FBI. You spend most of your time
analyzing things, rarely exerting any physical
prowess to capture your suspect. I'd like to see
your behavior in a gang shoot-out or hostage situation."

"Let's not argue. I meant no disrespect. I recall
hearing you were fairly high up in the Philadelphia police department." Rhett conceded, suggesting he'd be honored to work side by side
with someone of Connor's caliber. "I'm speaking
mostly of those cops who hang around in their
cars, waiting for someone to speed through an
intersection or fail to yield properly."

"Gosh, sounds like a lot of things to consider,"
I said, interjecting my way into the conversation.
If I didn't bring the topic around to Giovanni,
we'd get nowhere before someone interrupted
us. "So, you must have been close with Giovanni,

I mean, to attend his funeral. You said earlier that you'd known him for years, right?"

Connor said, "Mr. Ballantine told me in our interview on Monday that he'd become acquainted with Giovanni approximately three years ago. I verified the records. You worked together in the FBI before he joined ICE."

"That's correct. We had an unofficial mentor program in our division. Giovanni had been working for a couple of years when he transferred into mine, and I was assigned to look out for him. Customary practice, nothing peculiar there." Rhett confirmed that he'd only lost one other team member in the line of duty in the past. "Paying my respects to a solid agent. That's all."

"Does that mean you weren't working with him on locating Queen Tessa's talisman? Was this not part of your current caseload with ICE?" I knew he'd told me previously that he couldn't discuss active investigations.

"If you must know... yes, I approved Giovanni's transfer to ICE. He was a strong field agent, but his passions were elsewhere. He wanted to explore international opportunities, and though my division handles them, we primarily focus on American citizens." Rhett noted that ICE allowed for Giovanni to travel more frequently, including spending time in South Africa to investigate theft and fraud.

Connor continued to apply pressure on Rhett. "In the spirit of open communication, help me understand what you think happened to Giovanni. You've had a couple of days to process his death."

"To be honest, I'm not sure. Giovanni had a troubled personal life. His family, leaders of the Vargas mafia, as you well know, have many enemies. In his quest to find this missing African talisman, he could've inadvertently stumbled upon the person who'd stolen it. That individual might have murdered him." Rhett suggested a few other avenues to explore, but none made any sense.

I looked at Connor for advice. He knew what I was thinking, and given his slightly perceptible nod, I proceeded with my question. "Do you have a deeper connection with Giovanni Vargas that you're trying to keep hidden?"

Chapter 23

Rhett opened his mouth to speak but couldn't find the words. He pulled us closer. "Where the hell do you get off asking me a question like that?"

"How about you just answer it?" asked Connor.

"I will not. One, it's none of your business. Two, have respect for a man who just died." He began to walk away, then thought better. "Whoever has the talisman killed Giovanni. I'm certain of it."

I decided to forego his nonresponse to my question so I could pursue a different angle. We could always come back to it. "There is a big problem with your theory about Giovanni figuring out who had Queen Tessa's talisman and being killed because of it. I actually had it at the time he died, and I know for a fact that I didn't kill him."

Rhett's gaze widened, either in alarm or anger. "You've found it? That's impossible. How could you be involved?" He stepped to the side to let someone approach the casket line.

If Rhett had stolen it from my office, he was intentionally trying to confuse me. "My uncle put the figurine in his luggage for safekeeping. Through a series of mishaps, it wound up on my doorstep two days ago. I brought it to the sheriff's attention and locked it somewhere safe."

"I'm baffled. You said you had it *at the time*. Do you not have it anymore?" Rhett asked with a cautious smile.

Connor jumped in. "The much sought-after object was stolen again. So, your theory that Giovanni was killed because he found the person who'd stolen it doesn't hold water."

"And the fact that Uncle Zach was in possession of it means his death wasn't accidental. Someone engineered that car explosion. Anything you'd like to share?"

Rhett paused to digest the news. With his head cocked, he stumbled to respond but finally found the words. "I'm really not sure how to help you. Your uncle was always in the middle of things he shouldn't be involved in. I'm sorry for his unfortunate death. Truly, I am. But you have more information about this entire fiasco than I do. The agency told Giovanni to drop the case, but he refused."

"Speaking of Zach Danby," added Connor, leading the conversation down a different path. He was dangerously skirting the line of pushing his luck, especially if he'd be taken off the case by morning. "We understand you two had a volatile relationship, beginning with him dating your ex-wife, Ivy Natcher, when you two split up during high school."

Rhett looked over my shoulder and nodded at Fern, his ex-sister-in-law who'd just arrived with Ursula in the lobby. "Ivy and Zach hardly dated. We were all friends, and when she and I split up, he took advantage of the situation. Ivy left town after ending things with both of us. It was a very tough period for her, but she knew he wasn't the right guy. That's why we ended up back together again."

He'd taken the bait. I needed to lure him in. "Did you and Ivy stay connected while she left the country? What was so difficult for her that year?"

"This line of questioning is going nowhere. Let me be clear," replied Rhett, indicating he needed to pay his respects and leave the funeral parlor. "Ivy and I found our way back to each other. We had a wonderful marriage for almost twenty years. I was a fool to let her go, but it happened. Why she and Zach maintained their friendship, I'll never know. As far as I'm aware, nothing serious ever happened between them."

Connor threw me for a loop with his next statement. "We've pulled Zach's banking records. You cut him a sizable check earlier this year. When the Orlando police deemed his death an accident, no one thought to delve into Zach's financial situation. Once we learned of his money concerns and considered his death a murder, we discovered your connection."

Rhett balked, but eventually acknowledged it looked worse than it was. "I hadn't spoken with Zach in years, nor heard much about him other than random bits and pieces from Ivy. Then Ivy mentioned Zach had come across some African artifacts and was trying to earn money to offset his debts and the future of elephant rescue programs. That's when I got Giovanni invited to

Zach's dinner party at his place in South Africa. I attended to help Giovanni with his search for Queen Tessa's talisman. We saw the object, then it disappeared. But I didn't buy the talisman that day."

If Rhett knew anything about Renee or her connection to Queen Tessa, he wasn't revealing it. Connor instructed him to hold on one more minute. "Wait, why did you transfer money to him if you didn't buy it?"

Rhett explained that Ivy had asked Rhett to contribute to saving the elephants. She'd donated, but Tobias wasn't interested in further helping Zach beyond their initial gift. "That should prove I had no ill feelings toward the man. At least now. What happened between us was in the past. I did what I could to help him out of his debt, but he must've double-crossed someone and that damned curse on the figurine killed him. As for Giovanni, I don't know what occurred, but I'm here to pay my respects to a colleague. We're officially done speaking." Rhett stomped away from us like an irate child.

When he was out of earshot, I said, "You should have asked him if he had a birthmark!"

Connor slapped his forehead. "Sure, and then he knows we're on to him. We have no clue if Rhett is guilty, but we can't surrender our upper hand. We planted the seed about the talisman showing up. Now we wait to see what happens."

"Good idea. I sometimes jump into my questions. It's the way *Dark Reality* works… learn as much as possible and report on all the angles to the show's viewers. I don't always think about jeopardizing an arrest or conviction down the line." Evidence could be tricky, depending on its obtained method. I apologized to Connor before he headed out.

We agreed to connect the following day once he had time to talk to April about his involvement in the case. Connor was planning to tactfully search for Renee, mostly because she was his aunt. He hadn't yet processed that a member of his family could be a killer. In the meantime, I collected Emma and Ulan, then caught up on their school days. April and I also had a brief phone call. She was back and forth with the airlines, FBI, and Orlando car rental company to accumulate more information.

* * *

The next morning, I brought Ulan and Emma to school and confirmed Francesca would pick up Emma for dinner. Ulan had a late swim practice and then planned to meet Augie and some friends. I had agreed to monitor the art exhibition until it closed at eight o'clock and wouldn't be able to see them until it ended. Afterward, I drove to campus and completed the rest of the lesson plans for my summer class and deliverables to Fern on Braxton's university conversion. Despite wanting to focus on finding Giovanni's and Uncle Zach's murderer, work had to be my priority. Surprisingly, Myriam hadn't shown up all morning. She must've been genuinely sick for her to take the day off.

April let me know that she'd come by around noon to go through everything we'd assembled on the case. I volunteered to pick up our lunch, then headed to North Campus. When I arrived, Fern endlessly paced her office.

"Your carpet treads will wear through if you keep that up. What's going on?" I shut the door and sat adjacent to her desk. "Take a load off.

Let's work this out together. Please don't tell me this pertains to the art exhibition. I can't take on any additional work."

Fern shook her head. "No, it's not. April released Cain this morning. He is attending to his mother today, but he'll be back tomorrow to handle his part. I'm upset about my sister."

"Ivy? What happened? Did she decide to leave Braxton with Tobias, anyway?" I was curious to find out what happened with Cain, but that would have to wait for April

"Not yet. Ivy is keeping a secret from me. I pushed her to explain something the other day, but she told me it was in the past and not to worry about it." Fern loved her sister very much, and they hardly got to spend much time together once she married Tobias and left the country. She would be distraught if Ivy suddenly departed again.

I didn't want to involve myself in their family business, but since it might have something to do with my uncle's death, I couldn't remain silent. "Is this related to Ivy saying something about two pregnancies yesterday?"

Fern nodded. "Yes, I thought you'd picked up on it. She only has one child. Jordan wanted a brother or sister, but it never happened. Unless it did and I never knew it."

"Can I be honest with you, Fern? I have something awkward to discuss." I debated whether I was crossing one of those lines Connor had spoken about earlier. Was Giovanni's potential biological parentage information the sheriff's department wanted kept under wraps?

"Of course. We've come a long way, Kellan. What's going on?" Fern grabbed a tissue and blew her nose loudly.

"I have reason to believe that Ivy could be Giovanni Vargas's birth mother. No evidence, but Giovanni was searching for his biological parents, and Ivy disappeared during that period. She was in Eastern Europe, which is where he was born."

Fern looked up and cocked her head. "But why would you assume she's his mother? That seems like a distant connection."

"Normally, I'd agree. But if she's acting suspicious, and she said she had two pregnancies, she could be his mother. They're both looking for this cursed talisman. Ivy met Giovanni at my uncle's dinner party, then she and Tobias could've followed him here to confirm the truth." I paused to let the news digest before mentioning the bond between Giovanni and Rhett. "I'm not sure whether Rhett or my uncle could be his father. Do you know if Ivy's relationship with Uncle Zach was intimate?"

Fern was at least six or seven years older than her sister, but she'd lived in Wharton County while Ivy was a high school senior. "Ivy was so angry back then. You know how sisters can get with each other. I told her to be careful getting involved with two friends, but she insisted things were over with Rhett when she and Zach began their fling."

"Can you recall anything about the timing?" I counted back nine months from Giovanni's birthdate, which April had previously provided to me. "Do you know whom she was dating that month?"

Fern shook her head. "I can't be sure, but based on her reactions this week, and Rhett's connection with Giovanni, I suppose it could be true. I know she slept with Zach. I caught them in her bed one morning during her senior year."

I decided not to tell Fern everything about the fifty-year-old curse, even though Rhett would turn a half-century that year. If he were Giovanni's father, why would he kill his own son? I was still lacking important evidence. I mentioned the four-leaf clover while comforting Fern, but a knock boomed at the door before I could reveal all the details.

"Come in," she said, raising her voice slightly.

The door opened, and Jordan stepped several feet into the room. He'd put on a few pounds since graduating from Braxton the previous year, likely due to no longer playing on the baseball team. "Hi, Aunt Fern. I'm sorry to bother you, but Dad was gonna meet me on campus this afternoon. Any chance you've seen him?"

Fern indicated she hadn't talked to Rhett earlier. "Why would he come to my office, honey?"

Jordan said, "I checked with my mom, and she thought he was planning to stop by today. He wanted to follow up on something about one of tonight's exhibits before he met me for lunch."

I fully turned my head around at that point. From where he was standing, Jordan couldn't have seen me. "Hello! It's been a long time. I'm glad we finally ran into each other."

Jordan walked over and shook my hand. His baby face hadn't changed much. We briefly exchanged a few words when he said, "I guess I should try his cell again. It keeps going to voicemail. Maybe a case got in the way. Always did in the past."

Fern shuffled toward him. After placing her hand on his shoulder, she kissed his cheek. "Your dad has always loved you. He just gets caught up in his job. I'm sure you'll find him before long."

"I don't know. He's been extra weird the last few days. Every time we meet, he's focused on that guy who died three days ago. Giovanni Vargas. You'd think he'd pay attention to his only son who's in town." Jordan's sullen words accompanied his sadness and sloped posture.

Picking up on the clue, I jumped right in. "Was he particularly close to Giovanni? I know they worked together in the past."

Jordan nodded. "Yep. They've known each other for years. Dad's canceled visits to me in

New Orleans several times because of Giovanni. It's always an important case or some mentor program responsibility. I don't even know why I care anymore."

Fern squeezed his neck. "Hey, kiddo. Don't say that. Your dad loves you. He'll come around. If not, I'll talk to him."

"I don't want to put you out, Aunt Fern. I just can't really discuss it with Mom. She's frustrated with Dad for ignoring her for years too. And now that she's with Tobias, they have their own life." Jordan attempted a smile but couldn't fully deliver one. "I'll be fine. Just want to know I make Dad as proud as he was of Giovanni. I can't help it if I don't want to join the FBI. I feel bad the guy died, but I'm Dad's son. Giovanni is just a guy he's been mentoring. Ya know?"

Fern sent Jordan to reception to contact his father again. If he couldn't, she would have lunch with him. I told Fern I'd do some digging about the potential of Rhett being Giovanni's father. "You work on Ivy, and I'll pressure Rhett. Fair?"

Fern agreed. "I'm wondering if you're right about Giovanni's birth parents. It would explain why Rhett has cozied up to him the last few years. Perhaps he's hiding their real relation-ship."

"I'll go one step further. If either of those two can trace their roots back to this ancient feud between Queen Tessa and Governor Yeardley, and Rhett believes this curse is real, for whatever reason, one of the two, or both, resorted to murder to protect themselves."

Chapter 24

After leaving Fern's office and purchasing lunch to go, I returned to Diamond Hall. April arrived at the same time, and we devoured our sandwiches, a BLT and a chipotle chicken double-decker. When we started sharing lunch several months ago, neither of us could decide which we wanted, so we'd been splitting both. It had become our weekly routine. My newest motto was *'Couples who eat together, stay together.'*

"So, Fern told me you released Cain earlier?"

"Yep. We have little proof he's responsible for the break-in at his own house. Our evidence in Giovanni's murder is circumstantial. Bitsy is his alibi for immediately before you found the body, and she's not budging about the amount of time they were together."

"Speaking of Bitsy... have you gotten anything out of her and Sawyer? Or on his car rental changes? Or whether he saw anyone near Diamond Hall the day Queen Tessa's talisman went missing?"

"Slow the roll! I spoke with them both at the sheriff's office this morning. Sawyer claims Renee and her bodyguard were plodding through the courtyard. He wanted to ask her about the talisman, but by the time he got down there, they'd disappeared." April confirmed that the campus video footage captured Renee idling in front of Glass Hall at the same time Sawyer and I were chatting in my office. It'd also recorded Sawyer wandering around the immediate vicinity, purportedly looking for her. "As for Orlando, he clammed up. Told me it wasn't any of my business what he was doing there."

"I told you he didn't like questions. Now what do we do? Court order?"

"No probable cause." April indicated she'd convinced the Jaccards to remain in town for twenty-four hours. "Now that their role in Braxton's art exhibition is finished, they intended to leave tomorrow afternoon. But I made it clear they were both persons of interest in a murder case. I suggested publicly announcing their names as connections to our investigation, if they didn't change their travel plans."

"What about the blood on the documents in the classroom where Giovanni was killed?"

"It definitely wasn't Cain's blood. Bitsy confirmed she'd sliced her finger on one, and she was waiting to hear from her lawyer whether she should submit a blood sample. I've no doubt it's hers, especially since it wasn't a match to Cain's or Giovanni's."

"True. Confirmation would be better. What about the fresh spot on her purse? Couldn't you get a warrant to collect it from her?"

April grunted. "I tried, but Bitsy claims Sawyer donated it to some charity that had visited their B&B. He can't remember the name of the place. Given they're staying at the Roarke and Daughters Inn, I was going to follow up later to see if the Roarkes knew the name of the organization who took the purse. Bitsy couldn't recollect much either."

Maggie's family ran the B&B. If a charity had requested handouts, they'd know for certain. "I can call Maggie to ask for the name, if you'd like?"

April instructed me to stand down. "I'll talk with her and Connor this afternoon. But thanks."

"Does that mean you aren't kicking Connor off the case?"

She shook her head. "I had to. If he's related to a suspect, I can't risk anything with our investigation. He was removed officially two hours ago. I hope I made the right decision."

"Okay, so where does that leave us?"

"I've got some reports to review. You should go home and take a break."

Even though April told me not to pursue the organization's name, I had to find out for myself. Within fifteen minutes of her leaving, I pulled up at the Roarke and Daughters Inn. I'd ask some basic questions and convince Ben and Lucy Roarke not to disclose that I'd been there.

Flowering vines crept around the perimeters of the building's elaborate windows, contrasting the beige brick and iron-colored mortar. Roarke and Daughters Inn had once been the home of a former mayor who'd died at the end of the nineteenth century. Eventually, the three-story Victorian home was willed to one of Maggie's ancestors, and several decades ago it had become her family's home. When I entered the front hall, Maggie surprisingly stood behind the counter.

"Since when do you work here? I thought you were the only Roarke sister not to run this place?"

"Connor is on his way over. Now that he's been taken off the case, he scheduled a couple of vacation days to help my dad with overdue repairs. After he gets back from the doctor's office."

Ben Roarke had been involved in a massive car accident the previous year, and ever since then, the Roarkes were adamant about regular visits to Dr. Betscha to monitor some side effects. Dr. Betscha, Nana D's distant cousin, cared for most of Braxton's families and consulted on cases with the sheriff's office.

"So, why are you toiling away at the front desk?"

"I've been assisting this week while two of my sisters are on a girls' trip. What's going on?"

I explained what I'd heard about Sawyer and Bitsy Jaccard donating her purse to a charity organization several days ago. "I was hoping you might know its name. Not sure if we could still get the purse back, but it might be evidence in a crime."

Maggie said, "Connor just told me about that a little while ago. April called and asked him what he remembered from his interviews. But unfortunately, Bitsy's statement wasn't exactly true."

"What does that mean?"

"I was here the morning Bitsy and Sawyer talked to the people from the charity." Maggie explained that the Jaccards were jittery and snapping at each other all throughout breakfast. Finally, Bitsy told Sawyer that she didn't want to donate her purse, that it was in awful shape and she'd send them a check in the future. "Finally, he backed down and went to his room to shower."

"Why would they lie to the police?" I failed to understand their motivation. If Bitsy had gotten Giovanni's blood on her purse, she would've destroyed it or given it away as quickly as possible.

"Connor thinks Bitsy was paranoid it would resurface, so she tossed it in the trash outside." Maggie excused herself for a minute and stepped into the back office.

"If the purse was already thrown away, we've lost our evidence," I shouted loud enough for her to hear me.

When Maggie returned, a peculiar smile commandeered her face, and she carried an item
wrapped in plastic. "But my mother thought
she could salvage the thing. It was an expensive
piece."

"You kept it?" Thrilled at the news, I per-
formed an embarrassing happy dance.

"My mother intended to tell Bitsy she could
fix it, but my father insisted she keep quiet. If
Bitsy didn't care about its value, then she didn't
need to worry about what happened to it." Ben,
Maggie's father, wanted his wife to clean and sell
it, then donate the money to a homeless shelter.

"Did she?" Tracing Giovanni's blood would
be difficult if she'd wiped it off. Still possible,
though.

"Nope. We got extraordinarily busy the last
two days, so it sat on a closet shelf." Maggie verified she'd packaged it up an hour ago and was
waiting for April to send someone to collect it
for analysis.

I thanked Maggie for the update and extracted
her promise not to tell April, Connor, or anyone
else from the sheriff's department that I'd shown

up. "She'll kill me if I don't mind my own business."

"Oh, Kellan. She won't kill you. April has fallen for you hard. We can all see it." She paused long enough for the news to settle in, then sighed. "I'm glad things worked out for us. I have Connor. You're with April. Now, don't screw it up. Start listening to her more often."

"I'm doing my best. Thank you." After reminding Maggie to keep mum about my visit, I left the Roarke and Daughters Inn. No need to discuss my relationship with an ex!

If the blood on Bitsy's purse proved to be Giovanni's, then she had to be involved in the scheme to obtain Queen Tessa's talisman and eradicate all the descendants of Governor Yeardley. Could Renee have hired Bitsy and Sawyer to kill Giovanni? Was Bitsy responsible for the car switch in Orlando? Sawyer could've inadvertently led his wife to the talisman, Uncle Zach, and Giovanni. Given Bitsy's affair with Cain, Sawyer had the potential to be the next party eliminated. I wasn't sure who was playing whom, but something was clearly off between Bitsy, Sawyer, and Cain.

What I also couldn't comprehend was how Giovanni's birth parents fit into the puzzle. Figuring out their identity was crucial. Two warring factions were fighting one another, and my uncle had landed in the middle. His death needed to be avenged properly. His murderer should be held accountable. Renee was at the center of the situation. I needed to understand who descended from Queen Tessa and who descended from Governor Yeardley before the curse impacted our soon-to-be fifty-year-old.

I considered all the ways to check who had a four-leaf clover birthmark. It would require additional digging, but soon we'd obtain our answers. When a car pulled into the parking lot, I knew exactly who could help me. I scurried down the front walkway and waited for Tobias and Ivy to ascend the lower steps. "Good afternoon. I thought you looked familiar. Hard to know for sure from a distance."

Tobias walked side-by-side with his wife through the gravel parking area and let her scoot up the narrower incline of the pathway. Ivy carried a light sweater in her arms and smelled of a floral perfume. She commented on the beautiful landscaping throughout the front lawns of the Roarke and Daughters Inn. When Tobias approached, I pulled my right hand from my pocket and reached it toward him.

He greeted me amiably with a confident voice. "To what do we owe this pleasure?"

"I've known the owners for years. They saved something for me, and I finally got around to picking it up. Was just about to leave when you pulled into the driveway." I technically hadn't lied, but they needn't know about my hefty concerns with the Jaccards.

"It's an idyllic bed-and-breakfast," remarked Ivy, scanning the vast splendor of the two-centuries-old Victorian home. "Maybe we should buy one and fix it up, Tobias." She barely looked at her husband as she spoke the words.

When I noticed a ReedWell logo on an envelope sticking out of the pocket in Tobias's briefcase, I remembered that he'd met with Hampton the previous evening. I pointed at the paperwork and cautiously smiled. "Should I assume you've purchased a new business for your portfolio?"

A heartfelt look of pride engulfed his face. "We just came from the lawyer's office. I've brokered a deal with your brother and his wife. It'll take several weeks to execute contracts and file all the proper paperwork, but by midsummer, we will finalize the sale." He tenderly squeezed the back of Ivy's arm and tugged her closer.

"We're extremely excited, Kellan. This is our first foray into the industry. Thankfully, your brother's wife offered to spend six months consulting while we build the new management team." Ivy shifted her weight to balance Tobias's increasingly steady grip.

"Wonderful. I'm glad it's all worked out. Hampton and Natasha need a break from everything going on this year. I assume you've heard about her accident?" Although Natasha had said she'd known Tobias since her childhood, they might've only maintained a distant relationship.

"Such an awful misfortune. To lose a loved one, then almost fall off a cliff. I gather the assailant's trial is coming up this summer." Tobias glanced at his car, then back at his watch.

I nodded. "August, I believe. We're hoping it's a quick one. The evidence is quite strong."

Ivy said, "I can't imagine what it's like to know someone your entire life, only to have them turn out to be a killer." She pressed a hand against her chest and exhaled. "Have you heard anything about the recent murder on campus?"

"Not much yet."

"I understand from Fern that you've been instrumental in solving many homicides around here," noted Tobias as he steered us toward the front of the house.

"I tend to bump into them, to be honest. I suppose I have bad luck with these sorts of things." When we reached the porch, I asked if Tobias was still leaving the following day.

"Yes, my flight departs at noon. To return to South Africa for a business engagement this weekend, one has to leave at least thirty-six hours in advance from the east coast of the US."

Ivy added, "Of course, the flight isn't that long, but depending on where you stop, it adds delays. Plus, our favorite hotel is almost an hour from the airport." She turned to her husband. "Do you need help packing?"

Tobias shook his head. "No, I should be able to take care of it now. Then I'll head back out to meet with the lawyer to review the ReedWell paperwork. I'll message you when I'm on the way to the restaurant."

I was glad Tobias would depart soon, as it allowed me the time to ask Ivy about her relationship with my uncle. "Take care of yourself, Mr. Natcher. And please enjoy your last evening and the flight home. I hope you weren't too disappointed in Braxton's art exhibition this week."

Tobias laughed. "Not at all. I've only been here once or twice in the past when I accompanied Ivy on a trip to visit her sister and my stepson. I wish we could slow down someday soon, but alas, that doesn't seem to be in the cards."

I suddenly thought of something else important to ask. "Is Sheriff Montague aware you're leaving town? She prefers folks stick around until an investigation is closed."

Tobias indicated he planned to stop at the sheriff's office to sign his witness statement the following morning. "She'd like me to confirm everything I saw during Monday's incident. Nonetheless, she'll be able to reach me once I'm back home. I look forward to seeing Renee Hawkins and Rhett Ballantine get their comeuppance." Tobias turned to his wife apologetically, pleading for her compassion. "I know you hate when I trash your ex-husband, but he's mixed up in this seedy business."

Once Tobias entered the inn, I promptly addressed Ivy. "Do you think Rhett is responsible? He hasn't been incredibly open about his involvement here."

Ivy suggested we take a seat on the wicker sofas near the large bow window. "Rhett is a complex man. You must understand something, Kellan. He wields a tremendous amount of responsibility in the FBI. Men like Rhett can't afford to be friendly or let down their guard."

Ivy had a point. If Rhett were completely innocent of both murders, I'd face the truth—he was a stand-up guy who tracked down criminals and protected our country. "I understand. Would you mind if I ask a rather personal question, Mrs. Natcher?"

"If you're going to do that, Kellan, please call me Ivy." She relaxed into the sofa across from me and draped her sweater on its arm. "Fern speaks highly of you, and you've been a wonderful support to my son. Jordan respects you very much."

"I'm glad to hear it. I adore Fern, and Jordan is coming into his own." I considered the best approach to asking whether she'd given up a child for adoption after graduating from high school. "If I understand correctly, you and my uncle were particularly close over the years. Was this a platonic friendship, or had it… I mean… were you two… there isn't a straightforward way to bring up this topic." I dipped my head in shame, hoping she'd grasped the gist of my inquiry.

Ivy's cheeks reddened. "Well, I mentioned the other day that Zach and I were more than friends. If you're asking whether we were lovers, the answer is yes. But I don't understand the importance."

"I'll be as honest as I can. I'm fairly certain you aren't responsible for the murders of Giovanni Vargas and my uncle, but inexplicable coincidences have occurred this week. I feel compelled to dig deeper and hopefully exonerate a handful of potential suspects." I explained that Giovanni had been searching for his biological parents before he was killed on campus that week. After estimating his birthdate and suggesting that Rhett had bestowed a fatherly influence on the younger man, Ivy comprehended my roundabout method of asking whether she was his mother.

"Oh, Kellan. I'm not surprised you took such a leap. The year after high school was difficult for me." Ivy clarified everything she'd gone through during her late teens. After she and Rhett had broken up, Ivy and Uncle Zach dated. She was in love with both men for varied reasons. "I had poor judgment and foolishly slept with your uncle on our third date. It might've been revenge because Rhett had fooled around with another girl. Hard to say." Ivy had become pregnant in her senior year and carefully hid the first three months of the pregnancy.

"Were you able to identify the father?"

Ivy shook her head. "Truthfully, it isn't important anymore. The day after graduation, I left for Europe. I couldn't tell anyone, especially my parents, that I was going to have a baby. I flew to Greece and soaked up the sun on their beaches for a couple of weeks. Then I took a train to Poland to see the sights. In my fifth month, I miscarried."

I hadn't expected Ivy to reveal that unfortunate shocker. "I'm so sorry. I guess that illuminates why you said two pregnancies the other day."

Ivy patted my knee twice. "You're an intelligent man, Kellan. Jordan is my only child, and I must admit, I don't have a clue about Giovanni's biological family. Until you just told me he was adopted and searching for his birth parents, I knew nothing."

Ivy summarized more about her life before Tobias. When she and Rhett met at a homecoming game one fall, they rekindled their romance. She'd decided not to tell him about the baby, as she couldn't be sure whether it had been his or Uncle Zach's. Knowing Rhett disliked my uncle, she chose not to exacerbate the situation. Years later, Rhett grew obsessed with his career in the FBI. In her early forties, Ivy thought she was pregnant again.

"How did he take the news?"

"I wasn't pregnant. Early menopause. But I confessed the truth about the high school pregnancy. That's what ended our marriage. He felt he couldn't trust me, and I was tired of being the other woman to the FBI."

"So, you divorced and traveled around the world." I began to assemble the full picture of her life story. I couldn't fathom any links to the murders, but her input worried me that Rhett could be unstable or untrustworthy.

"Tobias and I met in Egypt on a pyramid tour. We grew fond of one another, so I sold my house and moved in with him in London. Our marriage has been marvelous, but after three years, I miss my son and sister. Some days, I worry whether I can keep up with all this travel." Ivy laughed and shared a couple of stories about her plastic surgery experiences and meeting people from all over the world.

"Do you think Rhett could've gone after Uncle Zach? Or is there any reason to believe he snapped and killed Giovanni?" I needed to rule him out as a suspect, and then I could focus on the Jaccards. If not them, I was back to the drawing board or assuming Renee had fooled us all.

Ivy considered my suggestion. "I know Rhett better than anyone. I'm ninety percent certain he's innocent. But he's had a couple of meltdowns in the past after complex FBI operations. I can't promise you something crazy didn't happen."

Ivy had no additional insight into the Jaccards, Renee, the talisman, or the strange events at Uncle Zach's dinner party. It was time to leave the Roarke and Daughters Inn and connect with April. Ivy had to return several calls and to meet her husband that evening. But first, I needed to finish an errand at my office.

On the drive back to Diamond Hall, Nana D checked in to determine whether I'd learned anything new about Uncle Zach's death. I provided her a mini update on the pros and cons of all my suspects, but she couldn't make heads or tails of the dilemma.

"Pish! I'm confident you'll flush the creeper soon enough. As for putting Lindsey or Kathy Endicott on your list, I highly doubt either has the guts to kill someone. Cain, on the other hand, has a wild side. I've seen and heard things over the years, and he's built shady connections." Nana D indicated that her gossip had come from Eustacia Paddington the previous year, when both women were indignant with Lindsey for two-timing them. "Cain likes the ladies. I heard he got one or two *in trouble*, if you get my drift. Lindsey has had to pay off some of his son's gambling debts too. Might not be related, but it speaks to his character."

I hadn't heard those stories about him. Then again, Lindsey had several wives and children. As far as I knew, he always did the proper thing by them. "I'll give it a thought. Right now, my money is on the Jaccards, Renee, or Tobias. He's a dark horse but still in the race. I can't decide who has more to gain."

"You'll sort it out like a miser with his money. Anyway, I was supposed to visit Kathy and Cain for dinner tonight, but she canceled. Something else came up. Keep me posted, brilliant one. And do me a favor, will you?" she added as I reached the parking lot and began ambling toward my office.

"Sure, what's that?"

"Bartleby Grosvalet called earlier. He requested additional support for Constance this morning. She refused to leave the lighthouse, and they don't think she's gonna make it through the weekend. You should visit her." Nana

D reminded me that the woman had been a good friend to us in the previous six months and that we owed her a proper goodbye.

"As soon as I can, I'll drop by. Thank you for the heads up. I love you."

While we hung up, I opened the office door and collapsed into my chair. It'd been a long day, and I needed an evening to analyze all the clues I'd gathered to date. Somewhere among them was a double killer, and if I focused properly, I could pinpoint his or her identity.

As I lifted my head from the desk, Myriam wandered into my office. She carried two cardboard boxes and suspiciously shut the door. Her face had turned a ghastly shade of white, and she struggled with breathing.

"Are you okay?"

"Yes," she squeezed out while taking a seat opposite me. "I need to discuss something important. I require your utmost confidentiality and a personal guarantee that you will not jump to conclusions like you usually do."

If she was trying to flatter me, it wasn't working. She had frightened me a little, though. "Of course. Is this related to Braxton or the recent murder or—"

"It's about Queen Tessa's talisman. I know to whom it belongs." Myriam lifted the cover off the box and pointed to several similar African figurines.

"Okay, I'll bite. You've piqued my curiosity." Like a morbid freakazoid!

"I found them in my attic. They belong to my father, Luther Castle. But in another box, I also discovered some paperwork from his immigration to this country in 1968." Myriam handed me the document from a folder she'd been lugging around. "Look at the signature and tell me what you see."

I scanned the document and zeroed in on her reference. I'd never felt such a terrifying chill in my life. "Your father is Ludovicus Casseldricken? As in the man who was supposed to have died in a shipwreck off the coast of South Africa?"

Chapter 25

"I may neither choose who I would, nor refuse who I dislike; so is the will of a living daughter curbed by the will of a dead father" Myriam leaned forward and rested her head on my desk, hiding any ability for me to read her expressions. "I won't challenge you to guess where it comes from. *Merchant of Vernice.* I always admired Portia. Not so much what her father forced her to do."

The shock of her potential relationship to Ludovicus Casseldricken continued to ricochet inside my body, the similarities between the two names suddenly becoming more obvious than when she'd first uttered the words. He'd faked his death to escape the volatile apartheid era and fled to the US. I had to ask for more details about Luther Castle's recent situation.

"I'm not sure what to say. Are you comfortable sharing more with me?" For the first time, a surge of pity for my boss soared.

Myriam mumbled something incoherent, then lifted her head. "I haven't yet confessed the truth to Ursula. But I will this evening. I'm sure you've guessed by now that I wasn't ill the last twenty-four hours. I've been rummaging through my father's boxes, piecing together some of his past."

"Look, we're not friends. Some days, I think if we broke down the walls, we could become something more than rivals. I can be a good listener. Why don't you try me, Myriam?" I turned my phone on silent and set it to the side. "No interruptions either."

Myriam hesitantly nodded and settled into an uncomfortable wooden chair. "My mother died when I was a toddler, and ever since then, my father and I have always been close. I'll tell you more about him."

Myriam's father was an only child and of German descent. He'd told her little about his parents, except that when they'd died and left him enormous wealth in the late 1960s, he moved to the US. Myriam never knew her father had changed his name during that process. Among some of his childhood memorabilia, Myriam had found his immigration paperwork and tons of newspaper clippings. Ludovicus Casseldricken had been shortened to Luther Castle, and he'd left behind a dying wife and lover to escape the destruction of their village. Ludovicus settled in Pennsylvania, began a new life, and married Myriam's mother.

Her parents were adventurous travelers who'd sailed all over the globe. Myriam had been educated in the finest institutions and visited many of the world's wonders. Ludovicus, then known as Luther, was an affluent man, and on an extravagant trip to Japan, they'd eaten at a restaurant hailed for preparing rare cuisines. Myriam's mother ordered fugu, a pufferfish known to cause a violent death worse than cyanide poisoning, if it wasn't properly prepared. In the restaurant, Myriam watched her mother suffer that fate, forever changing their family dynamics.

"It devastated my father. I remember him lamenting a family curse, but he'd share no details. I'd almost forgotten about it until this crazy drama with Queen Tessa's talisman arrived on campus." Myriam gathered several smaller figurines from the box and ran her fingers over their faces.

"Were these your father's dolls?" I knew in that moment why Myriam had developed such a tough, cold exterior.

"Yes, they were family heirlooms, but I was never allowed to play with them." Myriam continued to share her story.

Luther and Myriam spent every day together, and during that time, they studied Shakespeare and international cultures. Luther had inspired Myriam's penchant for quoting *The Bard* in all her conversations. When they'd researched Africa, Myriam's father's eyes always glistened. She'd never understood he was longing for a past he'd left behind. After graduating from college and becoming a professor, Myriam decided to tell her father she had fallen in love with Ursula. Her father had been agitated for weeks, constantly collecting newspaper articles from all over the world. The New York City World Trade Towers had just fallen that month, and she couldn't hide the truth any longer; life was precious, and love meant taking risks.

"When I introduced him to Ursula, a strange expression overtook his face, and within minutes, he suffered a stroke." Myriam paced the room after handing me some newspaper articles. "I'd always assumed my news had horrified him." Luther had been admitted to the hospital that night, and for the previous seventeen years, he'd been a patient at the Willow Trees nursing home.

"But now you suppose differently?" I scanned a few articles and saw that one of them rejoiced about Queen Tessa's talisman being found in Africa. Days later, the woman was mauled in an elephant stampede. The victim's name was unfamiliar and connected with none I'd come across.

"I think my father had a delayed reaction to the news article he'd read that day, not my words. His past had come back to haunt him." Myriam clarified that he'd never spoken again, and since his stroke, she'd visited him every Saturday morning in the nursing home, hoping he'd wake up. "He'll turn eighty soon, but a quarter of his life has been wasted in this unresponsive state."

I began to wonder whether Luther Castle was involved in the deaths of Giovanni Vargas and my uncle. "Are you certain he's been catatonic these last few months?"

Myriam quavered. "As far as the nurses tell me, there's been no change. He moves around silently, but rarely. He can't be responsible for what's happened on campus. At least, I'm hoping he hasn't been alert. I've been visiting him a lot this week, even told him that I'd discovered his secret and the talisman was somewhere in Braxton. Maybe he'll speak soon, and we'll know more."

I worried her revelations could also send him in the reverse direction. "Do you realize that if this is true, you have a half-sister named Renee Hawkins." I explained that Renee was Ludovicus's child with Gemma Hawkins, including what I learned about her.

Myriam clasped her chest. "I have a sister. I've always wanted to have a sibling."

I believed Myriam's story, assured she had nothing to do with any of the murders. She was not a woman who lied or killed others. But her revelation had made me view the fiasco in an entirely different light. If Ludovicus had two daughters, the descendants of Governor Yeardley would have a harder time breaking the curse. I believed Giovanni had been killed because of his connection to Yeardley too. There might be other reasons, and I'd continue looking into those options, but for now, something inside me insisted I follow this path. I immediately needed to determine the identity of Giovanni's biological parents. If anyone called dibs on killing Myriam Castle, it was me!

Myriam's phone buzzed. When she picked it up, I checked mine as well. Bitsy and Sawyer had called and left a message that they were on their way to visit me. What could they want?

I had no opportunity to respond as Myriam hung up her phone and gathered all the items from her father's boxes. "I need to get to Willow Trees. Can I leave these with you for now? Please, don't tell anyone what I've revealed."

"Sure, of course. Is your father okay?" I tossed the newspaper articles into the box and sealed it with the lid. I would read through them after she left. I could learn something important from many of the strange deaths Luther had tracked.

"No. He's missing. The nurse went to check on him and he wasn't in his room." Myriam promised to update me and rushed out of the building.

Had one of Governor Yeardley's descendants discovered Ludovicus was alive and living in Braxton as Luther Castle? What was happening in the war between the two sides? I called April to deliver the news, but she was behind locked doors and couldn't pick up the call. I left a message with another officer to have her contact me as soon as possible. He casually confirmed she'd picked up the purse from Maggie's family's B&B. When I read through Myriam's newspaper articles, I found little to help me decide any next steps. Four people had been killed in the twentieth century from bizarre deaths, but none of them had familiar surnames or relatives mentioned in their obituaries.

I headed to the courtyard to walk off the stress. While I crossed the bridge over the pond, Francesca verified that she'd picked Emma up from school and would drop her off at my mother's place after dinner. Emma wanted to play with her cousins, Hampton's children, and given the insanity closing in on me, it was for the best if she didn't come home that night. As Francesca and I disconnected, Bitsy and Sawyer approached the pond.

"I got your message. What's up?"

Bitsy said, "Sawyer and I have been reconnecting, and we've decided to leave Braxton tomorrow morning. We're on our way back to the bed-and-breakfast now." She fondled her husband's hand and rested her head on his shoulder.

Sawyer thrust a small box at me. "Just a token of our esteem for helping us get back on track. Maybe you ain't the meanest, toughest hombre to cross the Rio Grande, and you might be a little namby-pamby, but doggone it, you fixed our marriage."

What on earth was he talking about? "Come again?" I needed to prevent them from leaving until April finished testing the substance on Bitsy's purse. Was that why she hadn't picked up my call?

"It's like this, Kellan. Sawyer and I have been fighting lately because we thought we'd fallen out of love. But we hadn't. Just got ourselves too sidetracked." Bitsy clarified that he'd hired a private detective to follow her, and it had annoyed her to no end. When they finally discussed the source of their troubles that afternoon, she realized he was afraid to lose her.

"Bitsy dumped that varmint. Cain Endicott was a reckless distraction, so we're heading to Australia on a long second honeymoon." Sawyer dropped his wife's hand and hauled me in for an enormous bear hug. "Your kindness opened her eyes. You take care of yourself now."

Bitsy said, "Well, first we have to stop in Orlando to meet with the architect."

"Whoa, hold up! I can't let you leave without explaining a few things first." Bitsy had opened the door for me to find out what happened with the car Sawyer had rented. "I heard you were there a couple of months ago. Something about renting a car?" I worried I would get myself into trouble, but I couldn't let it go.

"What about it?" Sawyer narrowed his gaze. "I thought I told you I don't like questions, boy."

"I'm gonna level with you. My uncle's car exploded in Orlando. He was supposed to get the specific car that you never returned. Is there a connection between the two incidents?" I stepped back and waited for him to reply or shoot me with a hidden pistol.

"Seeing as how you've been a big help to us, I'll put your mind at ease." Sawyer explained that he'd bought land outside Orlando to build a second home for him and Bitsy. Since it was a last-minute decision, he kept the rental car longer so he could coordinate with the architects and bank to close the deal that week. "I can't help you much with your uncle's death. Bitsy and I thought he was a fine fella, and we're sorry for what happened to him."

Bitsy ran a couple of fingers through her curls. "Renee Hawkins and Rhett Ballantine are the two with the most connections to Zach and Giovanni. I suggest you focus on them. Never understood why they were so persistent about finding Queen Tessa's talisman."

"We really wanted to get our hands on that cursed idol, but it's not gonna happen. That thing disappears more often than I care to remember." Sawyer tipped his Stetson cowboy hat in my direction and slogged away.

"Bitsy, before you go... do you have a minute to talk about Ursula?" I waffled on whether to tell her about the purse April had collected from the Roarke and Daughters Inn. In the end, she should know they were still under suspicion, especially if they left the country early.

Sawyer volunteered to start their car. "Take care of yourself, Kellan. I'll be in the parking lot, Bitsy."

Once he exited, she said, "What about her? We're supposed to see Ursula and Myriam for dinner tonight."

"You might want to change those plans. Myriam's father is missing, and they will be at the nursing home for a while." I paused, then said, "Plus, Sheriff Montague wants to talk about your purse with the stain. The one you never really donated to charity?"

"Oh, you know about that, huh?" Bitsy folded her arms together and gritted her teeth. "It's not what you think."

"Tell me the truth, so I can figure out what really happened to Giovanni Vargas." I revealed how I'd come across Bitsy's purse and that the sheriff's office collected it from the trash.

Bitsy led me to a nearby bench. After we sat, she said, "Yes, Cain and I were in Glass Hall's basement classroom when I cut myself. Cain took me to his office in the other hallway and bandaged my finger, but then he heard a noise in the hallway." While Cain left, Bitsy waited around. She confirmed that Sawyer had called and asked where she was, but she hadn't directly gone upstairs.

"You went to see Cain in the classroom, but instead you found Giovanni, didn't you?" I knew she'd been lying about the stain that morning at The Big Beanery, but I couldn't prove it previously.

"I did. Cain was gone for at least thirty minutes, and I worried something had happened to him. So, I sneaked through the hallway and searched for him in a few of the rooms." When she'd gone into the classroom with all the non-displayed art, she saw the closet light. "I poked my head in and noticed Giovanni on the floor. The spear was sticking out of his stomach and the blood was everywhere. I must've bent down and gotten my purse too close."

"Are you saying you didn't kill him?"

"No, I swear it wasn't me." A trail of mascara tears traced Bitsy's cheeks. "I was afraid Cain had done it."

"Why didn't you call the police right away?" Was she so enamored by Cain that she'd overlook him being a killer?

"I assumed the police would discover Cain and I had been fooling around, and because I'd met Giovanni in South Africa at your uncle's dinner party, they'd think I was involved in his death."

"So, you what, just ran out of the room and back up to the lobby?" I tried remembering the timing of all the events, but it wasn't fully clear.

"Yes. I couldn't risk anyone seeing me, so I rushed up the other stairwell and slipped out the front entrance when no one was paying attention. Sawyer knew I was supposed to meet you any minute. He wasn't worried about me." Bitsy had decided to clean herself up in The Big Beanery's restroom rather than be caught at Glass Hall.

"Do you still think Cain is responsible?" I finally understood her timing and the brash response to my pointing out the blood on her purse.

Bitsy shook her head. "I can't imagine why he'd kill Giovanni. They'd only spoken on the phone about Queen Tessa's talisman a few times. Giovanni thought Cain was hiding a partnership with Zach."

"What about the break-in at Cain's place? I'd like to understand what you know about that."

Bitsy said, "Nothing. He was working on campus that day. I texted him while Myriam was freshening up in the restaurant's bathroom. We met in the courtyard, and after you caught us, he rushed home to get his briefcase. That's all. I really need to go now."

"I suggest you make a stop at the sheriff's office to clear this all up. If you don't, it'll look like you're hiding something, and you might find yourself in hotter water." I verified Bitsy knew nothing else, nor had she any secret children or clue about the four-leaf clover birthmark.

"Sawyer doesn't have one either. And I've seen every inch of his body, Kellan." She smirked and leaned in to hug me as we rose from the bench.

"I don't need to know that. But I guess we're done here. I sincerely hope you're not lying. You won't get away with two murders, especially not when one of them was my uncle."

"I promise. If I think of anything else, I'll let you know." Bitsy agreed to call April before she and Sawyer left town.

As the sun set behind her, I laughed at the absurdity Bitsy and Sawyer had brought to my life that week. I had only a few seconds to bask in it before my phone vibrated with a text message.

Ulan: *I'm gonna crash at Augie's tonight. We're having a video game competition. April said it's okay. Already have my backpack, and they'll lend me some clothes. Cool?*
Me: *Sure, just be safe. Don't leave the house and don't open the door to strangers.*

I expected a humorous response but received none. Teenagers got distracted easily. When April returned my call, I'd confirm she was fine with him staying over for the night. I briefly considered whether she'd want to sleep at my place since Emma was crashing at the Royal Chic-Shack, but I didn't think it was safe to leave the boys on their own overnight. I trusted them completely, yet with everything that had transpired, being cautious was more important than a night alone with April. We'd make up for it as soon as I solved the mystery.

When I pulled up in front of my house, I noticed a strange car parked across the street. With only a few other houses on my block, I knew everyone's vehicles. Two of the neighbors were away, so it made me a little suspicious. Someone sat in the driver's seat, but I didn't recognize him. Then I realized it was the same car that had been following me. I cautiously approached my front door, wondering whether I should call the police. I leaned forward to insert my key in the lock, but it was already open. I turned the knob and pushed open the door.

When I entered my living room, Renee lounged on the sofa in front of the fireplace. "Don't be afraid, Kellan. We need to talk. I've got important news to share."

"You've got a nasty habit of breaking into my home and office. This has got to stop." With one hand in my pocket, ready to dial 9-1-1, I scouted around for the nearest blunt or sharp object.

"I wouldn't do that if I were you," demanded a voice behind me. "How about you take a seat and hear us out first?"

Chapter 26

Renee's bodyguard lurked nearby while I sat on the couch. He glanced at his boss and cocked his head sideways. "I'll wait in the other room. Mind if I grab a glass of water, Mr. Ayrwick?"

Puzzled, I let out an obnoxious laugh. "Since you've already broken in and threatened me, why bother asking? Just take what you want. Then you can add theft to the growing list of crimes."

Renee removed her sunglasses and pinched the bridge of her nose. Both of her eyes were swollen and red-rimmed. "I assure you, neither he nor I killed your uncle and Giovanni."

"If that's so, why are you hiding in my house?" I leaned back and crossed my legs, relaxing enough to presume I wasn't next on their hit list.

"To tell you the whole truth this time, at least now that I've sorted most of it out." Renee stood and unfolded her walking stick. She slowly shuffled across the room, tapping against some of my furniture, and perched on the couch next to me.

"I had dreams of becoming your aunt one day. I think we can drop the pretenses and false apprehension."

Renee's bodyguard returned to the living room and studied us from the corner.

"Okay. I'm listening." I considered my safest approach to escaping the hostage situation, but nothing immediately became evident.

"Giovanni Vargas was my son. You'll undoubtedly have many questions." Renee positioned her cane to the side and rested a hand on my knee. "I could never have killed my own child."

If Giovanni were Renee's son, then he descended from Queen Tessa. But his four-leaf clover birthmark meant he also descended from Governor Yeardley. "You can't be serious. A dual heir never even crossed my list of theories."

"Let me explain what happened many years ago." Renee shared the story of her childhood.

After Renee escaped South Africa to attend college in the US, she rebelled against her mother's strict upbringing. Gemma Hawkins had been a staunch, religious woman who always feared someone would find out that Renee was Ludovicus Casseldricken's daughter. Renee being blind made the situation far worse, as her mother hardly ever let Renee out of her sight. Renee partied for that first year she was on her own, and one night, she'd gotten a little drunk at a fraternity house. Her roommate had pointed out that a hot guy had been watching her all night. When Renee woke up the next morning, she'd lost her virginity and asked him to escort her home.

"Were you attacked?" I couldn't believe someone had taken advantage of a blind girl, and no one had tried to stop it.

"No, no… it didn't happen that way. I'd met a couple of boys, and they were kind to me. I was a wild girl in those days. I vaguely remember flirting with one of them, and I knew what I was doing." Renee confirmed that it had been consensual, but she couldn't recollect anything about him. A month later, she discovered she was pregnant.

"Do you know the identity of Giovanni's father?"

"Not exactly. But let me finish conveying all the details." Renee confirmed that she'd immediately dropped out of school and traveled to

Europe. She considered getting an abortion, but her strict rearing forced her not to do it. She joined a sisterhood of nuns in Eastern Europe, where she'd given the baby up for adoption and later departed to the US. "A few weeks later, my mother called to tell me about the extent of her illness. I'd never told her about the baby, but it was time to return home before she died."

"And that's when you learned the truth about your father, an older half-brother, and the curse?" I considered what her news meant. Even though Giovanni was a descendant of Governor Yeardley, he still had to die to break the curse because he descended from Queen Tessa.

"Exactly. I've been trying to find the talisman and Governor Yeardley's descendants to defend myself in case one of them came looking for me. I always knew my son was out there, and I occasionally checked in at the nunnery to find out if he ever called them." Renee had always believed no one would ever find out about her son, but a small piece of her wanted to protect him just in case the truth ever came out. "If Yeardley's heirs discovered I had a child, they'd go after him too."

"This is a lot to handle." I was trying to sort it out and decide how much I believed her.

Renee motioned to her bodyguard to get the car ready. "I can only stay a few more minutes. Now that I know the killer has found and eliminated my son, I need to leave and safeguard myself. I only came by to tell you I was leaving the country and abandoning this insanity."

"But what if the killer has the talisman? Don't you need to get it back?" Was the killer Giovanni's father or someone else close to the man?

"Yes, but it's too risky. It's better to disappear and live my life in hiding. Now that my son is dead, I cannot shield him anymore."

"When did you discover you were Giovanni's mother?" I wavered whether it was my responsibility to tell Renee that Ludovicus was alive and she had a half-sister in Myriam Castle.

"Yesterday. I felt a strange connection to him at Zach's dinner party, but since I never saw or touched him, I didn't realize he was my son then." Renee indicated that she'd called the nunnery after the dinner party to demand the truth about what had happened to her child. "That's when I discovered he had a four-leaf clover birthmark on his neck as a baby. And when my body-guard overheard you talking to the detective at the funeral home, I learned about Giovanni's four-leaf clover birthmark."

"I never saw him there."

"You were distracted, and I blended in well," the man said before leaving to start their car.

I turned to Renee. "Did the nuns tell you any-thing else about Giovanni? Had he discovered your identity?"

"He called to ask, but they wouldn't give him my name. I'd ensured the adoption was sealed, and they could tell no one the truth of my iden-tity." Renee asked me to walk with her to the door.

As I led her to the porch, she latched tightly to my elbow. "Renee, is there anything you can tell me that might help me figure out what's go-ing on."

She waited for her bodyguard to approach the steps. "The nuns told me a man came to see them recently. He asked a lot of questions but wouldn't give his name."

"Did they provide a description?" I again de-bated whether to tell her about Myriam.

"He had a strange mustache. They referenced the lead actor in *Gone with the Wind*. That's all they could tell me."

"Rhett Ballantine. That's who went to the nunnery. He must be the last descendant of Governor Yeardley. Except he has a son named Jordan. Could he also be Giovanni's father?" It was making some sense. Rhett mentioned turning fifty years old soon, and he was desperately trying to save himself from dying beforehand.

"It's possible. I remember little. It was over thirty years ago, Kellan." After she slipped into the backseat, the bodyguard closed the passenger door, walked around to the front, and entered the driver's seat. Renee rolled down her window. "Please call me if you find out who killed my son."

I asked her to hold on for one more minute. "Listen to me. You can't leave just yet. I have something to tell you about your father, but I want to obtain proof first. Can you visit a detective tonight? His name is Connor Hawkins. He's your nephew. His father, Victor, was Gemma's son. You can trust him, and he'll protect you until I can come by later. It's important."

"It would be good to meet someone in my family now that I know my son is dead. We'll head back to my hotel room so I can check out, and on the way to the airport, we'll go to Connor's place." As I handed her the address, Renee smiled and thanked me. "I'll give it to my bodyguard."

After her car pulled away from the curb, I checked my watch and confirmed it was eight o'clock. April still hadn't called, but she needed to know everything I'd just learned. On my way back into the house, I contacted Jordan to find out his father's location.

"Hi, Kellan. I'm not sure. He was supposed to meet my mother and me for dinner tonight. My stepfather, Tobias, had a final meeting with your brother on the sale of ReedWell, so he couldn't join us." Jordan indicated he was at Simply Stoddard with his mother and aunt.

"Okay, please tell Fern and Ivy I said hello. If you hear from your dad, can you call me as soon as possible? I want to talk to him about my uncle. It's important." I couldn't tell Jordan that I suspected his father was a murderer, but I needed to keep Rhett from going after Renee that night.

I scarfed down a bowl of soup, eager to seek the truth. Once I let out Baxter, I went upstairs to my bedroom to change clothes. It had gotten colder that night, and I needed a heavier sweater. As I walked past Ulan's bedroom, I saw his back-pack on the floor. He'd told me that he had it with him at Augie's and April's house. Was he lying to me?

I dialed Ulan's number, but he didn't pick up. I sent him a few text messages and received no response. I worried as if he were my own son. Finally, my phone rang and lifted my spirits. April had finished her meeting and could chat.

"Sorry about the delay. We're testing the blood on Bitsy's purse. We should know by midnight. Lots to discuss. I can probably come by in an hour if you're free."

I explained to April what I'd learned from Bitsy and Sawyer, as well as Renee's revelation about being Giovanni's mother. "I have a strong feel-ing about Rhett Ballantine. As an FBI agent, he had the ability to fake my uncle's car explosion and pick the lock in my desk cabinet. I think he's responsible for everything."

"Let me read through Connor's interview notes from the morning Giovanni died. I might find something that proves Rhett sneaked into the basement to kill Giovanni." April put me on hold to direct an officer to bring her all the files.

When she returned, I said, "Even though I suspect Giovanni is his son, he's also a descendant of Queen Tessa, so he had to die to break the curse. It's sick and twisted, and I can't believe what Rhett has done."

"I'll get back to you in a little while. I guess I won't be there in an hour now! Sorry," April noted apologetically.

"It's okay. I have another urgent priority. Ulan lied to me about his backpack. And he won't pick up his phone. I'm heading to your place now to find out what's going on." I grabbed my car keys and raced down the front steps.

"Wait! Ulan isn't at my place. I just talked to Augie. He's by himself picking out his classes for the fall," said April, texting her brother to confirm Ulan hadn't been there in the prior three hours.

A nauseating pit bloomed in my stomach. "I don't understand what's going on. He knows I'm trying to help him. I hope he didn't go off on his own to do some snooping."

"Like you? I wouldn't get too worried. He's a teenager. They do foolish things sometimes." April confirmed that Ulan had left Augie's place three hours earlier by bike. "He wasn't planning to sleep at my place tonight. Augie is positive."

When April hung up, I called everyone in the family—Nana D, Hampton, Eleanor, my parents, and Gabriel, who'd returned earlier that morning from visiting Sam in Dallas. No one had seen or heard from Ulan all day. My cousin had gone off half-cocked and was going to get himself hurt. But where could he have gone?

By the time I finished checking with everyone, I pinged Connor. I was stumped, but he might have an idea that could help me find my cousin. I knew he would be busy talking with Renee, but I needed to interrupt them.

When I asked what Connor thought about Renee's news, he was confused. "Renee never showed up. I don't know what you're talking about. Maggie and I have been watching a movie all night."

I explained what Renee told me, suggesting she was running behind while checking out of the hotel. I also told him about Myriam's news and Ulan's disappearance. "Any ideas where he could be?"

"That's incredible. I can't believe Myriam and I are related to the same person. It's almost laughable," said Connor, controlling his tone and pontificating on Rhett's guilt. "I have no idea where Ulan could be, though. If he contacts me, I'll be sure to send him your way. I wish I could help, but April doesn't want me to get involved in the case anymore."

"I appreciate it. Maybe you could do some digging on the side?"

Connor agreed, and I hung up so I could try to reach Ulan one more time. His phone kept ringing just as it had the previous times before it eventually cut over to voicemail. This time, he picked up.

"Ulan! Where are you? Why haven't you answered your phone? I know you're not with Augie."

No response. In the silence, a steady water sound hummed in the background. Had he escaped to Crilly Lake? Was he visiting Constance at the Finnulia River lighthouse?

"Answer me, please, Ulan. I'm upset, but surely you have a valid reason for scaring me. Where are you?" I tried to keep my tone calm. My nerves were shot, and it wasn't easy to accomplish. I heard him mumble something. In the background was another familiar sound, but I couldn't distinguish it. Did we have a poor connection? "Speak louder. I can't hear you."

"Kellan," he said in a strained, panicky whisper. "You've got to help me. I've been kidnapped. Renee is here and—"

The phone went dead, and silence filled the vacant air around me. "Ulan! Ulan!" I screamed as a horrible terror struck my body.

Chapter 27

I continually dialed Ulan's number, but it rang endlessly. What had he meant by *Renee was with him and he'd been kidnapped*? Had she been lying to me the entire time? Were she and Rhett coordinating together to trick me?

I could only assume Renee had been an intentional distraction while Rhett went after Ulan. But why? What did he know? If he'd been hiding something from me all along, it must've been huge. The only thing I thought of doing besides calling April was to check online for his phone records. I scrambled to open my laptop and ran a GPS search on his phone through our cell carrier. If that didn't work, I'd use the *Find My Phone* app. I'd insisted that he keep it turned on so I could always reach him in an emergency. It was an emergency.

While running the program with one hand, I called and updated April on the other. "I have no idea what's going on, but we have to locate him.

He's gotten himself into danger and… and we just have to find him, April."

"I know. We will, don't panic. I'll get my team on it pronto. Hold tight. Give me ten minutes and I'll be at your side. I love you." Before hanging up, April insisted I remain silent and keep replaying the conversation repeatedly in my head. "You might recall a sound or a clue, okay?"

"Thanks. I love you too. Get here soon." I disconnected and waited for the trace to pinpoint Ulan's location. It wouldn't be exact, but it would get me close enough. When it finished, I recognized the coordinates. Ulan was somewhere on Braxton's South Campus. He must've been taken to Glass Hall, where the art exhibition was being held.

Why would someone kidnap Ulan? The only thing that came to mind was my cousin's mother. Uncle Zach's wife had died during childbirth, and my uncle never told us a lot about her. Could she have been descended from Governor Yeardley? If Renee had discovered something like that, she'd want to kill Ulan, so he never found out. It made little sense, but it was an avenue I'd never explored.

While jumping in my car, I focused on Ulan's panicked call. That's when I remembered hearing the campus bell tower chiming. I'd heard it in the background but didn't realize that was the noise. I checked my watch, and it was just after ten o'clock. It had been clamoring while he called me. Then I recalled the sound of water. Ulan could've been walking near the pond. Occasionally when the wind picked up, it would create waves against the bridge pillars or the side banks. It had gotten chilly that day, and the weather reporter had expected intense winds to prevail before midnight.

I drove to campus and parked in the lot near the cable car. Before running through the courtyard to reach Glass Hall, I quickly texted April that I'd traced Ulan to South Campus. She was going to send someone over as soon as possible. I didn't tell her I'd already raced there myself.

As I sprinted across the pathway and approached Glass Hall, my cell rang. I pressed accept without even reading the caller's name, hoping April had positive news.

"Kellan, it's Fern. Sorry to bug you so late, but something came up. I thought you'd want to know about it."

I switched it to speakerphone as I approached Glass Hall. "Fern, I've got to call you back. Emergency. Ulan might've been kidnapped, and I'm trying to locate him." Before I hit disconnect, I asked the security guard, "Has anyone been here in the last few hours? A blind woman and a teenager?"

He looked at me like I had three heads and laughed. "Nope. I haven't moved from this spot since my dinner break four hours ago. It's been quiet. But I did hear something by the running path over there. Near the pond. Maybe they're hanging out on the bridge?"

"Thanks!" I turned around and tore off for the pond, assuming my theory about the water noise on the call earlier was accurate. I realized I'd left the phone on when Fern called my name.

"Kellan... I'm so sorry. That's totally the priority. Call me back as soon as you find him. I'll tell you all about my call with Ivy. Tobias canceled dinner after they had an awful row."

As she finished speaking, I reached the nearest edge of the pond and looked toward the bridge. Most of the lamps were lit, so I had a decent view, but the tall trees in the background had created several shadows. While creeping toward the bridge, something floating in the water caught my attention. When the light hit it in the right way, I noticed a person's unconscious body.

"Oh my god!" I rushed across the wooden planks. As I slipped, I grabbed the railing. My phone fell to the ground, landing on the edge of the bridge between the wooden rafter and one of the pilings.

Fern's voice boomed through the speaker. "Are you okay? Listen, I'll hang up. Be careful. I'll tell you about the four-leaf clover birthmark later."

My head jerked forward as I dropped to the ground and reached for the body through the railing. I'd just gotten my hand around some of the victim's clothing and turned the body over when I realized what Fern had said. I also recognized the person floating in the pond.

"Who has the birthmark?" I shimmied myself between two of the poles and lifted and shoved Renee's body as far as I could toward the sandy, tall grasses on the perimeter. As I pulled myself out from between the two wooden poles, I watched her upper half reach the edge of the bank, so her face wasn't drowning in the water.

I reached between the wooden planks and piling for my phone, but the slippery texture of the bridge caused me to knock the phone over the edge. It careened toward the water.

Fern said, "I remembered you mentioning a four-leaf clover earlier, and when Ivy repeated it—"

When the phone landed in the murky pond, I lost my opportunity to know whom she was about to name. It had to be Rhett. He was her ex-husband, and she'd know if he had a birthmark.

I carefully gripped the railing and ran to the edge of the pond, screaming Ulan's name. Could he have sunk to the bottom? I didn't think it was deep enough, but I had to find out if Renee was alive. She could tell me where Rhett had taken Ulan. As I reached her body, I began performing CPR. After the first round of breaths, I felt the wrong end of a gun pressing into my back.

"Stand up slowly, Kellan," said a familiar voice.

I instantly knew it wasn't Rhett's. Tobias Natcher then held the gun inches from my head. I did as he asked, gradually rotating until I came face to face with Giovanni's and my uncle's killer.

Next to him, Ulan's mouth and hands were bound with duct tape. Tobias had one arm gripped around his neck tightly, and the other pointed his gun in my direction. "Move closer to that lamppost so I can see everything you're doing."

When I followed his instructions, he rammed Ulan to the ground in front of us. "Don't move, kid! I'm an excellent shot, and there are plenty of bullets left for both you and your cousin."

Ulan lay still on the ground, his enlarged and darkened pupils begging for help. I wanted to but couldn't risk being shot. April would be there soon enough, unless Tobias killed us before that happened.

When I realized my mistake about Rhett's role in the murders, everything suddenly fell into place. "You're Giovanni's father, aren't you? Fern was about to say your name when I lost my phone. Ivy must've told her you had a four-leaf clover birthmark."

Tobias grunted. "Yes, only I didn't know Giovanni was my kid until Renee heard about my birthmark." Tobias's sleeve had been torn during a fight with Renee when she tried to attack him earlier. In the process, Ulan had commented about his strange tattoo, not realizing it was a birthmark, which prompted Renee to remember some of the missing pieces from her night with him over thirty years ago. "Renee confessed the truth to me an hour ago. I would never have killed him... I can't believe Queen Tessa intended for her own blood to be destroyed for this curse to end!"

I processed everything that I'd learned, carefully looking around the immediate vicinity for a weapon and escape route. "Giovanni figured out I killed your uncle. He confronted me in that basement classroom. He never expected me to grab the spear and thrust it in him."

"You sneaked downstairs to find Queen Tessa's talisman, didn't you?"

Tobias nodded. "It was the only way to end the curse. Tomorrow is my fiftieth birthday. All I

must do now is get rid of Renee Casseldricken…
or Renee Hawkins… however she refers to herself, and it's all over. After I burn this doll, of
course," he said, pulling the cursed idol from
a bag he'd tossed on the dirty ground next to
him. The doll's diamond eyes sparkled from the
moonlight.

I suddenly felt overly optimistic about my
chances of getting out of the predicament alive.
But I had to be careful. "Before midnight, right?
Renee has to die, and you need to destroy Queen
Tessa's talisman?"

"Exactly. Now that Giovanni is dead, and Renee didn't have any other children, it can all conclude tonight. Then I can escape and live a long
and happy life." Tobias bent down and pulled the
talisman out of the velvet bag with his gloved
hands. "First, I shoot you. I don't care if you die
or not. As long as you and your cousin stay out of
my way, I can put another plug in Renee if she's
still alive. Once she's dead, I'll burn the figurine
and escape this horrible town. I have ninety minutes until midnight."

I swallowed the lump in my throat. "You blew
up my uncle's car, didn't you?"

"He got in my way. I bought this idol legally. He disappeared with it. Your uncle thought he escaped me on that plane, but I'd already arranged for someone to follow him. While Zach was talking to your mother at the airport, we fixed it so his car would explode." Tobias looked toward Renee and snorted. "I realized at Zach's dinner party that I'd slept with Renee years ago. Only I didn't know her connection with Queen Tessa back then."

"How did you figure it out?"

"I only suspected she was Queen Tessa's descendant when the figurine disappeared after the dinner party and I did a little research on the woman. I had her stopped at Immigration & Customs because she couldn't die until I knew the exact location of Queen Tessa's talisman."

Tobias confirmed that he'd arranged for one of his contacts to tail Renee on her flight from South Africa to Amsterdam. When she was distracted, his henchman stole her passport from her coat pocket. Once Tobias knew Uncle Zach didn't have the talisman with him in the parking lot, nor had another of his contacts found it in Uncle Zach's luggage in Orlando's Baggage

Claim, he green-lit the explosion and instructed the henchman to return Renee's passport. Tobias needed to follow her to find the talisman's trail, but once he'd overheard Kathy mention to Lindsey that she'd come across Uncle Zach's luggage, he hit the jackpot. Tobias first checked Cain's place but failed to find the talisman there. Luckily, one of his henchmen later eavesdropped on my conversation with April and learned the talisman was locked in my desk. He then coordinated to steal it when I'd left my office.

Tobias directed Ulan to crawl closer to Renee. Ulan wiggled across the dirt and flowerbeds until he was just a few feet from her. When Renee stirred and blinked rapidly, Tobias ordered me to step toward them too.

I did as he instructed. "And then you had someone change the car rental agency records. You're a horrible excuse for a human being."

"At least Ulan will get a generous settlement. If he survives." Tobias warned both of us not to move as he aimed his gun at Renee's chest. "Once I escape, I'll disappear forever. No one will find me. And I have you to thank for helping me track Renee down in Braxton. When I overheard you mentioning something about the Hawkins family coming from South Africa, and I understood all her connections to your friends and family, it hammered the final nail in Renee's coffin. Looks like the witch is unfortunately stirring. Pardon me, as I fix that situation more permanently."

Renee could only hear the conversation. She must've been confused and afraid without her vision, incapable of understanding what was happening around her. "Kellan, is that you?" she uttered a decibel above a whisper.

"It's still Tobias, sweetheart. But don't worry, you've only got a few minutes left. Say cheese as I take your picture." He cocked the gun while simultaneously winking at me.

"Wait! Before you do that, Tobias, ask yourself another question," I said, hoping my voice wasn't full of tremors. I'd been in dangerous situations before, but the latest was by far the worst. Even when Cristiano's sister tried to kill me, I had faith that he could stop her from taking that permanent step. Now, no one else was around, and Tobias thought he only had ninety minutes left to live.

"I'll bite. What's an extra two minutes when I'll have another thirty or forty years to remember this moment." He switched his focus off Renee for one second to peek in my direction. "Go ahead. Ask me this important question."

"Renee might not have any other children. But what if Ludovicus Casseldricken did? I suppose that would mean you could kill all of us and burn Queen Tessa's talisman, but she'd still come after you before midnight." In the background, only the eerie howl of the wind persisted. Except for the branch or twig that unexpectedly snapped as Tobias prepared to respond.

"That old fool? He died fifty years ago. His wife was childless, and his affair with the housemaid only produced Renee. You're just messing with me." Tobias stepped closer to his prime target and suggested she say her goodbyes.

"Unfortunately, you're mistaken. Ludovicus had another child, and she's alive and healthy, Tobias." I looked up when I saw a shadow appear on the ground near us. Someone was standing behind our assailant, but I couldn't see his or her face.

"Who? I want her name, Kellan." While breathing heavily and unexpectedly jerking his body, Tobias turned the gun on me.

At the same time, a man stepped out of the shadow and clunked Tobias with a heavy tree branch. The man dropped to the ground in a weakened state and stuttered his words. "Her nnname... isss Mmmyriam Cassstle, and... ssshe's my daughter." Ludovicus, who resembled an older, more masculine version of Myriam and went by the name Luther, trembled in front of me as he pulled himself to his knees.

When Tobias's gun flew across the ground, I dashed in its direction and threw myself into the flowerbed to reach it. Ulan had rolled himself closer to Renee to get out of any crossfire.

As I searched for the gun, the brawling continued behind me. Luther shouted, "Sssilent for the last ssseventeen yearsss... but I'm nnnot anymore. Nnno one comes... after my family and gggets away with it."

Tobias had thirty years on Luther and was able to break away from him, even with his head injury from being smacked by the tree branch. "You're alive! Not for long, old man."

As I found the gun and swiveled toward them, April rushed into the wooded area with a pair of officers. "You're outnumbered, Tobias Natcher. I highly suggest you give yourself up!" She cocked her head in Renee and Ulan's direction, instructing her officers to tend to them while she focused *Old Betsy* on Tobias.

Within minutes, an ambulance arrived. While the EMTs checked on Renee and Luther, I ripped the tape off Ulan and squeezed him so hard, he begged me not to flatten him.

"I'm so sorry, Kellan! That man forced me to send you the text that I was staying at Augie's place. He kidnapped me while I was riding my bike home."

"But why?" I asked, letting him wiggle out of the hug. "What did he have to gain by taking you?"

"Renee. He couldn't destroy the talisman without Renee. He made me call her and tell her I had the talisman. I begged her to meet me at Glass Hall, but only because he said he'd kill you and Nana D. When Renee showed up in the courtyard, they struggled. I mentioned seeing a four-leaf clover, and that's when he realized

Giovanni was his son. Tobias knocked Renee out and shoved her into the pond." Ulan wiped a few tears from his bloodshot eyes. "Did you figure out my clues?"

"You mean about the backpack?" April inquired, massaging his shoulder.

"That, and when Mr. Natcher wasn't looking, I stole back my phone. I waited until ten o'clock to call because I knew the bell tower would chime every hour. It was my best chance. Then he hit me and took away the phone." Ulan rubbed his arms, sensing the cooler weather beginning to chill him.

April tossed him her blazer. "Put this on, kiddo. Your cousin hates when I wear it, anyway. Maybe it'll look better on you."

"Thanks, April. Will Renee be okay? She's the only other person who can tell me what happened to my dad before he died." He slipped into April's coat and pleaded with us to be honest with him.

"I hope so, Ulan. I hope so." I glanced at April and shook my head. "Your blazer does look good on him. What if we went shopping together and you considered a slight wardrobe change? Not that I'm saying you aren't gorgeous to me no matter what, but—"

April held up one hand in my direction and the other pointing at the cursed figurine on the ground. "I've decided what we're gonna do with that thing."

"I'm stoked you found a new purpose for Queen Tessa's talisman!" I grinned widely, curious what she might say next. "Museum donation? Cautionary tale for unruly teenagers? Toy for Baxter?"

"Nope. Queen Tessa and I are gonna become buddies. I need her help to control you." April rattled off a few of her recent frustrations, beginning with me forgetting to tell her I'd worked out that Ulan was at the pond, not Glass Hall, and ending with me playing detective on my own again. "You're incorrigible. Unpredictable. Preposterous. Frustrating. Foolish. Absurd. Hairbrained. Half-witted. Outlandish—"

"But you love me, right?" I blinked my baby blues like a naughty puppy begging for clemency.

"But I love you, right." April then turned to Ulan and said, "Put that duct tape on your eyes, kid. I'm about to slobber all over your cousin. In public. For an exceptionally long time."

Chapter 28

"I never should've doubted that you'd uncover the truth, brilliant one." Nana D dropped a second helping of her famous cherry pie on my plate and encouraged me to eat as much as I wanted. "You captured Zach's killer, and now we move forward. The hole in my heart will never be filled because of this loss, but at least we have some closure."

Ulan sat at the far end of the table, struggling to keep his eyes open. "I've been up all-night thinking about what I could've done to stop Tobias before he killed Dad. I let everyone down."

Nana D grabbed the spatula off the table and gently whacked him on the shoulder. "Pish! Don't be such a fool. You couldn't have known what was going on. Your father chose to keep silent about his financial issues. He fell head over heels for Renee and wanted to bring her here to meet us. Love makes men do strange things."

Ulan rubbed his shoulder, then stared at our grandmother with one eye open and the other closed. "Why are you always hitting us with kitchen tools? That hurt!"

"Oh, what babies! I thought it would be a good thing for Kellan to finish raising you, but I don't know who complains more between the two of you." Nana D reminded us she would slap our bottoms silly if we didn't stop whining. "Be men. Not wimps. I barely touched you with a kitchen utensil. It's called a love tap. And some day, when you find the perfect girl, you'll fall in love and know what it's all about. Right, brilliant one?" She addressed that last part to me.

"Just go with it, kiddo. She's been flicking and swatting and pinching me for years. Nana D comes from a generation where you torture the ones you love." I ducked before she hit me with the spatula. Truthfully, it was rarely hard enough to leave an impression or turn my skin assorted colors.

"I'm gonna take a nap. Wake me up for lunch," Ulan replied, hugging both Nana D and me before he grabbed Baxter and scampered up our stairs. "I'm ordering a new phone for both of us too."

Nana D had come by at dawn to find out the full story, angry because she couldn't reach me by cell. Could I help that it was lost at the bottom of the pond? I'd only returned home with Ulan around three in the morning, which meant he and I had barely gotten any sleep before she was cooking breakfast and praising her two favorite heroes. She'd reminded me to find time for Constance Garibaldi too. I planned to visit her the following day, but earlier I sent a brief text to let her know I was thinking about her and would bring a plate of the Pick-Me-Up Diner's Baklava, her favorite treat. Constance replied with eight hearts and a hand-clap icon. No clue what it meant!

After April and I had smooched for what felt like an hour by the pond the previous night, her team read Tobias his rights and escorted him to the sheriff's office. He had been allotted his single call, which was to his wife. When Ivy learned what he had done, she told him where to go in no uncertain terms. April locked him in jail overnight, then took control of the investigation, so I could bring Ulan home and make sure he was okay.

The EMTs had taken Luther and Renee to the hospital. Once they left in the ambulances, April called Connor and told him what had happened. He drove to the ER to be with his half-aunt. She also called Myriam and told her they'd found her father. Myriam met him at the hospital, and once the on-call physician cleared him to leave, she brought her father back to Willow Trees. He was extraordinarily tired, needed his medication, and kept asking to meet Ursula. Connor had given April a brief update when he'd arrived at the hospital, otherwise I wouldn't have known much. My focus was entirely on Ulan for the rest of the night.

News had gotten out. My mother brought Emma home, and they stayed for a few hours to enjoy Nana D's breakfast. Even Eleanor, Manny, and Gabriel came by to check on us. Hampton called the house line to let us know that he'd canceled the transaction to sell ReedWell to Tobias and was back to the drawing board. Natasha had also wiggled her big toe that morning. The Ayrwick family stuck together, and whether a tragedy or a blessing impacted us, the group banded as one these days, something we hadn't always done historically.

While everyone was in the kitchen, my mother approached me in the dining room. "I'm so glad you're both okay, Kellan. You worry me too much these days, honey."

"Why's that, Mom? Everything turned out fine. We're home, no worse for the wear." I wrapped my arm around her shoulder and pecked her cheek. "I'm sorry to place so many burdens on you."

"I need to tell you something. Well, two things, but one's more important." She rested her hand on her chin, gently stroking the side of her cheek. "Which do you want first?"

I considered the options. My mother's news tended to be low key, but she'd always make a tremendous deal out of it. Once, she'd called me months after I'd moved to Los Angeles for graduate school so she could beg forgiveness for doing something terrible. I panicked. Had she accidentally pushed Dad down a flight of stairs? Mistakenly poisoned Nana D with her cooking? By the time we'd worked out that she'd repainted my bedroom in the Royal Chic-Shack without my permission, I'd sweat off three pounds.

"The more important news first, please."

"I approve of your relationship with April, but only because now I see she protects you the way she should." My mother paused to let her news sink in.

I'd figured out why she was reluctant to provide her blessing, not that I needed it. "Do you dislike April?"

She vehemently shook her head. "Of course not. It's just that... you keep putting yourself in the line of fire and almost getting killed. I blamed April. I thought if she had properly done her job as the sheriff, you wouldn't insert yourself into an investigation."

"What's changed?" I understood her perspective, even if she had it all wrong.

"Now I know she's just as perturbed about it as I am. You're incorrigible, Kellan. You always were as a kid... just like Nana D. Putting your nose where it doesn't belong. You can't be controlled. It's a sickness, my child." She grabbed the last muffin from the basket and ferociously bit into it. "It's gonna take someone like April to fix you. I'm glad she has your back. So… you have my blessing."

My mother's logic was totally backward, but I wouldn't argue about it. Just the fact that she was eating a muffin told me it had been a stressful situation. "I appreciate it. I love April, but we've only been together for six months. It's still early on… we need time to figure out what the future might hold."

"Okay, all I'm saying is you shouldn't wait forever. You're not getting younger. If you insist on putting yourself in so many dangerous situations, I'm glad you have a strong woman to watch out for you. Just don't get all masculine and domineering like your father and brothers. They couldn't let themselves be the little spoon. You've got the right personality for it." My mother took another bite of the muffin and swigged a gulp of her mimosa. "Hmmm… why have I been skipping carbs?"

"I've been around tough women my whole life. I think I can handle it." I closed my eyes and prepared for her second piece of news. "What's the other topic?"

"Oh, nothing too big. I've decided to retire from Braxton this summer. Your father and I are house swapping with Aunt Deirdre and Timothy. They're gonna stay at the Royal Chic-Shack, and we'll live in London for a year." As soon as she finished dropping her mammoth announcement, my mother exited the dining room with a refilled mimosa glass and asked when Nana D would make more muffins.

What was wrong with my family? How could my mother make such a rash decision to quit and leave town? Where did that leave my aunt's writing career and Timothy's London business dealings? Why did everyone around me lose their minds? It was as if they secretly took turns deciding who would punish me. That week, my mother had the honors. I was sure it would continue rotating until everyone got their fair share. As I stood from the table to check in with April, the front doorbell chimed.

"I've got it," I yelled while hustling to the door. When I peeped through the hole, Fern and Jordan stood on my porch, deep in conversation. I opened the door and greeted them.

"Your mom will be accepting, I'm sure. Your dad, he's not gonna take the one-eighty well, Jordan. I'd wait a few more days prior to dropping the news," announced Fern before realizing I was staring at them. "Hi, Kellan. Glad you're awake. We thought you might be sleeping."

"Ummm… if you thought I was sleeping, why did you come by?"

Jordan pushed past me. "Is she here?" He didn't wait for an answer and continued walking down the hall toward the kitchen. Before he entered, he turned back to me and said, "Thanks for finding out the truth about my stepfather last night, Kellan. It made my decision a lot easier."

I glanced at Fern. "What's going on?"

Fern stepped further inside and leaned against the wall. "Jordan and I had breakfast together. He unsuccessfully consoled his mother for a few hours last night. But once Rhett showed up, Jordan knew his dad could help Ivy."

"Ah, I see. That's useful information, but why are you here?" I hadn't meant to appear rude, but my brain was still fuzzy from the previous night's melodrama.

"Jordan needs to talk to his new boss. I hitched a ride with him to check on you. When Ivy told me last night that Tobias had a four-leaf clover birthmark, I just had to tell you. I never expected that he was connected with this whole cursed talisman business." Fern sighed heavily, then hugged me. "I'm so glad he didn't kill you. That would have been awful. I rely on you for so much these days."

"Thanks, Fern. I'm glad he didn't either. I wouldn't know what to do without you at Braxton." I knew she'd said something else I wanted to follow up on, but her phone rang before I could think of it.

While Fern excused herself to take Ivy's call, I remembered what I wanted to ask. Just then, Nana D exited the kitchen, carrying her treasured spatula, and approached me. "Did you hear the news?" Jordan directly followed her like a trained puppet.

I glanced sideways, then at the ceiling and the floor. "No. I'm as baffled about this morning's activities as is Baxter when he's barking at the basement door. Nothing makes sense. Upside down world today."

"You speak strangely sometimes, brilliant one."

"Do I get to call him *brilliant one*, I mean, now that I'm working for you?" queried Jordan, beaming about his own bulletin of joy.

Nana D gently flicked the spatula on his bum. "That depends… are you man enough to deal with me? Or are you gonna run away and cry like my previous assistants?"

Jordan jerked his head back. "Nah, I'm cool. You can't get rid of me that easily. Now that I'm not going back to New Orleans, I can enroll in Braxton's new graduate curriculum. By day, I'll work for you. By night, I'll earn my MBA."

Nana D gripped Jordan's shoulder and jostled him. "Good boy. See Kellan, that's been my problem all along. Too many female assistants. It's time I gave the job to a man!"

Before I could respond, Fern disconnected and joined us. "You won't believe what Ivy just told me." Her face was ashen, and her body trembled. "Tobias choked on his breakfast this morning. Although the guard applied the Heimlich maneuver, he still died."

The curse! It was the man's fiftieth birthday that day. "Do you know what time he was born?"

Jordan volunteered the answer. "Oddly enough, I do. He told me in the past it was just before midnight. I guess... technically, he wouldn't turn fifty until later this evening."

We all stood silent. Though we were in shock, we also wanted to be respectful about a man's death, even if he had killed two people.

Fern and Jordan left to support Ivy. Rhett was on his way to the Roarke and Daughters Inn to be with his ex-wife too. Before he arrived, he called to thank me for stopping Tobias. "Jordan gave me your house line. I figured out the identity of Giovanni's biological parents about twenty-four hours ago and was trying to update Renee last night. One of Tobias's henchmen ran Renee's bodyguard off the road, then drugged him. He'd been asleep all night on the side of the highway."

"How did Renee get on campus?"

"Tobias made Ulan call her, and she agreed to get in the car when Tobias's henchman showed up because she thought Ulan was in danger." Rhett confirmed the henchman escorted Renee to Glass Hall, and then Tobias paid the man to leave town. He then proceeded to tell me that Tobias's death was a sign that he should get back together with Ivy. "Maybe we'll move to New Orleans to be with Jordan."

I didn't have the heart to tell Rhett what his son had decided to do. Instead, I wished him luck in his goal of convincing his ex-wife to give him another chance.

Once everyone else left the house, and Ulan offered to watch Emma for a few hours, I headed to Braxton to finish a report I owed Ursula about what had happened on campus. She told me not to worry about it until Monday, but I needed a clear head for the weekend and wanted to get everything done as soon as possible. April and Augie were coming by that evening for dinner with Ulan and Emma. We were spending the entire weekend together as a weird, modern version of a family.

As I approached Diamond Hall, Cain called my name. "Got a minute?"

"Sure, what's going on?"

"Just wanted to say thank you for helping find the actual killer. I know you thought I had something to do with your uncle's death for a while."

Cain tried his best to offer his appreciation without overstepping any boundaries.

"I'm glad I could. I'm sorry if I made things more difficult for you and Bitsy." I wasn't sure if he knew she'd left town to repair her marriage with Sawyer.

"Nope. All good. This whole affair with Bitsy was a wake-up call. I need to take a chance and follow my dreams. Explore my passions." Cain explained that he'd resigned from his position as chair of the art department, effective at the end of the summer. "I'll give President Power a chance to find the new Dean of Academics and my replacement before I head out of town."

"Where are you going?"

"I've decided to pursue my own art career. I've been selling some painting and pottery, but abstract fear has held me back." Cain confirmed that he would move to New York City to take a chance on life, to do something to make him happy. "Bitsy promised to open a few doors for me. I'll see you around, Kellan. I think you should do the same too. You're a high-strung man! Stop trying to do everything. Make yourself happy."

When Cain sauntered away, I considered his advice. I also knew just what I needed to do, which I would accomplish as soon as I returned home. When I reached my office, I heard voices coming from down the hall. I strolled toward them and noticed Myriam and Ursula pouring themselves cups of tea in our department kitchen.

"Ah, my two bosses. What brings you to campus today?"

"I need to prepare a brief for the Board of Trustees. This is the seventh murder associated with the campus in a year. I've been the president for just as long. They'd like to understand what's going on." Ursula cocked her head in her wife's direction. "That one told me to sacrifice you."

"Me? I didn't kill anyone." My mouth fell to the floor.

Myriam said, "You've been back just as long, and you're in the middle of every single one of them. Really, you must consider that—"

Ursula cleared her throat. "Don't you have something else you'd like to say, Myriam?"

When Myriam rolled her eyes, I shouted, "Hey! That's my move!"

"We might have more in common than you realize, Kellan. Thank you for stopping Tobias Natcher from stealing Queen Tessa's talisman and almost killing my sister." Myriam reached a stiff hand in my direction and waited for me to meet her halfway. "*If you prick us, do we not bleed? If you tickle us, do we not laugh? If you poison us, do we not die? And if you wrong us, shall we not revenge?*"

I clasped her hand and shook it gently while contemplating the apropos quote from *Merchant of Venice*. "Truce?"

"Truce." Myriam confirmed her father was doing much better, including speaking at length since returning to Willow Trees. "He heard everything I said this week, and that's why he went to Glass Hall to view the art exhibit. But he'd seen Tobias threatening you and Renee near the pond. My father is excited to spend time with both his daughters now."

"How is Renee doing?" I asked, noticing as we walked back to her office that Queen Tessa's talisman was on her chair. "And didn't the police keep that horrific thing?"

Ursula laughed. "No, it wasn't really evidence, since he had purchased it. Plus, they have enough witnesses to put Tobias away for good."

Myriam said, "Renee is much better. She stayed at the hospital overnight, but we're going to visit her shortly. Then we'll take her to see Dad at Willow Trees."

I relayed news of Tobias's death from choking that morning. "I'm so glad you have your sister to get to know better, despite everything that's happened to your family."

"Murderers should be exterminated, thank you." Myriam noted that she was saddened to learn Giovanni was her nephew only after his death. "I would have liked to get to know him better."

"It's unfortunate. I'm so sorry. At least this dreaded curse is done with now." I considered whether to offer any physical support or encouragement in addition to my words.

Ursula's eyes popped. "You're assuming Tobias had no other children. We're hiring a lawyer and a genealogist to verify there's no secret offspring."

"Smart! Please tell Renee that I'd like to see her when she's better. Ulan would too, I'm sure." I turned to exit Myriam's office but was halted.

"Oh, Kellan. Visit me on Monday. I have some thrilling plans to discuss with you." Myriam glanced sideways at Ursula, who subtly smiled.

"I don't like the sound of that. Do I get any hints?" I guessed she wanted to drop some horrible new course in my lap, or she'd signed me up for a torturous club I'd have to advise.

Myriam sighed. "Just one. We're planning a semester abroad next year. A professor from a school in another country is teaching at Braxton, and in return, we're sending one of ours there. You'd be perfect for this opportunity."

"Why me?" I didn't want to leave the country anytime soon.

Ursula replied, "I like you very much, Kellan, but Myriam thinks Braxton could use a mini hiatus from your particular talents. Meaning, if there's gonna be another murder in your future, let it happen somewhere else."

I walked away. I had no words for their announcement. Instead, I finished my report and dropped it into a cubby in the mailbox rack. After stopping by the store to pick up the new phones Ulan had reserved for us, I headed to the Pick-Me-Up Diner to visit my sister, hopeful that I'd forget about traveling the globe sometime soon. When I found Eleanor and Manny, her fiancé and head chef, they were giggling in the back office. "What's up with you two?"

As if I hadn't received enough shocks for the day, Eleanor reached out her hand and showed me her ring-clad finger. "Isn't it pretty?"

I nodded. "Yes, but I've seen your engagement ring before, sis."

She slapped her forehead with the other hand. "Ugh! Look more closely, you fool."

When I pulled her arm forward, I realized it wasn't her engagement ring, but her wedding ring. "Wait, are you saying—"

"Yep, Manny and I got married a few weeks ago. No one else knows. I can't hold it in any longer. We decided we didn't need a big wedding while everyone was grieving for Uncle Zach. Now that we know what happened to him, we feel better about celebrating our news. You can throw us a surprise reception party in two weeks, okay? But keep it secret, please!"

I hugged my sister and new brother-in-law and congratulated them on their blessed union. We talked about their unexpected leap for several more minutes. I could've sworn Eleanor had something more to tell me, but she wouldn't take any bait I tossed out. Finally, I gave up and drove home. When Augie and April arrived, I asked the kids to decide on dinner and configure my phone. "We're doing takeout. I don't have the energy to cook or taste one of Ulan's creations. This family is gonna put me in an early grave."

Augie grinned and marched upstairs to find Emma and Ulan. As he ascended the steps, he turned to us. "You two kids behave now. Don't make me explain the birds and the bees to you, okay?"

After April scooted him away, we moved to the living room and collapsed onto the couch. I leaned closer and rested my head on her shoulder. Then I told her about Myriam's news and my family's proclamations. "So, anything else major happening I need to be aware of?"

"I received an important piece of paper in the mail today."

I smiled. "Is it what I think it is?"

"Yes," April said coyly. "Fox is officially my ex-husband. We're free of him, babe."

I pressed my lids down and asked an important question. "I've been thinking about this a lot. You can totally say no, but if we're serious about making a go of something together, you and Augie should move in with me. There's plenty of space, and we'd be quite the blended family."

April swiveled her head in my direction and cupped her hands on my cheeks until my eyes opened. "On one condition."

"What's that?"

"There is no talk of marriage or kids between us for at least a year. If we can live together that long without shooting, knifing, or poisoning one another, then we'll be ready to do something more permanent." She planted her lips on mine and wouldn't pull them away until excessively forced. "Deal?"

"Deal! But that leaves plenty of other ways to consider murdering someone, you realize?"

April punched me in the gut, a little harder than I'd expected too. "Since I've agreed that we're gonna cohabitate together, you get to inform the kids! Didn't Emma join the archery club? Maybe we should practice our skills this weekend, babe?"

Before I could respond, my doorbell rang. "I'll get it. Probably Nana D with another cherry pie. She's been making them all day for me."

"Doubtful. Nana D would walk right in and offer some sassy comment. Gotta be someone else."

I slipped into the foyer and looked through the peephole. Bartleby Grosvalet stood at my door with an envelope in his hands. What was he doing outside? He should be taking care of Constance Garibaldi, who I really needed to visit soon. I opened the door and waved him inside.

"No, really, I can't stay. I don't bring good news, Kellan." A heavy sadness hung between us, and immediately, I understood what had happened.

"Constance passed away, didn't she?" A lump formed in my throat.

Bartleby nodded. "It was peaceful, and she was content in the end." He handed me the envelope and promised to share the details of her funeral arrangements. "Constance wanted me to convey how much she appreciated you. I'm not sure what's in her letter, but right before she took her last breath, she made me vow to deliver it to you."

As Bartleby trudged down the steps, April sneaked up behind me. "Are you opening it now?"

"Yes," I said, offering a small prayer for God to protect the woman's soul. "I can't imagine what Constance left me in a letter."

I carefully slit open the envelope and read through her words. When I finished, my body froze. I barely rattled off to April, "She's provided instructions for a treasure hunt, but it comes with an enormous risk and the potential for a huge reward. It involves a secret about my family, specifically the Ayrwick ancestors and the village they hail from. Apparently, just like my mother, Myriam, and Ursula, she's decided we need to travel the globe too!"

What were these madcap women forcing me to do now?

Dear Reader,

Thank you for taking time to read *Legally Blind Luck*. Word of mouth is an author's best friend and much appreciated. If you enjoyed it, please consider supporting this author:

- Leave a book review on Amazon US, Amazon (also your own country if different), Goodreads, BookBub, and any other book site you follow to help market and promote this book

- Tell your friends, family, and colleagues all about this author and his books

- Share brief posts on your social media platforms and tag the book (#LegallyBlindLuck or #BraxtonCampusMysteries) or author (#JamesJCudney) on Twitter, Facebook, Instagram, Pinterest, LinkedIn, WordPress, Tumblr, YouTube, Bloglovin, and SnapChat

- Suggest the book for book clubs, to bookstores, or to any libraries you know

About the Author

Background

James is my given name, but most folks call me Jay. I live in New York City, grew up on Long Island, and graduated from Moravian College, an historic but small liberal arts school in Bethlehem, Pennsylvania, with a degree in English literature and minors in Education, Business and Spanish. After college, I accepted a technical writing position for a telecommunications company during Y2K and spent the last ~20 years building a career in technology & business operations in the retail, sports, media, hospitality, and entertainment industries. Throughout those years, I wrote short stories, poems, and various beginnings to the "Great American Novel," but I was so focused on my career that writing became a hobby. In 2016, I committed to focusing my energies toward reinvigorating a second career in reading, writing, and publishing.

Author

Writing has been a part of my life as much as my heart, mind, and body. At some points, it was just a few poems or short stories; at others, it was full length novels and stories. My current focus is family drama fiction, cozy mystery novels, and suspense thrillers. I conjure characters and plots that I feel must be unwound. I think of situations people find themselves in and feel compelled to tell the story. It's usually a convoluted plot with many surprise twists and turns. I feel it necessary to take that ride all over the course. My character is easily pictured in my head. I know what he is going to encounter or what she will feel. But I need to use the right words to make it clear.

Reader & Reviewer

Reading has also never left my side. Whether it was children's books, young adult novels, college textbooks, biographies, or my ultimate love, fiction, it's ever present in my day. I read two books per week and I'm on a quest to update every book I've ever read on Goodreads, write up a review, and post it on all my sites and platforms.

Blogger & Thinker

I have combined my passions into a single platform where I share reviews, write a blog and publish tons of content: https://thisismytruthnow.com/. I started my 365 Daily Challenge, where I post about a word that has some meaning to me and converse with everyone about life. There is humor, tears, love, friendship, advice, and bloopers. Lots of bloopers where I poke fun at myself all the time. Even my dogs have had weekly segments called "Ryder's Rants" or "Baxter's Barks," where they complain about me. All these things make up who I am; none of them are very fancy or magnanimous, but they are real. And that's why they are me.

Genealogist & Researcher

I love history and research, finding myself often reaching back into the past to understand why someone made the choice he or she did and what were the subsequent consequences. I enjoy studying the activities and culture from hundreds of years ago to trace the roots and find the puzzle of my own history. I wish I could watch my ancestors from a secret place to learn how they interacted with others; and maybe I'll comprehend why I do things the way I do.

Websites & Blog

Website: https://jamesjcudney.com/
Blog: https://thisismytruthnow.com
Amazon: http://bit.ly/JJCIVBooks
Next Chapter:
https://www.nextchapter.pub/authors/james-j-cudney
BookBub:
https://www.bookbub.com/profile/james-j-cudney

Social Media

Twitter: https://twitter.com/jamescudney4
Facebook:
https://www.facebook.com/
JamesJCudneyIVAuthor/
Facebook:
https://www.facebook.com/
BraxtonCampusMysteries/
Facebook:
https://www.facebook.com/ThisIsMyTruthNow/
Pinterest:
https://www.pinterest.com/jamescudney4/

Instagram:
https://www.instagram.com/jamescudney4/
Goodreads:
https://www.goodreads.com/jamescudney4
LinkedIn:
https://www.linkedin.com/in/jamescudney4

Genres, Formats & Languages

I write in the family drama, suspense, and mystery genres. My first two books were Watching Glass Shatter (2017) and Father Figure (2018). Both are contemporary fiction and focus on the dynamics between parents and children and between siblings. I wrote a sequel, Hiding Cracked Glass, for my debut novel, and they are known as the Perceptions of Glass series. I also have a light mystery series called the Braxton Campus Mysteries with seven books available.

All my books come in multiple formats (Kindle, paperback, hardcover, large print paperback, pocket size paperback, and audiobook) and some are also translated into foreign languages such as Spanish, Italian, Portuguese, and German.

Summary of Books

Father Figure (Contemporary Fiction / Family Drama)

Between the fast-paced New York City, a rural Mississippi town and a charming Pennsylvania college campus filled with secrets, two young girls learn the consequences of growing up too quickly. Amalia Graeme, abused by her mother for most of her life, longs to escape her desolate hometown and fall in love. Contemplating her loss of innocence and conflicting feelings between her boyfriend and the dangerous attraction she's developed for an older man, Amalia faces life-altering tragedies. Brianna Porter, a sassy, angst-ridden teenager raised in New York City, yearns to find her life's true purpose, conquer her fear of abandonment, and interpret an intimidating desire for her best friend, Shanelle. Desperate to find the father whom her mother refuses to reveal, Brianna accidentally finds out a shocking truth about her missing parent. Set in alternating chapters two decades apart, the parallels between their lives and the unavoidable collision that is bound to happen are revealed. FATHER FIGURE is a stand-alone emotional story filled with mystery, romance, and suspense.

PERCEPTIONS OF GLASS SERIES

Watching Glass Shatter (Contemporary Fiction / Family Drama)

The wealthy Glass family lost its patriarch, Benjamin Glass, sooner than expected. Benjamin's widow, Olivia, and her 5 sons each react to his death in their own way while preparing for the reading of his will. Olivia receives a very unexpected confession from her late husband about one of their sons that could shatter the whole family. Prior to revealing the secret to her children, Olivia must figure out which boy Ben refers to in the confession he left her in his will. While the family attorney searches for the mysterious Rowena Hector whom Ben says holds the answers, Olivia asks her sons to each spend a week with her as she isn't ready to let go of the past. When Olivia visits her sons, she quickly learns that each one has been keeping his own secret from her. Olivia never expected her remaining years would be so complex and life-altering, but she will not rest until her family is reunited after Ben's untimely death. We all need family. We all want to fit in. We're all a mix of quirky personalities. Will Olivia be able to fix them, or will the whole family implode? What will she do when she discovers the son behind Ben's secret? Check out this ensemble cast where each family member's perspective is center stage, discovering along the way who might feel the biggest impact from all the secrets. Through various scenes and memories across a six-month period, you'll get to know everyone, learning how and why they made certain decisions. Welcome to being an honorary member of the Glass family where the flair for over-the-top drama pushes everyone to their limits.

Hiding Cracked Glass (Contemporary Fiction / Family Drama)

An ominous blackmail letter appears at an inopportune moment. The recipient's name is accidentally blurred out upon arrival. Which member of the Glass family is the ruthless missive meant for? In the powerful sequel to Watching

Glass Shatter, Olivia is the first to read the nasty threat and assumes it's meant for her. When the mysterious letter falls into the wrong hands and is read aloud, it throws the entire Glass family into an inescapable trajectory of self-question. Across the span of eight hours, Olivia and her sons contemplate whether to confess their hidden secrets or find a way to bury them forever. Some failed to learn an important lesson last time. Will they determine how to save themselves before it's too late? Each chapter's focus alternates between the various family members and introduces several new and familiar faces with a vested interest in the outcome. As each hour ticks by, the remaining siblings and their mother gradually reveal what's happened to them in the preceding months, and when the blackmailer makes an appearance at Olivia's birthday party, the truth brilliantly comes to light. Although everyone seemed to embrace the healing process at the end of Watching Glass Shatter, there were hidden cracks in the Glass family that couldn't be mended. Their lives are about to shatter into pieces once again, but this time, the stakes are even higher. Someone wants to teach them a permanent lesson and refuses to stop until success is achieved.

BRAXTON CAMPUS MYSTERY SERIES

Academic Curveball: Death at the Sports Complex (#1)

When Kellan Ayrwick, a thirty-two-year-old single father, is forced to return home for his father's retirement from Braxton College, he finds the dead body of a professor in Diamond Hall's stairwell. Unfortunately, Kellan has a connection to the victim, and so do several members of his family. Could one of them be guilty of murder? Then he finds a second body after discovering mysterious donations to the college's athletic program, a nasty blog denouncing his father, and a criminal attempting to change student grades so the star baseball pitcher isn't expelled. Someone is playing games on campus, but none of the facts add up. With the help of his eccentric and trouble-making nana weeding through the clues, Kellan tries to stay out of the sheriff's way. Fate has other plans. Kellan is close to discovering the killer's identity just as someone he loves is put in grave danger of becoming victim number three. And if that's not enough to wreak havoc on his family, everything comes crashing to a halt when his own past comes spiraling back to change his life forever. In this debut novel in the Braxton Campus Mystery Series, readers discover a cozy, secluded Pennsylvania village full of quirky, sarcastic, and nosy residents. Among the daily workings of Braxton College and the charming Ayrwick family, Kellan weighs his investigative talents against an opportunity to achieve a much sought-after dream. When this first book ends, the drama is set for the next adventure in Kellan's future... and it's one you won't want to miss.

Broken Heart Attack: Death at the Theater (#2)

When an extra ticket becomes available to attend the dress rehearsal of Braxton's King Lear production, Kellan tags along with Nana D and her buddies, sisters-in-law Eustacia and Gwendolyn Paddington, to show support for the rest of the Paddington family. When one of them appears to have a heart attack in the middle of the second act, Nana D raises her suspicions and asks Kellan to investigate who killed her friend. Amidst family members suddenly in debt and a secret rendezvous between an unlikely pair, Kellan learns the Paddingtons might not be as clean-cut as everyone thinks. But did one of them commit murder for an inheritance? Kellan is back in his second adventure since returning home to Pennsylvania. With his personal life in upheaval and his new boss, Myriam, making life difficult, will he be able to find a killer, or will he get caught up in his own version of stage fright?

Flower Power Trip: Death at the Masquerade Ball (#3)

Braxton College is throwing the Heroes & Villains Costume Extravaganza to raise money for renovations to the antiquated Memorial Library. While attending, Kellan stumbles upon a close family friend standing over a dead body that's dressed as Dr. Evil. Did one of Maggie's sisters kill an annoying guest at the Roarke and Daughters Inn or does the victim have a more intimate connection to someone else on campus?

As Kellan helps the school's president, Ursula, bury a scandalous secret from her past and unearth the identity of her stalker, he unexpectedly encounters a missing member of his own family who's reappeared after a lengthy absence. When all the peculiar events around town trace back to the Stoddards, a new family who recently moved to Wharton County, the explosive discovery only offers more confusion. Between the special flower exhibit that's made an unplanned stop on campus and strange postcards arriving each week from all around the world, Kellan can't decide which mystery in his life should take priority. Unfortunately, the biggest one of all has yet to arrive at his doorstep. When it does, Kellan won't know what hit him.

Mistaken Identity Crisis: Death on the Cable Car (#4)

A clever thief with a sinister calling card has invaded Braxton campus. A string of jewelry thefts continues to puzzle the sheriff given they're remarkably similar to an unsolved eight-year-old case from shortly before Gabriel vanished one stormy night. When a missing ruby is discovered near an electrified dead body during the campus cable car redesign project, Kellan must investigate the real killer to protect his brother. Amidst sorority hazing practices and the victim's connections to several prominent Wharton County citizens, a malicious motive becomes more obvious and trickier to prove. As if the latest murder isn't enough to keep him busy, Kellan partners with April to end the Castigliano and Vargas crime family feud. What really happened to Francesca while all those postcards showed up in Braxton? The mafia world is more calculating than Kellan realized, and if he wants to move forward, he must make a few ruthless sacrifices. Election Day is over, and the new mayor takes office. Nana D celebrates her 75th birthday with an adventure. A double wedding occurs at Crilly Lake on Independence Day. And Kellan receives a few more surprises as the summer heat settles in Wharton County.

Haunted House Ghost: Death at the Fall Festival (#5)

It's Halloween, and excitement is brewing in Braxton to carve jack-o'-lanterns, go on haunted hayrides, and race through the spooky corn maze at the Fall Festival. Despite the former occupant's warnings, Kellan renovates and moves into a mysterious old house. When a ruthless ghost promises retribution, our fearless professor turns to the eccentric town historian and an eerie psychic to communicate with the apparition. Meanwhile, construction workers discover a fifty-year-old skeleton after breaking ground on the new Memorial Library wing. While Kellan and April dance around the chemistry sparking between them, a suspicious accident occurs at the Fall Festival. Soon, Kellan discovers the true history and dastardly connections of the Grey family. But can he capture the elusive killer - and placate the revenge-seeking ghost.

Frozen Stiff Drink: Death at Danby Landing (#6)

A winter blizzard barrels toward Wharton County with a vengeance. Madam Zenya predicted the raging storm would change the course of Kellan's life, but the famed seer never could've prepared him for all the collateral damage. Nana D disappears after visiting a patient at Willow

Trees, leaving behind a trail of confusion. When the patient turns up dead, and second body is discovered beneath the snowbanks, Kellan must face his worst fears. What tragedy has befallen his beloved grandmother? Kellan's brother Hampton learns essential life lessons the hard way after his father-in-law accuses him of embezzlement. While trying to prove his innocence, Hampton digs himself a deeper hole that might lead to prison. Sheriff Montague wants to save him, but she receives the shock of her life as the past hurtles forward and complicates her future. Between locating Nana D and solving the scandalous murder of another prominent Braxton citizen, Kellan and April's worlds explode with more turmoil than they can handle. Too bad neither one of them knows what to do about the psychic's latest premonition. The suspicious deaths happening around town aren't ending anytime soon.

Legally Blind Luck: Death via Curse (#7)

Surprising new family members. A hidden talisman. Deadly curses. Horrific murder. Months after tragically losing a loved one, Kellan learns his relative's death wasn't an accident. Someone discovered Queen Tessa's cursed talisman, and a rogue government agent will stop at nothing to retrieve the heirloom. Too bad it changed hands during an anonymous auction and found its way on campus. Moments before Braxton's controversial art exhibition opens, Kellan stumbles upon another murder victim. It appears he might be next on the avenger's list too. Will Kellan protect Tessa's true heir and prevent a killer's nefarious plan from ending the curse? Given all the suspects have ties to prominent Braxton citizens, he's uncertain whom to trust. Together, Kellan and Sheriff April are determined to solve the mystery via legal means or purely through blind luck.

Legally Blind Luck
ISBN: 978-4-86745-296-7

Published by
Next Chapter
1-60-20 Minami-Otsuka
170-0005 Toshima-Ku, Tokyo
+818035793528
28th April 2021

Lightning Source UK Ltd.
Milton Keynes UK
UKHW011913291222
414606UK00003B/24